Code Name
Elodie

BOOKS BY ANNA STUART

Code Name Elodie

ANNA STUART

Bookouture

Published by Bookouture in 2023

An imprint of Storyfire Ltd.
Carmelite House
50 Victoria Embankment
London EC4Y 0DZ

www.bookouture.com

ISBN: 978-1-83790-143-2
eBook ISBN: 978-1-83790-142-5

For Norman and the many adventures ahead...

PART ONE

1943

ONE

BLETCHLEY PARK, JANUARY 1943

Fran

Fran Morgan fumbled for her security pass, trying desperately to get it out of her pocket without removing the gloriously thick woollen gloves her friend Ailsa had given her as a Christmas present. The snow was crisp on the ground, her breath was a mist in the night air, and she had no wish to expose her poor fingers to the shocking cold. She looked pleadingly to the uniformed guard standing, arms folded, in front of the iron gates, his nose as red as his military cap.

'You know it's me, sir. I come in every day.'

His face was implacable. 'Rules is rules, miss.'

With a sigh, Fran finally pulled off her glove, fumbled out her pass and thrust it under his chin, hoping her fingers actually went blue in front of him. Mind you, the poor bloke had to stand out here all evening, so she shouldn't really complain. And she knew he was right, security was of the utmost importance. If the Nazis ever found out that the people working in this quirky old mansion in the middle of Buckinghamshire were systematically breaking their codes and reading their every message, they'd all be dead within hours.

'Thank you, miss. Go on in.'

She summoned up a smile and consoled herself that she'd soon be warming up – unless, that is, she was splayed out on the ice. Looking ruefully towards the frozen pond, where she could already make out figures skating merrily around in the moonlight, she pulled her glove back on and hitched her new skate-blades over her shoulder. Steffie had given both her and Ailsa a pair for Christmas and she was excited about trying them out with her dear friends.

She smiled as she walked through the gates, remembering the very first time she'd arrived here with those two young women. They'd seemed so different to each other back then, Fran with her family of Cambridge medics, Stefania the daughter of the military attaché to Rome, and Ailsa from fisher-folk up on the remote Scottish island of North Uist. And yet within weeks they'd become firm friends, moving into the sweetest caravan together and supporting each other through the ups and downs of the first three years of the war. And they weren't the only special people she'd met at Bletchley.

'Coming, Valérie?'

She turned to the woman who'd accompanied her here, but Valérie shook her head.

'I can't I'm afraid. Uncle Julien will be arriving any minute.'

Fran's heart tightened. Valérie was French and was always appearing with fine foods brought into the country from her network of uncles, aunts, cousins and, apparently, a formidable grandmother, operating out of Normandy. Recently, however, despite the terrible weather, activity in her family network seemed to have increased.

'You have a new uncle every week, Valérie.'

'Aren't I lucky,' she said lightly. 'And, besides, if I can't get to France, it's nice to have a bit of Her here with me.'

'You'll get to France, sweet one. It might just take a bit of time.'

Valérie nodded, her eyes shining with too many fiercely unshed tears, and Fran stroked her silky hair, longing to offer more concrete comfort. They both worked in Hut 3, disseminating the decoded Luftwaffe and Wehrmacht messages that came across from their partner Hut 6, and had been told last week that Roosevelt and Churchill had agreed to invade France in spring '44 – a little over a year from now.

When she'd heard, Fran had been both dismayed that the war would go on so long, and horrified at how they would prepare such a vast invasion in so short a time. What's more, the top men had also agreed to invade Italy this summer, penetrating what Churchill had recently called the 'soft underbelly of Europe' to prepare the way for the northerly landings. So many young men would be heading into enemy territory in the most vulnerable of ways in the coming year and the people at Bletchley Park must do everything they could to increase their odds of survival. It was a hefty responsibility.

'We have time,' Valérie said. 'And, if Uncle Julien is on form, we'll have wine too! Now – off you go to skate. And please don't bruise yourself too badly.'

She grinned at her and Fran tried to smile back, wishing, again, that there was more she could do. But Valérie was bouncing down the road away from the park, dark bob swinging insouciantly, and she could only watch her go, blessing the world for sending the fiery Frenchwoman her way.

A clock struck six and Fran shook herself. Steffie's shift would be finishing and if she was quick, she could meet her at the door of Hut 4, where she worked for the naval department. Ailsa was coming down on the bus from her job as a wireless operator at Whaddon Hall, a few miles away, and it would be good to forget the worries of the world for an hour or so and have some fun.

Turning away from Valérie's receding figure, Fran headed into Bletchley Park, hearing her feet crunch on the icy snow. The moon was full and cast a silvery light over the strange complex, dominated by a mishmash Victorian mansion and dotted with wooden huts housing the code-breaking and processing staff. Over to the far side, new concrete blocks were going up as the bosses recruited more codebreakers and information processors, but Fran avoided looking at them, hating their blank impersonality compared to the cosy huts. She picked up her steps towards Hut 4, which sat to one side of the mansion.

The snow-coated lawns were sparkling in the moonlight and from the pond came chatter and laughter. The happy sound lifted Fran's worries but then a plane flew across the moon, casting the whole park momentarily into darkness, and she shivered. Another followed and then another and she looked up to see the chilling shapes of Messerschmitts directly above. They were heading south and she wondered what poor city they'd been dropping their bombs on and shuddered to think of the women and children climbing out of the rubble of their precious homes, or – worse – *not* climbing out. She shook a fist angrily at the enemy planes. They had to stop the Nazis, whatever it took, because if Hitler won the war then the whole world was doomed.

'We're listening to you,' she hissed after the retreating aircraft, but at that moment, as if the pilot had somehow heard her, another plane swooped in and, to Fran's horror, its trapdoor opened and she saw a glint of silver against the stars.

'Get down!' she cried as the air filled with the scream of a bomb.

She saw it plunge straight for Hut 4 before she hit the snowy ground, burying her head beneath her arms as it exploded with a whump and a flare and the horrible sound of splintering wood.

'Steffie,' she whimpered. 'Oh God, Steffie.'

Steffie

Five minutes earlier

'That's the last of them for the logbook.'

Steffie Carmichael placed her final decrypt into the basket and stretched out her back, looking hopefully to the clock. Nearly shift end. She reached out to touch the skating blades hanging over her peg and smiled. Fran and Ailsa would be here soon and she could escape the fug of the hut and get onto the pond. She'd never skated before but her whole body, sluggish from ten long hours at her desk, was itching to move.

The skates were the only thing on the peg, as she was wearing both her coat and her scarf and would have pulled on the lovely woolly gloves Ailsa had given her for Christmas if she'd been able to work in them. She waggled her frozen fingers and cast a baleful look at the iron stove in the corner stolidly belching out more smoke than warmth. Harry Hinsley, head of section, called it 'the Führer' and the nickname had stuck. It was irreverent perhaps, but the dark humour appealed to the hut full of academics – and Steffie.

She glanced around as her workmates started to get up and, like her, try to stretch out hours of being hunched over five-letter blocks of typeface. Three years ago, when she'd arrived in Hut 4 and been sent to the secretaries' room as a typist, she'd dreamed of working in this main team, translating decrypts and turning them into Ultra – messages that made sense – and she was proud of herself for having made that happen.

She'd had to go via a lively stint in frontline Cairo, mind you, and had nearly lost her Italian fiancé, Matteo, unhappy at having a wife who was intent on risking her life doing war work. Thankfully, he'd seen sense and they'd spent the last three wonderful weeks while he was on British soil getting to know – and love – each other all over again. Matteo had assured her he valued her brain as much as her body and that he still wanted a future together and, slowly, Steffie was believing that she, too, wanted that. It was just a shame that any day now he had to go to Rome to spy on Italian high command.

'You off, Steffie?'

She shook herself out of her thoughts and nodded to Harry.

'I'm off. It's skating time!'

'You'll be back in here within ten minutes with a sprained ankle then,' Harry laughed.

'I will not! My balance is fantastic. I did gymnastics as a little girl, I'll have you know.'

'But did you do it on a pair of quarter-inch thick blades?'

She shrugged. 'How hard can it be?'

Reaching for the skates, she sneaked one of the blackout blinds up a fraction to glance out at the park. The snow was sparkling like diamonds beneath the bold light of the full moon and it looked wonderfully enticing. Through the thin glass, she could hear the happy calls of people on the pond and wondered if Fran and Ailsa were there yet. She was about to drop the blind again when the pretty view outside went strangely dark and the walls of the hut shook slightly. Planes. Nasty, German planes.

'They're low,' she commented.

Harry came over to peer out with her.

'Back off to the Fatherland after bombing some poor innocent out of their beds,' he snarled.

'As we do to them in Dresden and Cologne and—'

'They started it,' he snapped, and there was no arguing with that.

Steffie had had enough of this war. She'd had enough of people being senselessly killed in the name of a sick regime. She'd had enough of rationing and blackouts and people being parted from their loved ones – though she had to admit, she did love her job.

'We'll beat them,' she said. 'Every day we're reading more and more of their messages without them knowing we're even here and...'

She dried up as another plane came over and they caught a strange screaming noise in the sky above their heads – a noise they'd never heard here in Bletchley Park, but knew all too well from the newsreels in the local cinema.

'Bomb!' Harry cried, pulling her to the floor as a horrific bang filled her ears and the hut leaped.

The floor seemed to skew and they rolled towards her desk but it skidded away from them and somehow the wooden wall slammed up against their backs, knocking the wind out of her. The air filled with smoke and decrypts flew everywhere. Steffie caught the smell of cordite, heard cries of alarm from outside and braced herself for the end.

It didn't come. The hut steadied, the decrypts floated down like snow, and they were still here, still alive.

'The Führer!'

For a moment Steffie thought Harry was raging at Hitler, the megalomaniac at the heart of all this horror, but then she saw the stove on its side, door open and hot coals spilling onto the wooden floor and understood.

'Quick!'

She scrabbled to her feet, grabbing the fire extinguisher off the wall and fumbling with the catch, desperately trying to remember the fire drills to which they'd all paid far too little attention. The pin, thankfully, came out and she shot the foam onto the coals, covering the entire stove in putrid fluid.

'Nice work, Steffie.'

Walter Ettinghausen, one of the senior translators, pulled himself shakily up to join her, but now there was another plane and a second explosion sounded out, further away but still, surely, within the BP complex.

'Are we under attack?' Steffie gasped.

'Looks like it,' Walter choked. 'We need to get to a shelter.'

'There are no shelters at BP,' Harry said. 'If they're coming for us, we're sitting ducks.'

'And the whole operation is blown.'

They looked at each other through the dust. Steffie put a hand up to brush her hair from her face and saw it was trembling.

Matteo, she thought longingly, but he was in London, getting final briefings on his imminent trip to Italy. Would it be delayed if he had to go to her funeral? she wondered, and then told herself off. She wasn't dead yet and, if she had anything to do with it, she wasn't going to be. From somewhere among the howl of the fire sirens and the shouts of people outside, she thought she caught her name. Was that Fran?

'We have to get out,' she said, moving towards the exit, though it was hard with furniture strewn everywhere and the hut listing at a curious angle.

The far wall creaked ominously and her breath caught in her throat as she stepped into the narrow central corridor. Harry and Walter were at her shoulders and others were stumbling out of the offices either side, but it was down to her to reach for the handle, praying the fragile structure wouldn't collapse around their ears. Bracing herself, she turned it slowly. The hut shook but settled and the door swung open to reveal a large crowd beyond.

'Steffie!' A lanky figure threw itself at her and Steffie fell gratefully into Fran's arms as her fellow workers streamed out around them. 'Oh, Steffie, I thought you were a goner.'

'Me too. What happened?' Steffie looked back to see that Hut 4 had slid about four feet off its brick plinth, stopping when it butted up against the neighbouring telephone exchange, still miraculously intact. 'I thought it was a bomb.'

'It was,' Fran told her, pointing to where smoke was pouring from a crater in the trees.

Seeing it made Steffie shake all over again and she was grateful for Fran's strong arms to hold her upright. A few feet further over and that would have landed right on top of her.

'I nearly died.'

'But you didn't,' Fran said crisply. 'Come on, they're brewing tea in the mansion.'

Steffie turned her eyes up to the sky, searching for more of the dark shapes of death against the silvery moon.

'Is this really the time for tea? What if there are more of them? What if they've found out about us?' Something else occurred to her. 'I thought I heard a second bomb.'

Fran nodded grimly and pointed across the park.

'It was down by the entrance. Over there where...'

She dried up and looked at Steffie in horror as they both spotted the front of a large vehicle sprawled at an ungainly angle beyond the wire.

'Where the bus is,' Steffie finished for her. 'Where Ailsa's bus is!'

And then they were both running, Hut 4 forgotten in the horror of fresh tragedy.

Ailsa

The sound was deafening. The bus skewed wildly, brakes screeching in protest, and Ailsa Robinson felt her head flung against the window and tasted blood.

'Everyone down!'

She looked blindly about as they came to a juddering halt right before the gates of Bletchley Park. All those around her crouched obediently in the slim spaces between the seats, but a hot, smoky smell was filling the air and, after a year on war-torn Malta, Ailsa knew it all too well. There was no way she was staying here to be consumed by fire. Pushing herself up, she made for the front, clutching onto the seatbacks as the poor bus lurched terrifyingly.

'You there – get down!'

An officious older woman brandishing a clipboard stepped out and Ailsa glared at her.

'No,' she said. 'I don't want to be trapped in here if another one lands.'

'It's safer than out there.'

'Take it from me,' Ailsa said darkly. 'It's not.'

'How would you know?'

'Because I spent hours being dug out of a collapsed air-aid shelter on Malta last year. There's no way I'm doing that again and I don't want to see anyone else on this bus trapped either. Even you.'

The woman gaped at her and Ailsa took advantage of her confusion to yank on the door and throw herself out. There was a smoking crater where the gates to Bletchley Park had stood just moments before and the sturdy iron bars were nothing more than grotesque, spiky twists. The bus seemed intact, but for how long? She looked to the sky, her mind spinning. Who had bombed them? How had they known where to target? And were there more on the way?

Making for a clutch of trees behind the guard's shed, she leaned back against a trunk, fighting for breath. There was something running down her cheek and when she put up a hand, it came away red with blood. Her lungs felt tight, as if a Gestapo torturer had irons around them, and she dug her fingers into the cold bark for purchase.

'Ned,' she whimpered, but there was no way her husband of three short weeks would ever hear her.

He was on a boat heading for Ceylon via the Mediterranean

Sea. In around two weeks' time he would dock briefly in Valletta, the place where they'd met and fallen in love last year, and if it wasn't for the stupid pen-pushers at the Air Ministry, she'd be with him. They'd both been talked into taking a Japanese Morse course after their honeymoon at the start of January and passed with flying colours, but only one of them was being allowed to use their new skill.

'At least I'll know you're safe here,' had been almost the last thing Ned had said to her when she'd kissed him goodbye yesterday afternoon, and she shook her head at the horrible irony that he might, in fact, be safer in the heart of the war zone than she was in sleepy Buckinghamshire.

It was chaos up in the park. Sirens were wailing out and she could see the funny volunteer fire crew trying uselessly to feed their hoses into the iced-over pond. Did that mean more bombs had fallen in the park? The huts were wood and would go up in flames fast. Ailsa touched the skates that were still incongruously slung around her neck and felt tears sting her eyes.

'Steffie,' she whimpered. 'Fran.'

A man was hacking at the ice with a pickaxe and Ailsa thought she recognised the diminutive figure of Alan Turing and feared the genius codebreaker was not made for such heavy work. People were running towards the bus as the other passengers followed Ailsa's example and spilled out of it. She should go and help them, but she was shaking too much to be of any use.

Ailsa glanced up the road, terrified that she might see a platoon of Wehrmacht soldiers marching towards them. There would be no mercy for those who had listened in to German messages, who had decoded their precious Enigma and read all their commands. They would be executed straight away – and that was if they were lucky. Her parents would be so upset.

'Don't be stupid,' she told herself sternly.

The invasion of Britain had been cancelled two years ago. It was their turn to hit back now. Bletchley Park was recruiting more and more people every day to up the number of enemy messages they intercepted, but if the Nazis knew that... Very few people in the park were arrogant about their work but they all understood that it was a vital weapon in the Allied armoury and one they couldn't afford to surrender.

'Ailsa? Ailsa, where are you?'

Ailsa pulled her eyes from the road to see Steffie and Fran running along the side of the bus, banging on the windows and leaping up and down in a vain attempt to find her.

'Here!' she called, though it came out stupidly hoarse. She cleared her dry throat. 'Here, girls. I'm over here!'

They turned, waved, ran. Ailsa watched lanky Fran and curvy Steffie fight across the smoke-covered snow towards her. A smile pulled at the edges of her lips and she pushed herself away from the tree and held out her arms as they threw themselves upon her.

'You're hurt!'

Steffie touched her cut cheek and Fran lifted one of the skates around her neck to reveal a red stain on the, as yet, unused blade. 'Looks like this bit you.'

Ailsa attempted a weak smile and Steffie hastened to reassure her: 'It's not too deep, thank God. Honestly, Ails, we thought you were dead.'

'Not dead.' She grimaced. 'At least, not yet.'

They each took one of her hands and together they looked up to the sky, searching for enemy planes. For now, there were only stars, twinkling benignly above, but tonight the war had come right to the heart of Bletchley Park and they had no idea what it might mean for them all.

TWO

FEBRUARY 1943

Fran

Fran followed Valérie out of Hut 3, turning her eyes automatically to the sky to look for planes. Thankfully there'd been no more bombs since that dark January night and everyone in the park was finally starting to believe it had been a stray drop rather than a targeted attack. Even so, Fran only realised how tight her shoulders were when the sight of clear blue sky above allowed her to loosen them.

She glanced over to Hut 4, sitting placidly in place as if nothing had ever happened. The day after the bombing, a big group had got together and, with the aid of some railway jacks and a couple of sleepers, pushed the whole structure back onto its brick foundations. The hut had been remarkably unscathed by its experience but the trees to its left were blown to bits and it would take months for England's spring greenery to grow up and cover the ugly crater. The mental scarring, too, would take time to heal. For days they'd all believed the Nazis had discovered what they were up to here in Bletchley Park. But the skies had stayed clear and the airwaves had stayed full and, somehow, they'd picked up their usual routines with even more determination to win this damned war.

'The snow's melting.'

Valérie pointed to the path where sparkling white had given way to brown sludge. It wasn't anywhere near as pretty, but it was certainly easier to walk on and they traced their way past the new concrete blocks with ease. Fran gave them a suspicious sideways glance. The staff of Hut 4 had moved into Block A last week, deciding that with all the effort of sorting their desks and files after the bomb, they might as well make the leap into their new accommodation. Steffie said it was horrible – big, echoey rooms with none of the cosiness of the wooden huts.

Mind you, she also said it was warmer and less crowded and there was space for row upon row of files. As Fran was responsible for the ever-growing Hut 3 index, that was a tempting thought – though not tempting enough to want to give up the hut in which she'd been so happy for these last three years. She took Valérie's arm to hurry her past the ugly building and on towards the canteen. The smell of onions, tea and undefinable meat was drifting out on the breeze and Valérie screwed up her nose.

'I cannot wait for the invasion, Frances. I tell you, I'd rather die chasing Germans than have to eat your British food for another year.'

Fran nudged at her.

'It's hot and nutritious. What more do you need?'

'Taste!' Valérie cried, wrapping an arm around her waist, and adding, 'Luckily, I got some saucisson the other day, so I could cook for us later...'

'Sounds good,' Fran agreed. 'Oh, but Steffie and Ailsa are both on days this week, so they'll be around. Have you got enough for four?'

Valérie tossed her head.

'I do. But I do not really want to eat as a four, *chérie*.'

Fran sighed.

'Me neither. That is, I love it when we all eat together but it would certainly be nice to have some time alone with you.'

She glanced guiltily to the other people streaming towards the canteen for lunch, feeling treacherous for even saying that out loud. Steffie and Ailsa were her best friends in the whole world and she loved living in their caravan together near Bletchley Park. Steffie had found it when she'd stormed away from her lecherous landlord and Fran and Ailsa had seized the chance to join her, making a cosy home together. Last year, however, Steffie had been sent to Cairo and Ailsa to Malta, so Fran and Valérie had had the caravan to themselves for a while. She missed it.

'We could go to your digs?' she suggested half-heartedly.

'With the rats?' Valérie protested. 'And Mrs C hovering over us every minute? I tell you, she's as much of a scavenger as the rodents.'

'It's only because you have such lovely food, Valérie. Everyone's so hungry.'

'I know, I know. I am wonderful!'

Valérie tossed her black bob and Fran nudged her again.

'Don't get above yourself, girl. You're wonderful at finding endless family members with good contacts.'

Valérie stopped dead in the middle of the path, almost tugging Fran over, and clapped a hand comically to her head.

'Which reminds me – Uncle Claude is away, so his suite at Oddenino's is free. We're both off tomorrow, yes, so how about a trip to London, just the two of us?'

'Sounds perfect,' Fran agreed happily. Suspicious as she was of Valérie's French connections, they didn't half come in useful, and it was with renewed appetite that she headed in to see what the Bletchley Park cooks had managed to drum up for them to eat today.

'This is amazing.' Fran stretched out across the huge bed, luxuriating in the warm covers and soft mattress. The caravan was lovely but her bunk bed was narrow and she was always hitting her head on the struts, so Oddenino's Hotel was something else. 'Remind me to thank your Uncle Claude if I ever get to meet him.'

Valérie jumped onto the bed at her side.

'Oh, you will. Once this madness is over you will meet *all* my uncles and they will adore you, as I adore you.'

Fran wasn't so certain about that. It had taken her some time last year to realise that her gloriously tender feelings for Valérie were valid and, although her closest friends had been wonderfully supportive, she wasn't sure the rest of the world was quite as liberal.

'Are you sure, Valérie?' she asked nervously. 'Won't they find, you know, this...' she waved her hand vaguely across the two of them, 'a bit odd?'

Valérie kissed her.

'You are talking of a people who haven't been able to go to the postal office without running the gauntlet of a Gestapo officer on the street corner. Why would they find two girls living together odd after that?'

'It's not quite the same, Valérie.'

'No! It is fifty times more wonderful. They will understand. The French know how to love.'

'But not how to fight.' It slipped out before Fran could stop it and she cursed herself. 'Sorry. I'm so sorry. I didn't mean that. It's not the French who are the problem, but their cowardly leaders.'

'Pétain!' Valérie spat, and Fran was grateful her ire had

been directed towards the collaborationist president rather than herself.

Until recently, Marshal Pétain and his posse had been living it up in unoccupied southern France but last autumn, when the Allies had invaded French North Africa, Hitler had had enough of his cowering collaborationists and occupied the south as well. Loyal French men and women everywhere had been torn between pleasure at seeing the cowards get their comeuppance and horror at the rest of their beloved country being trampled by German soldiers.

'You realise,' the French girl went on, leaping up to pace the grand room, 'that ours is the only European government to have caved in to the Nazis. The only one!'

'I know, Valérie, but—'

'The Poles have a government-in-exile in London.'

'They do, but—'

'And the Norwegians and the Belgians, the Greeks, the Dutch. Even the Yugoslavs are here, but not the French. Oh no, we prefer licking Hitler's dirty boots while he sits at our own, beautifully catered, table.'

Fran pushed herself off the bed and went to Valérie, though she knew better than to reach out to her yet.

'The ordinary French people are doing their best to resist,' she said.

Valérie tossed her head.

'Some of them.'

'Your family.'

'My family, yes. We have a fine example in my grandmother.'

'You do?' Fran moved cautiously around to face Valérie. 'Would you tell me about her?'

Valérie sniffed but gave a quick nod and even a small smile.

'Grand-mère Elodie is an amazing woman, Frances. During the Great War, she lived in a little town not far from the

Somme where the bastard German invaders were camped. She and Grand-père ran a bicycle shop and every day of the war, Elodie took their horse and cart, rode to the battleground and brought back injured men to be treated in the local hospital. Twice she was shot, once in the hip and once in the shoulder. She used to show me the scars when I was a child, pulling down her blouse or wrenching up her skirt to reveal the puckered flesh.

'"Where's your decorum, Maman," my mother would plead, but Grand-mère Elodie would say, "Buried on the Somme with too many fine young men"!' Valérie beamed. 'She has bicycle shops all over Normandy now, and every one a shelter for *résistants*. Truly, she is a wonderful woman.'

'General de Gaulle will be proud of her,' Fran suggested.

Valérie tossed her head.

'De Gaulle is a paltry leader. He is trying his best, I grant you, but the "Free French" are too few and he is barely known and a bit weird. Have you seen his ears? They stick out miles. His nose too.'

'I don't think that's vital, Valérie.'

'Well, no, but Grand-mère says the man's a maniac, though a patriotic one.'

'She's met him?'

Valérie grinned.

'Of course. Grand-mère has met everyone. *She* is who we need leading the Free French, Frances, but would anyone listen to an old woman? No! They have to have a big man in a stiff uniform. Pah!'

She was getting worked up again and Fran racked her brains for something to help.

'He speaks well on the radio.'

'I suppose,' Valérie agreed begrudgingly, 'but is anyone listening?' She flung herself suddenly into Fran's arms. 'Churchill is preparing to invade, Frances. He and Roosevelt are getting ready to liberate France, which is wonderful, but we French should be doing it ourselves. We *want* to do it ourselves.'

'I know that,' Fran soothed, cursing herself again for letting loose this demon. Valérie was always spiky about her homeland – understandably. Fran couldn't imagine what it would feel like if Britain had rolled over to the Nazis. She hugged her tight, but Valérie pulled away, grabbing her shoulders.

'We *will* do it ourselves, Frances. We will.' Her eyes shone with a luminous intensity and Fran smiled fondly at her, but Valérie was already springing away, pointing at the clock. '*Sacré bleu*, look at the time! It's nearly seven o'clock.'

'Does it matter?'

'The table is booked for half past and we're still in our travel clothes!'

Valérie ran to their suitcase, flinging it open and scattering clothing.

'Table?' Frances was confused. 'Are you taking me out to dinner?'

Valérie froze halfway through pulling out a dark red dress, and gave a funny grimace.

'Did I not tell you?'

'Tell me what?'

'We're invited out.'

'What? With whom?'

'Uncle Bertrand and some wonderful French people.'

'Valérie! I thought we'd come here to have time together.'

'We *will* be together. And really, you will like them, Frances. They are just your type.'

'My type?'

'Pierre and Gilberte are journalists. Clever people. And fascinating... Until recently, they ran a bookshop in Paris and their cellar was the heart of the...' She looked around the room and then leaned in to whisper, 'the *Resistance*.'

'Ah,' Fran said. 'I see.' She swallowed. 'And we're going to dine with them? Is that wise?'

It was one thing Valérie's family running a Resistance ring, but quite another to be pulled into it themselves.

'Please come and meet them,' Valérie said, reaching for her hand. 'For me?'

How could she resist?

'Come on then,' she agreed reluctantly, 'but I wish you'd have told me. I'd have brought a fancier outfit.'

'You don't need fancy outfits to look utterly gorgeous, Frances Morgan.'

Valérie pulled her in for a kiss but she squirmed away.

'Valérie! We've got to get ready.'

'It is fashionable to be late, chérie.'

She kissed her hard and Fran felt her whole self respond, but, tempting as it was, she'd been brought up to be punctual and, with reluctance, she wriggled out of Valérie's grasp once more.

'Come on. If I have to meet these people, I'd rather get on with it.'

She busied herself getting ready, dabbing nervously at a small stain on the cuff of her blouse and wishing she'd brought a dress. Valérie looked beautiful in her claret frock and she felt dowdy in comparison. Still, there was nothing to be done about it and she was grateful for the smart coat her parents had sent her for Christmas to give her some style in front of this crowd of French résistants.

Her heart beat with nerves as they approached the York Minster, a pub in Soho that had been so thoroughly frenchified, it was now known as the French House. In fact, this part of London was full of French exiles, many wearing the American-made uniform of the Free French, and it buzzed with life. Valérie looked in all directions with a clear thrill and Fran could swear she walked taller for being among her compatriots.

'Here we are!'

The York Minster looked dark and dowdy on the outside, but the moment Valérie pulled open the door, a flood of light, warmth and French chatter spilled out. It was like an onslaught of vocabulary and Fran thought of her languages teacher back in school and wished she could see her now. She also wished, ruefully, that she'd paid more attention in lessons. She tried to speak French with Valérie regularly, but their careful conversation was nothing like the babble in here. Every table was full and the room smelled deliciously of garlic, cream and wine. Edging past the first tables, Fran caught sight of bowls of mussels and marvelled at the ingenuity of the chefs – then hoped she wouldn't have to eat any.

'Bertrand!'

Valérie grabbed her hand and pulled her to the back, where a small man in a smart suit was waving madly. Opposite him, a handsome couple were talking earnestly to two men in uniform, and Fran's nerves grew. She stood back as Bertrand and Valérie shared the obligatory volley of kisses, but the next thing she knew Bertrand was taking her hands and kissing her too, his big moustache tickling her cheeks.

'*Frances! Nous avons beaucoup entendu parler de vous et je suis ravi de vous rencontrer enfin.*'

It was noisy but Fran was pretty sure he'd said he was pleased to meet her.

'*Enchanté,*' she managed, and it seemed to suffice as he beamed and turned her to the rest of the table.

'This is Pierre Brossolette,' he said, switching smoothly to English. 'And his lovely wife, Gilberte.'

'Pleased to meet you.'

Frances offered her hand and they both rose to shake it. Pierre was a good-looking man in his forties, with a shock of dark hair marked with a striking stripe of pure white at the front. Gilberte was a tall woman with a wonderfully defined face and piercing grey-blue eyes. Both were lean and, if you looked closely, tired, but they shook her hand enthusiastically.

'Welcome to London,' Frances said.

'*Merci, merci*,' Gilberte replied. 'We are glad to be here. At least, we would rather be back in Paris, but we are grateful to have found sanctuary in Londres.'

'I'm sorry you had to leave.'

'So were we. We were doing important work but when the Gestapo arrested our son, enough was enough.'

Fran gasped.

'How old is your son?'

'Fourteen. Poor boy was terrified but he did marvellously. Told the bastards nothing at all and after three days they let him go. That's when we left France.'

'I don't blame you.'

'But we will go back.'

'Of course. Once we win the war—'

Pierre interrupted her.

'No, no – we will go back to *help* win the war. Or at least I will. Gil has the children to care for, but she will wage her own battles with words.'

Now that Frances liked the sound of.

'You're a journalist?' she asked, slipping into a seat at Gilberte's side.

'We both are. Pierre writes for the left-wing press and I for anyone that will have me. We are passionate about getting a good education for all French children, or we were before the war. For now, though, we are passionate about getting a *French* education for all French children.' She shook herself. 'But listen to me, going on like this. Some wine, Frances? Bread?'

She proffered a basket and Fran fell eagerly on the crusty baguette – white bread was a delicacy never seen in Bletchley.

'I'd like to write,' she admitted.

'Then do.'

Fran squinted at her.

'Who for?'

'For yourself, at first, to find your own style, then we can see where it might fit.'

She said it so simply, as if it was a perfectly natural aim and one she believed Fran capable of achieving. Fran, used to her own family who spent all their time telling her to get a job in the medical services, stared at her in astonishment.

'What?' Gilberte demanded. 'If you are serious, do it.'

'Yes,' Fran stuttered. 'You're right. Of course.'

Gilberte smiled at her.

'Forgive me. I am too brusque. Pierre is always telling me so, are you not, Pierre?'

'Gil sees the world in black and white,' he agreed, patting his wife's hand. 'It can be helpful sometimes but daunting for those with a finer appreciation for the greys in between.'

'Ah!' Gilberte threw her hands up. 'This from the man who *lives* in black and white. You never see the other side of any story bar your own, Pierre.'

'Not true. I love stories. It is politics where everyone else is wrong – especially those fascist bastards.' He leaned over, his eyes ablaze. 'I warned France, you know. I warned them as early as 1933 when the big-pig came to power. I warned them over and over, but they weren't listening. Too busy clamouring to appease the Nazis, to appease the men trying to narrow the world into the tiniest mould of Aryan "perfection" and killing off anyone who didn't fit as if they were mere bugs in a summerhouse! Bloody *Munichois*.'

'*Munichois?*'

Fran looked to Valérie for enlightenment, but she was wrapped up in urgent conversation with Bertrand and it was Gilberte who provided it.

'It is a term we use for those people who wished to see the Munich Agreement signed.'

'*Idiots*,' Pierre said, 'that's another term for them.'

Gilberte gave Fran a sideways smile.

'See – black and white!'

'And right, as we all found out to our cost.' He shook himself visibly. 'But here we are, so, Frances, let me introduce you to this pair.' He gestured to the men at the end of the table. 'This is André Dewavrin, who works for General De Gaulle.'

'You do?'

Fran looked curiously at the balding, bright-eyed man, who shrugged.

'For my sins, *oui*.'

'You do not like him?'

'No one likes him; he is quite objectionable. But he is wonderful too – the only man with the true vision of a free France.'

'And the drive to make it happen,' added the last of their number in, to Fran's surprise, an English accent. 'Forest Yeo-Thomas at your service, Frances, though please call me Tommy, everyone else does.'

'Nice to meet you, er, Tommy. You're English?'

He laughed.

'I am, though brought up in Paris, so the old French isn't too bad. And I love the country. Hated seeing it nicked by Jerry, so I've signed up to help kick him out and get all these poor exiles home.'

He gestured around the buzzing room and Frances followed his hand, trying to take it all in. She had, of course, always wanted to defeat the Nazis and the hateful ideology of fascism, but sitting in this little slice of France in the heart of Soho, she could see and feel another, more driving need to win the war – not just a political ideal or a sense of moral justice, but a burning desire for freedom.

She felt Valérie's hand on her knee beneath the table and placed her own over the top as she looked around her eclectic dinner companions. They were united by one key desire – to have their country back – and Fran felt a renewed surge of urgency about the fight ahead. The invasion was on the horizon and there would be many parts to play in making it a success; she could hardly wait to get back to Bletchley Park and get on with her own.

THREE

MARCH 1943

Ailsa

Ailsa woke and stared up at the ceiling of the caravan, so close to her face in the top bunk that she could see every detail of a spider's web gracing the nearest corner. Steffie and Fran were fast asleep in the bunks below and she drew comfort from their proximity, but it didn't bring her any peace. She put a hand over her churning stomach as if she might contain the anger roiling inside, though she knew already that it would continue until she somehow stopped the authorities being total and utter eejits.

'Why shouldn't I sail to Ceylon?' she'd demanded of her boss, Richard Gambier-Parry, yesterday afternoon. 'I was fine working abroad before, so I'll be fine again.'

'Ah,' he'd said, 'but you're married now.'

'So? Do I look different?'

'No, but—'

'Has stepping up to the altar changed my brain power? My ability with a wireless? My Morse speed?'

'Of course not, my dear. But you are married.'

'So...?'

'So, the air force doesn't permit married women to serve abroad.'

She could have screamed.

'What about married men?'

'That's different.'

'In what way?'

'Men aren't changed by marriage.'

'I think we just established that I'm not changed by marriage either.'

Gambier-Parry had looked pained. 'Children,' he'd said vaguely.

'I don't have any children.'

'But you could do.'

'Not with my husband in Colombo!'

His eyes had lit up.

'Ah, but if you joined him, then you might.'

'So you're saying this is all about sex?' she'd sighed.

'Mrs Robinson, please!'

He'd looked mortified but so what? This was her life they'd been talking about.

'You're saying,' she'd pushed on, 'that if I hadn't married Ned, I could have gone to Colombo, we could have had all the sex we liked and I could have got pregnant, but that would have been fine because it's not against air force rules?'

'It's against God's rules.'

'Aye, as it is for men, but I know for a fact that the military encourage brothels around foreign postings, so perhaps they've not got their rules quite right?'

Gambier-Parry had looked to the door, clearly desperate for someone to rescue him from the hysterical female in his office, and Ailsa had forced herself to calm down.

'Look, sir, you have to see the logic. I am, by your own admission, your best wireless operator, yes?'

'Well, yes, but you can operate a wireless from here too, you know.'

'I can and I am doing, but the government paid for me to go on a course to learn Japanese Morse.'

'Well, yes. That was bloody Tiltman going round recruiting people.'

'Because we need them. And now I can do it, and do it well, what on earth is the point of me not doing it?'

'It's dangerous in the East.'

'It's nowhere near as close to the frontline as we are here at Bletchley.'

'By strict mathematics, perhaps.'

'Usually the best way to judge distance. And besides, there are any number of women stationed on England's south coast who are, let's face it, within thirty miles of the enemy.'

'But on British soil.'

She'd nearly screamed.

'Ceylon *is* British soil, sir!'

He'd harumphed, then shaken his head ruefully.

'All the points you make are good ones, Mrs Robinson, but my hands are tied. The Air Ministry says no married women abroad, so no married women it is.'

'Even though they're desperate for wireless operatives on Ceylon? Even though they especially need people who know how to mend a set because theirs are always breaking and they don't have any decent engineers? I can do that, sir, you know I can.'

Richard Gambier-Parry had shaken his head again.

'You're determined, I'll give you that, though why you'd want to take yourself halfway around the globe when you can have a lovely job right here at Whaddon Hall, I have no idea.'

'I want to see the world, sir. I want to get to different places and experience different things. I've spent all my life so far stuck in the arse— sorry, back end of Scotland.'

'Fair point. Never been to the place but I hear its all midges and heather. Very well, Mrs Robinson, let me see what I can do, but I'm not making any promises.'

He hadn't looked like he meant it and she'd been forced to leave his office with nothing to show for the meeting but the boiling sense of injustice that was still churning in her guts. Now, she lay in bed watching the spider patiently mending a corner of his web and feeling every bit as trapped as the poor fly that was bound to bumble into the sticky thread.

She missed Ned terribly. Much as she'd enjoyed being back in the caravan with Steffie and Fran, she'd had only three weeks of married life and she was hungry for more. After marrying at Bletchley in the new year, she and Ned had managed to grab a few days in a quaint hotel in the Cotswolds before they'd been recruited for the course in Japanese Morse. That had been away in Bedford, so they'd had a room together, almost like an extended holiday, but with a lot more dots and dashes. They'd both naively assumed they would be posted together, but now the ridiculous, uneven air force rules were stopping them and, with no sign of the war ending, they could be apart for months. Maybe even years.

Ailsa's stomach lurched again at the thought of not looking into Ned's loving brown eyes for that long and she heaved herself onto the ladder and crept out of the bedroom before she could disturb the other two. She really did feel peculiar. She had to stop raging; it wasn't good for her gut. Still, hopefully it was nothing that a cup of tea wouldn't sort out, and perhaps a bite of breakfast. Today she would go to John Tiltman, the fiery Scot who'd recruited her onto the Japanese Morse course, and see if he could help. If anyone could shift things, John could.

Feeling better with a plan, Ailsa put on the kettle and opened up the caravan door to reach for the milk they kept beneath the step. But, as she bent over, she felt the contents of her stomach protest and barely had time to step into the longer grass before she chucked them all up. She leaned back against the wall of the caravan, wiping her mouth as she tried to gather herself. This was strange. She wasn't usually given to illness, especially not of the digestive kind. Her ma's cooking had never been the best and her body had long since learned to stomach the strangest things. She closed her eyes, feeling weak and horribly tearful, but her stomach wasn't done with her yet and she had to run for the grass once more as it retched up what little was left inside her.

'Ailsa? Are you well?'

Ailsa looked blearily around to see Fran in the caravan doorway, peering at her in concern.

'Do I look well?'

'No. Sorry, stupid question.'

'Stupid stomach, more like,' she said gruffly. 'Don't know what's going on. I thought I was just crabbit about the Air Ministry and, you know...'

'Their outdated, bigoted and brutally unfair posting process?'

Ailsa managed a weak smile.

'Exactly.'

'That would make me sick too, Ails, but it looks like more than that. Did you eat something dodgy?'

'No more than usual. Yesterday's spam pie was ropy, but you both had it and you're not being sick.'

'True, though perhaps that's the odd thing. It was disgusting.'

Ailsa turned back into the caravan, grateful for Fran's strong arm to help her up the step.

'Maybe a wee cup of tea will help.'

'Take a seat. I'll make it.'

Fran bustled around finding mugs and Ailsa collapsed onto the bench seat feeling comfortingly mothered. The bedroom door opened and Steffie emerged, her blonde hair exploding from her night-time plaits and her pyjamas askew. Ailsa smiled and stood up to hug her, but her damned stomach protested at the movement and, instead, she had to push past and run for the lavatory. When she was done, she turned round to see Steffie staring down at her.

'I see,' she said, nodding her head sagely.

'What do you see?'

Behind them the kettle whistled and Fran switched the gas off and came to join them.

'What do you see, Stef?'

Steffie pulled Ailsa to her feet and put an arm around her. 'You're being sick, Ails.'

'Very observant.'

'But you don't feel unwell?'

'I feel furious at the higher-ups but, no, not unwell like a fever.'

'Umhum. And, let's see, you got married two months ago?'

'Yes, but—'

'And had a lovely honeymoon, plus all that time in Bedford?'

'Yes.'

'With lots of lovely, erm, marital relations?'

Ailsa flushed. 'Maybe.'

'Course you did. You were glowing when you got back.'

'Steffie!'

'Oh, come on, it's exactly as it should be, but these things can have consequences.'

Ailsa stared at her. 'You mean... You mean, I might be...?'

'Pregnant, yes. Do you not think so?'

'No!' Ailsa shook her head violently. She remembered Gambier-Parry muttering 'children' as if that was a reason to deny married women everything possible. 'No, I can't be.'

'Why not?'

'Because... because I don't want to be. Because they'll never post me abroad if I am. Because if they don't, I'll be stuck here having Ned's baby without Ned.'

Tears were flowing now and she batted angrily at them. She didn't want to cry any more than she wanted a baby. That's to say, she did want a baby, of course she did, but not now. Definitely not now, with a war to win and a world to see.

'Fran?' she heard Steffie asking. 'You've got medical family, what do you think?'

Fran let out an indignant protest that Ailsa might have found amusing if she wasn't feeling shaky and sick and, frankly, terrified. With an effort, she pushed herself off the wall and faced her friends.

'I am *not* pregnant,' she said as firmly as she could manage. 'I am not pregnant because if I was, there'd be no way they'd let me on the boat to Colombo.'

She saw Steffie and Fran exchange worried looks.

'It doesn't really work like that, Ails,' Fran said. 'Bodies don't listen to what you want.'

'I know, but this body isn't pregnant.'

Steffie put out a hand to her.

'What if you get on the boat and then you find out that you are?'

'Then I'll deal with it out there. Women have babies all over the world and I don't see why I should be any different.'

'Because those women are in their homes, with their own doctors and their own mothers and their own friends.'

'And their own husbands,' Ailsa pointed out. 'My home is with Ned and nothing is going to stop me getting there, not even a baby.'

'But—'

She put up a hand.

'Not that there is a baby, right?'

'Ailsa...'

'Please, girls, for me, there's no baby. Right?'

Steffie and Fran looked at each other again but then came and wrapped their arms around her.

'Right, Ailsa,' they agreed.

They all knew it was a lie but, let's face it, their work in Bletchley Park had taught them that in wartime there were lies everywhere. This was one of the most benign and, until she got where she wanted to be, Ailsa was going to cling to it with all she had.

FOUR

MARCH 1943

Steffie

Steffie glanced up at the three-faced clock beneath the left-hand arch of Paddington station and saw the minute hand click forward. Time was visibly running out for her and Matteo. His train would leave in ten minutes and then she had to catch the underground to St James's Street for the mysterious meeting at which Harry Hinsley had asked her to deputise. She suspected it was a kindness from her boss to get her to London on the day Matteo left for enemy territory, and she was grateful, if nervous. The minute hand clicked again and she told herself the meeting could wait; for now it was all about Matteo.

'I hate goodbyes,' he murmured, pulling her close.

She clutched at him, running a hand over his chest as if she could somehow imprint the feel of him onto her palm.

'Me too.' She looked up at him. 'Should I have come with you, Matteo? Last year, I mean, when you escaped from hospital in Cairo?'

She'd been thrown when he'd asked her to escape to Italy with him and had instinctively refused, knowing the importance of the war job she'd been doing in Bletchley's Cairo outpost, reading enemy messages across the rabid North African front. Now, though, having to part with him again, she questioned her judgement. 'We could be living in the hills, you and I, without any of this terrible war.'

He kissed her. 'But, as you rightly pointed out, the war would still be here.'

'It's not our war.'

'No. But it threatens us anyway, and all those we love. You were the brave one then, my love; I was the coward. But, look, it's all turned good. I'm working with the British now.'

'And looking gorgeous too.'

She stroked his RAF uniform and reached up for another, longer kiss. Above them the minute hand continued its inexorable turn of the three clock faces. Then the tannoy crackled into life, announcing the imminent arrival of the train to Oxford and the airfield at Brize Norton.

'I'll miss you so much, Matteo.'

'And I you.' He pulled her close, whispering into her hair. 'But I'm sure your father will find a way to pass on a few messages, or at least to tell you I'm safe.'

Steffie nodded jealously. Major General Anthony Carmichael had worked for years before the war as the military attaché to Rome, a post that had brought the family a glamorous life in the Italian capital and introduced Steffie to Matteo when he was a rising young officer. Mussolini's treaty with Hitler had set them on opposite sides of the war for two heartbreaking years, but now Matteo was working as a double agent for the British and her father would be his primary liaison officer.

'It's not fair that Daddy will get to talk to you more than I will,' she said, kissing him tenderly.

'Believe me, I'd much rather it was you, my beautiful girl, but we'll be together soon. Once the Allies hit Italy, Musso will surrender and we'll be on the same side.'

'That sounds good.'

'It will be. Work hard for it, Steffie, my beautiful, clever, bold...'

A squeal of brakes and hiss of steam heralded the arrival of the train, and people on the platform began gathering bags. Matteo bent to his but did not get up again. Steffie looked down and saw him on one knee before her.

'My beautiful, clever, bold *wife*?' He held out the diamond ring he'd demanded she return on the terrible day when she'd refused to escape with him. 'Will you give me another chance, Steffie? Will you let me prove to you that I've grown up, that I'm going to work hard to help the Allies win this war, and that I'm going to be one hundred per cent proud of you for doing so too?'

'Matteo!'

People were turning and pointing and she felt very self-conscious in the red suit she'd worn to give her confidence in Harry's meeting. As she looked into Matteo's eyes, however, she found them so bright with emotion that her heart swelled and no one else mattered one jot. She'd refused his renewed proposal last new year, not ready to trust him, but these last few weeks together had been a wonderful chance to get to know him again, and to see that he was truly changed. War did that to men; to women too.

'All aboard!' The train panted to a halt and a conductor strode along the platform, adding, 'Best make your mind up, lass, or he'll miss his train.'

Steffie snapped out of her reverie.

'Yes!' she said. 'Oh, Matteo, yes!'

Then he was up and slipping the ring onto her finger and kissing her while the conductor kindly put his bag onto the train.

'Can't hold it much longer, folks. This war waits for no one, I'm afraid.'

Somehow, they forced themselves apart and Matteo

stepped onto the train, to cheers from those within. The door closed but the window was down and he leaned out, his fingers touching hers.

'I'll make you a worthy husband, Stefania, I swear it.'

'I know it,' she told him. 'I love you.'

'And I you.'

The train's wheels were beginning to turn and it wheezed away, pulling his fingertips from hers. She waved madly, but in a heartbeat, it was out of the arches of the station and she was left on the platform with only a beautiful diamond for company. She looked down at it, stroking her finger across the hard surface and marvelling at how very familiar it already felt. Tears threatened and she brushed hastily at them before they ruined her make-up.

She looked at the clock again. All she really wanted to do was find a dark corner of some café to absorb all that had just happened, but she had Harry's damned meeting to attend. He'd been kind to hand this to her, and brave too, as she'd doubtless be the only woman in the room, so she couldn't let him down by not turning up, or even being late. Giving the ring one last tiny stroke, she adjusted it on her finger, wiped her eyes with a hand-kerchief, and strode towards the underground station, focusing on the task ahead.

A short trip around the Bakerloo line took her to St James's Street and she strode past White's, her father's club, and on to number 58. It was a dull-looking building with a FOR LET sign outside, but she supposed that was good for a secret meeting and headed up to the door with all the confidence she could muster.

'Hello?'

The voice through the intercom couldn't have been more supercilious but Steffie could play at that game too and gave her name in her most cut-glass accent. The buzzer went and she entered a building that was far grander on the inside, giving the receptionist a steely nod of thanks as she showed her towards a room on the left of the entrance hall. There was no space for nice-Steffie if she was going to cut it here but, even so, she touched her fingers to her diamond for courage as she stepped inside. The room was large and dimly lit, with the long windows boarded up and a collection of men in much-decorated uniforms standing around a long table.

'Can I help you, miss?' asked a donnish man, stepping possessively in front of the rest as if his slim body might hide them from her.

Steffie eyed him, steely again.

'I hope, sir, that *I* can help you. I'm Stefania Carmichael and I'm deputising for Harry Hinsley at Bletchley Park.'

'Are you indeed? How... unusual.'

'Does no one else ever send deputies?'

'Oh yes. But not... No matter. If Harry has sent you, then you'd better come in. I'm John Masterman, head of the Twenty Committee.'

'Twenty Committee?'

'The only joke name of any government committee ever,' he told her proudly. 'Pun on the roman numeral XX – for double-cross. We do strategic deception, with the emphasis on strategic. The point is not simply to set up individual lies and deceits, but to build them together to make the enemy believe what we want them to believe. "Mystify, mislead and surprise," that's the aim. Do you know who said that, Miss Carmichael?'

Steffie shook her head.

'Stonewall Jackson, leader of the Confederate army in the American Civil War, tactical genius, and father of Battle Deception.'

'Right.'

'But he didn't have our resources, so our aim is to do it bigger, bolder and better. Welcome to double-cross! Tea's over there. Buns too.' He leaned in, suddenly conspiratorial. 'I find it ensures they all turn up.'

Steffie had no idea what to make of this curious man and his curious committee, but tea and buns sounded right up her street. It had been an emotional time at Paddington and emotion always made her hungry, so she headed for the side table to help herself while she took in the curious bunch of mainly older men who – judging from their multifarious uniforms – had been drawn from every branch of the services imaginable. She was attracting a lot of glances herself, mind you, and had to put her teacup down on the table in case her shaking hand made it clink against the saucer. She was wondering if the red suit had been a wise choice when a familiar voice said, 'Stefania?' and she spun round, astonished.

'Daddy? That is, er, General Carmichael.'

Anthony Carmichael smiled.

'Daddy will do. What on earth are you doing here, my girl?'

'I'm deputising for Harry Hinsley as the BP representative.'

'Are you indeed? How wonderful. Everyone, pay attention – this is my daughter, Stefania Carmichael. She's here for Bletchley Park and I hope you'll give her your fullest courtesy.'

There were murmurs of agreement and nods hello from around the table. Steffie gave a bright smile and took a seat next to her father, not entirely happy that it had taken his intervention to speed up her acceptance on this peculiar committee, but keen to make the most of it. She drew out her notebook and nibbled as quietly as she could on the very welcome bun, as the meeting got under way.

Steffie listened, agog, as the various members of the committee went through their plans. She heard about fake radio signalling to indicate invented or mislocated British units. She heard of mocked-up planes and tanks and, above all, of double agents feeding misinformation at a highly controlled and focused level. The British, she learned from a smiley-eyed

Scotsman called Tar Robertson, were controlling every agent that the Germans believed they'd planted on British soil. There were fifteen of them with one man, Garbo, running at least fifteen more entirely fictional agents all around the country. The committee had to decide on the 'chickenfeed' information these agents were permitted to give their German controllers to build their credibility so they could be used to help deceive the enemy about Allied battle plans. Bletchley's job in all this was to provide the feedback from Ultra – the name for decrypted German radio messages – on whether the enemy were swallowing the carefully planted lies and what that meant they were doing with their troops, ships and planes.

Steffie drank it all in, especially when it became clear that the current focus was on the invasion of Italy proposed for this summer. This was, she gathered, a critical operation in itself, but also an important dry run for the bigger invasion of northern France next year. As she took rapid notes, her diamond clinked against her saucer and she reminded herself that this morning she'd got engaged. Already, immersed in this vital work, it felt forever ago, but if this strategic deception succeeded, Italy could be brought over to the Allies fast. She had to concentrate.

The plan, it appeared, was to convince the Germans that they were going to hit Greece and Sardinia, rather than the more obvious – and correct – target of Sicily. Her father reported that there had been industrial action in northern Italy as the Italians grew weary of the war and Steffie was able, nervously, to chip in with some of the notes Harry had given her detailing recent Ultra indicating that Mussolini was trying to break away from Hitler. This was warmly received and Steffie sat back, relieved not to have messed up and, she had to admit, glowing from playing her part on this high stage.

She reached for her last sip of tea but almost disgraced herself choking on it when a smart naval officer stood up and

said, 'Mincemeat is all going to plan, John. We have the perfect
corpse.'

Steffie glanced to her father, who gave her a wink.

'It's a great one, this,' he said. 'We're planting a dead officer
with some fictitious documents. Listen up.'

'The body is now to be identified as Major Martin and it's
been decided he should be a marine.' There were murmurs of
protest but the officer put up his hand to stop them. 'I know we
wanted air force, but no air officer would travel in anything
other than dress uniform and that's far too tricky. It would have
to be tailor-made, and we haven't yet found a tailor prepared to
fit a corpse – and a frozen one at that.'

'Marines travel in battledress, do they, Montagu?'
Masterman asked.

'They do, sir, and, as I'm sure you all know, battledress is far
baggier and more, er, forgiving for the rigid form.'

Steffie tried to stop her eyes widening as she listened
eagerly to this Montagu and his seemingly bonkers plan.

'We've spoken to naval hydrographers and have found the
perfect spot to drop Major Martin so that he washes ashore in
the Spanish town of Huelva where there's a very active German
agent. The man has his nose in everything and is constantly on
the line to Berlin. It's proved a nuisance in the past, but should
play into our hands here. If a British officer washes up on his
beach, he'll know about it – and so will German high command.
And if that officer has a briefcase containing secret, top-level
documents chained to his wrist, they will be read.'

'Good stuff,' Masterman said, as easily as if this were a
cricket game. 'And do we have the documents?'

'We do, sir. Lieutenant-General Sir Archibald Nye, Vice-
chief of the Imperial General Staff, has himself penned a
marvellous letter to General Alexander in the 18th Army group
HQ. It's a one chap to another type of thing, asking for his help
with a few difficulties over the invasion of Sardinia. He's also

got a letter from Mountbatten to Admiral Cunningham, introducing Major Martin as a landing craft expert to explain his travel.'

'Two letters?' someone asked. 'Would that warrant a briefcase? Surely a chap would simply slide them into his top pocket?'

Steffie was distracted momentarily by envy over an outfit with pockets big enough to hold two letters, but Montagu had an answer.

'Indeed, but we need the briefcase to help protect them from the water, so we've added two proofs of Hilary Saunders' excellent pamphlet on the commandos with another letter from Mountbatten asking General Eisenhower if he would be so kind as to write a foreword for the US edition.'

'Marvellous. Smart thinking.'

'Thank you, sir. It's all about attention to detail, we believe, and, on that note, we're working on private documents to make Martin seem a, ahem, fuller human being.'

Everyone nodded earnestly.

'Theatre tickets,' someone suggested.

'Laundry receipts.'

'Invitation to the Cabaret club. I've got a spare, if you fancy it.'

'That would be excellent, thank you,' Montagu agreed.

Steffie looked around the crusty group, happily throwing ideas about for turning a corpse into a real human, and wondered at the number of fronts on which this war was being contested, including, it seemed, some entirely imaginary ones.

'Letter from his bank manager,' someone else was saying. 'I know old Forbes at Lloyds and can get him to put something together. A nice overdraft, maybe. Man's been overspending recently.'

'That's good,' someone else chipped in. 'But what on?'

'An engagement ring,' Steffie suggested.

She'd spoken without thinking, caught up in the general enthusiasm, but as everyone at the table turned to look at her, she buried her own diamond beneath the table and fought not to blush.

'An engagement ring,' someone across the table echoed approvingly.

Steffie swallowed, but there was no turning back now.

'He should have love letters. And a photograph.'

'He should,' Masterman himself said. 'There's nothing more personal than that. Good thinking, Sarah.'

'Stefania,' her father corrected for her. 'Her mother is Italian.'

'Of course. Sorry.'

No one in this room full of double-dealers, spies and deceivers so much as flinched at her dual nationality and Steffie smiled at her father. She liked it here and desperately hoped Harry would ask her to deputise again.

'A photo,' Montagu said. 'A photo of a pretty fiancée. Now where would we get one of those?'

Everyone looked back to Steffie.

'Me?' she asked.

'Would you?'

'Well, er, why not?'

'Great. I'll talk to you afterwards,' Montagu said, and sat down.

The meeting moved on to something about chickenfeed in Tunis and Steffie sat back, palms sweaty and head reeling. Only this morning she'd become a fiancée in reality; now, it seemed, she was to become a fantasy one as well. Life in the heart of the war was a very strange business indeed.

FIVE

APRIL 1943

Fran

'Aren't they marvellous?'

Peter Lucas swept his hand across the myriad maps and charts coating every concrete wall of the vast room.

'Marvellous,' Fran muttered.

The Cambridge don had recruited her to BP and for that she would be forever grateful, but right now she was finding it hard to share his enthusiasm. She was still smarting from having Hut 3 move into giant, impersonal Block D, so to find another department doing exactly the sort of data collation that she'd made her speciality was most discombobulating. Not that Peter had noticed.

'I knew you'd like them,' he said cheerily. 'Right up your street.'

That much was true, Fran reflected, as she was dragged round to look at an astonishingly detailed map of German radio networks, similar to her own maps of convoys in the Mediterranean last year. She'd been told they'd been critical in the success of the battle to control the seas and liberate besieged

Malta and she knew she should curb her silly pride and welcome the work of this new group.

They were called SIXTA – Hut 6 Traffic Analysis – and had been moved to Bletchley from Beaumanor Hall in Leicestershire. Peter had brought her along to their section to welcome them, but she wasn't feeling very welcoming. An ATS sergeant, so fresh-faced that she should surely still be in school, stepped up to add a new pin to the chart and Fran felt old for the first time in her twenty-three years.

'Do you see the patterns?' Peter asked eagerly as the girl skipped away. 'The pins represent enemy wireless stations. These here are arranged in a *stern* – that's German for star – and it represents an enemy HQ operating with two or three outstations. And this here is a *kreis* – a circle – with several outstations of equal status communicating with each other. Through direction-finding this lot can accurately pinpoint all the enemy comms and, by extension—'

'Where their units are,' Fran filled in.

'Exactly! And by tracking the sender and receiver's codes and matching them with other data, they can also work out *what* those enemy units are. All that information, without so much as a dot of Morse read, a code broken, or a message translated. Marvellous!'

'Marvellous,' Fran echoed again, with so little enthusiasm that even Peter picked it up.

'Are you all right, Fran?'

She shook herself.

'Sorry. Yes. Just rather a lot to take in.' She spotted a large, well-thumbed book on the table below the chart and hastily picked it up. 'What's this?'

'They call it the Bird Book. It's all the Luftwaffe call signs. They change the sign for every unit at midnight using a fixed rotation detailed in here.'

'We have the German book?'

'We have a copy of it, laboriously constructed throughout most of 1940 and '41. It doesn't seem to have occurred to the Nazis to change the patterns every year so it's still, thankfully, in use. Nothing if not methodical, the Germans.'

Fran pulled a face. She flicked through page after page of three-letter call signs, arranged in tiny grids, and marvelled anew at the work that went on at Bletchley and its outstations. What diligent man or woman had constructed all of this? It was a work of extreme patience and attention to detail and definitely rivalled the Hut 3 index of which she was so proud.

Fran tutted at herself. Why was she making it all about her own achievements when everyone knew that winning this war would be a collective effort? It was hard though, and sometimes she yearned for her first months here back in 1940 when she'd taken on the task of turning a handful of shoeboxes full of rough notes into a well-organised index worthy of her year of experience in the Cambridge University Library. She'd felt so alive then, so much part of something important, but now, with the African campaign nearly sewn up, she was barely ticking over and it wasn't the same.

There was even a fancy central index now. Block H had Hollerith stamping machines to mechanise the process and an 'expert' from their Letchworth Factory had arrived to get it all running. He was acquiring a staff of WRENS to punch out thousands of cards a day and it put Hut 3's neat wooden cabinets with their hand-filed cards well into the shade. Fran was starting to feel distinctly outdated amid all this modern technology.

Peter took her arm.

'You know that we're preparing to invade Italy?'

Fran looked around.

'Of course I know, Peter.'

'And, after that, northern France.'

'Yes. I know. So what?'

'Invasions take a lot of coordination. A lot of maps and charts and indexes.'

'Good job we've got the Holleriths then, isn't it?'

Again he chuckled.

'I hear tell they're good enough for long-term research, but not a patch on a manual system run by a well-informed librarian when it comes to immediate demands.'

'Really?'

He gave her a nudge.

'You're so transparent, Miss Morgan.'

'I am?'

'You are. It's endearing – and amusing.'

'Well, I'm glad—'

'Oh, come on, girl, think about it – with the Holleriths crunching the dull data and SIXTA doing all this mapping, it frees up our top minds for higher level tasks.'

Fran swallowed.

'Higher level?'

Peter guided her out of the room and down the concrete corridor to their own, equally soulless rooms. The sign on the door still said 'Hut 3', however, and the people were still the same inside and Fran felt herself relax, especially when she spotted Valérie working away at a report, her pencil in her mouth and a frown of concentration on her lovely face.

Valérie had originally been brought into Bletchley Park as a telegraphy expert to help set up SLUs – Special Liaison Units – in France, but after Dunkirk that had become impossible and she'd shifted to working with the battlegroups in Africa. Now that Rommel had been driven out of that continent, she'd been asked to turn her attention to the Italian invasion, but Fran knew that she was feeling sidelined. Fran was beginning to feel the same.

'There's a committee been formed to collate all information relevant to an invasion,' Peter was saying, and she forced herself to concentrate. 'Oscar's on it and he tells me he's been singing the praises of Hut 3's battle order maps.'

He waved and a dapper man at the far desk rose and came over.

'Peter's told you my scheme then?' he said eagerly.

'Not fully.'

'Right. Well, I'm on this Western Front Committee, you see, run by a chap called Thomas Boase. It's an excellent concept, having a group to pull together everything relating to the invasion of Fortress Europe, but it's drowning in information, from all sorts of sources. What they need is someone to coordinate all their findings and Thomas asked me if I knew of anyone that might fit the bill.'

Fran's eyes widened.

'And you said...?'

'I said you. You did a meticulous job with the Mediterranean convoys and your index is a thing of beauty. You seem the perfect man – sorry, woman – for the task. Are you up for it?'

'I'm up for it!'

'You're sure?' Peter asked, his voice teasing. 'You don't feel too old, or outmoded, or—'

'All right, all right. I've been a bit grumpy recently, I know.'

'A bit?'

'But it was only because I was feeling ineffective.'

Peter grinned.

'I know that. Well, you're ineffective no more. Report to Mr Boase in Room 149 – top floor of Block B – on Saturday at 9 a.m.'

'Saturday?' Fran squeaked. That was her day off. Or rather, it had been. But war didn't take days off and at least this way she'd be useful once more. 'I'll be there.'

. . .

By midday on Saturday, Fran's mind was reeling – and she loved it.

'There's so much to do!' she raved to Valérie, who'd come into Bletchley Park to meet her for lunch. 'It's a total mess.'

Valérie knew better than to ask any more details but gave her hand a squeeze.

'I'm delighted. You needed a mess to get your teeth into. You've been a pain in the *postérieur* recently.'

'Thanks very much.'

'My pleasure. It's only the truth, you know.'

Fran did know and supposed she should appreciate her girl-friend's honesty. Certainly, the meeting had been exactly what she'd needed. The group had been going since the middle of last year but now that Churchill and Roosevelt had agreed rough invasion dates, their task was more urgent.

Fran had sat there, taking it all in as they'd discussed the vital importance of knowing every last detail of the enemy's battle positions before sending Allied men in against them. Thomas Boase, an earnest Oxford art historian, planned to produce a three-service report detailing German troop and equipment locations along the whole Western Front, including all the fortifications of Hitler's formidable Atlantic wall.

'Lives will be on the line,' Boase had said, his cut-glass accent making the words sound no less sinister. 'It's up to us to make sure that line is drawn as accurately as possible.'

It was exactly Fran's sort of task and she'd eagerly agreed to take on the hefty job of keeping the maps and charts up to date, as well as compiling the weekly report from their meetings. She thought now of the stars and circles on the walls of SIXTA and how she might incorporate them into her wider-ranging charts and felt a glow of satisfaction.

'You look smug,' Valérie said, pulling her back into the present.

Fran grimaced.

'Do I? Sorry. I'm just glad to be busy again.'

'I can imagine. It's good to be doing important work.' She grabbed her hand. 'But it's good to relax too. This way, please.'

Fran was startled. 'What are we doing?'

'We're going boating.'

'Here?'

She looked in astonishment as Valérie stopped by a small boat sitting in the reeds at the edge of the Bletchley pond.

'Here,' Valérie confirmed, going over to the nearby shed, taking a key from her pocket and opening it up to pull out oars.

'It's barely twenty feet across.'

'So it shouldn't be too hard to master. Come on – it'll be fun. And it's a lot warmer than skating.'

That much was true. It had been several days after the bomb back in January before Fran, Steffie or Ailsa had dared attempt skating again and, although it had been great fun, Fran had found herself sprawled on the ice far more often than she'd liked. If she was honest, she'd expected that, as the tallest, strongest and most naturally sporty of their three, she'd be best at ice skating and had not enjoyed being proved wrong.

Ailsa had natural balance from her years of Scottish dancing and had taken to it like the proverbial duck. Steffie had also been neat on her feet and shown a reckless courage at flinging herself across the ice that had turned out to be remarkably effective. She'd been less good at stopping but, as usual, there had been plenty of young men ready to catch her if she came flailing towards them. They seemed to flock to her, not that Steffie, brimming with love for her renewed fiancé, ever noticed – which only made them flock more!

Fran looked at Valérie and was glad she, too, had been granted the privilege of love, albeit in a rather more unconventional way than either of her friends. She laughed as the petite Frenchwoman wobbled into the boat, oars thrashing about wildly as she tried to get them into the rowlocks.

'Let me.'

Clambering in, Fran took control. No one brought up in Cambridge escaped a rowing boat and although the sculls she'd learned in at school had been finer than this stocky skiff, the principle was the same. They were across to the far side in moments and she spun expertly to go back again, enjoying the familiar motion. As she reached the centre of the water, however, her stomach rumbled loudly and she lifted the oars to glide to a halt.

'This is all very nice, Valérie, but there's not as much food on the pond as in the canteen.'

Valérie tossed her head.

'What they serve in the canteen is not food. Do you know, yesterday they tried to give me a mauve sponge? Mauve! That is not natural.'

'It was violet-flavoured and really quite nice. Well, it was with plenty of custard at least.'

'Custard!' Valérie threw her hands in the air, rocking the boat alarmingly. 'You English and your stupid thick, hot, lumpy custard. I swear you would eat one of my rats if I put enough of that on it.'

'Highly nutritious,' Fran said mildly.

The boat rocked again and she laughed. Valérie's eyes narrowed dangerously.

'Your palate is clearly too rough, then, for a *pain au chocolat*.'

'No!' Fran looked eagerly to Valérie's haversack as she opened it up. 'I could definitely manage a *pain au chocolat*.'

'Are you sure?' Valérie held up two of the crumbly, buttery, exquisite-smelling treats. 'Because I'm happy to eat them both myself.'

'Very sure. Please, Valérie. I'll be super-lovely to you for the whole rest of the week, I promise.'

'Super-lovely! I'll take that. And there's more where this came from, if you keep that promise.'

Fran gratefully took the pastry but didn't bite into it.

'Where *do* they come from?'

Valérie's shoulders tightened.

'Did I ask you details of your precious meeting?'

'No, but this isn't work.'

'It might be.'

'What?' The girl took a deliberate bite of her pastry. 'Valérie, what do you mean?'

'Can't talk,' she mumbled, through crumbs.

'Really?' Fran dipped an oar into the water and brought it up with a nicely threatening puddle in its curve. She aimed it at Valérie.

'No! My *pain*!'

Valérie pulled violently away, trying to protect her treat from a dousing and the boat rocked alarmingly.

'What do you mean, it might be work?' Fran demanded again. 'What are you planning?'

'Nothing. I'm planning nothing. Can I help it if Grand-mère Elodie sends me treats?'

'As long as that's all she's sending you,' Fran said, waving the oar.

Valérie threw her hands up.

'Put that damned thing back in the water, Frances. This isn't super-lovely, or even vaguely lovely.'

'I don't want you putting yourself in danger.'

'Why?'

'Why? Because I'd miss you, you stupid woman. Because I love you.'

Valérie gave a long, slow grin.

'Do you know, my Frances, that is the first time I have truly heard you say that.'

Fran flushed.

'Yes, well, it's true so, you know, don't put yourself in danger.'

'I think,' Valérie said, standing up, 'that I am in danger already, from you.'

She leaned over to kiss her and Fran felt the glorious crush of her emotion, tinged with the warmth of butter and the tickle of crumbs, and gave in to it. But just then, the boat gave up the battle with Valérie's extravagant movements and tipped them both, pastries and all, into the pond. They came up spluttering and spitting, to see half of Bletchley Park gathering round to point and laugh.

'You're certainly in danger now,' Fran growled, grumpy all over again and cold, wet and hungry into the bargain.

Valérie, however, threw back her hair in a shower of droplets, and laughed and laughed, and Fran could not be cross for long. She worried about the pull the mysterious Grand-mère Elodie had on her girlfriend, but at least she was here, safe at her side, and as long as it stayed that way, little else mattered.

SIX

APRIL 1943

Ailsa

Ailsa let herself into the caravan and sank down on the bench seat, drawing the letter from her bag and smoothing it carefully out on the table as she read the words for about the hundredth time.

> This letter is to confirm the appointment of Corporal Ailsa Robinson of the WAAF as senior wireless operative stationed at HMS Anderson, Colombo, Ceylon.

It still said the same thing, it was still her name – her *married* name – and sooner or later she was going to have to actually believe it. John Tiltman had been touchingly indignant on behalf of one of his top pupils and he had somehow got the military ruling overturned, which was exactly what she'd wanted – wasn't it? She glanced around the cosy caravan with its neat cupboards, gingham curtains, and postcards taped to the wall. If this was really happening, then there would soon be a postcard from Ceylon here in her place. It was, frankly, mind-blowing.

Ailsa looked out the window at Gloria's hens clucking innocuously around the farmyard. One looked back at her and she grimaced at it.

'Be careful what you wish for, hen.'

The bird looked impassively back, as if to say, *I thought you might have learned that last year*.

'True,' Ailsa told it. 'Malta wasn't quite the dream destination I'd imagined it might be.' She remembered the craters in the runway the day she'd arrived, the rubble in the streets and the people desperately digging their loved ones out from beneath it. 'But it was amazing,' she went on. 'I saw such glorious sights and worked with such wonderful people – and met Ned.'

Fair enough, the hen seemed to say before it went back to its pecking, and she had to remind herself that talking to animals was a sure sign of madness. Malta *had* brought her Ned though, and now Ned was on his way to Colombo and so, it appeared, was she.

'Tiltman must really rate you to have got this sorted,' Richard Gambier-Parry had said when he'd handed her the letter earlier. 'Well done you. I hope you enjoy it. Fly the flag for women and all that.'

'Thank you, sir,' she'd stuttered, stunned. She still felt much the same way now.

Ailsa reached up to the shelf above her head, where they kept an old atlas, guiltily aware that she had no real idea where Colombo was. In truth, she'd been so certain the crusties in charge would continue to block her posting that she'd tried not to think too much about it. Now she laid the atlas on top of the letter, found the grid reference on the main map of the world and traced her fingers along one, two, three squares. Then four, five... Oh my goodness!

She stared at the little island in the middle of the vast expanse of the Indian Ocean. It was past Africa, past Arabia, even past India, snuggling in at its base, much as Sicily did with Italy – only approximately five thousand miles further away. Ailsa gulped.

'Ailsa? Are you all right?'

She looked around to see Steffie and Fran standing over her. She'd been so wrapped up in the astonishing map that she hadn't heard them come in.

'Quite all right, thank you.'

'What are you looking at?'

'Erm.' She'd instinctively placed a hand over the atlas, and she forced herself to unpeel it. 'I'm looking at Ceylon. Lovely place apparently.'

The girls weren't fooled. They leaped over, Fran grabbing the atlas and Steffie pouncing on the letter beneath.

'You got it. Oh, Ailsa – you got it.'

They all looked at each other and for one horrible moment Ailsa thought she was going to cry, but then she pulled herself together. There might be a lot of sea to cross to reach Colombo but Ned would be there, and she'd go round the whole world to get to him if she had to.

'I did. I'm to get a boat from Glasgow and round into the Med, then through the Suez Canal. Remember you telling us about the Suez Canal, Steffie, when you first explained why the Med mattered so much in the war? Well, now I'll actually be travelling through it.'

'Through it and way beyond. Gosh, Ailsa.'

'Gosh what? You're both looking at me like I'm mad. And maybe I am. I was talking to a hen before you got here, but everyone does a bit of that, right? I mean, I hear people talking to their wirelesses all the time, especially when they're not working. I'm not mad. I know it's a long way. A lot of sea. An awful lot of sea if I'm honest, but it's not like I'm not used to the sea, is it? I grew up on an island surrounded by the stuff. And last year I was on Malta and that was fine. Well, not fine. There was the whole nearly being shot and then being trapped in an air-raid shelter thing, but I made it out. So I'll make it out of Colombo too. Right?'

She stopped her blethering and the others blinked at her.

'Right,' they both said, but they didn't sound very sure.

'There's just one thing...' Steffie said.

'One quite important thing,' Fran agreed.

Ailsa shifted and her hand went instinctively to her stomach, where she could feel a tell-tale hardening beneath her hand.

'This?'

'That.' They both nodded.

'It's fine. The sickness has gone and I feel totally well. Better than ever.'

That wasn't strictly true. She was still ridiculously tired, but the book she'd snuck out of the library said that ought to pass and, let's face it, she'd be sitting around on a boat for weeks so she could get all the sleep she wanted. Steffie slid onto the bench and put an arm around her.

'I know you want to see Ned, Ails. I understand that, of course I do. I'm missing Matteo dreadfully and I'm so scared for him, trying to spy on Mussolini. It's a dangerous thing to do and that's before we start invading and all the Italian soldiers have to face our guns. I mean, I know Matteo is working for the British, but how's a Tommy with a gun meant to know? He'll be in full Italian uniform so they'll shoot him and... and... Sorry, this isn't about me, is it.'

'It's about love,' Fran said, sliding in opposite them. 'It's about wanting to be with your other half. Wanting to keep them safe.' She reached for Ailsa's hand, but it didn't come naturally to either of them and she gave it a pat adding, 'Which, Ailsa, is exactly what Ned would want for you – safety.'

Ailsa bit her lip.

'Ned wants us to be together. I bet he'll get a copy of this letter – what with being my husband and therefore, you know, in charge of me.' They all sniggered but then Ailsa sobered again. 'The point is, he'll be excited I'm going to join him and upset if I don't go.'

'Not once he knows that you're pregnant, Ails.'

'With his bairn. Why should he miss out on seeing it born? That's the same sort of prejudice as me missing out on a posting because I'm married.'

Fran squinted at her.

'Not really, Ails. One is a point of principle because you can still do your job perfectly well with a ring on your finger. The other is a point of medical practicality because I'm not sure you can do your job with a baby coming out of your—'

'Thank you, Fran!'

She shrugged.

'Telling the truth, that's all. Valérie says that's always the best way.'

Her face clouded momentarily and Ailsa looked curiously at her.

'Everything all right there, Fran?'

'Fine, thank you.'

'Nothing rocking the boat?'

Steffie laughed; Fran glared. The story of her and Valérie tipping themselves into the pond had shot around the park like wildfire and they'd been the butt of many a joke.

'If you must know,' she said stiffly, 'I think Valérie wants to have more to do with her *résistant* friends in London and I don't want her to – because it's not safe. So...'

Ailsa sighed.

'I understand, honestly I do, but Colombo *is* safe. I doubt I could be further from Nazis than out there.'

'Or further from us,' Steffie said in a small voice.

'Now that I don't like,' Ailsa agreed, 'but my position is confirmed, so what can I do?'

Fran and Steffie looked at each other, then back at Ailsa.

'Tell them you're pregnant,' they said as one.

At that, however, Ailsa shook her head. She'd fought for this posting and now that she had it, she was going to grab it with both hands and pray that Mother Nature sorted out the rest.

'My wee bairn, going all that way. I swear to God, my heart can't take it.'

Mirren MacIver clung to Ailsa in a way that Ailsa could swear she'd never done before, not even on her wedding day. They were a family used to nothing more demonstrative than an approving nod of the head and she was finding all this contact a bit overwhelming, especially right now. Not that she was regretting anything. Not that she was wondering if it was too late to say no. Not that she was trying not to look at the large, grey ship in the Clyde dock that would transport her down the Atlantic and across the Mediterranean and along the Suez Canal into the mysteries of the East. Oh no. It was just that saying goodbye was always tricky.

She patted her ma's shoulder awkwardly.

'I'll be back, Ma, I promise.'

'You'd better be, lassie. And it had better be soon. Get this war won, will ye, and we can surely all go back to normal. That's to say...'

She stopped herself and they all looked uncomfortably around, unwilling to address the thorny subject of where Ailsa and Ned might live after the war. Clearly in Mirren's head the best possible plan was for them to take a house on the island, but there was precious little work there for anyone not in the fishing trade and Ailsa couldn't see Ned with a net and galoshes. She had no way of putting that into words, though, and certainly no way of explaining that Mirren and Hamish's grandchildren might not grow up three doors away.

She dug her fingers into her coat to stop herself from touching them to her belly, but even so she could feel it hard and tight beneath her clothes. She hadn't actually been to a doctor, worried that her condition would have to be declared to the WAAF authorities, but there seemed no doubt that she was in the family way and she couldn't even tell her family. She hugged her mother closer.

'It's right, lass,' Hamish said, though his voice was tight with what might be tears. 'It's right that you're with your husband.'

'Just a shame you have to go so far to reach him. Could you not both have got a nice posting in Scotland? There's plenty of activity around these docks, is there no'? Bound to be work for, you know, other stuff.'

Her parents had dutifully not asked what she did and she was grateful for that, though she longed to be able to tell them. What would they say if they knew she was using the ham radio skills she'd picked up from a primary school teacher on North Uist to pluck Nazi Morse out of the airwaves in the hope of stopping them in their deadly tracks?

The ship's horn sent out a loud hoot, making them all jump, then laugh nervously.

'That'll be your call to get on board, lass,' Hamish said, but as he bent to pick up her bag, his other hand reached for hers. 'You take care, aye? You don't go getting bombed, or shot at or, or...'

'Trapped in any shelters,' Mirren filled in, clutching at her other hand. 'We feared we'd lost you once, my sweet bairn, and we dinnae want to fear it again.'

'No. No I won't. I... I'm sorry.'

She suddenly felt desperately guilty for putting them through this.

'Ah, don't be sorry, lass – you're doing your duty in the defence of our country.'

She gave her father a weak smile of thanks but was horribly aware that it wasn't quite true. She could as easily have served her country from the safety of Bletchley Park. But then she remembered the bomb that had fallen so close to her bus in January and reminded herself that while Hitler was still alive, nowhere was safe.

The ship honked again and the three of them shuffled to the gangplank.

'Mrs Ailsa Robinson,' she said to the sailor standing at the bottom with a clipboard.

He ran his pencil down his list of names and Ailsa held her breath, thinking for a moment that he wouldn't find her, wouldn't let her on.

'Ah yes, here we are. Cabin 126. Welcome on board.'

Well, that was that then. Ailsa turned to give her parents a last squeeze and then hefted her duffel bag onto her shoulder and took her first step up the gangplank. It wobbled and she gripped at the handrail and hesitated.

'What if she's sick?' she heard her ma say to her pa, and then the robust answer, 'She won't be sick, she's from fisher-stock.'

There was no turning back after that and Ailsa headed up the gangplank as fast as her distinctly un-fisher-like legs could carry her. She only stopped at the top to look down on her parents, scarily shrivelled below her, and wave as cheerily as she could manage. She'd wanted adventure, but was this an adventure too far even for her? Only time would tell.

SEVEN

APRIL 1943

Fran

'There he is!' Valérie grabbed at Fran's hand and pointed across the smart hotel lobby at a man on the far side with as much awe as if he were Cary Grant or Humphrey Bogart. 'General De Gaulle!'

Fran squinted at the man, struggling to see the appeal. Even sitting down, De Gaulle was clearly unusually tall and held himself very straight-backed, his long nose sharp in the light from the wall-lamps and his ears amusingly prominent.

'Are you sure that's him?'

'Totally. Look at his fancy uniform. And, besides, Uncle Claude said he would be sitting beneath the portrait of Napoleon.'

She gestured to the heavy oil painting over the man's head which, sure enough, portrayed the great French leader. The one, Fran thought, who had been defeated by Wellington and ended up imprisoned and embittered on Elba – not that she'd point that out right now. To one side of Napoleon was a second portrait, this time of Joan of Arc, also, it had to be said, a failed saviour of France but she supposed that wasn't the important point.

De Gaulle had several people around him and appeared to be haranguing them in stentorian French. Fran caught the words *'patriotisme'*, *'fierté'*, and *'bravoure'*, as well as repeated use of 'La France'. It sounded good, she had to admit – grand. It would be most odd if people went around talking about 'The England' but she had to admire these people's guts, especially when La France, at least the free part of it, was concentrated in a corner of the Connaught Hotel around a leader almost no one had ever heard of until he'd started broadcasting defiance across the BBC.

That was how they'd secured the invitation to dine with the near-mythical leader of the Free French. Pierre Brossolette was a regular voice on the BBC French service and had got to know De Gaulle well. Pierre was 'away' at the moment – details very much not forthcoming – but Gilberte had been working with the general on his most recent broadcast and had suggested Valérie and Fran come and join them this evening. Fran, exhausted from doing her indexing job in Hut 3, as well as extra hours collating information for the Western Front committee, hadn't been keen but Valérie had been so excited at the prospect that she hadn't had the heart to say no. Now that they were actually here, however, the Frenchwoman was hanging back like a shy toddler.

'Shall we go over?' Fran said.

'In a minute.' If Fran wasn't much mistaken, her girlfriend was holding onto the coving on the wall nearest them and she looked at her fondly.

'This isn't like you.'

'It's General De Gaulle, Frances. He's a hero.'

'He's a man doing his part to win this war, as you, Valérie, are a woman doing yours.'

Valérie shuddered.

'I could never speak on the BBC.'

'Really?'

'*Sacré bleu*, no! I'd have no idea what to say.'

'Lots about *fierté* and *bravoure* and La France, I'd suggest.'

Valérie stuck her tongue out at her.

'It's all right for you, Fran. You're confident and articulate and—'

'And you're not?'

'Not if there's a microphone in front of me.'

'Or, it seems, a French general. Come on, I thought you said Grand-mère Elodie had met him?'

Valérie stiffened.

'I did.'

'So would it not be good, next time you see her, to chat about the great man?'

'It would,' Valérie agreed cautiously, letting Fran unpeel her hand from the wall, but they'd only taken two steps before she froze again. 'But what will we say?'

'Try "*Bonsoir, Generale*," and we'll take it from there.'

'*Bonsoir*,' Valérie muttered earnestly, as if it was the smartest word in the world. '*Oui*.'

But still she didn't move, and Fran was grateful when Gilberte Brossolette came in behind them.

'Frances! Valérie! Shall I introduce you?'

There wasn't so much as a moment's pause for a reply before she took their arms and swept them forward. General De Gaulle looked up and, to Fran's surprise, leapt to his feet and flung his arms out wide in welcome. Valérie's eyes shone and she took a step towards him.

'Jean!'

'No,' Fran started. 'We're—'

But De Gaulle was brushing past to shower someone behind them in kisses. Valérie's face dropped and for a moment Fran felt actual hatred for the leader of the Free French, but already Valérie was recovering.

'*Mon dieu! C'est Jean Moulin.*'

'Who?'

Gilberte pulled Fran in close.

'Let's just say that he's something important in southern France, shall we?'

She looked sternly at Valérie, who nodded, her eyes still on the new arrival. He was far smaller than De Gaulle, coming barely up to his ostentatiously uniformed shoulders, and had bright, darting eyes beneath a heavy brow. He'd swept a chic trilby off his dark hair, wore a silk scarf tied jauntily around his neck and couldn't have looked anything other than French. Resistance, no doubt about it.

'And who are these lovely ladies?' Moulin asked, pulling away from De Gaulle to look at them.

De Gaulle turned round.

'No idea. Gilberte?'

'This is Mademoiselle Valérie Rousseau. Her grand-mère is Elodie Rousseau who runs the bicycle shops in Normandy.' Both men picked up on the name and De Gaulle looked instantly more interested. Valérie shone with pride. 'And this is Miss Frances Morgan, who works in Buckinghamshire with Valérie.' Again the inference, again they picked it up. These, Fran realised, were men who were used to living their lives in allusions and half-truths and she felt a guilty thrill at being here with them. There were many ways to fight a war, and Bletchley Park wasn't the only arm of the Allies keeping secrets.

'We thank you, ladies,' Jean Moulin said with a bow. 'We all have our part to play in winning this terrible war.'

'And liberating France,' De Gaulle said, and Fran saw instantly that this was his sole purpose. She supposed that was what made him so appropriate for his self-appointed job. 'Now, shall we eat? I hear Chef has got hold of some horsemeat for a *bourguignonne.*'

There were murmurs of appreciation around the small group and Fran fought to suppress memories of the ponies their neighbours had kept in the field behind their Cambridgeshire house. There was a war on and dietary scruples, like so much else, had been bombed into oblivion.

They dined in a private room at the back of the hotel, the conversation around the table fast, lively and all in French. Fran battled to keep up as De Gaulle lectured them on Blitzkrieg, a military tactic he had apparently been urging the French to adopt in the interwar period with no luck. 'So when Hitler Blitzkreig-ed all over us, that showed Pétain!' he finally concluded, moving on to a spirited condemnation of the man who had once been his mentor and had now 'lost his marbles, in fact, all his balls'.

'I hear the war is almost won in North Africa,' Moulin interjected at one point and Fran was grateful for something positive. Both her brothers were working in a field hospital near Algiers and she absorbed all the news the BBC could offer about the situation out there. Everything suggested that the last dregs of German defence were about to give up and she couldn't wait to hear that Rob and Ben were free of the threat of enemy fire.

'The Free French forces fought well in Libya,' she offered in nervous French.

Moulin smiled at her. De Gaulle pounced.

'*Very* well! That showed the Americans. Bloody Roosevelt tried to stop our forces from fighting out there, you know. Terrible man. No idea how to run a country. The Free French in North Africa have been bold and brave and efficient. I don't believe in empire – waste of time and resources – but, *mon dieu*, those equatorial states have stepped up at a time of crisis.'

'And are ready to host the French government as soon as the last German is off African soil,' Moulin said.

'Hmm.' For once De Gaulle didn't seem to have much to say.

'It is important, Charles,' Moulin said quietly but firmly. 'It is one of the conditions of the *conseil.*'

Fran looked to Gilberte, sitting on her left, for an explanation.

'*Le conseil de la résistance,*' she whispered. 'Jean is trying to unite the various groups in the south and my Pierre the same in the north.'

Fran stared at her.

'In the occupied zone?'

'Hush! Yes.'

'Is that not terribly dangerous?' Gilberte gave a Gallic shrug but tears shimmered at the edges of her eyes and Fran gave her hand an awkward pat. 'Pierre must be a very brave man.'

'He is. He has to be. We all have to be.' She shook herself. 'But listen to me – this is not dinner conversation. Tell me, Frances, have you thought any more about writing articles?'

'I wish I could have done but I've been far too busy.'

'I understand, but you are staying the night here in Londres, yes?' Fran nodded. 'And you are off duty tomorrow?'

'I am,' Fran agreed cautiously.

Gilberte clapped her hands.

'*Parfait!* How would you like to come to Broadcasting House with me?'

Fran gaped at her.

'The BBC?'

'*Oui.* My good friend Maurice Schumann is putting out a report on the French service and I have agreed to go along with him. You can come too if you'd like. Valérie as well.'

Fran turned to Valérie, who was listening, rapt, to De Gaulle and Moulin. The waiters were bringing in the bourguignon, and in their presence the men had switched smoothly from discussing the *conseil* to comparing the merits of Brie and Camembert.

'Valérie!' Fran nudged her in the ribs and she drew her eyes away from her heroes with evident reluctance. 'Would you like to come to the BBC with Gil and me tomorrow?'

Valérie frowned.

'The BBC? *Non, merci.*'

'But...'

'I have someone I have to meet, *ma chérie.* I'm sorry.'

'An uncle?'

Valérie smiled, then gave her a cheeky wink.

'An uncle, *oui.*'

'If I didn't know better, Valérie Rousseau, I'd worry that you were chasing after men.'

'Only for what they can do for me, and for France. All else is for you, *ma chère* Frances.' She kissed her openly on the lips and Fran flushed but De Gaulle was too busy digging into his food to notice and Jean Moulin simply smiled. 'But you go, Frances. You will love it.' She leaned across her to offer Gilberte a kiss too, though this one on the cheek. '*Merci, mon amie. Merci beaucoup.*'

Then she was tuned into the Frenchmen once more. Frances blinked, feeling, as she often did with Valérie, as if she'd been caught up in a small whirlwind. This one, however, had landed her in a very exciting place.

'I'd love to come,' she told Gilberte firmly, already looking forward to the next day.

Fran approached the iconic walls of Broadcasting House with something of the awe that she'd seen in Valérie standing before General De Gaulle last night. She winced at the boarded-up hole in one side of the mighty building where a bomb had blasted into it in '41.

'It looks rotten, torn apart like that,' she said, pointing upwards.

'A bomb won't stop Auntie,' Gilberte said calmly, guiding her past the damage and round to the main doors. 'Here we are.'

Fran looked up at the curved frontage, like a ship cruising forward across the airwaves. She took in Eric Gill's statue of a ten-foot Prospero, sending Ariel – spirit of the air – out into the world, then the art deco facade above, leading up to a huge clock and the giant aerial that was the symbol of the BBC. She glanced to Gilberte, who gave her a knowing grin and sashayed through the big doors, leaving Fran to scuttle in her wake.

Inside was every bit as impressive. The curved reception area was graciously decorated and exuded an aura of calm importance, not dented by the tape and stern 'no entry' signs across the upwards stairs. Since the bomb, Gilberte told her, the BBC had been running its core programmes out of big studios in the basement and now she checked them in and handed Fran a pass, before making for the downward stairway. Fran followed, gazing in wonder at the pass. Beneath the letters *BBC*, it said *Miss Frances Morgan, guest* and she fastened it onto her lapel with pride.

In the basement, it was a hive of activity. They were asked to wait in a cavernous studio, complete with stage and chairs. Several technicians were setting up four microphones and after a few minutes someone came out and set a sign in front of them.

'*It's That Man Again*,' Fran read excitedly. 'Does that mean Tommy Handley's here?'

She looked eagerly around. Handley's goofy satire on wartime Britain was a big favourite in Bletchley Park and she couldn't believe she might actually see a recording in progress. Gilberte shook her head.

'You British and your peculiar sense of humour. I doubt he'll be here yet, but maybe when we come out. Ah, Maurice!'

A side door opened to release a slim-faced man in heavy

specs, and a babble of French chatter poured out. Maurice and Gilberte kissed and then Gilberte turned to Fran.

'This is Frances Morgan, budding journalist.'

'Oh now...' Fran tried to protest but Maurice seemed to see nothing odd in the claim.

'Miss Morgan, *enchanté*. Welcome to our cave – our portal into La France.' He shook her hand heartily and gestured around the basement. 'What you are looking at here, is a weapon of war.'

Fran frowned.

'In what way?'

'In the most important way. The BBC, like the newspapers, is a weapon of the mind. It is a manipulator of public opinion. It informs, it boosts morale, it keeps spirits up. Everything, even something as apparently benign as *It's That Man Again*, tells the nations – yours and mine – that we will not give up anything to the Nazis, not even our sense of humour. That gives them the strength to battle on even as their rations are being cut, their homes bombed and their sons shot.'

Fran sucked in her breath, her thoughts going instantly to her two brothers, working to save lives so close to the front line.

'Herr Goebbels understood that early on,' Maurice went on in his silky, radio-perfect voice. 'The Germans have been producing cheap wireless sets for years, getting them into homes across the country so that they can trickle poison into every single ear. They are censoring everything and manipulating each news item to their own advantage. Ordinary German housewives will believe that Germany are fighting a noble cause and that they are winning.'

'And us?'

Maurice looked at her sharply.

'The British do it differently. The BBC believes in the truth. They think that the people will trust them more if they don't lie, and it seems to be working. Hell, even the French trust them now, so it must be!' He gave a sharp laugh and added, 'We have to. The Nazis have taken over all our radio stations, so where else is there to turn?'

'I'm sorry.'

'Don't be sorry, Miss Morgan, just keep doing what you're doing. The BBC is solid, and in a world where so much else can be swept from beneath you at any time, that counts for much.'

Fran looked around the big studio, noting the people popping in and out of the smaller side ones in an endless round of activity. She pictured the wireless set they had in the caravan, the ones sitting in every office in Bletchley Park, and in almost every home in the country, families gathered around them waiting to hear what was going on in this most global of wars.

'I can see that,' she agreed, 'and I'm keen to watch you broadcasting.'

'I had best be sure, then, that I, how do you say – pull my socks up?'

Fran smiled.

'I'm sure your socks are in excellent shape.'

'You are too kind. This way, please. My slot, *Les Français parlent aux Français*, will be on shortly so if you come through here...' He took them into the French offices, steering them between desks and into the recording studio. 'Then you will catch it all. You speak French?'

'*Un peu.*'

'*Bon!*' He winked at her, waved them into hard chairs in the corner, and slid expertly into a seat behind a microphone set on a desk with some complicated-looking equipment. A producer buzzed around, adjusting things, and Fran had to surreptitiously pinch herself to believe she was really here. She hated the war but, goodness, it was throwing up some amazing opportunities.

'Right.'

Maurice turned up a dial to let them hear what was

currently being broadcast and a plummy voice filled the studio, asking the public for 'urgent assistance'. Fran leaned curiously in.

'This is a chance,' the man assured his listeners, 'for you all to do your bit towards the final push on Herr Hitler and you can do it from your own homes – from your cupboards, your albums and your attics. If any of you have ever been to any part of France on your holidays or for work trips, please dig out all post-cards, photographs, maps and articles and send them to us at the War Office. It will help us build up an invaluable picture of the area to which your sons, your husbands, your fathers and your nephews will be heading one day, when the time is right, to take the war into Fortress Europe and defeat the Nazis once and for all. Here's the address to send them to...'

Fran stared at the speaker, wondering which studio the man was speaking from, not that it mattered. The key point was that someone had thought to ask for pictorial evidence of the land-marks of northern France and that that evidence could be invaluable to the Western Front committee. Gilberte reached out and squeezed her hand.

'Enjoying it?'

'Loving it!' Fran agreed.

This morning was giving her a glimpse into another world – a world she might, if she could prove herself worthy, visit more often once the war was over and she was looking for a new job. It had also offered her a new way to do her current job well and she could hardly wait to get back to Bletchley Park and tell the committee of this huge resource they could feed into their burgeoning files.

'Take the war into Fortress Europe,' she echoed under her breath.

It was what they were all working towards now and as she settled in to listen to Maurice broadcasting to the people of France who were bravely working to welcome them, she vowed, yet again, to do her very best to make the scary events ahead of them succeed.

EIGHT

APRIL 1943

Steffie

'Oh yes!' Ewen Montagu held the photo up to the sparkling lights in the theatre bar. 'This is perfect. Isn't this perfect, Charles?'

He waved the photograph at Charles Cholmondeley, his partner in the planning of Operation Mincemeat, and Steffie winced at having herself in a bathing costume shown to the great and the good of London.

'Stop wafting the photograph around, Ewen,' Delilah said, plucking it out of his fingers and spiriting it away in her evening bag. Steffie shot her a grateful look.

Delilah was Ewen's secretary and a smart, no-nonsense girl who looked as if she'd be far more at home in jodhpurs than an evening gown.

'Why?' Ewen protested. 'Major Martin is proud of Pam, his lovely fiancée.'

'And you're not Major Martin!' Delilah slotted an arm through Steffie's and said, 'Honestly, Ewen's become obsessed. I swear he's living the poor major's life.'

Steffie laughed. It came out rather too loud but was easily lost in the chatter of the pre-theatre folk in the bar. If she was honest, she felt she was living Pam's life at times. From the moment she'd sat with Ewen over coffee after the Twenty Committee meeting a month ago to start dreaming up the girl who'd captured their intrepid traveller's heart, she'd felt the lines between herself and Pam blurring.

The two letters she'd written from Pam to her Bill had come straight from her own feelings about Matteo, though channelling them through a made-up character had helped create some distance. 'Pam' had written on headed paper from the Manor House, Osbourne St George, Wiltshire – Ewen's brother's address – telling Bill Martin how much she'd hated saying goodbye at the station and begging him to 'please don't let them send you off into the blue in that horrible way they do nowadays'.

'Now that we've found each other out of the whole world,' she'd gone on, 'I don't think I could bear it.' Steffie had actually wept as she'd written those words, knowing that poor Pam was about to be shattered by the tragedy of her fiancé's plane being shot down over the Straits of Gibraltar. The fact that Pam was fictional and her fiancé an already dead tramp reincarnated as a trusted courier had not dampened her sorrow one bit. Even now, she couldn't stop herself looking around the Prince of Wales Theatre and feeling sad that this would be the last happy night Major Martin would spend. Ewen had invited her to join him, Charles and Delilah at the Sid Fields show so that Martin could carry the ticket stubs in his pocket – yet one more device to make the man convincingly real for the German agents to find at the other end. She'd been honoured to be included and was looking forward to the show, but the whole thing felt surreal and suddenly she wished she could be here with Matteo, laughing and cuddling. The five-minute bell rang out, as if admonishing her, and she swallowed and fought to pull herself together.

'Are you all set then?' she asked Ewen.

He glanced around but everyone in the theatre was collecting their friends to head into the auditorium and no one was paying them any attention.

'All set. He's dressed and ready to go – not that it was plain sailing.'

'Ever tried to dress a frozen man, Stefania?' Charles gave a comedy grimace.

'Charles!' Delilah admonished, and he grinned.

'It's not easy, I can tell you. Thank the Lord we went for battledress as we needed all the wiggle-room we could get for the poor chap's stiff limbs. And the boots!'

He and Ewen exchanged rueful looks. The bar was all but empty now and the usher on the door was looking pointedly at them. Charles cheerfully lifted his still half-full pint glass and waved them all in close.

'You cannot get boots onto feet that are frozen solid at right angles to the legs. We had no idea what to do. We couldn't defrost the poor chap or he'd start decomposing way too early to be convincing in the sea in two days' time.'

Steffie tried to picture two men trying to fit battle boots onto a corpse, and got a fit of the giggles.

'What did you do?' she choked out.

'Thought about it for a long time and, in the end, got an electric heater to defrost his feet and ankles enough to gain some movement and ram the damn boots on. We figure if the coroner picks up a discrepancy, they'll put it down to damp socks or some such. Besides, Martin will be washing up in a tiny town and our chaps say Spanish coroners won't have a clue.'

'Your chaps sound rather arrogant, if you ask me,' Delilah said crisply. 'Now come on, or we'll have everyone tutting at us as we find our seats.'

Charles rolled his eyes but downed the last of his beer and led them all through for Major Martin's last, fabricated, night of fun. Later tonight, he and Ewen would pack the major's body into a specially made lead container, add tonight's theatre stubs, plus Steffie's photo and letters and the briefcase containing the vital correspondence confirming the invasion would be in Sardinia not Sicily. Then they would fill it with dry ice and drive him through the night to the mouth of the Clyde, whence he would catch his submarine, HMS *Seraph*, to his final destiny off the coast of Spain.

Rommel's forces were still just about holding their bridge-head in Tunisia but had their backs to the sea wall and Ultra decrypts suggested the legendary general was asking permission to abandon the troubled continent and shore up forces in Europe instead. So far, Hitler was resisting but it could only be a matter of time before the troops on the ground caved in and when they did, it was imperative that they moved to Sardinia not Sicily. Major Martin's fictitious delivery was vital. Steffie settled into her seat in the theatre and glanced to Ewen, Charles and Delilah as the show started and they laughed innocently at the opening lines. Soon the curtain would be going up on their own performance and they could only pray that the enemy audience would drink it in.

'Matteo,' Steffie murmured.

The sun was warm on their skin and the soft waves of the Mediterranean lapping at their toes as they lay together on the sand, hands entwined. Her body, when she squinted down at it through the translucent light, was that of her teenage self, but Matteo was murmuring to her about how proud he was of her work and how he couldn't wait to marry her tomorrow in a church on the rocks.

'But Matteo,' she said, 'I don't have a dress yet.'

'I'll marry you exactly as you are, Stefania Carmichael,' he replied, stroking a hand across her stomach and leaning in to kiss her. But before their lips could meet, something bumped up against her foot and she sat up to see a bloated corpse bobbing in the shallows. It was wearing the uniform of a marine and trailing a briefcase that was scattering pictures of herself across the blue water like black-and-white confetti.

'Major Martin!' she shouted, and at that point she woke up to find she'd dribbled onto her desk and most of Hut 4 were laughing at her.

'Nice snooze, Steffie?' Harry Hinsley teased.

'No,' she said crossly.

'Shame. There's a message come in on the teleprinters for you from an E. Montagu.'

'Ewen?' She leaped up, all embarrassment forgotten. 'Where is it? What does it say?'

'Ooh! You're keen. I thought you were all set to march down the aisle with your Italian?'

'I am,' Steffie said, cross again. 'If, that is, we can invade Italy without losing too many precious British lives and kick the Nazis out before he's found out as a...' She dried up, doubly furious that she'd nearly spoken state secrets out loud. Even here in the sanctity of Hut 4, you couldn't be too careful. 'Anyway,' she went on, 'the point is that there are critical operations afoot and Captain Montagu is a key element with what could be key news, so may I have it please?'

Harry had the grace to look ashamed. He held out a slip of paper and Steffie snatched it eagerly from him.

'Major Martin safely delivered for his fish supper,' it said, beautifully cryptic.

Steffie shook away the image of his corpse bobbing against her toes. That had been a dream, a stupid dream brought on by too many long hours in the office. Major Martin was in the sea and they had to hope that he hit the shore where he was meant to, that the Spanish authorities were as corrupt as they believed, and that the German spy got hold of his briefcase – and believed what was in it. As the rest of Hut 4 went back to their desks, Steffie collared Harry.

'A word, please – in private.'

'Of course.'

As head of hut, he had his own office and ushered her inside, still looking shame-faced.

'Sorry about the teasing. Brandy?'

'Don't worry about it, Harry. And yes, please.'

'Good news?'

'Sounds like Operation Mincemeat is in action.'

'Operation Mincemeat?'

'You know – the one to land a corpse in Spain? To convince the Germans that—'

'Oh yes. Sorry. It's been so hectic here that I'm not paying enough attention to the Twenty Committee stuff.'

'You should. It's vital.'

'Agreed.' He poured them both large brandies and handed hers over. She lifted it and drank a silent toast to the poor tramp who was inadvertently doing vital work for the British government. 'It's so vital, it needs someone better than me on it. How about you take over permanently, Stef?'

'Take over what?'

'As Bletchley Park rep on the Twenty Committee. I hear you did a great job, and you clearly appreciate the work, so why not?'

'Really?' Steffie sipped her brandy, trying to take this in. 'I'd love to, Harry – if you think they'll accept me.'

'They'll do what they're told. They need the ears Bletchley Park are giving them and yours are the sharpest ears around.'

Steffie felt a glow spread through her and set her brandy hastily down.

'Thank you, Harry. That means a lot.'

'What it means is that the job will get done. In fact, I was talking to Denys Page about it the other day. He runs ISOS, reading the Abwehr traffic, and he's done his shift on the committee too. He's fed up with the disruption of the constant trips to London and would love the chance to hand them over.'

Steffie couldn't see how anyone could be fed up with that, but kept her peace.

'What are you thinking, Harry?' she asked tentatively.

'I'm thinking, Stefania Carmichael, that if we transfer you to ISOS, you could be at the coalface, reading what the German secret service believe we're doing – how they're taking what our agents are telling them, how they're reading our battle plans, where they think our troops are – and report that straight to the Twenty Committee. It would cut out half of the shilly-shallying so the whole thing would be far more efficient.' He smiled, clearly pleased with himself. 'What do you say?'

'Me, reading Abwehr Enigma?'

Steffie gaped at her boss. The Abwehr was the German military intelligence agency and their messages circulated at the highest level.

'That would be the plan,' Harry confirmed.

'In German?'

'If you're up to it. I seem to remember you're pretty fluent.'

Steffie wasn't sure 'fluent' was the word for her finishing school German, but it was good enough for operational messages and she could soon brush it up.

'I can read German,' she said determinedly. 'And then I'd feed the info straight into the Twenty Committee?'

'Exactly.'

She swallowed; it sounded amazing, apart from one thing.

'I'd have to leave Hut 4?' She could still remember turning up in the funny little hut when there were only a handful of them laboriously working through codes and she'd been sent through to the secretaries' room. How far she'd come! A rush of pride overcame her sadness and she cleared her throat. 'I'll miss you all, but I want to do this and I want to do it well.'

'I know you do, Stef. And we'll miss you too, but, hey, we'll still see you in the Drunken Arms, right?'

'Too right. That's where we'll toast the victory.'

'One day,' Harry agreed. 'And sooner for having you on the job.'

Steffie pulled a face at him, awkward before all this praise, but as she stood up from her desk, she felt far taller than she ever had in even her biggest heels. This new role was an honour and one she vowed to do justice to – not just for herself, but for the whole of Europe.

NINE

JUNE 1943

Ailsa

Ailsa looked at her handkerchief in dismay. She'd only got it out of her bag a few minutes ago and it was drenched already. She'd thought it was hot on Malta but that was nothing compared to the Indian Ocean. She supposed she should have expected it but, packing in a chilly caravan in soggy Buckinghamshire, it had been hard to imagine anything like this. The air seemed full of water and her pale skin flared to the colour of her red hair almost the moment she stepped out of the shade.

Luckily, as long as she kept to the right side of the big ship, shade was always available and it was only now land was in sight that she'd been unable to resist the lure of hanging over the rail to see her new home. And her husband.

'Ned,' she breathed.

Back in Bletchley she had missed him but had been distracted by her work and her friends. On the thirty-day trip she'd had little to think about but being reunited and the closer she got, the more the hours seemed to drag. She couldn't believe another human being had the power to make her ache with longing like this. It both awed and scared her. Too often in this war, she'd seen what losing loved ones did to people and it was terrifying. Sometimes it felt like sitting in the waiting room at the dentist's and hearing someone in the chair shouting out in pain, filling you with the dreadful anticipation of your own suffering to come.

Ailsa gripped the railing and prayed that Ned would be there when she landed. There had been times on her month-long trip when she'd feared she might not make it and she had no way of knowing if his ship had done so. The only thing stopping her from going mad had been the views along the way. She'd loved their brief dock into Valletta, her home for over a year, and the Suez Canal had been crazy enough to distract her from either the past or the future. It had been a most peculiar creation, a flat, featureless line of a man-made river, with desert either side and only warships and cruisers to alleviate the blankness of the landscape.

Often Arabs had come to the east bank to watch the progress of the ship, their robes white against the sandy earth. At first Ailsa had stepped up to the rail to wave, but as soon as the ship had drawn close, the men had lifted their robes to expose themselves to her shocked eyes. The first time, she'd looked around, unsure if the heat was playing tricks with her, but another girl had caught her eye and grimaced.

'They always do it, I'm afraid. No idea why. It's not like we could jump ship and swim up to them even if we wanted use of the wrinkled goods on show.'

Ailsa had laughed out loud and introduced herself to the WREN, who was called Daisy and was full of the joys of her adventure. She'd been good company down the Red Sea – not, to Ailsa's disappointment, red at all – but had left the ship at Djibouti, bound for an outpost in Kenya.

'Kenya! Me!' she'd giggled to Ailsa. 'Can you believe it? Until Herr Hitler decided to try and conquer the world, I was sewing press-studs in a factory in Manchester, and now look at me – halfway across the world.'

'Magical, isn't it?' Ailsa had agreed.

'Well, not the Hitler bit. That man is a proper villain! But the rest, yes. What about you, what were you up to before the war?'

'Living on a tiny island in the Hebrides with no chance of anything more than marriage and kiddies ahead of me.'

'But aren't you...?'

For a moment Ailsa had thought she'd been rumbled, but thankfully Daisy had been pointing to her wedding ring.

'Oh. Yes. I met Ned on Malta and I'll be joining him in Colombo. It turns out it wasn't the marriage bit that was the problem, but the men on offer.'

'That's so romantic,' Daisy had sighed. 'I hope I meet a handsome officer in Kenya to sweep me off my feet beneath the banana trees.'

'I hope you do too,' Ailsa had said, 'but I'm sure you'll have fun whatever – and do important work too.'

Daisy had cocked her head on one side.

'I suppose so, but it would be poor show not to come out of this lot with a husband. You must be proud.'

It had been a curious way of looking at things, to Ailsa's mind. She loved Ned to bits and was delighted she'd met him, but she was far prouder of her wireless work than of getting someone down the aisle. Still, it took all sorts. And now the docks of Colombo were getting so close she could see the men cleaning the decks of the many military vessels lined up on either side and every minute stuck onboard without Ned felt like an hour.

She pressed a hand to her belly, glad that, thanks to losing so much weight during the hunger-months of the siege of Malta, there was still enough room beneath her WAAF uniform to accommodate her growing belly. Even so, the belt was starting to feel tight and it was always a relief when she got into her cabin at night to take her skirt off and slide into the forgiving folds of her nightie. There were three other girls in her cabin, but they were all too busy eyeing up the sailors to pay any attention to Ailsa's waistline. Quite what she'd do in another month or so, she had no idea but she figured she'd deal with that when she got there. The important thing now was to get off this ship and find Ned.

Leaning down, she checked on the trusty duffel bag that she'd thrown her clothes into four years ago when she'd stormed off North Uist to join the WAAFs. That move had taken her to Bletchley Park and the two young women who had become her greatest friends, and she wondered, with another ache, what Steffie and Fran were up to right now. It was mid-afternoon in Ceylon, which would make it morning tea time back in England, not that anyone in Bletchley Park had morning tea these days. Well, unless Gloria had baked a cake with rations swapped for poached rabbits, or Valérie had received some of those tasty Madeleine things from one of her uncles, or the NAAFI had got a lucky delivery or... Ailsa stopped herself. She was in Ceylon now, actually in Ceylon, and from the bump of the ship they were docking. As soon as she was ashore, she could send a postcard to the girls – well, after she'd given Ned a long, hard kiss.

She hitched her duffel bag onto her shoulder as the sailors ran around securing the ship with giant ropes. The sun was shining across the busy dock, bleaching it into a mass of hazy figures against the green hills behind, and she squinted furiously into the crowd. Her whole body was shaking with anticipation and she worried she might lose her balance and tumble off the narrow gangplank. A dip in that bright blue water wouldn't go amiss, but it probably wasn't the best way to reintroduce herself to the man she'd married back in January snow in Bletchley.

'Ailsa? Ailsa! Here. I'm here!'

She shaded her eyes to catch sight of a man leaping up and down in the crowd, waving both arms. He was wearing tropical whites and looked unutterably delicious.

'Ned!'

She almost considered diving into the water to get to him faster.

'Patience girl,' she muttered, sounding, even to herself, like her mother.

'Good things come to those who wait,' Mirren MacIver had always said, but had Ailsa not proved that good things come to those who march right out there and grab them? She smiled and forced herself to stand back until, at last, her name was checked off on a list and she could escape the ship.

Ned was at the bottom and swept her into his arms. She clutched at him, feeling the familiar shape of his surprisingly broad chest, drinking in the scent of his soft hair and reaching up to touch her lips to his and lose herself in his kiss.

'Oh, Ailsa, I can't believe you're really here, that we're really together.' He pulled back to look at her. 'My wife! You're so beautiful.'

Ailsa pushed damp hair self-consciously out of her eyes.

'I'm sticky and sweaty and red as an over-ripe cherry.'

'You are all those things,' he agreed, 'and still beautiful. I've missed you so much.'

'And I you, Ned.' She drew him down for another kiss. 'Tell me we don't have to share a billet?'

He shook his head, his eyes dark.

'We have a banda.'

'A what?'

'A banda – a straw hut. Small and primitive but lovely and all ours.'

'Take me there now!'

He laughed and pulled her close in for another, deeper kiss.

'Goodness,' he said eventually. 'Where are my manners?' He took the duffel bag from her shoulder and looked around. 'Do you have anything else with you?'

Ailsa put a hand to her stomach, unable to keep her secret any longer.

'I am, er, carrying something, but I'm afraid you can't take it off me.'

Ned's eyes widened.

'You don't mean...?' Ailsa nodded. 'You're not...?'

'I am.'

'You're having a...?'

'Sssh, Ned!' She put a finger up over his lips. 'No one knows.'

His face fell.

'You mean you're out here on, on false pretences?'

She laughed.

'Of course I am. Goodness, I had enough trouble convincing them to let me off Blighty with a wedding ring on my finger, let alone with a... you know.'

'But Ailsa, what will happen when they find out?'

She shrugged. It was a habit she'd noted in Valérie and she found it most useful.

'I suppose they'll try to send me home, but it'll be too late.'

'It will?' Ned looked pale now. 'When are you due?'

'I'm not sure exactly. I haven't been to see a doctor.'

'Ailsa!'

'I couldn't be sure they wouldn't tell Bletchley Park, could I? But I'm perfectly healthy, Ned, really I am and, if you remember correctly, there are only three weeks in which I could possibly have conceived...'

'Oh, I remember,' he said, clutching her close again.

'So by my calculations I must be due sometime in late October.'

'Right. Yes, I see. That makes sense.' He shook himself.

'Actually, no, none of this makes sense. That's to say, it fits together logically but it's still impossible to comprehend. I'm going to be a father? We're going to be a family?'

It sounded glorious like that, and Ailsa cuddled in against him, the endless hours on the boat already forgotten in the joy of being in his arms.

'We're going to be a family,' she confirmed.

He kissed her over and over.

'I'm so glad,' he said. 'So very glad. We are also, however, going to be in deep trouble. Commander Keith will not like this.'

'Commander Keith,' Ailsa said, 'won't have much choice. And, besides, unless he gets as close to me as you just have—'

'Which he better not.'

'Then he won't notice for a few weeks. A bit of padding and I'll just look like I've been at the black-market pies.'

Ned shook his head.

'Lord help us, Ailsa Robinson, my beautiful, bold, bonkers wife! I've missed you so much, but I have a feeling life is about to get considerably more interesting now you're back.'

'Oh, I hope so,' Ailsa said. 'Now, take me to this banda and get these damned clothes off me.'

'Yes, ma'am!'

Later – quite some time later – Ned took Ailsa out of the cosy hut that would be their marital home for the foreseeable future and across to HMS Anderson, the naval base where they'd both work. Set up on what had, before the war, been a lush golf course, the large collection of long, straw-roofed buildings sat in open land cut into banana groves, only the vast aerials dotted about the complex giving any indication of its function as a listening station.

Ailsa looked up at the big metal towers and felt the rush she always got from the idea of messages scrambling around on the airwaves. She didn't believe in magic – not even the selkies all the islanders back home swore were real – but this, to her, was as close as it got. From Colombo she would be able to listen in to the intimate communications between Berlin and Tokyo – two great powers exchanging evil across vast distances. More importantly, thanks to Bletchley Park, she'd be able to pass them on to someone who could work out what they were saying and turn their plans against them.

'It's amazing,' she said to Ned, unable to stop gawping. There were the familiar English sights of a tennis court and a cricket square, but they were set against palms and etched with the sound of crickets and strange birds, and were far, far too coated in sunshine to ever be in England. 'This would blow my parents' minds. They thought they'd been on a great adventure making it to Bletchley for our wedding, but would never be able to even conceive of this place.'

'And now they'll live it through your letters.'

'The bits that get past the censors.'

'And your accounts of it once the war is over and we're home.'

'With our baby.'

Ned stiffened and looked nervously around.

'I thought we weren't going to talk about that here, Ails?'

'We aren't,' she agreed. 'I'm sorry. I'll shut up now.'

'Best do because we're here – the office!'

He gave her a wry smile as he threw open the door of a big wooden hut and ushered her inside. Ailsa had a sudden flashback to the day he'd introduced her to the listening station on Malta, plunging her into a hole in the corner of the castle square and leading her through tunnels in the rock to an office overlooking the bay of Valletta. Today's office was humbler in appearance but as a lizard darted across the earth floor before them, pausing halfway up the wall to give them a curious stare, she drank it all in.

'Mrs Robinson?'

A large, sharp-eyed man stepped out of an office and looked her up and down. Ailsa automatically sucked in her stomach though she knew already that that had little impact on the baby bump.

'Reporting for duty, sir.'

'Good. Decent trip?'

'Not bad, thank you, though I'm glad to be on dry land again and can't wait to get on to the wireless.'

Commander Keith nodded.

'About that...'

Ailsa's stomach clenched beneath Baby Robinson.

'Is everything all right, sir?'

'I'm not sure.'

Ailsa felt Ned tighten at her side and resisted the urge to lace her fingers into his. She was here as his colleague now, not his wife.

'In what way, sir?'

'It's your set. Our operatives have been struggling with it. Something about the dipole antenna?'

'Oh!' Ailsa felt relief flood over her. 'Oh yes, they're tricky wee things. I know exactly what to do.'

'You do?' Keith brightened. 'In that case, Mrs Robinson, come right this way.'

He held out a hand to usher her deeper into the office and she followed him gladly, glancing back only for enough time to throw her dear, anxious husband a cheeky wink. She was back at work, doing her bit for the war effort, and, boy did it feel good.

TEN

JUNE 1943

Fran

'Frances! Frances, *c'est moi.*'

'Valérie!' Steffie groaned from her bunk opposite Fran's as the hammering on the door woke them both. 'Does that girl never sleep?'

Fran jumped out of bed, revelling in the warmth of the June morning as she ran to the door and pulled it open.

'Is everything all right?'

'Everything is wonderful, Frances.' Valérie bounced in, kissed Fran, and sniffed the air. 'No coffee?'

'We were asleep. Steffie's doing something mysterious in London later and it's my day off.'

These last few weeks had been a long slog at Bletchley Park as the war ground on with seemingly endless information to process. At a conference in Washington last month, Churchill and Roosevelt had set the date for the invasions of both Italy and Normandy, and a team had been appointed to prepare a workable invasion plan.

As a result, the Western Front Committee had stepped up

its work. Fran was squirrelled away at the top of Block B at least two days a week now, sorting through various reports, maps, plans and, of course, the postcards that she'd been mad enough to suggest they collated at BP. The public had been enthusiastic in their response to the appeal for information and the War Office, who hadn't anticipated such a deluge, was delighted that someone was happy to take it all in. There was a sense in the air that things were going to start coming to a head, but it wouldn't be fast and she'd been looking forward to a lazy day away from it all.

'Surely not a moment of a day off is to be wasted?' Valérie said now, hands on hips.

'Sleeping is not a waste,' Fran retorted.

'It is. Especially today.'

Fran looked sideways at her girlfriend.

'Why? What's happened?'

'You have an *invitation*!' She pronounced it the French way, drawing out the a in the middle, and making it sound even more alluring.

'An invitation to what?'

In answer, Fran waved a telegram under her nose.

'Pierre Brossolette is back in England and speaking at the Albert Hall tonight, and Gilberte has two guest passes. She wishes to know if we would like to join her.'

'In the Albert Hall?' Fran was finding this rather hard to take in.

'*Oui! Réveille-toi* – wake up! She particularly wants you, my Frances. Something about it being a fine journalistic opportunity.'

Fran felt a thrill rush through her.

'I'd love to, Valérie.'

'*Excellente*. I thought as much. Coffee then?'

She tipped her head appealingly on one side and Fran laughed and kissed her.

'Coffee,' she agreed. 'Or what passes for it these days.' She lifted up the tea tin. 'Can I tempt you to tea instead?'

'*Sacré bleu*, no! I'll take the disgusting roasted barley stuff over that nonsense. I still don't understand what you English see in tea.'

'Not just us,' Fran protested. 'All of India and China too. I was looking up Ceylon in the encyclopaedia the other day and I reckon Ailsa will be working right alongside tea plantations. She'll be able to pick her own fresh for breakfast!'

'Poor girl,' Valérie said with a comedy shake of her head.

'Did someone say Ailsa?' Steffie asked, coming out of her room in a silk dressing gown. 'Is she well?'

'As far as we know,' Fran assured her. 'No news.'

'Shame. You making tea?'

Valérie slapped a hand to her forehead and Fran nodded.

'Tea and coffee, it seems.'

'So if it's not about Ails, what's all the fuss?' Steffie asked, sinking onto the bench seat.

'Valérie and I are invited to the Albert Hall.'

'Ooh, fun! What for?'

Fran looked to Valérie.

'It's an evening to commemorate two years since Charles De Gaulle first broadcast to the Free French on the BBC. He is in Algiers now...' She pulled a sad face.

'Setting up a provisional French government in North Africa,' Fran reminded her gently, 'as you wanted.'

'I wanted a French government in *France*, but, *oui*, I take your point. Anyway, with De Gaulle gone, Pierre Brossolette is to be his voice on the BBC. They are going to broadcast it direct from the Albert Hall and out to the *armée secrète* across La France.'

Fran turned slightly to hide a smile. She swore Valérie became more French in both her mannerisms and language whenever she was talking about De Gaulle or the Resistance.

'The Albert Hall is very smart,' Steffie said. 'It'll be evening dress, I imagine. What are you going to wear?'

Fran stared at her in horror. 'Oh God, I've got no idea. Is it posh frocks, Valérie?'

Valérie spread her hands wide.

'Of course.'

'I don't have any posh frocks.'

'I do.' Steffie smiled. 'I've got this divine dark green one that would look perfect on you.'

'Here?'

'Not here, at the parents' place, but, look, if we get the train up together you can come to mine for lunch. Mummy's bored stiff so she'd love to have you.'

'Lunch?' Valérie's eyes lit up. 'I'm in. Grand-mère Elodie always says that there are few problems that cannot be tackled over lunch, and the Albert Hall is not until six o'clock, so we have plenty of time. We can catch the last train back to Bletchley. *Parfait!*'

Fran looked from Valérie to Steffie, both eagerly making plans, and felt that the quiet day off she'd been planning had been swept from under her. Still, it sounded a lot more exciting now and she ran to wash while the kettle boiled.

Two hours later they stood in front of Steffie's home, an imposing, three-storey townhouse in Hammersmith.

'You live here?' Fran breathed.

'No,' Steffie said, giving her arm a squeeze. 'I live in the caravan with you. But Mummy and Daddy live here, yes. Oh, and Roseanna, my sister. She's a bit of a live wire.'

'Good,' Valérie said stoutly. 'Who wants their wires dead?'

'Hmm,' was all Steffie said, as she stepped up to the door, let herself in with a large key, and called, 'Cooee! It's me.'

'Steffie? Steffie-poo, is that you?'

'Steffie-poo?' Fran giggled.

Steffie glared at her.

'Don't you dare ever call me that,' she hissed, as a pretty young woman, the spit of Steffie, save for her more extravagant – and low-cut – dress, came bouncing out of a door and threw her arms around her. 'Hello, Roseanna. You look well.'

'I am well, sweetie. Soo well. I'm in love.'

Roseanna clasped her hands over her ample bosom and let out a Shakespearean sigh. Fran dared not look at Valérie for fear of getting the giggles. She'd known Steffie came from a well-to-do family, of course, but hadn't realised the scale of their wealth.

'Who's the lucky man?' she half heard Steffie asking as she took in the gracious, panelled walls, and the wide staircase and tried to peek into the rooms to either side.

'Barney Fotherington. Remember him? He used to be a terrible oik when we all ran around Blaire House together, but, oh Steffie, he's turned into the most divine man. Officer in the Hussars. Gorgeous uniform. I'm quite smitten.'

'That's lovely, Rosie,' Steffie said. 'I'll look forward to meeting him. But for now, here are my friends, Frances Morgan and Valérie Rousseau.'

Roseanna turned the full beam of her smile on them.

'Divine to meet you. Rousseau? You're French? Oh, my dear, tell me you know Charles De Gaulle?'

Valérie's shoulders straightened.

'As it happens, I do.'

'Marvellous! What's he like? He sounds splendid on the wireless. I swear half the girls I know have a crush on him.'

Valérie glanced at Fran, who raised an eyebrow at her. Why wreck the girl's illusions?

'He's very sexy,' Valérie said earnestly. 'Very tall and handsome. And he exudes power.'

Again Roseanna's hands went to her bosom.

'I knew it! You can tell from his voice. A friend of mine

listens to him in her bedroom – says she pretends he's in there with her. Can you imagine! You must introduce me, Miss Rousseau.'

'I'm afraid he's gone to North Africa now that it's liberated, to form a provisional French government.'

'Oh?' Roseanna's pretty face fell. 'What a pity. Ah well, good job I've got Barney. Come in, come in.'

She took Steffie's arm and led the way up the grand staircase, Fran still trying to take it all in. There were portraits on the walls as grand as those in the Cambridge colleges she'd grown up around, but this was a private house. How on earth had Steffie coped in the tiny caravan with her and Ailsa, when she was used to this sort of luxury?

'Please stay for lunch,' Roseanna was saying, 'Cook's bound to bring out something nice if we have guests, especially a French one.'

Valérie beamed. She didn't seem in the least bit fazed by the grand surroundings, which suddenly made Fran question the Rousseau family status. If they had shops all over Normandy they must be doing well. Valérie's clothes were so chic and her family clearly knew everyone of importance. What on earth would they make of poor provincial Frances Morgan?

'Fran,' Valérie hissed, nudging her in the ribs, and she blinked and realised they'd entered a tastefully pastel, tall-ceilinged drawing room and a well-groomed older lady was standing before them. 'This is Lady Carmichael.'

Lady, she thought – Steffie had kept that one quiet too.

'Terribly sorry, Lady Carmichael,' she said hastily. 'I was just taking in your marvellous portraits.'

'It's Julianna, please. I don't hold with all these English formalities. And do you really think they're marvellous? I find them a bit dark and heavy myself – and impossible to match to curtains.'

She waved them all onto duck-egg blue couches, ringing a

handbell and telling a maid – an actual maid – to bring them tea. Fran glanced at Valérie, but her girlfriend refused to meet her eye and Fran waited, amused, to see what would happen when the hated drink arrived.

'So, do you two live with Stefania in her caravan?' Julianna asked.

'I do,' Fran said. 'And Ailsa, but she's in Ceylon at the moment.'

'Ceylon, heavens! What is the war doing to you girls? I hear the sun out there plays havoc with the skin.'

'Ailsa is a wireless operator so I expect she'll be indoors a lot,' Fran offered, feeling embarrassingly ignorant of what Ailsa actually did. This was the bind with not being allowed to discuss your work, you ended up sounding like you didn't care about your friends.

'Even so,' Julianna said. 'It can't be good for you, and how is the poor girl meant to find a husband stuck all the way out there?'

'Oh, she's with her husband,' Steffie said. 'She met him on Malta.'

'Malta! How unconventional. Ah well, at least she's married.'

She looked pointedly at Steffie, who held out her ring finger.

'I'm engaged, Mummy. There's not much more I can do until Matteo comes back.'

'*If* he comes back,' Julianna said darkly. She looked to Fran and Valérie. 'He's spying, you know – keeping an eye on Mussolini, Lord help him.'

'Mummy! That's top secret.'

'Oh, not with these lovely girls, surely? They work with you, Stefania, in... well, wherever it is you work.' She pouted at Fran. 'Neither Stefania nor her father will tell me anything.'

Fran refrained from saying that she could see why.

'So many secrets in a war,' she murmured hollowly.

Julianna gave a sad nod.

'Still, so many men in lovely uniforms too,' she said, perking up. 'You have to meet Barney, Stefania – he's quite transformed. Roseanna has done so well. He's in the Hussars, you know. A sergeant major and soon to be promoted, so I hear.'

'Do you?' Roseanna gasped. 'Do you really, Mummy?'

She went leaping across to press for more information and Steffie rolled her eyes at Fran and Valérie.

'Remember I told you that in Cairo, the officers' clubs were a hot-bed of gossip? Well, it's the same here. There's no one more indiscreet than those at the top. It's embarrassing.'

Valérie leaned in.

'Is Matteo truly spying on Mussolini?'

Steffie gave an awkward shrug.

'Something like that. I pray every day that he's safe, but it's a dangerous game he's playing, not so much with Musso, perhaps – I think he might be past caring – but if any of the Nazis around him suspect anything...'

She bit her lip and Valérie pressed her hand.

'I understand, *ma chérie*. I, too, have loved ones operating undercover. It squeezes the juice from your heart even to think about it, does it not?'

'It does, Valérie,' Steffie said. 'Thank you. It means a lot to have someone who understands. Who in your family is resisting?'

'Who isn't?' Fran chuckled.

Valérie shot her a glare, but Steffie simply said, 'Marvellous. You must be very proud.'

'I am,' Valérie agreed. 'Of them, if not of myself. Grandmère Elodie is running an entire comms network out of bicycle shops across Normandy aged seventy-eight while I, at a fit and healthy twenty-six, compile meaningless reports in Buckinghamshire.'

'Nothing at Bletchley is meaningless,' Steffie said.

Valérie looked unconvinced but now Julianna was waving the maid to set down an immaculate China tea set.

'Tea, everyone?'

Fran looked at Valérie, Valérie looked back at Fran.

'Divine!' she said, and took the cup from Julianna as if it was the finest treat she could imagine.

Fran shook her head – yes, there really was a lot to learn about Valérie Rousseau, and she only hoped she had the rest of her life in which to do it.

Later, stomachs filled with delicious beef the Carmichael kitchen had somehow conjured up, and heads spinning with a fine claret which Steffie's father, Major General Carmichael, had dug out of his cellar – much to Valérie's approval – they took a taxi to the Albert Hall. It was a rare indulgence on war pay but with Fran in Steffie's evening gown, and ridiculously strappy heels to match, there was no way she was walking. She stepped out in front of the iconic circular building feeling very exposed. Grand people were pulling up all around them and a handful of press had turned out to report on the occasion. She tugged self-consciously on her dress and was relieved when Valérie, stunning in an elegant black gown that Fran could swear said 'Dior' on the swiftly hidden label, took her arm.

'You look amazing, Frances. They will all be wanting to know who the belle in the forest-green gown is. Smile – we might be in the papers.'

She flashed a grin at a photographer as his bulb went off in their faces. Fran flinched, but as a voice called their names from behind, she realised that the press had pounced on Pierre Brossolette, arriving with Gilberte on his arm, and felt a rush of pride at being in their party. Pierre looked magnificent in dapper evening dress, the white streak in his dark hair matching his outfit to perfection. Gilberte wore white too, and together they looked as if they had stepped straight out of a Hollywood poster. Fran was glad of Steffie's gown now and went into the foyer, keen to take it all in.

'I hope you brought a notebook,' Gilberte whispered to her.

Fran patted her evening bag, the largest one Steffie had been able to find to accommodate her leatherbound book and pen.

'I did, Gil, but what am I making notes for?'

'For anyone and everyone, *ma petite*. The British press, they are out there, *oui*, but are they in here? *Non!* This is a French ceremony, for French people – and their honoured guests – so I am sure there will be papers wanting to buy an article from the inside.'

'What sort of thing will they be looking for?' Fran asked, looking eagerly around.

'Colour,' Gilberte told her. 'And, how do you call it – texture?'

'So...?'

'So what dresses people are wearing, how the music sounds, how Pierre looks, how people react to his stirring words. You are a woman, Frances, so I'm afraid people will only take you for women's magazines and columns and for those they expect a certain amount of...'

'Fluff?' Fran suggested.

'Fluff! *Oui*. The perfect word.'

Fran looked ruefully down as she caught her fine heel in the edge of the carpet.

'I'm not sure I'm the right person for fluff, Gil.'

'Me neither, Frances, me neither, but needs must... And, if you are clever with it, you can use the fluff to hide a few, shall we say, sharper observations.'

She winked and Fran nodded and surreptitiously took out her notebook.

For the next hour, she scribbled furiously as the higher

echelons of the exiled Free French listened to French music and drank a French toast to De Gaulle and, finally, sat back for Pierre's speech. Fran saw Gilberte squeeze his hand before he got up to take the microphone and made a note of this touching human detail of his well-hidden nerves.

He stood before the ranks of people, his white lock of hair shining beneath the lights, and spoke with passion of the importance of French involvement in the struggle to liberate their beleaguered country. He called out to the *armée secrète* in towns, villages and woods all across France and told them to be brave and to be ready. 'We are coming,' he said, in melodious French. 'We cannot yet say where or when, but we are coming, and you must be poised to rise up and join us to fight together for the liberation of La France.'

The crowd clapped wildly and Frances saw the BBC sound engineers frantically adjusting their levels and made a note of that too. She had to make readers feel that they were here, sitting at her side, and she fought to remember her high school teachings about using all the senses to note three-dimensional details. Who knew if the piece would be good enough for anyone to publish but she would give it a damned good go and at least, if it was rubbish, she would know to stop wasting everyone's time with the quietly flowering ambition inside her.

She was quite worn out by the time the curtain came down and they could retire for a drink.

'Champagne!' Gilberte declared, marching up to the bar. 'That was a triumph, Pierre.'

'It seemed to go down well,' he agreed modestly. 'And a drink would certainly be welcome, though—'

He stopped, his eyes fixed behind Fran and, as she turned, she saw Maurice Schumann pushing through the throng around the bar to reach them. The waiter had stepped up to take Gilberte's order, but she put up a hand to ask for a moment.

'Maurice? What's happened?'

'It's Jean,' he said. 'Jean Moulin. They've got him. The Nazi bastards have got him.'

Gilberte let out a cry of distress and Pierre put an arm instinctively around her, although he was visibly shaking himself. Fran felt Valérie's hand creep into her own and clutched at it. None of them was in any doubt what the Nazis would do to one of the most wanted men of the French Resistance and it was a stark reminder, among the glitter of the Albert Hall, of the dangers under which they were all operating. Gilberte turned to the waiter and shook her head. There would be no champagne now, for Jean Moulin was in the Nazi torture chambers and, without him, the fragile alliance of the Resistance was in as much trouble as the poor man himself.

ELEVEN

JULY 1943

Steffie

Steffie glanced up at the clock, horrified to see that two hours had shot past since lunch and it was now close to the time the new arrivals were expected. She was not looking forward to them. It had taken her a good month to brush up her German and get her feet under the table in ISOS, so another shake-up was not welcome. The worst thing was, they were Americans.

A week ago, the Secret Services in Britain and America had signed an agreement allowing unprecedented sharing of both information and personnel. It was being hailed among the agencies as a huge step forward and certainly the Twenty Committee seemed chuffed about it.

'It's the start of a very special relationship,' Steffie's father had assured her last week. 'They have vast resources and we have vast experience – it's an excellent match.'

Steffie wasn't so sure. Her own dealings with the Americans had been coloured by her experiences in Cairo last year when she – and Fran and Ailsa in Bletchley Park and Malta respectively – had been arrested under suspicion of spying because information had been leaking out via a useless American code. Bonner Fellers, the US attaché in Cairo, had been merrily reporting British positions into Washington in a code so weak that both the Italians and Germans had been reading along almost word for word, with near disastrous consequences.

They hadn't quite found out in time to stop Rommel taking Tobruk – a dark day for the Allies – but thankfully after that, the Germans had been robbed of their 'Gute Quelle' and General Montgomery had been able to turn the tide before Rommel reached Cairo. It had been a scary time and had not given Steffie much respect for American protocol or intelligence, so she wasn't keen on welcoming them right into the heart of BP, especially with the invasion of Sicily so close.

Not just close, Steffie reminded herself with a lurch in her gut, but tomorrow. Troops would even now be boarding their landing craft, ready to sail on Sicily under cover of darkness and launch a dawn attack. The success of the invasion – not to mention the safety of every one of those young people – would be immeasurably improved if Operation Mincemeat, backed up with reports from their double agents, had convinced the Germans Sicily was not the main target.

It was looking hopeful. Reports from the ambassador in Spain told them that Major Martin had washed ashore exactly where they'd wanted him to, in the Nazi-rich town of Huelva. The coroner had, bless him, concluded that the marine had died in a plane crash several days before arriving on the beach and the existence of a briefcase with vital documents in it had been confirmed.

Stewart Menzies had sent counter messages insisting that the documents be retrieved as a matter of utmost state security and for a nasty moment they'd thought the Spanish had obeyed far too scrupulously as the documents had been returned to London at some speed. Fortunately, the boffins in SOE's laboratories had been able to establish that they had been opened and, presumably, read, so everyone took that as a good sign. Then, two weeks ago, Steffie had worked on Abwehr decrypts confirming that German troops were being moved from Sicily to Sardinia, and they'd all prayed the enemy had taken the bait. They wouldn't know for sure until the soldiers hit the beaches tomorrow morning, however, and it would be hard to sleep tonight.

Steffie looked around the ISOS offices, already fond of her new team. Denys Page was an easy boss and, the Abwehr Enigma having been cracked early in 1941 by the genius Dilly Knox, they knew its ways well and rarely took more than an hour or two to crack the new settings every midnight. The result was a stream of decrypts providing an insight into the Germans' most secret manoeuvres.

The Abwehr were a puzzle, a pleasingly loose archaism sitting awkwardly within the Nazi system. They were part of the military, rather than reporting direct to the government as in Britain, and were run by an ageing aristocrat, Admiral Wilhelm Canaris, a star of First World War intelligence, back when it was all whispers in gentlemen's clubs. Canaris wasn't even a Nazi party member, but Hitler seemed to have the reverence of a natural snob for the man and trusted him far further than he could throw him, which was all to the good for the Allies.

Canaris was in control of a network of rather louche commanders who sat in their offices in the not-unpleasant cities of Lisbon, Madrid and Rome enjoying the high life, happy if they had reports to send in to justify their continued pleasures, and not concerned about where the intelligence came from. As Britain had imprisoned or turned every one of the agents they'd ever sent into Great Britain, and created a few more within their own control besides, this made their reports wonderfully malleable.

Amid all this dubious traffic, however, there was a truly solid piece of intel – the weekly *Lagebericht West* situation report provided by *Fremde Heere West*, the branch of the Wehrmacht high command to which the Abwehr reported. They were responsible for assessing the resources and intentions of Allies, so this was where Steffie's liaison with the Twenty Committee came to life. This was where she could glean whether their deceptions were being believed. So far, for Sicily, the signs looked good.

Steffie touched her finger to her diamond ring, as she must do a hundred times a day, trying to feel Matteo through its sparkling beauty. For all she knew he might be on Sicily, right in the line of fire, and the thought of it curdled in her stomach. If it hadn't been for this damned war, they'd have been married three years now, possibly with little ones on the way, or already here. Steffie blinked at the astonishing thought and her arms curled instinctively around an imaginary baby.

'Ha,' she said, unable to imagine herself as a mother, or even a wife.

But then, when she'd got engaged, she'd been unable to imagine herself as a trusted government worker, decrypting German secret service messages to feed into a top-level committee. You win some, you lose some. Steffie smiled softly and picked up her next decrypt, but then the door opened and Denys walked in with two tall young men at his shoulders.

'Team ISOS, can I have your attention to welcome our new recruits.'

Steffie rose reluctantly to join the circle around the men. One was blond with a perfect tan, even teeth and blue eyes that twinkled with self-assurance. The other was dark, with fine features and a quieter manner. He looked nervously around and, when he caught Steffie's eye, smiled shyly. She smiled back automatically and then had to remind herself she was suspicious of these newcomers.

'Let me introduce you all to Eugene Johnson and Leonard D'Angelo,' Denys said. 'They've been doing great work over in the US with Operation Magic – producing their equivalent to Ultra on the Japanese code – and now they're here to help us out as things get busy and to provide vital liaison into the US decrypts.'

'Of Japanese messages?' someone asked, looking sceptical.

'Correct,' Eugene, the blond one confirmed, stepping forward. 'The Japanese could prove very useful when it comes to an invasion of Europe. Their ambassador in Berlin – General Oshima – is intimate with Hitler. He has lovely long conversations with him, which he dutifully reports back to Tokyo.'

'And which we listen to,' Leonard said.

'And these conversations include things like troop positions?' Steffie guessed.

'Exactly that,' Leonard confirmed, in a way that made her feel top of the class. Ridiculous.

'Well, the more information the better,' she said and then felt stupidly prim. 'Shall we find you desks?' she added to cover her confusion.

'That would be excellent thank you, Stefania.' Denys nodded approvingly. 'I thought Eugene in the corner here to work with Simon, and perhaps Leonard next to you.'

'Next to me?' Steffie squeaked.

'Is that a problem?' Denys asked, one eyebrow raised.

'No, not at all. I just... I quite like to work alone.'

'I understand that,' Leonard said, his voice low and fluid. 'No problem. I'm sure I can fit in over there somewhere.'

He gestured to the far side of the office, between the filing cabinets, and Steffie felt bad. She'd only arrived in ISOS herself a month ago and everyone had made her feel welcome, so she owed it to these young men, so far from home, to do the same.

'Not at all, not at all. Please, take this desk.'

Leonard slid into it and looked across at her with eyes as dark as Bournville chocolate.

'I'll be quiet, I promise.'

'You don't have to be. I'm sorry. I'm on edge with the invasion of Sicily due.'

'They briefed us on that when we arrived. Tomorrow, right?'

'Right. It's an important time for Italy. I hope we can take it without too much... damage.'

'To people or places?'

'Both. It's too beautiful a country to destroy with war.'

'You know it?'

She nodded.

'My father was the military attaché to Rome, so I grew up in Italy.'

'No! I'd love to go to Rome. *Ho sentito che è una Bellissima citta.*'

Steffie gasped.

'You speak Italian?'

'*Naturalmente.* My family are New York Italians – the fiercest kind. I was brought up on a strict diet of spaghetti, chianti, and a rabid love of the "motherland". And you actually lived there!'

'My fiancé still does.'

She wasn't sure why she said that, but it felt important to get Matteo into the conversation before... Well, before nothing. This was merely a fellow human making conversation.

'Your fiancé is Italian? That must be hard.'

'It is. Well, it was. He's working for the British now, so we are, at least, on the same side, but it doesn't make it any easier not being with him.'

'I can imagine.' She waited for him to tell her about a sweetheart back home in New York, but he simply turned to Denys as he brought in some decrypts and said, 'Can't wait to get stuck in.'

'Steffie will show you the ropes,' Denys assured him. 'She's one of the best in the business.'

He was gone again before she could even register the compliment and, face burning, she set about showing her new recruit exactly how the Bletchley Park system worked. He was fluent in German, having apparently taken a degree in European languages, but no expert in how Enigma worked. It took some time to explain, making her realise how much she'd learned over the last three years, and she looked up like a mole emerging into daylight when Denys appeared again to suggest they call it a day.

'It's late, Steffie, and the poor man is newly arrived from the US.'

'I'm so sorry.'

'Not at all,' Leonard said with a smile. 'It's been fascinating, hasn't it, Eugene?'

Eugene sauntered over and perched on Steffie's desk.

'Totally fascinating, and it's cool working with chicks too, especially such pretty ones.'

He winked at Steffie, who instinctively leaned back.

'Watch it, Eugene,' Leonard told him. 'She's got a fiancé.'

Eugene did a comic eye-roll.

'Course she has; the best ones always do! Still, you're not married yet, are you, sweetheart?'

'I consider myself...' She ran out of words. What did she consider herself? Taken? Claimed? Committed? They all sounded prim. 'That's to say, I'm very much in love, thank you.'

Eugene put his hands up.

'It's a fair cop. Can't blame a man for trying. Now, where do you get a drink around here?'

Denys laughed.

'We'd better take you to the Drunken Arms. Coming, Steffie?'

Steffie hesitated. Eugene was still perched proprietorially on her desk and she wasn't sure she wanted to spend her evening fending off his overconfident advances. On the other hand, Leonard seemed interesting and the rest of the team were gathering up their things to go along so it felt churlish to refuse. Besides, if she went back to the caravan, she'd only sit there fretting about the invasion so she might as well pass the time somehow.

'Just the one then,' she said and reached for her bag.

It was busy in the pub and they had to fight their way through to the bar.

'You mean they don't come to your table?' Eugene asked, bemused.

'What table?' Steffie said, gesturing around the packed room.

'Good point. Come on then, this one's on me. Beer, Leo?'

Leonard nodded and looked around, quietly ushering a giggling group of WRENS aside with his long arm to make a space for Steffie against the wall.

'Thank you.'

'My pleasure.'

'Do you like England?' she asked.

'Not had time to tell yet. I think I will, though we've been warned it's a bit different to home.'

'Warned by who?'

Leonard took a small brown booklet from his inside pocket and Steffie read the title: *An American serviceman's guide to England*.

'They've given you a guidebook about us? What does it say?'

'Take a look.' He handed it to her. 'It's full of useful advice. For example, I'm told we're not to tell anyone around here that they look like a bum.'

'A bum?' Steffie giggled. 'Lordy, no! That's a, a...' She self-consciously patted at her behind and he flushed.

'A fanny?'

'No! A bum.'

'Course. Sorry. Over our way, that means a down-and-out, a homeless chap, you know?'

'A tramp?'

'No! A tramp's a lady of, well, loose morals.'

'Lordy,' Steffie said again. 'This is going to be complicated.'

Eugene brought her a gin and lime, and handed Leonard a pint of beer, before, thankfully, disappearing to chat to the group of WRENS, who were far more welcoming to his advances than Steffie had been. Denys and Simon joined them in their corner and laughed as Leonard took a tentative sip of his pint.

'Help! What is that?'

'Bitter,' Denys said. 'Very nice.'

Leonard held his glass up to peer into the amber liquid.

'You're sure it's edible?'

'Sure,' Denys agreed, chinking his own glass against the visitor's. 'Cheers.'

Leonard gamely took another sip, and then another.

'Not so bad when you get used to it, I suppose.' He glanced over his shoulder to where high-pitched giggles were greeting some tale Eugene was telling, turning into excited pleadings as he produced several bars of chocolate from his briefcase. Leonard sighed. 'That's another thing we were told not to do,' he said, gesturing to his compatriot, 'show off, especially when it comes to our resources. You folk have been on rationing for ages, right?'

'Feels like forever,' Steffie agreed. She waved the booklet at Denys and John. 'Look – they've got a book to tell them all our peculiar ways. What else does it say, Leonard?'

'Call me Leo, please,' he said, and then looked self-consciously back at his book. 'It says that you value age over size in your architecture.'

'Does it?' Denys asked, considering. 'I suppose that might

be true. A beautiful old building is beautiful whether it's a cottage or a castle.'

Leo grimaced.

'In the US it's all about whether its tallest, or longest or widest. We're not very subtle. Hey, this bitter stuff grows on you. We got told you Brits, for all your soft-spoken politeness, are plenty tough and perhaps it's drinking this that does that to you.'

'I think you'll find,' Simon said drily, 'that it's having Nazis twenty miles across the Channel that does that to us.'

Leo looked momentarily thrown but then gathered himself.

'Not for long, buddy. Not for long.'

It was a good night in the end. Far too good. Steffie rolled into the caravan with only enough energy to brush her teeth and say goodnight to an amused Fran before she fell fast asleep. She woke the next morning with her head pounding and her mouth as dry as a sandstorm and peered blearily at the clock. Only 6.30 a.m. – time for a touch more sleep, surely? Then she remembered.

'Sicily,' she cried, sitting bolt upright and clonking her already sore head on the bunk above.

'Sicily,' Fran echoed, her tone telling Steffie that she was in the know about the invasion.

They both leapt up, scrambling to dress and get into the park. Steffie felt guilt wash over her for living it up in the Drunken Arms while men were crossing the Mediterranean to face German guns on the very beaches on which she'd sunbathed as a teenager.

Please let it be all right, she said to herself over and over. *Please, please let it be all right.*

She and Fran were into Bletchley Park within twenty minutes, going their separate ways with a quick hug.

'Anything in yet?' she asked Denys as soon as she got into the office.

He turned, unspeaking, and horror hit her but then he smiled.

'Plenty. Monty's men have landed in Cassibile and taken Syracuse. They've been radioing in their position and the first reports on the German network show we've taken them utterly by surprise. They're scrambling to get units to Sicily, but it will take them far too long. The Americans have taken the port of Licata and we'll be driving Jerry out way before he can form a decent defensive position. It's not a done deal yet, but I'd say the first hand is ours, Stef.'

She sank into her chair, shaking with delight, and then remembered – Montagu. Picking up the phone, she dialled through to his offices in Whitehall. He picked up on the first ring.

'Ewen, it's Steffie.'

'Yes?'

'It's worked. It's definitely worked. The troops have landed to minimal opposition. Major Martin did his job and did it perfectly.'

His whoop of joy echoed down the phone, playing havoc with her sore head, but she didn't care. If the Allies could take Sicily, then they had a strong base from which to attack Italy, Europe's 'soft underbelly'. The Twenty Committee had created a perfect deception and she was proud to be a part of it. Now they could leave Sicily to the troops on the ground and turn their attention to the next – and far greater invasion – across Hitler's fearsome Atlantic Wall and into the heart of Nazi-occupied France. Steffie rubbed her hands and went to find some Epsom salts and make a cup of tea. Let the real work begin!

TWELVE

JULY 1943

Ailsa

'Oh, my goodness, it's Fran!' Ailsa pointed at the newsreel showing in the old-fashioned cinema in the centre of Colombo and several people hushed her. 'Sorry,' she said, unabashed, 'but that's my friend right there, next to the speaker's wife.'

She pointed again. The grainy footage showed a handsome man with a lock of white hair making a grand speech in what the caption said was the Albert Hall. A lot of VIPs in evening dress were listening to him and there, in the middle of them all, was Fran.

'Are you sure, Ails?' Ned whispered. 'It doesn't seem likely.'

'I'm sure,' she whispered back. 'That's Valérie next to her. She must know the man – Pierre Brossolette. That's possible, right? In fact, now I think about it, I swear she said something about meeting him in London before I left.'

Ned took her hand.

'You miss them.'

She squeezed it.

'I do, aye, but I'd still rather be here with you.'

'I don't blame you – it's far more glamorous.'

He gestured around the rickety 'cinema', furnished with threadbare seats and a projector that wheezed its way round the newsreels, often losing the thread and having to be started again. The bugs made your legs itch and flew across the screen, but everyone put up with it, keen to know what was going on elsewhere in the war.

'Exactly,' Ailsa agreed, leaning in to kiss him, just as he wiped sweat from his brow. 'Yuck!'

'Sorry. It's hot tonight, isn't it?'

'It's hot every night.'

It was evening and dark outside – save for the million and one fireflies who lit up the sky with their fairy lights – but out here in Ceylon, even when the sun went down it left much of its heat behind to prey on you. Plus, there was the humidity. HMS Anderson was in the south-west of the island so subject to the Yala monsoon season for most of May to September, drenching you when you were least expecting it and filling the air with moisture all the time. Ailsa had learned to sleep naked with the thinnest sheet to cover her and, even then, she usually cast it off when the sun came laughing back up. She'd bought a wide-brimmed hat to keep the rays off her pale face but it was impossible to avoid it all the time and even her peely-wally skin was starting to turn slightly brown.

The hardest part was working. The sweat ran down her legs in a most unladylike manner but, worse than that, it ran off her brow and into her headset, tangling the Japanese Morse that she already had to work hard to understand. Someone had brought in a load of towelling headbands, the sort you saw tennis players wearing, and they worked a treat, though even then you often saw people going outside to wring them out.

It was worth it though. Ceylon was beautiful. Tea grew on

the gentle slopes behind the listening station and last weekend she and Ned had braved a walk up in the hour before dusk and watched in fascination as the local women picked the tiny leaves and placed them into baskets balanced on their heads. There were pineapples too – a fruit Ailsa had never tasted before and couldn't get enough of. A girl would come to the station gates every day at noon and you could nip out and buy them fresh from the tree and dripping with the sweetest juice, like elixir from heaven. Just thinking of them made Ailsa's mouth water and she wondered if any sellers might be out when they emerged from the cinema.

They'd caught the 'Liberty Boat' – a battered bus that drove people into town from HMS Anderson – and Ned had promised her dinner in the Grand Oriental hotel, but right now she'd take a street pineapple instead. She tugged at her dress, feeling the bugs flying around beneath her skirt and trying to wrap its folds around her legs to protect them. She'd had to come out in plain clothes because Ned had been made an officer so wasn't allowed to be seen with someone of a lower rank, even if he was married to her. Honestly, the military was so full of stupid rules sometimes that Ailsa wanted to tell them to stuff off and do their own listening! But then she reminded herself that without them she'd never be here, eating pineapples, watching fireflies dance and swimming in the softest sea.

The Indian Ocean was amazing, especially for Ailsa, brought up alongside the battering seas of the Western Hebrides. There was a beach called Mount Lavinia, apparently named after a local girl the original British governor had fallen in love with, though with not a mountain in sight there was a rather coarse interpretation of the name among the troops. Whatever its origins, it was a long stretch of sand, backed with palms and kissed with soft waves and Ailsa loved it. There was an elegant old hotel right on the beach – once the loved-up governor's residence – and with prices pleasingly low out here, she and Ned could afford to sit on the terrace with a cold dram at least once a week, feeling like lords.

Ailsa pulled her thoughts back to the newsreel they'd come to see. It had moved on from the Albert Hall to report on the situation in Sicily where, it seemed, British and American troops were taking the island, forcing the Germans back over the Straits of Messina into Italy. The reporter said, in his plummy English voice, that Hitler had summoned Mussolini to see him, and Ailsa tried to imagine the conversation that might take place between the two dictators.

These were the men whose power games had sent millions of ordinary people out of their regular lives into terrible danger, and she couldn't begin to imagine them chatting over a cup of coffee like ordinary mortals. Steffie had met Mussolini and described him as 'charming if lecherous', but he was surely far more than that. These bastards (Ailsa had been brought up not to curse but, really, there was no other word for them), with their brand of insular hatred for anyone outside their own mould, were wrecking the world and the sooner they were stopped, the better.

She shivered, her skin crawling with more than Ceylonese bugs, and Ned looked at her in concern.

'Are you well?'

'Nothing wrong with me bar a healthy dose of hatred.'

He put an arm around her, then took it away again – it was far too hot for cuddling – and gave her a quick kiss instead.

'Fair enough. We'll get them, Ails, don't you worry. We'll be heading up Italy soon and once we hit them in France too, they'll be caught in their own miserable trap.'

'I hope so, Ned. Because if we don't, what sort of a world will our baby be born into?'

'Don't even think about it.'

He put a protective hand over her belly, which was now

pronounced. Luckily, there was a shortage of tropical uniforms and she'd happily taken an overlarge one, but the simple white skirt and blouse left scant room to hide a growing waistline and it was only a matter of time before someone pointed it out. Still, with guns and tanks and blinking rocket launchers in the world, surely someone having a baby was the least of anyone's worries?

The newsreel was coming to an end and Ailsa stood up gratefully. The velveteen fabric of the seat was clinging to her damp legs and the bugs flew up in an indignant cloud as she escaped the close confines of the cinema. Her mind went back to Fran, sitting in the Albert Hall in a fancy frock, and she smiled.

'I really think that was Fran, Ned,' she said as he ushered her out into the marginally cooler air of the street.

'I hope so, for her sake. I'd love to go to the Albert Hall.' He looked around bustling Colombo. 'For now, however, the Grand Oriental will have to do. At least it has fans. Shall we?'

He offered her his arm and she took it, forcing herself not to bend down and scratch at the bites on the back of her legs. She'd learned from bitter experience that it only made them worse and she didn't want to go home scarred from her time on this beautiful island.

Reaching the hotel, she headed for the Ladies – something she seemed to have to do more and more often as baby grew – and when she pulled her skirt up, she looked at her legs in horror. They were covered with bites, standing out like angry red lights all over her ivory skin, and instantly the urge to scratch was overwhelming. She splashed cold water onto them, little caring that it got on her skirt too and as it brought some relief, she went out to join Ned. He'd secured a perfect table in the corner of the opulent dining area, right below a coveted fan, and she sank gratefully into her seat.

'All right Ailsa?' he asked. 'You look a bit pale.'

'I always look pale.'

'True, but more so than usual.'

'I got bitten,' she admitted, stretching one leg out to show him.

'Bitten? Help, Ailsa, you've been mauled.'

'Only by bugs, thank heavens.'

'Even so... Should we go home?'

'No, let's eat. They'll go down soon enough and the fan is lovely.'

Ned accepted this and they ordered, but it was all Ailsa could do to concentrate on her surprisingly delicious beetroot curry. Far from going down, the bites seemed to be stinging more and more as the night went on and when Ned suggested skipping dessert and heading home, she agreed. There was some calamine lotion in the banda that would surely help ease the itching and she lay back gratefully as Ned dabbed it with infinite care onto every single bite. It took a while and it didn't seem to help much but eventually, with the sound of the crickets buzzing through her prickling skin, she fell into a fitful sleep, dreaming of Mussolini and Hitler taking tea with Fran in an evening gown.

She awoke the next morning to Ned shaking her, only it didn't look quite like Ned. His face wouldn't stay in focus properly and he was speaking in a strangely slurred way.

'What's up, Ned?' she asked, but she sounded slurred too.

It was very hot and, when she tried to sit up, the room tilted alarmingly and her stomach protested, ejecting last night's beetroot right onto her poor husband.

'Sorry,' she tried to say, but her tongue was thick in her mouth and she had to lie down again.

She saw Ned's face loom over her, his eyes dark with worry, and heard him say something about a doctor, and then he was gone and she could sleep again, only this time Fran was dancing with Mussolini while Hitler played a fiddle with curious skill.

Sometime later, she was shaken again and flung out an arm to ward off the interruption.

'Ailsa, please, let the doctor examine you.' She fought to the surface of her peculiar dreams and saw a sharp-eyed man in the uniform of the medical corps waving a stethoscope in the general direction of her chest. She looked to Ned, scared now, and he took her hand. 'It's all right, Ailsa. It will all be all right. The doctor will make you better.'

The doctor poked and prodded her, then turned to Ned, saying something about malaria or, if they were lucky, tropical fever.

I'm here, Ailsa wanted to tell him. *It's* my *fever, tell* me *about it*, but it was far too exhausting to speak the words out loud.

She heard Ned raise his voice, which wasn't like him at all, and forced herself to concentrate through the strange, hot cloud that was enveloping her.

'I asked you here because of her fever, not because of her... other condition.'

'Her other condition, as you so delicately put it, may be germane to her fever. And it's certainly germane to her ability to work at HMS Anderson.'

'No, it isn't,' Ailsa shouted, but it obviously didn't come out as she'd intended, for both men ignored her.

'It's not your place to "report" her,' Ned was saying angrily. 'It's your place to care for her.'

The other man blustered something about systems and lines of authority that was far too convoluted for Ailsa's struggling brain. Then he gave her a shot in her arm and the confusion receded into blissful rest.

For the next few days, she drifted in and out of sleep, the world slowly coming back into focus enough for her to see the spots on her legs as they, thankfully, began to shrink from one ugly red mass, into individual sores, and finally mere pinpricks. Her fever subsided and her mind reformed enough for her to know that, although she had thankfully avoided malaria, her cover was officially blown.

'That doctor is going to tell Commander Keith I'm pregnant, isn't he?' she asked Ned when she was well enough to sit up and drink some clear chicken broth.

'He already has,' Ned said heavily.

'And...?'

'And to say he's not happy would be an understatement, especially when the doctor told him you were six months gone and would most likely have known before you sailed from Britain.'

Ailsa waved this away.

'I'll claim innocence. Naive wee girl from the islands, no one ever told me, all that.'

Ned grimaced.

'Good luck. I've had the full rant about why marriage is a danger to the forces.'

'Honestly. These military men. They've spent so much of their lives hanging around with each other that they think women are some sort of plague. I've seen them sidling up to the poor wee girls on the street corners in Colombo though; they want them well enough when they're horny.'

'Ailsa! That sort of talk won't help.'

'I know. I'll be good.' She reached for his hand. 'I'm sorry, Ned. All I wanted was to be with you and for us to have our baby together.'

'I know, my gorgeous girl, and I'm so happy that you're here – both of you. It was a bit mad, but that's you, Ails, and I love you for it.'

She smiled at him.

'I don't know what all the fuss is about. It's not so complicated, you know. Women have babies all the time, in Ceylon as well as in Britain, and it doesn't need to be a big deal if people can stop being hysterical about it.'

'Tell that to Keith.'

'I will,' she said. 'Get me out of this bed and I will.'

'A baby! A bloody baby! Honestly, Mrs Robinson, what are you trying to do to me?'

'Nothing, sir. I'm sorry. It just happened.'

He raised a sardonic eyebrow.

'It didn't *just happen*, did it.'

'Well, no, but we were newly married and you know...'

'I know! Thank you. But there's a difference between, well, that, and shipping yourself halfway across the world pregnant.'

'I didn't realise.'

Again the eyebrow.

'I'm married, Ailsa. I have children. I'm not stupid. You willingly put yourself and your baby in danger coming out here.'

'It's war, sir, there's danger everywhere. I was trapped in an air-raid shelter in Malta and I was bombed in a bus right outside the gates of Bletchley Park. Who's to say Colombo is more "dangerous"?'

He gave a heavy sigh.

'Fair point. But surely you can see that it doesn't look good to the higher-ups?'

'A married woman carrying on family life while doing a sterling job for the war effort? I'd say that's a perfect story – it's all about how you present it.'

'Hmm. I admire your optimism, but I fear the Air Ministry isn't going to see it that way. This is precisely why they don't let married women travel – and why they certainly won't now.'

'If we tell them...'

'If!' He threw up his hands. 'This is why we don't let women run the forces. It would be chaos.'

'If women ran the forces,' Ailsa said drily, 'there would be no war and we would all be happily at home having babies in the blissful comfort of world peace.'

Keith screwed up his face.

'You have an answer for everything, don't you?'

'Sorry, sir.'

Another sigh.

'The question is, what am I going to do with you? Doctor says you're too far gone for me to ship home, but I can hardly have you on base.'

'Why not? It's only a baby, sir. It won't stop me doing my job – and doing it well.'

'Is it safe?'

Ailsa put her hands on her hips.

'Come on, sir. You just told me you've got a family. I bet your wife was busy right up to the birth?'

Keith rolled his eyes.

'She was chopping down a hazel when she went into labour.'

Ailsa smiled.

'Well then, I can surely sit at a wireless set and listen in to the Japanese?'

Keith got up, pacing.

'It's unorthodox.'

'So is listening to the enemy from a wooden hut on a golf course in Ceylon, sir. These are unorthodox times.'

A laugh burst out of him.

'For a woman, Ailsa Robinson, you've got balls. And, as you rightly said, you're damned good at your job.' He opened his office door and peered out. All eyes snapped guiltily away and he shook his head. 'Set Five is on the blink. If you can mend it, you can stay.'

'Yes, sir!'

Ailsa saluted and made for Set Five, already reaching for her tools. She wasn't going anywhere. There was an enemy to listen to, and while there was breath in her ever-expanding body, she'd be here listening to them.

THIRTEEN

AUGUST 1943

Steffie

Steffie couldn't concentrate on her lamb cutlets, however delicious they were. Her father was treating her to lunch before the next meeting of the Twenty Committee, and had told her he'd been speaking to Matteo. She was so jealous.

'He sends you all his love, darling, and says keep up the good work.'

'He's safe then? No one's rumbled him?'

'Nope. You know your Matteo, he's charm personified, and he knows so many people from the old days. They'll trust him and they'll be right to do so – he's working for their good, especially now.'

'Why?'

Anthony Carmichael leaned in.

'Because all hell has broken loose now the Germans are out of Sicily. The Fascist Grand Council have thrown Musso out and the king's backed them. Musso's been taken away "for his own safety" and Badoglio is prime minister. Remember him? Funny man.'

'I do. Mummy used to take me to play with his daughter, Alicia, and he'd always bring cakes home.'

'There you go! Solid chap and, most importantly, keen for an armistice.'

'That's wonderful.'

'It is,' her father agreed, 'but it will have to be done with the utmost caution. If Hitler gets wind of it, he'll unleash his fury on Italy.'

Steffie's heart clenched.

'Can Matteo not come home? Has he not done his bit?'

'He has and very well. Too well to lose him now. He had the foresight to see this coming and has been cosying up to Badoglio for weeks, getting information we urgently need to make this happen in the best possible way. You should be proud of him, Steffie.'

'I *am* proud of him, Daddy. I'm just a bit fed up of a world in which we have to be proud of those we love instead of being *with* them.'

Anthony laughed.

'Wisely put, my girl. But come on, eat that lovely lamb up – we've got a meeting to get to.'

Steffie felt herself glow at the 'we' and dug dutifully into her precious meat before following her father out of his club and ten steps down the road to the rickety Twenty Committee HQ. The others were gathering and Steffie said easy hellos to the men and one woman – taking the minutes, of course – who were already in the smart room. The mood was buoyant.

'Sicily has been a triumph!' Masterman announced to muted cheers. 'The troops have rampaged across the island and the Germans have fled, tails between their nasty Nazi legs. An almost flawless campaign.'

'Save for Patton,' someone put in.

Masterman harrumphed.

'Indeed. Damned man kicked some poor soldier out of bed

in a field hospital, despite him having raging malaria. And then slapped another lad with shell shock because he doesn't believe in it.'

'Those poor boys,' Steffie said.

'Well, quite. He's old school, I'm afraid. Likes to think he takes no nonsense, which is all well and good as long as you can actually distinguish what's nonsense. Anyway, Eisenhower has sent him off on leave and no doubt he'll be back in time for the big push. The important thing is that Sicily was a success, especially here at double-cross. A huge clap on the back to Montagu and the Mincemeat team. The PM's delighted. I had a message from him the other day: "Mincemeat swallowed whole". Chuffed he is, very chuffed.'

Ewen flushed with pleasure as several men got up to shake his hand.

'It was Steffie too,' he said, and she got her share of nods.

'Good work,' Masterman repeated. 'And to the double agents backing up the information into Admiral Canaris's credulous lot. All-round intel, that's the ticket. If every source is feeding them information that leads to the same conclusion, then it's far more likely to be believed. That's what we're here for and now it's time to turn our attention to the Channel. We'll be committing around 150,000 men to the northern invasion, British, American and a whole host of others besides, and the fewer German tanks they face, the greater their chances. It's a big old game, gentleman – and lady – and we need to play it well.'

There were murmurs around the room. Someone said something about it being a better game than last time and, looking around the table, Steffie realised that every one of these men was over fifty and must, therefore, have fought in the Great War. They had a new role now, behind the front lines, but they wouldn't have forgotten how it felt to face the guns and there was a set to their chin as they considered the invasion ahead.

'But that's for next year,' Masterman said. 'For now, we have Italy to consider, and the PM has asked for our help. Badoglio is looking for an armistice but it's going to have to be done with speed to get it signed before the invasion on September ninth. With the utmost secrecy too – which is where we come in. We're sending representatives to Lisbon to negotiate, and I need a fluent Italian speaker to go with the delegation. Carmichael, I thought of you?'

He looked at Steffie's father, who nodded.

'Carmichael is a good choice,' he agreed, 'but you're looking at the wrong one. My gammy leg makes flying dashed painful, I'm afraid. Stefania, however, has no such concerns and is even more fluent than me. She knows Badoglio too – used to play with his daughter. She's the perfect choice.'

There was a pause in the room. Steffie's father stared Masterman down and won.

'Excellent. Thank you, Stefania. We'll give you all the requisite permissions for Bletchley Park and you should prepare to leave tomorrow. There's not a moment to lose if we're to get this stitched up in time.'

'Tomorrow?' Steffie gulped.

'Is that a problem? I'm sure we can—'

'It's not a problem. I'll be ready, John. Thank you.'

Less than twenty-four hours later, Steffie stood on the tarmac at RAF Cranfield, quietly simmering. At her side stood Leo, very smart in full dress uniform and trying to be nice to her. She wasn't feeling receptive. Travis had been happy to release her for this diplomatic mission but had suggested that she take her colleague with her as a US representative.

'As a man, more like,' Steffie had retorted, stung. 'I can do the job, you know. I've been speaking Italian since I was in my cot and I've been to plenty of diplomatic bashes too. I won't hash it up because I'm female.'

'Of course not. That's not the point here, Stefania. This is all in the interests of Anglo-American relations. They don't like to be left out of anything and D'Angelo speaks Italian so he's the obvious choice. Are you uncomfortable travelling with a man?'

'I'm uncomfortable not being trusted to do my work.'

He'd sighed.

'I'll be sure to tell D'Angelo he's coming along as your assistant, nothing more.'

'Thank you,' she'd said, because it had seemed the only option, but she was still cross.

'I know you don't want me here,' Leonard said now, leaning in to speak in a low voice as a bevy of top ambassadors and military bods arrived in smart cars and began boarding the plane. 'And I'm sorry, it honestly wasn't my idea, but I have to tell you now, I am *so* excited.'

Steffie glanced at him, caught by the boyish enthusiasm in his voice and saw his eyes were shining.

'Why?'

'When I was a kid, I dreamed of coming to Europe. Rome, obviously, and England, but places like Lisbon too. They have so much history, so much culture. I did my degree in European languages as a way in to all that and the more I learn, the more it fascinates me. In New York everything is fast and shiny and thrilling, but it's not got much depth. I don't like war, but I can't believe what I'm getting to see because of it.'

Steffie softened; she understood that.

'Last year I was stationed in Cairo,' she told him. 'I loved it.'

'Cairo! Gosh – that must have been neat.'

'Neat? Oh, you mean good.'

'Good, yes, cool.'

'Cool!' Steffie shook her head. 'Cool means... Oh, it doesn't matter. It was excellent – until I was arrested as a spy, of course.'

'What?'

She laughed.

'Long story. Come on, we're boarding.'

As she stepped onto the small plane bristling with top men, she had to confess to feeling somewhat glad to have Leo with her. They took places at the back together, behind the American General Bedell Smith and the British General Strong, who were chatting away about the merits of Islay versus Speyside whiskies, and for a moment Steffie felt more as if she were on a school trip rather than a vital national mission. Once they landed in Portugal, however, there was no doubting the import of their mission. Big staff cars awaited them and they were conducted with top security to a small boat to take them across the vast Tagus river and into its capital.

The bigwigs settled themselves in seats at the rear, but Steffie made straight for the prow, keen to see Europe's most westerly city, and it was well worth the discomfort of the spray. Lisbon was sparkling, the bright sun reflecting off the mass of houses rising up a steep hill from the riverfront for at least half a mile. Many of the houses were white but in between were walls of pretty blue, green and red, and the buildings of the great square for which they were heading were painted an exuberant yellow. Above them, a medieval castle and cathedral stood on a rock of a hill, incongruously craggy against the brighter buildings below.

'Lisbon was almost totally flattened by an earthquake in 1755,' Leo told her, coming to stand at her side. 'I read a book about it once. The buildings on the rock were all that survived so everything else has been rebuilt since.'

'Like Messina,' Steffie said fondly.

Lisbon reminded her of the pretty port on Sicily where she'd spent several happy holidays, save that it was far larger. They were coming into dock at the Praça do Comercio and Steffie could see the elegant yellow buildings more clearly.

They stood on three sides of a vast square, running round to a towering archway in the centre. Beneath them, smart arches were home to many stalls selling vibrant fruit and vegetables, homespun textiles and bright pots. Everything in Lisbon, it seemed, was colour and life, and Steffie was sad to be hustled into another diplomatic car and driven west along the seafront, away from the centre.

She couldn't stop herself looking up every single, steeply sloping street to her right as the grand centre gave way to narrower alleyways full of bars and cafés. Around every one ran yellow trams, climbing the hills with seeming ease, people hanging out their windows and off their steps as they hurried about their business, calling to friends in their rat-a-tat language.

Many of the houses here were tiled with vibrant Moorish patterns and Steffie longed to get out and wander, but there was a job to do and she couldn't afford to indulge herself in more than a few longing looks. The embassy was some way out, in a more spacious, quieter diplomatic section. It was a suitably grand, marble-fronted building, running up one of the now familiarly sloping streets so that the lower end was a whole storey higher than the upper. Inside, all was hush, the bustle and heat of Lisbon absorbed by thick walls and heavy furniture, though Steffie caught a glimpse of a lush courtyard garden at the rear and was glad there might be somewhere to escape to if the business got too much.

Awaiting them in a high-ceilinged reception room were three Italian generals, jostling with each other for central position, and a long, extravagantly dressed banqueting table laden with a luncheon surely far too heavy for the bright summer day. Steffie felt a momentary panic as she was separated from Leo to sit with the generals, but what had she told Travis about being able to do her job?

'You can do this,' she told herself sternly and then, turning to the man on her right, realised she knew him.

'Signor Castellano!'

'*Brigadier-General* Castellano,' he corrected her, but he was smiling and went on, in Italian. 'Is that little Stefania Carmichael?'

'Not so little now,' she shot back, slipping easily into the language. He gave a gracious bow of his head.

'Indeed, indeed. The years are sliding away from us. Last time I saw you, was, let me see, New Year 1940, I believe.'

'My engagement party.'

'Of course! You are married now?'

She shook her head.

'Not yet. Matteo and I have been separated by the war.'

General Castellano shook his head.

'Too many have. I told Musso not to throw his lot in with the Germans, but would he listen? Still, here we are now – ready to negotiate a friendship with Britain once more.'

'And America,' Steffie said, glancing to Leo, who was chattering away with one of the other generals across the table.

'And America,' Castellano agreed heavily. 'You did well to get them on your side.'

'On the right side,' Steffie countered.

'Let's hope so. Because if the Nazis win, it will not go well for the nation who abandoned them as allies, will it?'

'They won't win,' Steffie said stoutly.

'I pray you are right, but we must get this armistice watertight, or we will have a foretaste of Nazi displeasure. We will need Allied troops around Rome and ready to invade from the seas if it is to work without terrible retribution. I hope you are ready for these talks, young lady, because there are many lives hanging on their success.'

It was a theme he was to return to time and again over the

next week of negotiations – once they had actually started. The first afternoon was hampered by the Allied delegation demanding a single spokesman from the Italian one and the Italians being unable to decide which of them was the most senior. It was a classic piece of military nonsense and, in the end, Steffie had little choice but to march up to the three high-ranked men and tell them in Italian to sort themselves out.

'You're making a mockery of your position before you even start,' she urged Castellano. 'What does it matter which one of you speaks? You're not in a strong position here. They can all get in their plane and fly back to the freedom of Great Britain, leaving you to face Hitler alone, so make your pick and get on with it.'

She'd been astonished at her own daring, but they'd hung their heads, as meek as children, and agreed that Castellano should take the floor. Steffie had looked over at Leo, who'd been trying desperately not to laugh, and been pleased once more that he was here. He did no more than make polite conversation with the bristling Italians in breaks, leaving the official translating to Steffie, but after dinner he was there to escape with her and see the city.

Leaving the diplomats nodding over brandies, they would hop onto a yellow tram to head into the bohemian bars of the Bairro Alto or the local cafés of the Alfama district beneath the castle. There, they'd sip wine and listen to the melancholy strains of *fado* music and the excitable chatter of the locals as the sun went down over the sea.

'It feels almost magical here,' Steffie said over a nice bottle of *vinho verde* in a bar overlooking the sea one night.

She and Leo were winding down from a long day of treading the same ground. The Italians wanted more military backup in Rome than the Allies were prepared to commit and were pushing for more details of the invasion than the Allies were prepared to give. There was also the small matter of the terms. The Italian appeal had come so fast that there had been no time for the Allies to write a full contract and they'd settled on a 'short term document' that gave eleven military conditions for the armistice, plus a sly twelfth one stating that political and financial settlement would be negotiated later. Much had been done to downplay that final term to the Italians and Steffie didn't like it. She had a feeling that, when it was finally pinned down, the Allies would be harsh on the country she'd grown up in. But then, they'd thrown their lot in with the Nazis, so perhaps it was what they deserved.

She sipped her wine, shaking off the rigours of the day and sinking into the embrace of the soft Lisbon night. Portugal was, of course, neutral and it was almost heartbreakingly glorious to be in a country that, to all intents and purposes, was functioning as usual. It was the little things – the lack of air-raid sirens or blackout blinds, the absence of bomb damage, people walking the streets without the encumbrance of a gas mask – that made Steffie realise how used to it all she'd got, and how sad that was.

'Everyone here feels so free,' she said wistfully.

'It's been a long haul in England, huh?' Leo asked.

'I guess so. You forget what normal life feels like after a while, and seeing it here...'

She blinked back a stupid tear.

'Y'all sure are brave, you know. Americans are whining about war privations already and the only part of our land that's been attacked is a harbour way out in the Pacific. I couldn't believe it when I landed in England and saw what you guys have been going through. Even seeing one house bombed breaks your heart, let alone street after street of them.'

'We don't have much choice, but thanks.' She poured them both more wine. 'Tell me about your family.'

He looked shy.

'Not much to tell. My dad's a barber. That's to say, he runs a chain of barber shops. Not a big chain. There are five of them, one run by him, one by his best friend, two by my uncles and one by my sister.' Steffie raised an eyebrow and he laughed. 'See – I'm used to feisty broads.'

'Broads?'

'Dames, you know – women.'

'You have some odd words.'

'So do you. It took me ages to work out what a tap was, and a pavement, not to mention a lavvie. Hey, perhaps we should talk in Italian – we'd probably confuse each other less.'

Steffie laughed but shook her head. Italian felt too intimate, too like Matteo. God, she missed him. He'd love it here. She'd have to bring him after the war – whenever that was.

'Your sister sounds fun. And your mother?'

'Mom's in a wheelchair.'

That surprised her.

'I'm so sorry.'

He shrugged. 'It's been that way since... For a long time. She's a smart lady and she runs all the accounts for the shops. She and Pops make a great partnership.'

He smiled fondly, his whole face softening.

'Are you a barber too?' Steffie asked.

He shook his head.

'I tried but I'm terrible with scissors. Much better with languages. I take after my mom's side, even sketch a bit like her.'

'Sketch? You mean draw? Paint?'

'A bit of both, yes, though I'm no Picasso. It's words all the way for me. I'd landed a job as a European liaison officer for a big polio charity before I was called up and I hope I can go back to it once this is all over. I'm full of ways to make them more efficient.' He smiled self-consciously. 'But enough of me. Tell me about yourself, Stefania Carmichael.'

'What's to tell? I'm just a society girl who was on her way to becoming a wife and mother before the war got its hooks into me and I discovered, well, that there's other stuff I enjoy, I guess. Not numbers so much, but letters definitely – patterns and languages.'

'You're a natural translator,' he said. 'You pick up all the important bits without cluttering.'

'I do?'

'Yep. And you're a mighty fine negotiator too. There's not many could stand down a set of bickering generals like you did, girl.'

'It was all such a waste of time.'

Leonard grimaced.

'If you ask me this whole fandango is a waste of time. Castellano's never going to agree to anything without Badoglio, and the Allies aren't going to back down on revealing their military secrets in case it all falls through. We're at an impasse.'

Steffie nodded.

'But at least the wine's good.'

Leo laughed.

'It certainly is. Here's to breaking the impasse!'

They drank with enthusiasm, but without effect. The next day, as anticipated, Castellano stood up and said he had to consult with his PM. With much humming and haahing and a long break for sustenance, it was agreed the negotiations would reconvene in three days' time – in Sicily.

'Am I to come?' Steffie asked General Strong, glancing out the window as a yellow tram went past. She'd loved Lisbon, but Sicily...

'Of course, my dear,' he assured her, 'or we'll never understand each other. Ever been to Sicily?'

'Once or twice,' she said, thinking of running on the beaches as a girl and then lying on them hand in hand with Matteo as a young woman. It would be very different this time, but it was getting her closer to her fiancé both politically and physically. Bringing the Italians onto the Allied side would be a vital step in ending this damned war and Steffie was determined to do her best to make it happen.

FOURTEEN

AUGUST 1943

Fran

Fran looked around Room 149 trying not to feel too helpless in
the face of a veritable mountain of paperwork.

'Why didn't I keep my stupid mouth shut?' she said to the
empty room.

In reply, a stack of postcards slid to the ground, scattering a
hundred people's holidays at her feet. Fran picked the nearest
one up feeling strangely voyeuristic.

My dearest Susan,

*I am writing this from the promenade at Arromanches where
we had so many happy holidays together when you and Tim
were children. I scattered your father's ashes off the end last
night, and I confess I shed a tear as he drifted out to sea, but it
is what he wanted and I feel better for having done it. Afterwards, I treated myself to a small Muscat in the Bar Michel,
where we always used to have our last night tea, but it wasn't*

the same on my own. I catch the boat home tomorrow and look
forward to seeing you and the little ones.

All my love,

Mum (Granny Rose)

It was a touching piece of writing that pushed a lump into Fran's throat. It was dated 1938 so poor Rose must have been on her own for five years now, if she was even still alive. It had obviously touched Susan too for her to have kept it all this time and was a sign of how desperately the public wanted the invasion to succeed that they were prepared to give up such treasures. They had all had enough of this war.

Resolutely, Fran turned the postcard over and scanned the picture of the beach at Arromanches or, as it was about to become on Allied maps, Gold. Churchill was back from meeting Roosevelt and the Canadian prime minister, Mackenzie King, in Quebec where the outline plans for the invasion of Normandy had been approved and the date agreed as 1 May 1944. Three rough areas had been identified for the landings – Omaha at the base of the Cotentin peninsula, Sword at the port of Ouistreham, and Gold around Arromanches in between.

General Eisenhower had been put in charge of all US troops in the European theatre and General Montgomery named as commander of the 21st Army Group of the British forces. Plans were solidifying from jingoistic speechifying into actual troops on the ground, and sometimes Fran couldn't quite believe she was one of the handful of people in Europe who knew the details. If her mum and dad could only see her now, they'd stop trying to persuade her to drive a damned ambulance.

Fran knew that her parents, both medics, only had her best

interests at heart but they didn't seem to be able to separate her best interests from theirs. She spoke to them once a week from the public telephone in Bletchley and was working up the courage to tell them she wanted to become a journalist, but she could already imagine their response.

'A journalist, Frances? Writing gossip columns and fashion features? Really, darling, we'd hoped for so much more.'

She ground her teeth, then told herself not to put words into their mouths. They'd changed their tune since Robert, her elder brother, had come home on leave from his field hospital in Algiers and raged against the pointlessness of mending broken men instead of stopping them getting broken in the first place. Fran was delighted both he and Ben, her younger brother, were now home, and horrified that they would almost certainly be part of the medical corps heading onto the beaches on what everyone was now calling D-Day. Well, everyone except Valérie. She and her French friends were calling it Jour-J which, to Fran, sounded slightly less harsh. Any which way you looked at it, though, it was going to be gruesome.

She picked up three of the cardboard boxes she had purloined from stores and, taking a big pen, wrote *Omaha*, *Gold* and *Sword* on them. Granny Rose's postcard could provide vital visuals for Gold and she placed it into the correct box and moved on. It was going to be a long afternoon.

An hour later, however, Fran almost jumped out of her skin at a knock on the door. She dropped her postcard – a particularly helpful view along the front at Lion-sur-Mer – and went over.

'Who is it?' she called through the wooden door.

'Frances? It's me.'

'Valérie? Are you all right?'

'No. I am bored.'

Fran suppressed a smile.

'Aren't you on shift?'

'Yes.' A pause. 'But my work is boring and pointless and
Hut 3 is no fun without you there.'

Fran's smile broadened.

'Hang on a minute.'

She unlocked the door with the key around her neck and
sidled out. Valérie tried to look behind her and she slammed the
door shut. The French girl jumped.

'Top secret work, is it?'

'You know it is, Valérie, like all the work around here. No
one is allowed to see what anyone else is doing.'

'Not even wives?'

'No. And you're not my wife.'

'I am not?'

Valérie's dark eyes swam with hurt and Fran groaned. She
was obviously in a funny mood.

'Much as I wish you could be,' she said gently, taking
Valérie's elfin chin in her hands and leaning down to kiss her.
'Now, is there something I can help you with?' She glanced at
her watch. 'It'll be lunch in an hour. Shall we meet at the pond?
Have another go in the rowing boat?'

She laughed but Valérie didn't.

'I was thinking,' she said instead, 'that I could join you here,
in your mystery room.'

'You were?'

'You are always complaining that you have so much to do
and I thought, why not help?'

'You did? I mean, I suppose you could.'

Fran's brain raced. There *was* an awful lot to go through
and a second pair of hands would be welcome but with Fran
spending so much time in Room 149, could Hut 3 afford to lose
Valérie too?

'You don't want me,' Valérie said, with a pout that made
Fran smile again.

'I was thinking more, my dear grump, that Eric might not be

able to spare you.'

'I'm no use to Eric. The SLUs run like clockwork these days so all I do is run reports on the inter-country comms. Any old WREN could do it.'

'Valérie!'

'It's true.'

'Well, then, I suppose we could ask.'

'We could?' Valérie's eyes lit up and she grabbed Fran's hands. 'We could! We should. Shall we go now?'

Fran knew already that when Valérie was in this sort of mood, it was better to run with it.

'Hang on – I have to lock up.'

'Lock up with your important key?'

Fran refused to rise and simply turned to secure Room 149.

'There's just one question,' she said, when she was happy it was safe.

'Whether you want me?'

'No. Stop it, Valérie – petulance doesn't suit you.' Valérie threw her an exaggerated pout, all lips and big eyes, and Fran smiled. 'Yes, well, maybe it *does* suit you.' She dropped a swift kiss on those deliciously full lips. 'But it's not exactly grown-up. The question is – who do we ask?'

Her first port of call was Thomas Boase, head of the Western Front committee.

'A second pair of hands is fine by me,' he said, 'but as to who that is, I couldn't say. Seems like one for Travis.'

Fran quailed at the thought of knocking on the door of the Head of Bletchley Park, but Valérie had no such inhibitions and had her there before Fran could think twice about it.

'Can I help you?'

Valérie nudged urgently at Fran and she edged inside.

'Sorry to disturb you, sir, and I don't know if this is something for you personally but we weren't sure who to come to.'

'Ask on, then.'

'Right. Well, I'm working in Room 149.'

'Ah. Excellent. Important stuff. Is there a problem?'

'I'm snowed under, sir. There's a lot to get through and, as you well know, there's something of a deadline.'

'That's putting it lightly, Miss...?'

'Morgan, sir. Frances Morgan.' Fran was aware she'd turned bright red and was not handling this at all well. 'So, the thing is, sir, I wondered if I could have someone else to help?'

'I see.' He looked to Valérie. 'And you thought Miss Rousseau would be the person for the task?'

Valérie stepped forward.

'You know my name?'

'I do. You work in Hut 3 and your family are from... Bayeux, is it?'

Valérie nodded.

'That's right, sir.'

'And run bicycle shops across Normandy, yes?'

'Erm, yes, but why does that matter to you?'

'It's my job to be aware of my staff, Miss Rousseau.'

'You didn't know Frances.'

Fran tried not to let that sting.

'Miss Morgan is not French.'

Valérie blinked.

'Right. I see. Is that a problem?'

'Your work has been exemplary, Miss Rousseau so, no, it is not a problem.'

'Thank you.'

'I cannot, however, have you working in Room 149.'

'Why not?'

Fran tried to tug on Valérie's blouse to make her stop but it was no use.

'Because the room contains sensitive information about the invasion of northern France. Were it to involve attacks on, for example, an area where you had family, you might – just *might* is all I'm saying – be tempted to warn someone.'

'I wouldn't!'

'It would only be human nature, would it not? Imagine if you knew that we were about to drop bombs on a village in which a loved-one lived? Might you not wish to get word to them to leave?'

'Not if I was told not to.'

'Hmm.' Travis sat back in his chair. 'Have you heard of the Gunpowder Plot, Miss Rousseau?'

'Of course I have. I've lived in England long enough to see your strange customs with the guy and the bonfires and that ridiculous sticky toffee stuff.'

Fran saw Travis suppress a smile.

'Good. What you may not know, however, is that it came close to succeeding – to blowing up the Houses of Parliament at the state opening, with the king and all his most important officials inside. The plotters had everything in place, but one man wrote a letter to his friend, Lord Monteagle, suggesting he stay away. Monteagle took it to someone else who alerted the authorities and – boom! Or rather, no boom. They put on an extra search of the building and found poor old Guy Fawkes crouched in the cellars with barrels of dynamite.

'One letter, Miss Rousseau, changed the course of history, one letter written with the best of intentions. Not treason, not sabotage, just a word of warning to a loved one, and one of the most audacious plots in British history was foiled.' Travis steepled his fingers together as Valérie stared at him, struck dumb for once. 'You understand my caution?'

'Yes,' she stuttered. 'But I wouldn't. I mean, I won't...'

'Valérie, enough.' Fran pulled harder on her blouse. 'I'm sorry, sir. We shouldn't have bothered you. We'll go now.'

Travis put up a hand.

'One moment, Miss Morgan. If you need help in Room 149,

I shall see to it that someone is assigned to you. The task is administrative?'

'Yes, sir. It's very simple.'

He smiled.

'There, you see, Miss Rousseau – your considerable brain would be wasted on it.' He got up and came round from the desk, placing a hand on her shoulder. Fran saw the prickly Frenchwoman flinch and wished she'd never agreed to this mad meeting. 'I understand your desire to be useful,' Travis went blithely on, 'but Hut 3 is doing invaluable work and you are a key part of it. Please, do not think this means that we do not trust you, simply that...'

'You do not trust me.'

Fran saw Travis's eyebrow twitch with a first show of impatience.

'Valérie!' she hissed.

'Simply that,' he pushed on with studied calm, 'we wish to protect you. Now, if you don't mind...'

'Of course not, sir. Thank you, sir.'

Fran dragged Valérie from the office, mortified. She didn't stop until they were out of the mansion and round the back of what used to be Hut 3.

'Well, that was embarrassing.'

'Not for you, Frances. You were not accused of being a security risk, a potential traitor to the cause of liberating La France.'

Fran swallowed. Once Valérie started talking of 'La France', things were bound to get heated.

'Travis was only being sensible.'

'Sensible, pah! You British are all so sensible.'

'Is it such a bad thing?'

'It is a block to passion, to rage, to true feeling.'

'That's not true. It's just what's needed in the real world. We are all passionate about winning this war, Valérie.'

'But you do not truly understand, tucked away on this

island, safe with your seas and your navy and your fancy Spitfire pilots.'

Fran felt anger rise in the pit of her stomach; Valérie wasn't
being fair.

'And yet, here we still are, fighting. Do not mistake sense for
a lack of care, Valérie. And do not be rude about the one
country still working to save your own.'

Valérie gasped. 'How dare you!'

'No, Valérie – how dare *you*.'

Valérie stared up at her, hands on hips and eyes flaring.
Fran stood tall, refusing to back down, and suddenly the French
girl folded, her fury draining visibly from her and tears welling
in her dark eyes.

'I'm sorry. I'm sorry, Frances. I want to help, to do something more than reporting on comms vans at the front line. I
want to be *on* the front line.'

Fran grabbed her shoulders.

'But don't you see, Valérie, it's the comms that will help us
win. The work at Bletchley Park is a huge advantage for the
Allies – *huge*.'

'I know. I do know that, Frances. It's just so... dull.'

Fran shook her head and opened her arms. After a
moment's hesitation Valérie stepped into them and wept against
her shoulder.

'I think you'd find,' Fran said softly, 'that crouching in a
trench, clutching a gun and waiting for an enemy advance
was dull too. This is war. It's all horrible, but it has to be
done.'

Valérie looked up at her.

'You're right, Frances. I know you're right. But look what
I've done now.'

Fran frowned down at her, puzzled.

'What have you done?'

'Got you a damned assistant. Travis will send you some

pretty young WREN, with blonde curls and long legs, and you'll be shut in that room with her every damned day.'

Fran burst out laughing.

'And will come home to you every damned night, you fool.' She stroked Valérie's hair out of her damp face. 'What's really wrong, Valérie?'

The French girl wriggled against her.

'I don't know. I feel, you know, *pas dans mon assiette.*'

'What?'

'Not in my plate. Out of sorts?'

'Ah!'

'You see! I cannot even express myself in your strange English ways.'

'The plate thing is pretty strange, Valérie.'

'Not to me, not to *us*. Oh, never mind the plate. This is a critical moment in French history and I am on the sideline.'

'That's not true. You're in the heart of it. You're part of the team making it happen.'

Valérie smiled at her.

'You are very kind, Frances.'

'I am very right.'

'Hmmm,' Valérie half-agreed, then buried herself in Fran's arms again and all she could do was to hold her and hope the mood passed. Their work, cocooned in a strange park presided over by a semi-Gothic mansion and filled with quirky academics, *was* vital to winning the war and the sooner Valérie realised that, the better.

FIFTEEN

SEPTEMBER 1943

Ailsa

Ailsa scanned the rainbow of fruit and vegetables laid out on the rough market stalls in the centre of Colombo and hugged herself with the wonder of it. If only her parents could be here to see this, perhaps then they would understand what had driven her to leave North Uist. Her home island was beautiful, but beauty took many forms and Ailsa was loving discovering more of them.

'What's this?' she asked, pointing to a curious fruit, like a waxy pink pear, polished to a high sheen.

'Jambu fruit,' said the stallholder, a big local woman dressed in a tunic as bright as her wares. 'Very soft, good juice. You try.' She whipped out an enormous knife and, with a deft hand, cut the fruit in half to expose a pale centre. 'Here.'

Ailsa took it, but had no idea how to go about eating it. She put her mouth tentatively to the edge and nibbled. The texture was curious, like cotton wool, but the taste was delicate and sweet.

'Nice,' she said.

'You want?'

It would be rude not to.

'Yes, please,' she agreed. 'Two please.'

'One for husband?'

'That's right.'

'Good, good – jambu fruit very fruity!' She laughed heartily then, noticing Ailsa's huge belly, laughed even more. 'But you don't need that, *akka*. When you due?'

'Too soon,' Ailsa said ruefully. 'Maybe three weeks?'

'Three weeks! Wonderful, wonderful. And never too soon, lady. You want baby out as early as possible – smaller then!' She pulled a graphic grimace and Ailsa pulled one back. 'Don't worry, Amaya have what you need. Cheena goraka.'

She held up another curious fruit – or possibly a vegetable, it was hard to tell, especially for a girl who'd been brought up on turnips and cabbage. It looked like a miniature, deeply grooved pumpkin and seemed to come in red, orange and yellow.

'What is it?' Ailsa asked, taking it in her palm.

'Cheena goraka,' the woman – Amaya – repeated. 'A sour fruit. Good in curries – tasty. And it will help bring baby out, if you eat it with chillies.'

She added a tiny but dangerous-looking bright-red shard of a bulb. Ailsa stared at it distrustingly. She'd been subjected to a few Ceylonese curries in the HMS Anderson canteen and they seemed to be designed to explode in your mouth.

'If you're sure,' she said uncertainly.

'Very sure. Very good.'

Amaya stuck several of both the gorakas and the chillies into Ailsa's basket.

'Now, what else? Madan? Pineapple?'

'Pineapple!' Ailsa snatched eagerly at the one fruit she knew – and loved. 'Definitely a pineapple, please.'

She lifted up her hat to wipe the ever-present sweat from her face and glanced skyward. The sun was heading to its zenith and beating down with fiery determination. The monsoon had thankfully moved round to the north-east but it was still searingly hot. Ailsa felt light-headed and thought perhaps she should have had more breakfast. Her hair was damp and her simple cotton dress was clinging to her as if she'd stepped through a waterfall, not down a market street.

'You need this,' Amaya said helpfully, pointing to her gaily coloured turban. 'Much more comfortable.'

'Really?'

'Yes, yes, yes. Here.' She came out from behind her table of produce and took Ailsa's arm, guiding her to the next stall, full of glorious textiles, where she spoke in rapid Singhalese to her neighbour. The second woman nodded, smiled at Ailsa and then lifted her hat off her head. She took hold of Ailsa's red hair, exclaiming.

'Such a pretty colour! Like a sunset.'

Ailsa smiled, flattered despite herself.

'It's hot.'

'Hot, yes. Very hot. This one I think, to match your eyes.'

She pulled a pale blue scarf off a rack and, with astonishing speed, wound it around Ailsa's head, somehow catching her heavy hair up into its soft coils as she did so. Ailsa felt a slight breeze against her neck and the relief of the tendrils that usually dangled in her eyes being lifted away.

'That feels good.'

'Why you think we all wear them, *akka*? Look – you are one of us now.'

She lifted up a mirror and Ailsa stared in astonishment. With her hair pulled away, her face looked as exposed as a statue – though with far more freckles – and the blue brought out her eyes in a startling way. She put up a hand to the fabric.

'I look... different.'

'You look beautiful, akka. And far cooler.'

'Yes, thank you.'

'And, see – you can still wear your hat.'

The scarf-seller plonked it back on top and Ailsa glanced in the mirror again, expecting to look ridiculous but instead finding that she seemed... What was it? Local?

One of us, she heard Amaya say; she liked the sound of that.

'Thank you,' she said again and paid, wondering what Ned would make of his exotic wife when she returned.

Would they let her wear her turban at work? She felt conspicuous enough as it was. The rigid rules on wearing uniform on base meant she'd had to sew a panel into the front of her skirt to make space for her bulging belly. The commander looked at her askance every time he came into the big wireless hut, but the other operators merely teased her.

'Someone's not on war rations, hey, Ailsa?'

'Who let the elephant into the base, hey, Ailsa?'

It was light and good-humoured, backed up by the fact that they were all coming to rely on her to mend their sets when the tropical weather played havoc with reception. Not only that, she was getting into the swing of Japanese Morse and had been taking it down with greater speed and accuracy. The other day they'd had feedback from Bletchley Park that messages from AR were requiring very few amendments. Keith had read that one out in his morning briefing, only realising as he did so that AR was the pregnant woman he hadn't wanted on his base. Ailsa had said nothing, but the others had crowded round congratulating her and she'd been unable to resist a slightly smug look at her boss.

'Wait until the baby comes, and we'll see how good your Morse is then,' was all he'd said. Sitting, head swimming, in the middle of a foreign market, Ailsa had to concede his point. Nothing was feeling easy right now. Pulling herself out of her thoughts and back into the bustling market, she returned to Amaya.

'Do you have any juice?'

'Juice? Yes! Of course, juice.' She indicated a row of jugs standing in the shade, muslins over the top to keep the flies out. 'Mango? Papaya? Pineapple.'

'Pineapple please.'

Amaya looked at her in concern.

'You sit here, lady.' She ushered her onto a stool. 'Drink this.'

Ailsa gratefully accepted the cup, sucking down the sweet juice as if were manna from heaven. The baby stirred in her belly and she placed a reassuring hand on it, though in truth she was starting to be concerned about the birthing – not that she dared admit it to anyone, not even Ned. It had been her choice to come out here. She'd known she was pregnant and, against the advice of her dearest friends, had travelled anyway. She'd been determinedly insouciant about women having babies everywhere, but now that she was actually getting close, tendrils of fear were reaching into her supposedly bold heart.

Those women are in their homes, with their own doctors and their own mothers and their own friends, Steffie had said.

Ailsa drank more of her juice, picturing Steffie and Fran's kind faces, and thinking of the caravan with its quintessentially English charm. She imagined lying in a bunk with them either side of her, a safe refuge, and for the first time she truly wished she was back there. But Bletchley was a full month's sail away and there was no going back, not with Baby Robinson ready to come into the world at any time.

'You need a doctor,' Ned had told her the other day.

'Not that horrible military one,' she'd said, remembering the sharp-eyed man who'd reported her to the commander.

'He cured you of your fever.'

'Time cured me of my fever.'

'And a dose of penicillin.'

'Aye, well, I still don't want that doctor. He didn't like women. He insisted on talking to you instead of me.'

'You were babbling like a lunatic, my sweet.'

'Even so. Anyway, it's not a doctor I need, it's a midwife.'

'Right, yes. Good thinking. Let's find one of those then.'

It hadn't, however, proved that simple. They'd found out that there were two British midwives on the island, but further enquiries had revealed that one had been posted on the other side of Ceylon, and the other had gone back to England to work in London's East End.

'I'll find a local one,' Ailsa had said blithely, but HMS Anderson was a way out of Colombo, surrounded by nothing more than tea plantations and tiny villages. She wasn't sure how to go about hunting down a midwife among the shacks and, with only a few weeks until baby was due, she still had no one lined up to assist her.

Looking up from her juice, she saw Amaya serving two local women, all jabbering away in high-speed Singhalese. The babble of their voices mingled with the shouts of the stallholders, the bleating of goats in a nearby pen, and the phut and rumble of the few rickety vans traversing the capital. Ailsa drank the last of her juice, willing her mind to stop spinning. Baby seemed to be kicking hard at her taut belly and, although her lovely turban was keeping her neck cool, sweat was trickling down her back and between her thighs. At least, she hoped it was sweat.

'Don't come now,' she gasped, dropping the cup and putting both hands around her belly to keep her baby safe inside.

She was half aware of Amaya turning, calling something, but then the rainbow of the market turned upside down and, with a clatter, she fell off her stool. Strong arms caught her and she felt herself cradled against an ample bosom as she fought to hold onto consciousness.

'Ma,' she muttered.

Those women are in their homes, with their own doctors and their own mothers and their own friends, Steffie said again in her head.

She had eventually sent a letter to her parents, telling them the happy news, but it would have taken a month to get back to the Clyde and then a while longer to reach North Uist, with at least the same again for any reply to get to her. She could send a telegram, of course, when baby was safely born. *If* baby was safely born, she thought weakly and then told herself off. There was another human relying on her now, even if she hadn't met them yet, and she had to be strong.

With an effort, she collected her thoughts and peeled herself off Amaya.

'I'm so sorry. It's the heat and the baby. It's not coming, is it?'

'I don't think so, but I'm no expert.'

'Me neither,' Ailsa whimpered.

'Worry not. I have sent for my friend, Suranga. She expert. She midwife.'

'Really?' Ailsa's world swam back into focus. 'There's a midwife here?'

'Of course there is midwife. We have babies too you know.'

'I know,' Ailsa agreed happily. 'That's what I told everyone. Thank you, thank you so much.'

'Ah, it's nothing! We women, we have to stick together, yes?'

'Yes.'

'And here is Suranga. Suri, over here! A new patient for you.'

'So I see.' A small woman, far younger than Ailsa had been expecting, came bouncing up to them. She was wearing the same sort of bright tunic as Amaya but carried a large bag with a red cross on the side and looked Ailsa up and down with a professional air. 'Eight months gone?'

'About that.'

'Chest constricted? Belly tight? Need to go to the lavatory all the time?'

'All of those,' Ailsa agreed.

'Sounds right. Don't you worry, I've got you now. Come with me and we can do a proper examination.'

She offered Ailsa a strong arm and Ailsa leaned gladly on it.

'Oh, but I have to pay Amaya.'

'Later, later,' Amaya said, waving her away. 'Baby first.'

Ailsa nodded gratefully and let Suranga lead her across the market and into a nearby church. It was blissfully cool inside, but a suffering Christ peered sternly down at them and Ailsa looked around nervously.

'Here?'

'This way. Mother Mary looks after us.'

She steered Ailsa between the wooden pews and into a side chapel, separated off with a patterned curtain. Inside, under the kindly eyes of a statue of Mary, was a surgical bed and trolley of neatly laid-out equipment.

'Needs must,' Suri said with an easy smile. 'Our maternity hospital was commandeered by the air force, so we have had to, how you say – improvise?'

Ailsa nodded.

'It's lovely.'

'And blessed by God, which always helps.' Suri winked. 'Now, up on the bed with you, Ailsa. When were you last examined?'

'Erm.' Ailsa hefted herself onto the bed. 'I haven't really... been examined, that is. I was on the boat out here before I realised I was pregnant.' Suri raised an eyebrow and Ailsa flushed. 'Well, before I admitted I was pregnant. And here... A military doctor saw me when I had a fever but I don't think he actually examined me, simply spotted that I was pregnant and backed off as if it might be infectious.'

Suri laughed.

'Doctors can be like that. No matter. Baby is moving?'

'Oh, yes. Often.'

'Then I'm sure all will be well. Lie back and relax.'

It was a peculiar situation to find herself in, but Suri was so calm and gentle that Ailsa lay back, stared up at the bonnie carving on the ceiling of the Lady Chapel, and let her do her work.

'All well,' she said eventually. 'Baby feels healthy and is getting ready to turn.'

'Turn?'

'So they are born head first. It is a good thing – easier for you and safer for baby.'

'Right. Good.'

'I will check you again in another week, but I'd expect your son or daughter to be with us in around three weeks.'

'You'll check me again?'

'Is that all right?'

Ailsa could have wept with relief.

'That's wonderful. I can pay. I'm happy to pay. Can you be with me for the birth too?'

'It would be my honour.'

'Thank you.'

Now Ailsa was weeping, pathetic, cathartic tears. Suri held her hand and quietly passed her a handkerchief.

'Worry not, Ailsa. I will keep you and baby safe and healthy, I promise.'

The words were music to her ears.

'I can't believe I found you, Suri.'

Suri cast her eyes to Mary, who looked benignly back. Ailsa, who had been brought up in the fiercest Presbyterian tradition, felt awkward before this most famous of saints, but if Mary had a hand in bringing her to these kind Ceylonese women and this authoritative midwife, then she'd happily afford her a prayer or two. Beyond the walls of this chapel, beyond the confines of HMS Anderson, beyond the shores of Ceylon, the war was raging on. She still had her part to play in it, she was sure of that, but right now she had her own battle too and was over-joyed to have finally found someone to fight it with her.

SIXTEEN

SEPTEMBER 1943

Steffie

The whole tentful of negotiators held their breath as General Castellano lifted the pen then, with a frown, set to reading through the terms of the armistice again. Steffie could hear her heart beating loudly and feared everyone would turn to stare, save that she suspected hers was not the only one going like the clappers.

The Italians had been readier to come to terms on Sicily, as if the scent of their homeland had made them yearn to protect it more. And they all knew, after three bitter years with the Nazis, staying on their side was not the way to do that. The armistice was fraught with danger, especially in the short term, but it was the only way forward. Mussolini was in prison, the fascist party had been disbanded to singing in the streets of Italy, and this was the logical next step. But still General Castellano, representing the Italian government, hesitated.

Sign it, Steffie willed him. This armistice was the first step for the Allies in the plan for the full penetration of mainland Europe and, although it had been rushed through to be

completed before the invasion of southern Italy, it was solid.
Well, solid for the Allies. Steffie had overheard the British and
American generals talking the other night and gathered that
Eisenhower had seen the financial and political terms alluded to
in the coy twelfth condition of the provisional armistice and
thought them so harsh that he was pushing to sign the short
document first. Steffie's heart ached for Italy, who would pay a
stern price for her poor choices, but right now she couldn't
dwell on that. They had to secure the armistice and invade.
Europe was desperate for liberation and much depended on this
crucial moment.

The signs from Bletchley were good. When they'd arrived
in the army camp in Cassibile, Steffie had been able to hook up
with an SLU – a Special Liaison Unit running wireless coms
from an adapted van – and exchange messages with Bletchley
Park. It had been her first time on the coding end of the system
and she'd been allowed use of the Typex machine in the back of
the old army van to encrypt her own message and then decrypt
the reply.

She had to admit, it had been exciting seeing her words
turned into a jumble of letters and then the same in reverse. It
had been so easy and she could see why the enemy felt secure
in their communications. The process of breaking Enigma was
laborious and seemingly labyrinthine and she, too, would be
unable to comprehend that a load of tweed-jacketed academics
working out of a crooked country house could possibly crack it.
But crack it they had.

Yesterday ISOS had told her that the Abwehr Ultra was
suggesting the Germans were planning a retreat to northern
Italy following the loss of Sicily. Hitler was apparently fed up
of defending the isolated boot of his supposed ally's land and
looking at withdrawing to a strong defensive line above
Bologna. That would be tricky to break when the time came,
but taking the south would be a morale-boosting start and

would give the Allies several key ports from which to land troops in safety.

Even better, if southern Italy was free, Matteo would be too. Steffie might even, somehow, be able to see him before she went home. Marry him. Her mother would be furious, but Julianna's social needs were far down the list of priorities right now. First, though, Castellano had to sign the armistice.

'Where are the financial and political terms?' he asked, and Steffie snapped out of her dreaming to translate.

'Coming,' General Bedell Smith said shortly. 'But they will not stop military action, so it is best if we proceed on outline terms.'

Steffie translated, feeling treacherous. Castellano and, by association, Prime Minister Badoglio were being tricked here, but tricked in a good cause. Montgomery and the American general, Mark Clark, were poised on Sicily to attack. Castellano had toured their considerable ranks yesterday and knew that he had all that might on his side, if he would only put pen to paper.

'The paratroopers are ready?' he asked.

Steffie translated but Bedell Smith had understood and nodded impatiently.

'Ready. They will land around Rome as soon as the armistice is announced on September eighth, to coincide with Italian troops storming the four aerodromes around the city.'

Steffie translated the American's words. Castellano winced.

'General Carboni does not believe that we have the military capacity to take all four with the speed required.'

Bedell Smith waved this away.

'You have a week.'

'But we cannot arouse German suspicion. They are already sniffing around. Badoglio was summoned to see their commander two days ago.'

'And, I hope, assured him of his continued loyalty?'

'Of course, but it is hard to know if he was believed.'

Steffie fought to keep up with the translations as the men jibed at each other.

'Come, Castellano,' Bedell Smith snapped. 'We are here, on your doorstep, with men prepared to give their lives to liberate your country and you are hesitating over your own part in the operation?'

Steffie felt the sting of the words as she put them into Italian and glanced to Leo, who gave her an encouraging nod. These were not her words, but her translations.

'Not hesitating,' Castellano shot back, 'but being realistic. Rome is a great city, with many citizens, and we need to protect her at this most critical of moments.'

'Which you will do by letting the Allied armies in. Now – sign or I'm out of here, and my troops with me.'

Steffie swallowed and reported his words, inserting several 'the general says,' to be sure it was clear whose ultimatum this was. Brigadier-General Castellano looked up at her, worry in his ageing eyes, but then gave a fatalistic shrug and, with a grand flourish, signed his name across the crucial paper.

'It's done.'

'Excellent!' Bedell Smith snatched up the paper and checked it. 'Now – photographs. And some of that fine wine we had last night to celebrate.'

The sparring forgotten, he shook hands with the whole Italian delegation and summoned the photographers, getting Castellano to hold the pen again and standing, all smiles, at his right shoulder, General Strong on his left. Steffie, keeping well behind the camera, thought the British general looked uneasy but perhaps that was because he'd not taken part in the final negotiations. She hoped so. She needed this to go well, for Matteo's sake and for the sake of winning the war.

. . .

For the next week, the whole of Sicily was a hive of activity as the Allies prepared to invade. An attempt was made to fly the negotiating team home but, to Steffie's relief, it was overruled on the grounds that the planes were better deployed bombing Italy and, instead, they were moved up the coast to the British army camp outside Messina. She kept well out of the way, glad to have Leo for company, and went often into the town.

It was a battered shadow of the city she knew, but it kept its weary head proudly high. The golden statue of the Madonnina del Porto still stood determinedly over the entrance to the port to bless all who came in – especially, Steffie thought, if they were in Allied colours – and the elaborate clock in the Piazza Duomo still rang out its twelve-minute salute to midday, the statues dancing blithely above the war-damaged square. The Church of Christ the King kept watch from the hillside, the giant word DUCE painted defiantly across it, although Il Duce was now gone into the bowels of an Italian prison.

The one place that was livelier than she remembered was the sheltered docklands along the elegant seafront and she was drawn to it again and again, sickened by the changes the war had wrought on the pretty town. She'd holidayed here so many times, when the buildings were all bars and dance halls, not barracks for armies. This was where Matteo had first told her that he loved her, after they'd danced until the sun had risen over the sea.

'We'll be together forever,' he'd assured her that rose-tinted morning, but now the docks bristled with invasion craft and Matteo was somewhere in Rome with a prime minister she could only pray was ready for the German reaction to Italy changing sides.

Messages from Bletchley Park had been less encouraging in the last two days. Ultra was indicating that Hitler had done a U-turn and no troops were being moved out of southern Italy. Indeed, battalions around Rome, and particularly the aerodromes the Italians were meant to be taking, had been fortified. Steffie reported it all in, but General Montgomery, focused on his invasion into Calabria, was not in the mood to listen.

Steffie often thought back to the invasion of Sicily three months ago, where the Germans, tricked by Mincemeat, had been wonderfully unprepared. With the Italian coup happening so fast, there had been no time to set up a similar trick here and Steffie's gut churned constantly with nervous anticipation. She yearned for the liberation of the country she'd grown up in, and yearned even more to see Matteo. Her nights were broken by images of him shot or bombed or, worst of all, tortured as an enemy spy, and her days weren't much easier, so she was glad to find herself and Leo distracting employment with the SLU.

They, too, had moved to Messina, ready to land in Italy once the first wave had secured the beachheads so that BP Ultra decrypts could be delivered direct to the Allied commanders. The brave wireless operators deserved a break before that and Steffie was glad to take on their work for a few days. She watched them as they lazed in the sunshine, smoking and chatting as if they were on holiday, not the brink of battle, and felt renewed admiration for everyone on the frontlines of this endless war.

It was a relief when 8 September dawned – the day of the armistice announcement and the start of the invasion with the paratroopers into Rome. The troops were ready, the generals were ready; they just had to pray that the Italians were ready too. Eisenhower had sent notice that he would announce the armistice on Radio Algiers at 6.30 p.m. and Badoglio was standing by to make a parallel announcement on Italian radio. The press corps were taut with excitement, knowing something was coming, and all was set. But then, around midday, Steffie got a message direct through the SLU.

```
Abwehr sources in Rome say Italians
panicking. Aerodromes around Rome firmly
in German control. Badoglio looking for
delay.
```

She took it straight to Montgomery.

'Goddamned Ities,' he snapped. 'Got no spine.'

'That's not true, sir,' Steffie objected. 'It looks as if the Germans have wind of what's going on. They're shoring up battalions around Rome and may well move to seize the city the moment the armistice is announced. That would be bad for us all.'

'I'm well aware of the strategic importance of Rome, thank you, young lady. I shall get messages direct to Badoglio and see what the hell is going on.'

'Yes, sir, thank you, sir.'

Steffie escaped, flustered but relieved that he'd listened. Perhaps it was best to delay the announcement of the armistice so that the Italians could at least hold the capital in a pretence of unity with the Germans. There would be time enough to turn on them when the situation was more secure, she reasoned to Leo as they paced the camp.

Eisenhower, however, did not agree.

'The announcement goes ahead,' Montgomery told them a few hours later. 'It's been signed for a week now and it's time the Italians stood by it. Badoglio has been informed.'

Steffie ran for the telegram office in Messina and composed a sharp message to her father.

```
I want my fiancé back. Now.
```

She hoped that this message, read by strangers as the rantings of a hysterical female, would tell her father, as Matteo's handler, to order him out of the capital, and she could only pray he got it in time. She panted back to the camp shortly after 6 p.m. to find everyone crouched around the wireless. Sure enough, smack on the dot of half past six, Eisenhower's American tones came across the airwaves of Radio Algiers, announcing the 'unconditional surrender' of the Italian nation to the Allies.

'Is it on Radio Italy?' Steffie demanded of her SLU friends.

Someone turned the dial with expert precision. An Italian aria drifted out of the set with not a whisper of the prime minister.

'This isn't good,' the operator said, not that Steffie needed him to tell her that.

Please let her father have got to Matteo in time.

She crouched by the set, listening to banal Italian radio until her head swam with it. Finally, at 7.45, Badoglio hit the airwaves, his voice shaky as he did his best to tell his people that the armistice was a positive move. It was bravely done but already reports were flying in of German troops storming Rome and it was clear that little mercy would be shown.

Sure enough, a few hours later, Ultra arrived from Bletchley Park revealing that Hitler had issued an order allowing German soldiers to summarily execute any Italian officer who resisted arrest. This was clear licence to shoot anyone in a uniform, for how was a dead man to protest that he'd had his hands aloft? Eisenhower, alarmed at the chaos, stood down his American paratroopers and Rome was left to stand alone against the Nazi fury.

'We'll get them,' Montgomery told the men as they were loaded into the landing craft in Messina docks. 'We'll be straight up that west coast and into Rome within a couple of weeks. Tell the blasted Germans to take a good look at the Colosseum because they won't be there for long.'

The troops cheered wildly but Steffie listened with a cold

heart. The Germans were there now and, for Matteo and his fellow officers, a couple of weeks might be too long.

The invasions, at least, went well. Reports flew in that Montgomery had rapidly established a beachhead in Calabria and was marching north to join the American, General Clark, in Salerno. Fighting there had been harder, but the Germans had been driven back and the mood was optimistic. With the SLU gone, Leo, Steffie and a lone wireless operator set up a message centre in Messina and made themselves useful enough not to be sent home.

'I might get to Rome sooner than I'd hoped,' Leo said a few days into the attack.

'Don't count your chickens,' Steffie told him grimly. 'It's a long way up that coast.'

'Chickens?'

'Never mind.'

The confusion in language would have been funny at another time but nothing was funny right now. On 10 September news came in that the Italian, General Calvi, had signed the surrender of Rome to the German, Field Marshal Kesselring. All that had been achieved with the celebrated armistice, it seemed, was the loss of Italy to the Germans who were now shoring up their defences and turning Rome into a Nazi fortress.

A telegram came for Steffie from her father.

```
Fiancé told. Sure he will be with you
soon. Fret not.
```

'Fret not!' she scoffed to Leo. 'My fiancé is somewhere in that carnage and Daddy says to "fret not". The man's mad.'

'You said your fiancé is a clever man?'

'He is. And a cunning one too, with plenty of contacts. He nearly managed to escape Allied capture last year.'

'What went wrong?'

Steffie hung her head.

'I told on him.'

'For all the right reasons, I guess?'

'So I told myself and it felt like I was right when he came over to our side, but now he's in Rome, not as an Italian soldier but as a British double agent. If they find out, they'll, they'll...'

'He'll get away,' Leo promised. 'Hug?'

'Please,' Steffie agreed gratefully, taking comfort from his brotherly arms.

Leo had become a good friend over the last week and she was grateful for his support, but the bad news kept on coming in and still there was no news of Matteo. On 12 September, German paratroopers busted Mussolini out of prison and spirited him away to Salo in the north to set up the Repubblica Sociale Italiana – a puppet government if ever there'd been one. With 'Italy' established in the north, there was nothing to stop the Germans turning the south into a killing zone and horrible tales came flooding into Messina.

One village was destroyed and the mayor and parish priest burned alive. In another, fifty Jews were massacred and in Rome the Jewish population were ordered to pay fifty kilograms of gold to save their souls – though for how long was anyone's guess. Over on Cephalonia, an island held for the Axis by Italian troops, soldiers were summarily executed in groups of ten for days and days, until some five thousand bodies littered the island and a pall of meat-scented pyre-smoke shrouded it from view. And amidst all this horror, still nothing of Matteo.

In a frenzy of worry, Steffie sent a telegram to Fran.

Any sign of my fiancé in the lists of the dead?

It could have been a request for information from the

British papers, but Steffie was pretty sure Fran had access to more direct intel and was briefly comforted when the answer came back.

No sign. Stay strong.

She was trying to hold onto the hope that Matteo would make it out, but with the death toll rising across Italy it was hard. Badoglio and the king escaped to Brindisi, taken by the Allies, and Steffie prayed Matteo had managed to inveigle himself into their entourage but, if so, she got no word. Each day of silence was agony.

Then, late one afternoon as she was battling to process messages, someone came running.

'Do we have a Stefania in camp? Stefania Carmichael?' He stopped and looked around. 'This is a joke, right? That's a woman's name.'

'And we have a woman. Haven't you noticed? You'd have to be blind not to; she's a looker.'

Steffie didn't even register the compliment, she was so busy scrambling out of the tent to find the man before he moved away.

'Me,' she cried stupidly. 'That is, I'm Stefania Carmichael. Who's asking?'

The soldier looked her up and down.

'There's a man on the docks shouting your name – and I can see why now. He doesn't look in a great way, love. If he doesn't make it, you know where I am.'

Steffie pushed furiously past him and ran. She could hear Leo calling her but there was no way she was stopping. She burst out of the camp and onto the docks, looking wildly around. It was far quieter now, with the bulk of the invasion force in Italy, and it didn't take her long to spot a commotion on one of the pontoons.

'Matteo?'

She ran again, shoving past the guard at the barrier with a gasp of 'That's my fiancé.' But was it?

'Matteo!'

There were two medics standing over someone lying on the pontoon. Oh God, was it him? Was he alive?

'Steffie?' The voice was faint, but unmistakable.

The doctors stood aside and there he was, her dear fiancé, prostrate and wrapped in a blanket, shaking visibly, although the sun was beating down. She fell onto her knees at his side.

'You made it.'

'I made it. I had a message. Your father.' His words were coming out on rough breaths and Steffie glanced fearfully to the doctors, who looked away. She forced herself to turn back. 'Knew you were here. Had to get to you.'

'And you have. Hush, my darling. I'll keep you safe now, I'll make you better.' His hand clawed out of the blanket and she clutched at it. 'We'll get you to a hospital, get you sewn up or, or whatever you need.'

The blanket was hiding his wounds and she reached for the edge to take a look, but his hand convulsed in hers.

'I had to get to you, Steffie. I had to kiss you. One. Last. Time.'

'No!' She was aware that a small crowd had gathered at the end of the pontoon, that the doctors had retreated into it and that Leo was there, talking intently to them. None of it mattered. Matteo had made it to her and she had to save him. 'Listen to me, Matteo. You're not to die, you hear me? We're going to be together forever, remember? We're going to get married and have mini Steffies and Matteos, and a lovely house and lots of friends and, and...'

'And an influential job for you?'

The attempt at a joke gave her hope.

'That's not important. Really, it's not. I'd like it but *you* are what matters, Matteo. *You* are the key to my future, whatever else it holds.'

'I don't think I can be, *tresoro*. I think your key is rusting away.'

His breath caught on a paroxysm of coughing and she drew him into her arms.

'Please, Matteo. I love you.'

'I love you too, *tresoro*. So, so much. You are my heart, my life, my wife.' He coughed again and Steffie saw a horrible hazel light wash across his chocolate-brown eyes. 'Kiss me, Stefania Mancini.'

She bent, pressing her lips to his, willing her warmth across his cold skin and her breath into his battling lungs. She felt him smile against the kiss and held him close but he was limp in her arms. *No!* her body screamed and she kissed him harder but the response was gone and finally she pulled herself away and looked down at him. His eyes were the colour of amber now and stared into the blue skies of Sicily, vacant of life.

'No!' Steffie shouted to the cruel heavens. 'Not him. You can't have him!'

But it was too late. He was gone and she could only hold his empty form and weep tears onto his dear face as the world as she knew it collapsed into dust around her.

SEVENTEEN
OCTOBER 1943

Fran

'I don't know what I can do to make it better.'

Fran cuddled into Valérie's arms on the bench seat. Autumn had come raging into Bletchley and it was cold in the caravan, though not half as cold as it was when Fran thought of her poor, bereaved friend.

'There's nothing you can do, *chérie*,' Valérie said, 'save be there for Steffie.'

'But that's it, Valérie. I'm *not* there for Steffie.'

'Because she's in London with her family, which is as it should be.'

Fran sighed.

'You're right of course, except that I don't think Steffie feels that way. I spoke to her on the telephone last night and she was miserable.'

'Of course she was miserable. Her fiancé died in her arms; it's enough to make anyone miserable.'

Fran rolled her eyes.

'I know that. I mean she sounded miserable at home. She

says her mother's driving her mad. Would you believe, she's been inviting single men to the house! It's been three weeks since Matteo died, Valérie, *three* weeks, and already the woman is trying to replace him.'

'That sort do,' Valérie said dismissively. 'Marriage is a transaction to them, a way of keeping the circle of acceptable acquaintances tight.'

Fran looked askance at her girlfriend, reminded of Travis's comments about her family in Bayeux. It had made her realise how little she knew about the woman she loved.

'Are your family rich, Valérie?'

Valérie shifted against her.

'Not rich. Not, you know, aristocracy.'

'I thought you didn't have aristocracy in La République any more?'

Valérie waved her hand in a deeply familiar gesture of dismissal.

'Of course we do, we just call them *bourgeoisie* nowadays.'

Despite her concern for Steffie, Fran smiled. The French were ever practical with their ways around rules, even their own. But did that mean...?

'Are your family *bourgeoisie* then?'

'My family are *résistants*.'

'Now,' Fran agreed, refusing to give up, 'but what about before the war? Do they all run bicycle shops?'

Valérie shifted.

'Maman runs the bicycle shops with Grand-mère Elodie and a handful of cousins. Our immediate family have not done much in the bicycle line – well, not until recently.' She gave a cheeky shrug, then hurried on. 'My father is a lawyer, my brother a civil servant – we have many of them in France – and my sister is at university in Paris studying to be an architect.'

'Quite *bourgeoisie* then?'

'*Un peu*. Does it matter? Your parents are doctors.'

Fran shook her head.

'It doesn't matter, Valérie, but I like to know things about you.'

'Because you love me?'

'Because I love you, yes.'

Fran still wasn't really used to saying those words, though every time she did so it felt more natural. It wasn't because they weren't true but because it still felt a little risqué – and a lot scary. Loving someone exposed you, put you at risk of hurt, like poor Steffie.

'I'd hate it if you died,' Valérie said suddenly, as if she'd read her mind. 'You won't, will you, Frances? You won't die?'

'One day I will.'

'But not for a long, long, long time. Not in this war. It has taken too much already; it cannot take you.'

She looked panicked and Fran stroked her face.

'It won't take me, Valérie. How could it? I'm nowhere dangerous, not like Ailsa.'

She glanced up to where a postcard from their friend was stuck proudly to the wall. It had arrived last week, covered in stamps and with several words crossed out, but it had been enough to drink in the picture of a palm-lined beach and, more than that, to see Ailsa's signature and know that she was well. Fran missed her, all the more so now, with her heart aching for Steffie.

'There were bombs here,' Valérie reminded her.

'A one-off. Bletchley is the epitome of safety, especially for me. All I do is sit around with maps and plans of the fighting that other poor souls will do.'

For a moment Fran regretted mentioning Room 149. She had been sent a young WREN to sort the postcards, much to Valérie's chagrin, but thankfully today she was too distracted by thoughts of Fran's impending death to pick up on it.

'It is best that way. You are safe here.'

'As are you.'

'Hmmm.' Valérie got up, taking Fran's teacup and bustling to the sink with it. Given the French girl was all but allergic to washing up, Fran was instantly suspicious.

'Valérie? You are staying here.'

'I am. At the moment.'

'What does that mean?'

'Well obviously Bletchley Park won't always be here, will it? When the war ends, there will be no need for it any more.'

'That's true, but you sound like you—'

'How about we go to see Steffie?'

Fran was stunned into silence.

'When?'

'No time like the present, is that not what you English say?'

'Well, yes, but...'

'We know where she lives and we are not on shift until this evening.'

'That's true.'

'So, if we hurry, we can catch the nine thirty train up and the four thirty back. Plenty of time for you to see poor Steffie.'

'And you?'

'Oh, Steffie won't want me. I can go and see Uncle Claude. Perhaps he will have something for me.'

'What sort of something?' Valérie waved her hand but this time it did not make Fran smile. 'What sort of something, Valérie?'

'Cheese? Wine? Chocolate? Would you not like some chocolate, Frances?'

Fran wasn't convinced chocolate was Valérie's main aim, but the thought of being able to actually see Steffie was far too appealing to worry what her girlfriend was up to right now.

'Let's go,' she agreed, and ran to dress.

.   .   .

'Hello?' Steffie's sister peered curiously at Fran, but then something must have clicked. 'You're Steffie's friend! Francesca, was it?'

'Plain old Frances, I'm afraid, but I'm Steffie's friend yes. Is she in?'

Roseanna scoffed.

'Of course she's in. She's always in. I've tried tempting her out but it's hopeless. She even turned down cocktails at the Ritz the other day.'

'She's lost her fiancé, Roseanna.'

'I know. It's tragic, really it is, but it doesn't stop you having a margarita or two, does it?'

'It would stop me,' Fran said sternly. 'Can I see her?'

'God yes, please do. Come in, come in.' Roseanna waved Fran inside and turned to yell up the stairs in what was surely a most unladylike manner, 'Stefania – someone for you.' No reply. Roseanna ushered Fran into the duck-egg blue drawing room and grimaced. 'She'll be holed up in her room as usual. One moment.' She went back into the hall, climbed three of the stairs and yelled again, 'Steffie! It's a friend of yours.' Something muffled came back, then, 'No, none of them. Someone from that funny place you work in. Says her name's Frances.'

There was a pause, then the sound of a door flying open and footsteps pounding down the stairs. Steffie skidded into the drawing room and flung herself at Fran.

'Fran! Oh Fran, it's so good to see you. How did you get here? Why are you in London?'

'To see you, of course.'

'That's so kind. Thank you. Thank you so much.'

Fran hugged Steffie, worried by how thin she felt. None of them had much flesh on them with wartime rations but Steffie had always clung on to her luscious curves – until now. Fran could feel her ribs through the thin fabric of her crumpled dressing gown and her pretty face, when she finally pulled back to look at her, was lean and sharp-lined.

'I'm so, so sorry about Matteo, Steffie.'

Steffie nodded, tears welling up in her blue eyes.

'It was awful, Fran, so awful. He made it all the way to Messina on a fishing boat to try and get to me. He knew he was dying. He was shot in the back fleeing Rome and had a punctured lung, or so the doctor said. They think he'd have been bleeding internally too, said it was a miracle he lasted as long as he did.'

'He loved you.'

'He did. He smiled, Fran, before he died. I kissed him and he smiled. I felt his lips curving up against mine and then, just like that, he was gone.'

'He's at rest now.'

Steffie sighed.

'People keep telling me that, but it's not much use. I mean, I'm glad he's not in pain, obviously, but Matteo was never one for resting. He had so much energy, so much spirit.' She was crying again now and Fran held her helplessly. 'It's such a waste, Fran, such a terrible, horrible waste.'

'It sounded hellish over there.'

'It was a cock-up from start to finish. The Italian leaders were too timid and the Allied ones too bullish and the normal soldiers and civilians were caught in the killing. It's all very well for the top lot, isn't it? It's all easy for Badoglio and Castellano and Bedell Smith. They swoop in in their smart planes and cars, posture around "negotiating" and then stay safe in their bases while everyone else takes the flak – literally. I hate them, all of them.'

Fran bit her lip.

'That's not like you, Steffie. You don't hate them really.'

'I *do*. They didn't think things through carefully enough

and Matteo was killed as a result – and thousands of others besides. It's cruel.'

'It's war, Stef.'

'Not out there it wasn't. Out there it was a massacre, and it's still going on. I heard Montgomery tell the troops they'd be in Rome in a couple of weeks but that was a month ago and now the Germans have shored up their defences and the poor lads are dug in with winter coming. It was terribly slapdash. When I think about the time and care we put into Operation Mincemeat—'

'Operation what?'

Steffie slapped a hand over her mouth.

'Nothing. Sorry.' They exchanged a rueful look and for the first time Fran saw a spark of the old Steffie. She was still in there, somewhere beneath the inevitable grief, and Fran ached to help her back out again.

'Is there anything I can do?'

'Yes!' Steffie sat up, straightening her dressing gown and smoothing back her wild hair. 'Yes, there is.'

'Wonderful. What is it?'

Steffie looked at her solemnly.

'Get me back to BP.'

'What? But—'

'Please, Fran. I know I'm meant to be on compassionate leave, but I'm going mad here. I've got nothing to do but go over and over it in my head, and all Mummy and Roseanna can suggest is parties, as if I can slip off my grief with my dressing gown and start again. I don't want parties, Fran, I want to work. I want to help the men who are still alive.'

Fran nodded.

'I can understand that. So, you want me to bust you out?'

Steffie gave the glimmer of a smile.

'If you possibly can. Talk to Denys Page for me, will you?

Tell him I'm ready. I'll do whatever I have to, see a head-doctor, take a test, anything. I want to be back at BP.'

'I'll see what I can do,' Fran promised, and then Steffie was in her arms, crying again.

She had no idea if this was wise, but it was what Steffie wanted and that was good enough for her.

Two hours later, she left her friend calmer, with her hair washed, a day dress on and some soup inside her.

'You're a miracle worker!' Julianna told her. 'You've been so good for my poor girl. You will come again, won't you?'

'If it will help,' Fran said evasively, avoiding the wink Steffie sent her way.

She wasn't sure she'd be welcome in the Carmichael household if she succeeded with Steffie's request but so what?

As soon as she was back at Bletchley, she reported for her shift and slid away to 'take some things to Room 149,' doing so via ISOS in Block G. Denys Page came out to see her and asked very kindly about Steffie.

'It was so terrible what happened,' he said, wringing his hands. 'I never would have let her go if I'd known it would lead to so much pain.'

'And then her fiancé wouldn't have had the comfort of her arms for his last breaths. I don't think she regrets that, sir, and she was glad to do her job. She'd, er, still be glad to be doing her job.'

'Sorry?'

There was only one way to say it.

'She wants to come back to work, sir. Compassionate leave is driving her mad and she says she'll feel far better if she can be at BP.'

'It's only been three weeks, Miss Morgan.'

'Yes, but she says it feels like forever. She hates that the

Nazis have taken Matteo from her and she wants to come and do something about it. She has more reason than most, sir, to want the invasion to succeed and she'd love it if you'd give her a chance to prove that.'

Denys looked her up and down and nodded slowly.

'I'll see what I can do.'

Four days later, as Fran was pottering around the caravan, dishing up a dubious-looking corned beef hash for Valérie, there was a knock at the door and Steffie came tumbling through.

'Steffie! You're back.'

'I am. Thank God. I got a summons to Harley Street yesterday and hot-footed it along straight away. Some idiot doc poked and prodded me and asked me a load of stupid questions, but I must have answered them right because he pronounced me "fit to fight". Then he got all in a fluster about his choice of words and babbled away about how I wasn't to fight, "obviously" and I said, "Why obviously?" and he said because I was a woman, and I said, "Believe you me, sir, right now I could shoot down fifty bloody Nazis." He nearly changed his mind then, so I had to turn on the charm and it must have worked because here I am.'

She spread her hands wide.

'Here you are,' Fran agreed, squeezing her tight.

'Welcome back,' Valérie said.

'Valérie! Good to see you.'

'And you, Stefania. We have all been very worried about you.'

Steffie wrinkled up her nose.

'It's not been good, I can tell you, and I'm still not, you know, dancing the full waltz. I can't promise I won't cry a bit sometimes, but I'll do my best.'

'Ah, Stefania – cry all you want to. We will cry with you, that's what friends are for.'

Fran gave Valérie's hand a squeeze, loving her even more for the simple sentiment, and Steffie gave a teary laugh.

'Oh, I've missed you lot.'

There was another knock at the door and they all looked over as Gloria burst in.

'Is that Steffie? Oh, Steffie, my poor, poor dear girl. How I have ached for you.' Their kindly landlady crushed Steffie to her ample bosom and Steffie gave in gladly to the embrace. 'You're so thin, girl! Goodness, we can't have this. Alfie,' she said, turning to her husband, who'd followed her into the van, 'the girl's wasting away. Fetch the rest of that rabbit pie.'

Valérie's eyes lit up.

'It's not for you,' Fran whispered.

But, in the end, there was more than enough for everyone, plus some very strong apple wine that got even Valérie's approval, especially towards the bottom of the bottle.

'You are not so bad, you English,' she muttered, praise indeed.

'All we need now is Ailsa,' Steffie said, tearful again.

'She's made it to Ceylon,' Fran said, pointing to the postcard.

Steffie rose too and peered at it for a long time, before lifting it and twisting herself around to read the few words left untouched by the censor's blasted pen.

'She says she's well. Do you think she is? I hope she is. I know people have babies all the time but not our people. I worry about her. I can't cope if she dies too.'

Gloria threw an arm around her.

'She'll be fine. She's tough, that lassie, and she's got her head screwed on. She'll have found a good midwife, you mark my words.'

'She might even have had the baby by now,' Fran said.

'No!' Steffie looked shocked. 'She'd send us a telegram, surely?'

'Of course. Yes, of course she would. She *will*.'

'Alfie,' Gloria said. 'Best get onto a new batch of elderflower champagne. I'll warrant we're going to need it.'

'Will do,' Alfie agreed gruffly. 'And on that note, I think it might be time for us to retire and leave these girls to get some rest. They have work to do, you know.'

'We have work to do,' Steffie echoed joyously, 'thank the Lord.'

Later, however, as they lay in bunks, Fran and Steffie opposite each other on the bottom and Valérie tucked into the top, it being far too late for her to go back to her own digs, Steffie sighed into the night.

'Thank you, Fran. I kept telling them I was ready to go back but no one believed me.'

'Thank Denys,' Fran mumbled sleepily.

'Oh, I will. We cannot make the same mistakes in France that we made in Italy. Everything has to be perfect to give our troops the best possible chance. The fewer women who have to suffer as I've suffered, the better. The work we're doing at BP is vital, girls – vital.'

'It is,' Fran agreed.

There was a pause.

'There's certainly vital work to be done,' Valérie said.

The words were vehement but the tone peculiar. Fran fought to work out why but the apple wine and the late hour and the sheer relief of having Steffie back in one piece claimed her and she fell fast asleep before she could do so.

EIGHTEEN

OCTOBER 1943

Ailsa

'Twister's a-coming.'

Ailsa looked over to her colleague, wondering what on earth he was talking about. Hank was an American, whose words seemed to take forever coming out of his mouth, and he was standing at the window opening of the big wooden hut that served as their wireless room, peering at the sky.

'Twister?' she asked.

'Yeah, you know – cyclone.' She shook her head and he looked at her in astonishment. 'Great spiral of wind, tiny at the bottom, gigantic at the top, travels across the earth faster than any man can run, or any animal either. I've seen horses swept up in a twister in moments.'

'Horses?' Ailsa stared at him, horrified. 'And there's one coming here?'

She felt very naive. She'd thought about the dangers of war before demanding to come to Colombo and she'd had an inkling about the power of the sun, but the number of poisonous bugs and reptiles had astonished her and now, it seemed, the weather was dangerous too. She looked to Ned, but he was deep in a message, headset firmly on, and she didn't want to disturb him. Not yet anyway. She rubbed nervously at her belly. There was no way she was outrunning anything; she could barely even waddle to the primitive lavatory.

'It won't hit us,' Hank said, smiling at her. 'It'll be out at sea. They usually are.'

Ailsa felt relief wash over her.

'Thank goodness for that.'

'But it'll send chaos our way for sure. The wind's getting up already. We should batten down the hatches.'

He ambled off to find Keith and the next thing Ailsa knew, the window shutters were being closed and there was a sound of rapid banging as the local housekeeping staff ran around hammering nails into the wood. Ned's message was finished and he yanked off his headset and looked around at the frantic activity.

'What's going on?'

'Something called a twister – a big wind, basically.'

'A storm?' Ned said. 'Are we evacuating?'

'No idea.'

Ailsa shifted on her hard seat and wondered if she had the energy to go to the loo. She could hear the wind starting to howl across the straw roof and when she looked out of the side window before it was secured shut, she saw the palm trees across the one-time golf course bending and whipping their leaves around. She swallowed. She'd been used to winds on North Uist, but nothing like this. The air felt wild, raw.

'I think we should go home,' Ned said.

Ailsa took a last look at the palms as a big leaf was ripped off the nearest one and whisked away, twirling madly in the darkening air.

'I'm not so sure,' she said. 'Our banda is nowhere near as solid as this place.'

'True.'

Ned looked around the big hut. It was made of wood but the walls were thick and strong. Ailsa thought of how nice she'd made their first marital home, with bright local textiles on the bed and bonnie bamboo plates and bowls from the market. She thought of the photos on the wall, one of her parents looking cutely sheepish before the photographer, one of her, Fran and Steffie, caught laughing in the Drunken Arms by an aspiring journalist with his own camera. She couldn't bear the thought of her treasures being whipped into the tropical air by this crazy wind and suddenly felt very, very far away from her actual home.

Fran had sent her a telegram with the terrible news of Matteo's death and she had longed to be able to comfort poor Steffie. She'd sent a long letter, but it hadn't been the same as being with her friends and, right now, with the wind shaking the walls of her primitive listening station halfway round the world, she desperately wished she could be in the caravan drinking tea with them.

'Come on, Ailsa,' she muttered to herself. 'You made this bed, now lie in it.'

She spotted her wireless set.

'Might as well get some work done,' she said to Ned.

He was looking closely at her, concern in his kind eyes.

'Are you sure you're happy here?'

'As happy as a sandboy. I'm with you.'

Ailsa had no idea what a sandboy was or why he should be happy and, even if she did, it probably wouldn't be true. Her belly was aching, low down, and a ripple of pain shot across it. She clenched her teeth, smiling at Ned and burying herself in her headset. She'd been having these cramps on and off for a week now. Suri said it was the body practising for when it was time to go for it and a good sign of a healthy and speedy birth ahead.

'As long as it's not too speedy,' Ailsa had laughed.

Suri had promised Ailsa that if she telephoned the Colombo post office her cousin, who worked there, would get a message to her immediately and her brother, who had a motorbike, would bring her out to HMS Anderson.

'What if it's at night?'

'Call the nightwatchman. He knows who I am.'

She'd written both numbers down for Ailsa and she had one copy taped to the wall of the banda and the other to the side of her wireless set. She touched her fingers to it, then reached for the dial. The airwaves were badly stirred up, but it was still possible, with fine-tuning, to find the frequency between Berlin and Tokyo. Her ears pricked up and she leaned instinctively into her set, reaching for her message pad as a transmission started to come in. The preambles she recognised as being from the ambassador's office. General Oshima sent regular reports to his masters in Tokyo, often quite long and usually – so they'd been told – very valuable. She had to concentrate.

Lifting up her pencil, she tuned out the howl of the wind and the shaking of the walls and tuned in the dots and dashes of Japanese Morse, turning them into 'kana' letters that the decoders back in BP would turn into English. It was a long, laborious system, far slower than the shooting of a gun or throwing of a grenade, but it could blow the enemy apart just as effectively and Ailsa was proud to be playing her part, even if her belly was horribly sore now.

'Settle down,' she murmured to the baby, her pencil whipping across the message pad.

The baby wasn't listening. In fact, the baby was pressing against her lower back with the strength of a creature four times its size. She tried to stretch out without taking one hand off the dial or the other off her pencil, but nothing helped. Another pain shot across her belly and with it a ripple of unease.

'Not now,' she said, through gritted teeth.

The message was long, even longer than usual, and must surely be important. She knew the ambassador was an intimate of Hitler's and whatever was being said here could make a huge difference to the war. She had to concentrate. Outside, the winds were, if possible, getting even stronger and a bit of straw dislodged from the roof and landed on her message. The signal faltered but as long as Ailsa kept the dial steady, it held. This was no time to be having a baby.

The rising storm had, at least, brought some coolness to the air and, for the first time since she'd arrived on Ceylon, Ailsa felt a shiver run down her spine. She welcomed it. The message ground on and she battled to concentrate. It was all too easy to mix up dots and dashes and there would be no point in taking down the message if it made no sense – that would waste everyone's precious time.

Another pain. Ailsa had a strong suspicion that this was more than a practice for the birth but Suri had said that even a speedy first-time delivery would take hours and there was no point sacrificing the last of the message to pace around being uncomfortable. She dug her feet into the sandy floor of the hut and wrote on but was very relieved when the operator at the other end started the elaborate sign-off procedures that always concluded Japanese communications.

A pain, sharper than any yet, ripped through her and she cried out and lost her thread. It wouldn't matter now. The core of the message was done and she was glad to let go of the dial and tear off her headphones. She stood up, desperate to stretch the ache out of her poor back and, to her astonishment, water gushed from between her legs. She stood there, staring at the puddle on the floor and shaking with the rattle of the winds, not knowing what to do. It was Ned who reacted first.

'Oh, my goodness. You're in labour. She's in labour!'

He looked frantically around as others leaped up and came over.

'Thank you, Ned,' she muttered. She wasn't keen on giving birth with the entire listening station watching on.

'We need help,' Ned babbled. 'We need…'

'We need Suri,' Ailsa said. She felt calm now, glad that the moment was finally upon her. Of course, with the storm it wasn't ideal, but it was happening anyway and all they could do was to get on with it. 'Phone the post office, Ned, like we agreed.'

She pointed to the paper taped to the side of her wireless and he nodded and snatched it up, dashing for the telephone at the far end of the big room. Personal calls weren't usually allowed but this was an emergency and the duty officer nodded him on. Commander Keith, at least, was away meeting the governor, so they didn't have his disapproval to contend with.

The other two female radio operators were clucking around, ordering a bamboo screen brought over and setting it up in a corner. Someone ran for bedding and was blown back in with such a pile of blankets that Ailsa felt like the princess and the pea when she was helped on top. They were damp from the rain that had chased in on the wind, but at least that kept her cool.

Ned came back, standing awkwardly at the edge of the 'birthing room'.

'Did you get through?' Ailsa asked from her nest.

He shook his head.

'Telephone line is down. Could we reach them by wireless?'

'They won't have a receiver,' someone said.

Ailsa heard herself give a whimper. Finding Suri had been the miracle of the last few weeks and now, at the critical moment, there was no way of fetching her.

'I could go to Colombo?' she suggested.

'No way,' Ned said instantly. 'It's far too dangerous. I'll go. I'll bring her back.'

'Don't leave me, Ned.'

Panic flared in Ailsa and she reached out a hand. He hesitated at the screen.

'Can I come in there?'

The panic was replaced with annoyance.

'Of course you bloody well can,' she snapped. 'You were with me when baby got in, weren't you, so you can damn well be here when he or she comes out. I'm not doing this without you, Ned.'

'Right. Fair point.' He looked self-consciously back at the other operators, then stepped in at her side. 'I'm sorry. English reticence. Foolish.'

She pushed herself up on the blankets and smiled.

'I think we kissed goodbye to conventional proprieties when we decided to have a baby in the middle of a golf course in Ceylon.'

'*You* decided,' he said grimly.

Ailsa flushed.

'I'm sorry.'

Ned shook his head and bent down and kissed her.

'Don't be. I'm glad you're here. I just wish the damned storm wasn't. How the hell are we going to get this midwife?'

'I'll go,' someone called over the screen in an unmistakable American drawl. 'It's time we put the jeep through its paces, right?'

'Really?' Ned leaped up again and went to the 'door'. 'You'd do that, Hank?'

'Can't have the little lady stuck here without her nurse, can we now. Tell her to hang on in there and I'll be back with the cavalry before she knows it.'

'Thank you,' Ned told him. 'You're very kind. We appreciate—'

'Ned!' Ailsa shouted. 'We're done with the proprieties, remember? Now, get in here.'

. . .

Within the hour, Ailsa could see why they called it labour. She'd stripped down to just her oversized blouse but, despite the cool winds, she was still sweating like a navvy. Her body was as sore as if she'd been digging trenches for the entire day and the contractions were coming barely two minutes apart. She had no idea how she was going to endure this for hours more. She swiftly abandoned her nest of blankets, pushing herself up to pace, the movement the only way to counteract the needles sticking into the entire centre of her being.

The wind was shouting a protest outside the hut and, with the wirelesses out of action now the airwaves had been swirled into chaos by the twister, everyone else had retreated to the far side to boil coffee on the gas stove and wait to celebrate the new arrival at HMS Anderson. It was all right for them, Ailsa thought. She was being ripped apart, as if the twister was not out at sea but right inside her.

'Aaah!' she shouted, glad of the storm to cover her undignified yells.

She clutched at Ned's hand, trying to transfer some of the hideous pain to her husband and perhaps she succeeded as he was certainly grimacing.

'You've got a hard grip, Ails.'

'And you've got a bugger of a bairn. Where's Suri?'

'I don't know,' Ned said, his voice squeaking as she squeezed his hand once more. 'But if she doesn't get here soon, baby might beat her to it.'

'God, I hope so. I can't take much more of this.'

But it turned out, she could. Another hour ground by until, at last, the door burst open and the wind sent in sand, leaves and a soaking wet midwife.

'Where's the patient?' an authoritative voice demanded.

'Here!' Ailsa shouted and smiled for the first time since her waters had broken, as Suri's bright face poked around the screen.

'Excellent. And making good progress it would seem.'

She came closer and Ailsa saw that the poor woman's turban had been whipped off, presumably as Hank's jeep had bumped her out to HMS Anderson, and she pushed a cloud of dark hair impatiently away from her face.

'I'm sorry to bring you out in this,' Ailsa managed.

'Oh, don't be. It's only a storm. And it's an excellent omen. A baby born into this will be tough.'

'It will need to be,' Ailsa said, glancing around the unconventional birthing room and thinking that her mother would have a fit if she could see her now, but then another pain came and she could think of nothing at all bar trying to climb the walls to escape it.

When it receded, Suri tapped perkily at her watch.

'A nice big contraction. Shouldn't be long now. Shall we take a look at you?' She lifted the hem of Ailsa's blouse. 'Ah, yes! We're close.'

'You can tell?' Ailsa panted.

Suri laughed.

'I can see the top of baby's head and it doesn't take a pro to know what that means. Time to bear down.'

'Thank God!'

'I could, er, leave you to it?' Ned said hopefully, but there was no way Ailsa was letting go of his hand.

She bore down, Ned at her side, stroking her hair and Suri between her legs, shouting eager encouragement.

'One more, Ailsa. That's it. One more push and... Aah!' A lusty wail filled the hut. 'It's a girl. You have a daughter, Ailsa, Ned – you have a beautiful, perfect daughter.'

Suri cut the cord and placed the most unimaginably gorgeous bundle into Ailsa's arms. The girl was kicking out at the air, howling her indignation, but as Ailsa held her, gazing down with astonishment that this tiny human had come out of her, she stilled. Her eyes opened, palest aquamarine, and she looked straight up into Ailsa's.

'She looks like you,' Ned said in wonder. 'She's even got your hair.'

Ailsa stroked the damp auburn wisps on her daughter's head in awe.

'What will you call her? Suri asked.

'Rowan,' Ailsa said, thinking of the red-leaved trees of home. 'Rowan for her red hair.'

'And her red temper, no doubt,' Ned said teasingly, but he nodded. 'Rowan. I like it. It suits our beautiful child of the storm.'

Ailsa looked up at the ceiling, but it seemed that at some point in all the chaos of Rowan's birthing, the winds had dropped and shafts of weak sunlight were coming through several gaps torn out of the thatch. Suri fussed around, encouraging her to feed and checking on the afterbirth – a disgusting-looking lump that she suggested Ailsa ate.

'Goodness, no,' Ailsa said. 'There may be a war on, but things aren't that bad.'

Once she was all cleaned up, she nodded agreement to the screen being pulled back so that the others could see the new arrival. They crowded round, glasses full of some strange local spirit, toasting them raucously, and Ailsa looked to Ned and smiled.

'We did it, Ned.'

'We did,' he agreed. 'May I?'

He took Rowan tenderly into his arms and walked her into one of the shafts of sun, pointing the baby up to the light, which she gazed on in wonder.

'It's tough out there right now, little one,' he told her softly. 'But we'll sort it. I promise you, we'll sort it and make the world a safe place for you to grow up in.'

Ailsa watched him, happy tears welling in her eyes as she

sank back against the blankets. It had, perhaps, been madness to come to Colombo pregnant but, boy, she was glad she had. She snuggled up to Ned as he brought Rowan back, a family now, and they had a few brief moments of bliss before the door flew open and Commander Keith marched in.

'What on earth is going on in here?' he demanded, striding forward. Clocking Ailsa and Rowan in the improvised blanket nest, his jaw dropped. 'Who turned my listening station into a maternity ward?!'

'She did,' Suri told him, pointing to Rowan, who kicked out a tiny leg and gave a happy gurgle of agreement.

Keith looked down at her, his face softened, and he gave a chuckle.

'Fair enough. Welcome, baby. Good to have you here, healthy and well – but don't get too used to it. You and Mummy are going home as soon as it's safe.'

Ailsa looked nervously to Ned, who shrugged and gave her a soft kiss. They both knew it wasn't going to be safe for quite some time yet and, for once, Ailsa was guiltily glad of it.

NINETEEN

OCTOBER 1943

Steffie

'This is potential gold dust, Steffie. Actually, scrap that – who wants dust? This is potential gold.'

Denys Page waved a sheaf of papers at Steffie and she glanced across to Leo, seated in a chair opposite their boss. She'd been summoned into his office the moment she'd arrived on shift and had rarely seen phlegmatic Denys more animated.

'What is it, sir?'

'It, Steffie, is a detailed report from General Oshima on his recent visit to the Atlantic Wall.'

Steffie felt her eyes widen. The Atlantic Wall was Hitler's defence all along the coast of north and western France and knowing more about it could be of immeasurable benefit to the invasion planners.

'Came in from Colombo two days ago,' Denys said.

'Colombo?' Steffie squeaked. 'Do you know the operator, sir?'

'The operator?' Denys squinted at the top of the paper. 'Says here it's an AR. Does it matter? Whoever he is, he did a good job. There was a corker of a storm around Ceylon that night so it's a miracle he got any of it.'

'*She* did, sir.'

'Sorry?'

'I believe the operator is a she.'

'Is she indeed? Then she's a clever girl. It's very long and very complicated. The bods in the Japanese section have translated and emended it as best they can, but they don't know the situation on the ground in France so I've volunteered our services. I've asked Leonard to take it on but it's pretty tangled so he's going to need help.'

Steffie looked sideways at Leo. She'd found it hard to face him since Sicily, embarrassed that he'd seen her wailing like a banshee on the dockyard. He'd slid away through all the horrible fuss of getting Matteo to the field morgue and then burying him overlooking the sea, and Steffie wasn't surprised. She'd been a snotty wreck the entire time. Not that she blamed herself. Why shouldn't she shout her grief out to the world that had brought it upon her, especially in Sicily, land of hot emotions? Several local women – self-appointed mourners – had turned up at the funeral to wail with her and, although Leo had been there, he'd kept well back and she'd felt awkward in his presence ever since.

'Steffie?' he asked tentatively now. 'Are you up to it?'

She rounded on him.

'I was allowed to grieve, you know.'

He looked startled. 'Of course you were. I assume you still are.'

'Naturally.'

'I don't want to put you under pressure if you need to, you know, take your time.'

Steffie bristled. 'I chose to come back, Leonard. I asked to come back. I'm more than "up to it", thank you.'

'I know you are.' Leo put his hands up. 'Sorry. I didn't mean to offend.'

Steffie drew in a deep breath. 'And I didn't mean to overreact.'

Denys stepped hastily between them.

'Lovely. That's all settled then. Here you go. Start immediately. You won't be able to work on it full-time with all the usual Abwehr traffic still at full flow, but get it done as fast as you can. Thank you both.'

He waved them away and they retreated to their desks.

'Who's AR?' Leo asked.

Steffie smiled despite herself.

'Ailsa Robinson. She's a friend of mine. She used to live in the caravan with Fran and me, but she's gone out to Colombo to be with her husband.'

Leo stared at her.

'You live in a caravan?'

'Erm, yes. Not, like a gypsy one or anything, just in a farm-yard. It was better than any of our billets.'

'I bet,' Leo said with feeling. 'My landlady is a dragon. She won't let me have a bath without checking the water's below the line and she turns the lights off at 9 p.m. I've had to break a gas lamp out of stores to read in the evenings.'

Steffie laughed. The sound surprised her and she clapped her hand over her mouth, feeling instantly guilty. How could she laugh with Matteo gone?

'Shall we get on with this report then?' she demanded.

Leo jumped but nodded. 'Good plan, partner.'

She winced at the word. Stupid Americans.

'I'll take these first two sheets, and you the next two and so on?'

'It might be better to do it together.'

'Or it might not,' Steffie said shortly and, grabbing the first two sheets, retreated to her own desk and put her head down.

She was here to work not to chatter, and she wasn't having
Leonard D'Angelo trying to charm her or cheer her up. No, as
he would say, siree.

The report was, indeed, tangled, but she was glad to lose
herself in it and the detail was astonishing. The Japanese
general had seen fit to tell his masters in Tokyo every last
battery and troop station, despite the fact that they must surely
not give a fig what was going on in the English Channel. One
thing Steffie knew for sure – their own invasion planners would
give all the figs in the world for it. It was, as Denys had said,
pure gold and she was so glad she was back in Bletchley Park to
make it ready for their consumption. Her heart was no less
broken, and she still woke up with tears on her cheeks every
morning, but it was made that bit easier for having Fran's steady
breathing across the bedroom, and for having work to get up for.

She made it through her first two sheets and looked up to
ask Leonard for more. He was working away, chewing on his
pencil as he frowned in concentration. He wore his hair longer
than English men and it kept flopping over his eyes so that he
had to brush it constantly away. He looked deep in his work and
she hesitated to interrupt him. Besides, there were only ten
minutes of her shift left. Best if she left him to it and tidied her
desk instead.

'Steffie!' someone called from near the door. 'Someone for
you.'

Steffie went over.

'Where?'

'At the gates. Security says there's a madwoman jumping up
and down, asking to see you and a Miss Morgan. Says it's
urgent.'

Steffie frowned. A madwoman? Looking for her and Fran?
Who could it be?

'I'll go and see,' she said.

Leonard jumped up. 'I'll come with you.'

She frowned at him.

'Why?'

'Well, you know, a madwoman. She might be dangerous.'

'I doubt it's anything the guards on the gates can't handle,' she said, but he looked genuinely concerned so, with a sigh, she accepted the offer.

They set out across the park together. The cold weather had really come in now and with the wind up, brown and yellow leaves were blowing all across the park. Steffie tried to imagine Ailsa taking down the message she'd been working on in a tropical storm, but with such an English scene before her it was impossible. She hoped she was safe.

'Steffie!'

She caught her name called on an excited shriek and turned towards the gates – newly sturdy structures to replace the bomb-blasted ones – to see Gloria jumping up and down like the madwoman she'd been called. She broke into a run.

'It's fine,' she told the security guard. 'She's my landlady.'

'Lucky you,' he laughed.

Steffie ignored him and shot out the gate.

'Gloria? Is all well?'

'All's wonderful! She's had the baby, Steffie. Ailsa's had the baby. A telegram arrived this afternoon. My heart fair sank when the boy came into the yard but there was no black line around it and it wasn't death – it was birth! It's a girl and they've called her Rowan and mother and daughter are both doing well.'

Gloria finally stopped for breath and Steffie's brain caught up with her words. She threw her arms around her kindly landlady and Gloria jumped her up and down with the energy of her woman half her fifty years, suffusing Steffie in wonderful, heady joy. It had been far too long since she'd had any good news and this was the best.

'I have to get Fran,' she gasped.

Turning into the park she saw, with a start, that Leonard had followed her out of the gate.

'Who's this?' Gloria asked.

'Leonard D'Angelo, ma'am,' he introduced himself, giving a small bow.

'An American! Well, I never. Nice to meet you, Mr D'Angelo.'

'Leonard will do just fine, ma'am. And you are?'

'Ooh, where's me manners!' Gloria, Steffie noticed, had gone all coy and she looked to Leonard again. He was a good-looking man, she supposed, if you liked them clean-cut and well-turned-out. Which she did, of course. Not that she was looking, only trying to see him through Gloria's eyes. 'I'm Gloria Taylor, Leonard, but you can call me Gloria.'

He gave another bow.

'Congratulations on your good news, Gloria. Is, er, Ailsa your daughter?'

'No! Leastways, not biologically. I confess, I do think of all three of my caravanners as sort of my own girls, though.'

'Do you?' Steffie asked. 'Oh Gloria, that's lovely.' She hugged her again, revelling in her natural warmth. 'Goodness, look at me, all teary.'

She dabbed self-consciously at her eyes and Leonard offered her an immaculately laundered handkerchief. She took it reluctantly. What sort of a lily-liver must he think her? She was meant to be a strong career woman, equal to the men and all that; she couldn't go around weeping all the time.

'Ailsa is Steffie's friend from this funny place you all work,' Gloria told him.

'AR!' Leo said, looking to Steffie, who nodded.

'Oh, she's a sweetie that one,' Gloria was going on. 'But fiery too. Red-headed, you know.'

'Red-headed?'

'She means Ailsa has ginger hair,' Steffie told him. 'She's

Scottish, from up in the islands, and she can be pretty stubborn when she wants to.'

'But lovely too,' Gloria said, every inch the proud mother. 'And now she's got a daughter. Oh, I wish I could see her.'

'Perhaps she'll send a photograph, ma'am.'

'Perhaps,' Gloria agreed, 'but it'll take forever coming all the way round the world.'

'Half the way,' Steffie corrected but what difference did it make? It would still be ages before they knew more – which reminded her... 'Fran! I best go and find Fran.'

'Bring her back to the farm,' Gloria said. 'The elderberry champagne won't be ready yet, more's the pity, but Alfie's got a lovely cider coming right. That'll do, won't it? Will that do?'

'Of course it will do, Gloria,' Steffie said, kissing her and making her blush. 'You're a wonder.'

'Get away with you! A wonder, indeed. We know produce, is all. We're farmers,' she told Leonard.

'That must be rewarding.'

'It is! You must come and see the farm. Ooh, why don't you come now? Help us celebrate.'

'I wouldn't want to intrude.'

'It won't be intruding. You Yanks have come over here to help fight our war, so the least we can do is be hospitable, right, Steffie?'

What could she say?

'It's their war too, Gloria, thanks to Japan. But you're right, it would be lovely to have you, Leo.'

Her words sounded stiff to her but the others didn't seem to notice and they went off together, middle-aged Gloria hanging off Leo's arm like a giddy girl. Steffie had to smile but then she remembered Fran and, turning back into BP, ran for Block D, battering on the door until a startled WREN answered.

'Can you get Frances Morgan for me, please?' she asked. 'Tell her it's important. A matter of life and death.'

The WREN's eyes widened and she ran off at speed. Steffie felt a bit guilty and even more so when Fran came tumbling out, looking stricken.

'What is it? What's happened?'

'Something good, Fran. Something fantastic.'

'Really?' Fran sucked in air. 'That's a relief. What is it? Is it Ailsa? Has she had the baby?'

'You're good!' Steffie said admiringly. 'And she has. A girl. A niece for us.' That wasn't strictly true but if Gloria could look on them as her sort-of-daughters, they were most definitely sort-of-sisters. 'Alfie's breaking out the cider,' she told Fran. 'Can you get away?'

Fran wrinkled up her nose.

'I said I'd do a bit of overtime on Room 149 but, hell, that can wait. It's not every day a baby's born.'

Steffie looked at her.

'I think you'll find it is.'

'Yes, yes, but not *our* baby. Can I bring Valérie?'

'Of course. Leonard's coming.'

'Leonard?' Fran raised an eyebrow.

'Not like that,' Steffie snapped. 'Gloria invited him. I think she's got a crush on his All-American charm.'

'Don't blame her,' Fran said mildly. 'He's not my type, clearly, but if he was, he would be – if you see what I mean.'

Steffie laughed and gave her a gentle shove.

'Go and get Valérie, idiot, and let's celebrate.'

They tumbled into the farmhouse to find Gloria and Alfie jabbering away to their American guest. Four different ciders were on the table and they were urging a bemused Leonard to choose his favourite.

'They're all delicious,' he said. 'D'you know, cider was one of the first products to take commercial hold in America back when you Europeans were colonising us.'

'No!' Gloria gasped.

Steffie smiled. Leonard always surprised her with his random bits of history but Gloria was looking at him as if he were an oracle. She winked at Fran, who giggled.

'It's true,' Leonard went on. 'The apple was one of the few seeds hardy enough to make the journey across the Atlantic and a Mr Johnny Appleseed planted trees all along the frontier. Everyone was drinking it before the German settlers came along with barley and converted us to beer.'

'Well, I never!'

'But then prohibition struck and all the poor cider farmers had to grow eating-apples instead. The industry's never quite recovered. What we call cider now is really just apple juice and not a patch on this, so they all taste wonderful to me, thank you.'

'Our pleasure,' Gloria said, almost tearful, but then she glanced up and saw Fran. 'Fran! Has Steffie told you the news? Is it not marvellous? A baby girl. Here's the telegram, see.'

She handed it over and Fran and Steffie crowded round, drinking in the brief words.

```
Baby  Rowan  born  safely  on  10.10.43.
Storm-blessed. Mother  and  daughter  well
but missing you. Ned.
```

'Storm-blessed?' Fran queried, handing it on to Valérie.

'Oh, my goodness!' Steffie gasped. 'We've been working on a long message that came in from Ailsa. Denys said it had been scrambled by a storm. She must have given birth not long after.'

She glanced to Leo, who smiled.

'Doubly important work, then.'

'I guess so.'

For a moment, Steffie felt blindsided by the enormity of what war had brought them all to, but then Gloria was up again.

'Look what Leonard has brought, girls. Alfie!'

Alfie leaped up obediently and grabbed a bottle from the pantry.

'Champagne,' he said. 'Actual, real champagne, from actual France.'

Valérie giggled, then turned to Leonard and said with something like awe, 'How did you get that?'

He put up his hands.

'Not me. I simply, erm, procured it from stores. I've been saving it for a special occasion and this seems pretty darned special to me.'

'Are you sure?' Steffie asked. 'I mean, you don't even know Ailsa.'

'I'm certain. Sitting here with you lovely folks talking about her, I feel I do know her. And besides, any birth is worth celebrating with far too much death around us.'

He seemed to be looking pointedly at her and Steffie flushed.

'You prefer me happy.'

He frowned. 'Sorry?'

She shook herself. The others had got up to mine the pantry for food, leaving only her and Leonard at the kitchen table.

'Nothing,' she said. 'I... I know you must think I'm a right moaning Minnie.'

'A what?'

'Crying all the time and that.'

'Hardly all the time, Steffie. And you've lost your fiancé. I'd think it stranger if you weren't.'

'You would? It doesn't stop me doing my job, you know.'

'I never thought it did. Truly. Grief is a terrible thing and you're doing amazingly.'

'But I was a wreck. On Sicily.'

'Oh, Steffie, of course you were a wreck. The man you loved died in your arms. I felt so desperately sorry for you.'

'You did?'

'Of course. What did you think I'd feel?'

'I don't know. You kept your distance.'

'You looked like that's what you wanted, and I understood. I'm sorry. I would have loved to comfort you, but we're told you British are more reserved than that.'

She gave a choking laugh. 'Your guidebook?'

He tapped his jacket pocket.

'Never go anywhere without it! But I think, seeing you lovely people together, that it might be wrong about the reserve thing.'

Steffie considered.

'It just takes time to give our trust. After that, there's no stopping us.'

'Good to know.'

She looked sideways at him. 'You didn't think I was pathetic then?'

'If you want to know, as I saw you weep, the one thing I was thinking was, *I hope, someday, someone loves me enough to mourn me that much.*' He bit his lip. 'I'm so sorry Matteo died, Steffie. I'm so sorry you had to suffer, and I hope that somehow time heals.'

Steffie smiled back.

'Thank you, Leo. I hope so too. And, you know what, the one thing that helps is friends like these.' She looked around the table as the others settled back into place with a spread of pies and pickles and felt her tears recede. Her grief was still raw but she knew Matteo would have marked this moment in style and wanted to do the same in his memory. 'Come on,' she said, 'let's open that champagne and celebrate!'

TWENTY
NOVEMBER 1943

Fran

Fran prised a pin marked *716th division* from her map of northern France and replaced it nearer to the coast. Direction finding from the rapidly expanding SIXTA unit had identified a number of new enemy locations as the Germans moved into winter positions and it was up to Fran to chart them all. The whole of Room 149 was now covered in maps, but this, the overall one of the planned invasion site, was the hub.

She stood back and surveyed it with a mixture of pride and unease. Unless the Germans were fooling them, they believed they had over 80 per cent of their units accurately pinpointed and their relative strengths known. Many of them were still down near Calais, which was encouraging, but they could move up into Normandy at any time. The map was never complete. Fran remembered her father telling her about the painters of the Forth road bridge on a trip to Scotland one summer.

'It's an endless task, Fran. They have to keep the paint fresh enough to stop rust penetrating the steels but it takes so long to paint it that the moment they get to the end, they have to circle round and start again.'

To twelve-year-old Fran that had seemed excruciating and now, at twenty-two, she knew exactly how it felt, and why you did it. You couldn't let your guard drop, because if you missed one bit you might bring the whole structure down.

She rubbed at her eyes and wondered if she could sort a few more postcards before she clocked off. Her WREN had proved herself to be far more efficient than her baby-blue eyes had promised and they'd made excellent headway into the first batch but they kept on coming. The other day, Boase had asked her if she'd mind transferring into Room 149 permanently. With the days growing cold and dark and Christmas on the horizon, everyone was suddenly very aware that the invasion was set for next spring. They had to be ready.

'If that's what's needed, sir,' Fran had said.

'I think so, Miss Morgan. We'll get you two more helpers to do the bulk of the sorting so that you can concentrate on the weekly reports. The higher-ups are delighted with them. Invaluable was the word I heard the other day. They're going to Churchill and Eisenhower, so the more accurate we can make them the better.'

Fran had nearly passed out at the thought of the PM reading her reports and scrambled to agree that time to focus on them would be helpful if that were the case.

'Eisenhower says that knowing this much about the lay of the land is of inestimable value. He's planning parachute drops behind enemy lines before we send the boats in and knowing the safest places to land them will really help. He's also pressing SOE to step up the influx of secret agents into the area. The Resistance groups are doing amazing work and some chap's pushing for us to arm them to be ready to rise up to help the troops when D-Day comes.'

'Pierre Brossolette?' Fran suggested, thinking of his glorious speech in the Albert Hall last June.

It had been widely published, especially after the terrible news had come in that Jean Moulin was dead at Nazi hands and Pierre had stepped higher up in the Resistance leadership. Fran had diligently written several of her own articles about it and given them to Gilberte to submit on her behalf. A magazine called *Home Chat* had apparently asked for her one about 'Resistance fashion', but she'd heard nothing since.

'Not him, no. Some chap called Yeo-Thomas.'

'Tommy!'

'You know him?' Boase had looked at her in astonishment.

'My, er, friend is French. She's introduced me to a few people around De Gaulle.'

'Has she indeed? You're full of surprises, Miss Morgan. Well, this Tommy has talked Churchill into an audience and demanded more arms for the Resistance. Convinced him they're a solid force we can use on D-Day.'

'Good for him.'

'If you say so. The point is that everything is coming together – reconnaissance, direction finding, Ultra, Resistance information – and it's coming together here, in Room 149. Keep up the good work.'

Well, she could hardly have refused after that, could she? So here she was, moving pins around the map and passing the information on to the PM himself; she could only pray it was correct.

A knock at the door jerked her out of her musings and she went over, hoping it wasn't Valérie again. She had not been happy at Fran being moved permanently away from Hut 3 and was becoming increasingly irascible. Fran understood, but it didn't make it any easier to deal with.

'Hello?' she said cautiously.

'Erm, hello. Is that...? Oh, never mind who you are, I've got a report for you.'

Fran squinted at the door.

'Steffie?'

'Fran! It *is* you. I thought it was. What on earth are you doing in there?'

'If you have a pass, I can tell you.'

'I do.'

Fran opened the door a crack and peered at the pass her friend pushed through the gap. It checked out and, with a huge smile, she ushered her inside.

'Welcome to Room 149.'

Steffie looked around her slowly, taking it all in.

'This is amazing, Fran. And you work here?'

'I run it,' Fran said, then, fearing she sounded boastful added, 'That's to say, I coordinate it. I'm just an indexer for all the information everyone brings me.'

'There's no "just" about it,' Steffie said firmly. 'I imagine the different bits of info are only any good when they're matched together. Talking of which, I've brought this for you – it's a report to Tokyo on their ambassador's tour of the Atlantic Wall.'

'Really?'

Fran reached eagerly for the sizeable buff folder, scanning the pages of detailed description. 'This is amazing.'

'Isn't it though. And even better, look who took it.'

'AR – Ailsa Robinson?'

'I reckon so. It's the message she was taking down the day she gave birth to Rowan.' Steffie perched on the nearest table, being sure not to dislodge a scale model of Arromanches-sur-Mer that one of the new WRENS was making. 'Look at us, Fran. This report was plucked out of the airwaves by Ailsa in Colombo, untangled by me in ISOS, and now slotted into place for the commanders by you here in Room 149. We're really doing something, Fran. We're really helping.'

Fran gave her hand a squeeze.

'I guess we are.' She looked more closely at her friend. 'Are you coping, Stef? It must be so hard after, you know...'

'Matteo dying? It still hurts, especially when I wake up in the morning and remember all over again that he's gone, and it still feels like the future is this horrible gaping hole, but that's for after the war. Right now, I have to put my head down and work.'

'Not all the time,' Fran said, stroking her hair. 'Shall we head home and see if we can find a new way to massacre a tin of corned beef?'

Steffie laughed.

'That sounds scrummy.'

She stood in the corridor while Fran stashed the precious report in the filing cabinet and locked the room, then, arm in arm, they headed home. The air was icy and a handful of stray snowflakes drifted across the night as they turned away from Bletchley Park. They both pulled on the gloves Ailsa had given them last year.

'Soon be Christmas again,' Steffie said.

'Then 1944.'

'And D-Day.'

They looked at each other, swallowed, and picked up their pace for the relative peace of the caravan. Fran let them in to the welcome sight of post on the table, delivered by Gloria along with a pot of jam.

'Blackberry,' Steffie said, unscrewing the lid and sneaking a fingerful. 'Delicious.'

Fran barely even noticed. Her eyes were fixed on a large envelope bearing her name and a stamp that read: *Home Chat*. With trembling hands, she prised the flap open and lifted out a pristine copy of next week's magazine. On the front was a simpering woman wearing a woolly hat and scarf in a peculiar shade of mauve and the caption promised the reader the pattern to knit themselves something similarly gross. Fran sniffed but opened it to the contents page and there, halfway down, readers were pointed to an article on page 23, entitled '*Pièce de la résistance* – Paris chic in wartime', by Frances Morgan.

'What's that?' Steffie peered over her shoulder. 'Oh my goodness, Fran, that's your name. That's... that's your article?'

Fran could only nod and thumb her way to page 23, where she found an article that, on a quick scan, held approximately half of the words she'd sent in. They were almost exclusively the ones about what the great and good of France had been wearing to hear Brossolette speak. The man himself featured only for his good looks and striking hairstyle. A few passing mentions to the bravery of the *résistants* had made the cut but otherwise this was little more than fluff. Fran sighed.

'It's sort of my article,' she said.

'How exciting.' Steffie took it, poring over the piece. 'I didn't know you knew about fashion, Fran.'

'I don't!'

'But, hey, you look gorgeous in your pic. I told you that frock would suit you.'

She pointed to the tiny picture of Fran at the bottom of the article and Fran blushed to see a full-length image of herself looking tall and, even she had to admit, rather elegant in Steffie's forest-green dress.

'Smoke and mirrors.' She read out a line at random. '"Gilberte Brossolette's eyes sparkled with tears to match the delicate diamonds in her ears as she watched her husband step onto the stage." It's hardly award-winning, Stef.'

'It's very vivid. And, more importantly, you idiot, it's published. That makes you a writer – an actual, published writer.'

Fran felt a warmth steal through her.

'It does, doesn't it!'

'And a paid one, too. Look!'

Steffie had delved into the envelope and produced a cheque for thirty shillings. Fran stared at it. It was hardly a fortune but it was money all the same and, more than that, proof that someone valued her writing. She hugged Steffie.

'Thanks so much, Stef. Do you mind massacring corned beef by yourself? I have to show this to Valérie.'

'Of course you do,' Steffie agreed easily. 'I'll be fine; I've got jam!' She lifted the jar and shooed Fran to the door. 'Go, go, go!'

Fran needed no further urging and, clutching the magazine to her chest, traced her way back past Bletchley Park and down the crumbling street to Valérie's dubious digs.

'It's late,' was the first thing Mrs Cousins, the stingy land-lady, said when she opened the door.

'Good evening to you too, Mrs Cousins. Is Valérie in?'

'Course she's in. I told you, it's late. If you were a gentleman caller, you'd be out on your ear, but as it's you, you can have half an hour. Quiet though. I've had a busy day serving in the station kiosk and I need my sleep. There's a war on, you know.'

'I know, Mrs Cousins, thank you, Mrs Cousins.'

Fran crept through to Valérie's room at the back, smiling to herself at the thought of how little Valérie's grumpy landlady knew. As soon as she got into the bedroom, she gave Valérie a long, searching kiss.

'Wow,' she said when Fran let her come up for air. 'What was that for?'

'Mrs C's glad you don't have "gentlemen callers".' They both giggled, then Fran added, 'And I have something to show you.' She felt suddenly uncertain. 'It's not anything fancy or clever or, or intellectual.'

Valérie put her hands on her hips.

'Let me see.'

'And it's not what I, you know, want to be known for. Not my style, as it were.'

'Frances Morgan – let me see, now!'

Fran drew in a deep breath and handed over the magazine, opening it to page 23. Valérie's eyes darted across it and fell on Fran's name and picture at the bottom.

'That's you! *Sacré bleu*, Frances, that's really you. You're an author!'

'Hardly an author,' Fran tried to protest, but Valérie was covering her in kisses and she couldn't get the words out. 'It's only a silly piece on dresses,' she said as soon as she could.

'It is a silly piece on *French* dresses,' Valérie corrected her, beaming. 'I am turning you into a Frenchwoman, Frances.'

'Is that what you'd like?' Fran asked nervously. 'I mean, do you want to live in France after the war?'

'I want to live in France now,' came the harsh reply.

Fran backtracked.

'I know that, Valérie. It's hard.'

'It's unbearable.' The vehemence took Fran by surprise and she drew Valérie down onto the bed. 'I'm sorry, my love.' Valérie looked at her, her dark eyes full of something horribly like guilt. 'What? What have you done?'

'I daren't tell you.'

'Why?'

'You will be cross. But you have to understand, Frances, you have to see how it feels to be me, an exile in your county while my own is trampled on by bloody jack boots.'

'I do understand. Or, at least, I try. I remember how awful it felt back in 1941 when we thought the Germans were going to invade England. I hated it and that was before they even came. It must be so much worse for you.'

'It is, Frances. It is so much worse. You are right. And that is why I have to do it.'

'Do what?'

It was all Fran could do to keep her temper. Valérie took a deep breath.

'Go to France.'

'What? When?'

'Soon. Maybe very soon. I, er, went to see Yeo-Thomas.'

'When?'

'When you were with Steffie, before she came back to BP.'

Fran stared at her.

'That's ages ago, Valérie.'

'I know! Nothing happened. I was going mad. I thought they didn't want me, but it turns out they were doing battle with Travis who didn't want me to leave BP.'

'I'm not surprised. You're a valuable worker, Miss Rousseau, as he told you himself.'

'Maybe, but I don't feel valuable. I have had messages from Grand-mère Elodie in Bayeux. My brothers have had to flee into the hills with all the other young men to avoid the Service Obligatoire. A lorry came, Frances, to take them away to dig German defences. Pah! As if they would do that! So they fled and now they live wild with the Maquis and prepare to fight. They do good work, but it leaves Grand-mère without help in the town. I can be that help, Valérie. I grew up there. I know the land, the people. I can be one of the secret army, ready to help Eisenhower when he lands his troops.'

Valérie was shining as Fran had not seen her do for far too long. That was incredible, but not at the expense of her life.

'It'll be dangerous, Valérie. You could be killed by Nazis.'

'Or killed by boredom here.'

'That's just vanity.'

'What?' Valérie yanked away. Fran swallowed but this was important.

'Our work at BP may feel boring at times...'

'Does!'

'Fine, does feel boring at times and it also feels anonymous. The secrecy that's crucial to keeping Ultra working for us means that we can't tell anyone what we do and that's not much fun. I'm sure it feels far... cooler – is that the word the Americans use? – to stomp about saying that you're a *résistante*, but it doesn't actually make you more effective to the war effort.'

Valérie scrambled off the bed, pushing Fran away.

'You think I do this to look good?'

'No, Valérie, but to be able to stand up and be counted, yes. And I understand.'

'You do not!' Valérie hissed. 'You do not understand at all. This is not about me, this is about La France. It is about standing shoulder to shoulder with my family and defending my country.'

'Which you are doing from here.'

'No.' Valérie's eyes blazed fury. 'Here I am hiding. Or I was. I heard the other day that BP have signed my release and I have been accepted into the SOE programme. I will soon get a call to report for training.'

Fran grabbed at Valérie's hands.

'Don't do it, Valérie. You don't need to do it. You don't need to ride your horse and cart onto the battlefield.'

Valérie frowned at her.

'What does that mean?'

'You know what it means. Your grand-mère was very brave doing what she did in the Great War but not all heroism comes with a gun. You are a brave, bold, intelligent woman, Valérie – you *are* Elodie. You don't need to go to France to prove it.'

Valérie stared at her, looking deep into her eyes as if searching for the truth of Fran's words, but then Mrs C rasped 'time's up' through the door and she yanked back.

'I do,' she said. 'My family need me.'

'*I* need you.'

'Not as much.'

Fran felt ice steal around her heart.

'Oh I do,' she said, 'but it seems you do not need me.' She picked up her magazine where it had fallen to the floor and looked sadly down at page 23. She'd brought it here, keen to share it with her girlfriend, but her girlfriend was not so keen on sharing in return. 'Good luck, Valérie. I hope La France appreciates you more than you think I do.'

'She will,' Valérie flared back and, stung, Fran fled the house.

She ducked past the curious Mrs C and made for the safety of the caravan and her own pillow to weep into. She'd thought she was a critical part of Valérie's life but it appeared that she, like Bletchley Park, was not enough for the fiery Frenchwoman.

'Fran?' Steffie whispered from the opposite bunk. 'Is something wrong?'

Fran sucked in a deep breath.

'Let's just say you're not the only one on your own now, Stef.'

A hand reached across the slim space between them and grasped hers, warm and sure.

'You're not on your own, Fran.'

Fran clutched at her friend's fingers gratefully. Grief, she'd learned, came in many shapes, especially in wartime, and she held on to Steffie and let the tears slide down her cheeks into the darkness.

TWENTY-ONE

DECEMBER 1943

Ailsa

Ailsa peered hopefully into the majestic baby carriage they had bought off a friend of Suri's for a song.

'She's asleep!' Baby Rowan opened her blue eyes and gave her a cheeky smile. Ailsa groaned. 'One more turn might do it.'

She glanced across the golf course to where the NAAFI hut of HMS Anderson was decked out in palm leaves and vines – the closest they could get to holly and ivy – and willed her daughter to drop off. Rowan, however, was determined to enjoy the party too and resisting all their efforts to lull her to sleep.

'She's as stubborn as her mother,' Ned said, leaning across the perambulator to drop a kiss on Ailsa's lips. 'And I love you both to bits. Can you believe that this time last year we weren't even married yet and now here we are, a family?'

Ailsa kissed him back.

'Rowan's the best Christmas present we could wish for.' He nodded fondly and Ailsa looked at him in the blazing sunshine of the strangest festive period she'd ever known. 'You're glad then, Ned, that I came out here?'

'Gladder than I can say. I still think it was stupid, mind, but good stupid.'

Ailsa laughed.

'I'll take that. Ooh, look – her eyes are closing. Don't stop!'

They circled past the NAAFI, glancing enviously in at their colleagues dancing to a lively local band and helping themselves from a feast of a buffet, and Ailsa thought back to last Christmas, spent with Fran and Steffie in the caravan. They'd drunk Alfie's fig wine, snuggled up together against the cold, and had a snowball fight with Gloria and Alfie's grandchildren. Ned had still been on his way back from Malta to marry her. It couldn't have been more different to now.

'I think we've done it,' Ned whispered. 'I think she's fast off.'

Ailsa blinked herself back into the present and looked down at her daughter, even more beautiful now she was asleep. Rowan had turned eight weeks old a few days ago and was a lovely baby. Not a good sleeper, that much was true, but contented when awake, and a ready feeder. Already she was taking some goat's milk, leaving Ailsa free to leave her for a few hours. Suri had assured her that she knew several excellent nurses and Ailsa was going to meet them in the new year with a view to going back to the wirelesses part-time – if Commander Keith let her.

For two weeks she'd been coming in for the odd hour with Rowan lying in her carriage. Keith fretted about having a child in the office, but they needed the sets fixing and no one else was as good at it as Ailsa. Besides, she'd caught her boss playing coochie-coo with Rowan and hoped that meant he'd softened to having them both around. She was hoping to broach the subject of returning to work while he was in a festive mood, so made keenly for the NAAFI, manoeuvring the perambulator through the doors and into a spot near the wall. The noise made them both wince but disturbed Rowan not one jot and Ned clicked the brake onto the big wheels and offered Ailsa his arm.

'Shall we, wife?'

Ailsa took it gladly and they headed into the crowd, saying 'Merry Christmas,' to everyone they met. The room felt giddy, happy. It was nearly the end of 1943 and all the indications were that 1944 would bring the end of the war. Besides, it was Christmas, a time of peace and joy and, giddy herself, Ailsa pulled Ned onto the dance floor for a jive.

They came off, hot but happy, and made for the buffet, where Ned fetched them two glasses of a vibrant punch. Ailsa smelled her favourite pineapple juice and took a big drink, then nearly choked it up down her best dress.

'It's got quite a lot of rum in,' Ned said, laughing at her.

Ailsa nodded, her eyes stinging.

'Smaller sips?' she gasped.

'Might be a good idea. Ah, Merry Christmas, sir.'

'Merry Christmas, Ned.' Commander Keith pumped his hand vigorously. 'And you too, Ailsa.' He leaned in to give her a quick kiss on her cheek and, with the rum still tickling her throat, she fought not to splutter all over him. 'Where's the little one?'

'Asleep in the corner,' Ned said, looking at Ailsa in amusement as she tried to decide if another sip of the punch would make things better or worse.

'She's a good baby. You've done well with her, both of you.'

'Thank you, sir.'

'Yes, thank you,' Ailsa agreed, recovering at last. 'I'm sorry she's been a bother for you but it won't last for long. I'm going to meet—'

'It won't,' he said, cutting her off. 'Because there's a boat setting out for Blighty on January fifteenth.'

'What?' Ailsa's head whirled with far more than rum punch. 'You mean? Oh no, sir, please. I'm meeting a local nurse in the new year. She can have Rowan for me and I can come back to work. Properly that is, on the sets not mending them. You won't even know there's a baby here.'

'Living on naval premises?'

'We could move out,' Ned said, as panicked as Ailsa. 'Would that help, sir? I'm sure we could get a billet off site.'

Keith shook his head.

'Ailsa would still be employed by us and, although you managed to get the rules stretched regarding married women, those around mothers are not navigable even by someone as skilled as yourself. I'm sorry.'

'You're not,' Ailsa flared. 'You've been trying to get rid of me from the moment I arrived.'

'Ailsa!' Ned hissed, but Keith threw up his hands.

'Guilty.' He leaned in. 'But truly, Ailsa, it's not because of you. I think you're a wonderful woman and you're quite the best operator on site – apologies, Ned.'

'None needed, sir. It's true. So why can't she stay?'

Keith grimaced.

'This is the military, lad. Rules are rules and I've been under huge pressure over this one. I've held the higher-ups off as long as I can, believe me, but with this ship going, they want you and the baby on it. If you're not, I will be.'

Ailsa bit her lip.

'I'm sorry, sir. I didn't realise.'

He shrugged.

'Maybe one day, lass, the world will be a more enlightened place, but for now...'

'Rules is rules?'

'Afraid so. But, hey, you've got three weeks together yet, enjoy them. More punch?'

'A lot more,' Ailsa agreed grimly, gripping Ned's arm.

Christmas had just got considerably less joyful.

Fran

Fran sat tight on the pew between her two brothers and fought to focus on the beauty of King's chapel as the choir sang out 'Hark the Herald Angels' in perfect harmony. It was hard. All she really wanted to do was cry and the purity of the young voices was not helping her resist. She muffled a sob and felt Rob's hand close over her own.

'Peace on earth would be nice, right?' he whispered into her ear.

'Wonderful. Will we ever get it, Rob?'

'We will. Evil like Hitler and his hateful followers cannot last.'

'Are you sure about that?'

He grimaced and Fran held his hand tight and looked to the glorious arches above. She wasn't sure about anything any more. Valérie was gone. She'd left Bletchley Park a few days after their argument and Fran had heard nothing from her since, not even a Christmas card. She'd bought her a pretty locket, then agonised for hours over whether to put a lock of her hair into it, before realising that she had no address to send it to and taking it miserably back to the shop. She'd spent the money on scarves for her brothers instead and was happy to see them both wearing them for this Christmas Day service.

The huge chapel was packed and, as the service wound up, there were many friends to greet. It was charming, but a world away from her current life. For years she'd studied and played among the elegant environs of Cambridge and she greeted a handful of old schoolfriends readily but it all felt put-on.

'What are you doing?' a girl in ATS uniform asked her.

'Administrative work,' Fran said. 'For the government.'

'Admin? Lovely. I'm manning anti-aircraft guns in Hyde Park. Dashed hard work, but one has to do one's bit, doesn't one?'

'One does,' Fran agreed, gritting her teeth.

It was the secrecy of Bletchley Park that she was sure had ground Valérie down. Pushing paper didn't seem nearly as exciting as shooting guns at planes, blowing up rail tracks, or driving makeshift ambulances like her damned grand-mère Elodie. It could bust open German supply lines every bit as effectively though, and Fran was proud of what she did. She only wished Valérie had been too.

'What are you up to, Fran?' another girl asked, this one in the coveted dark blue of the WRENS.

'Government work,' she said this time, trying to sound mysterious.

The girl wrinkled her nose.

'You always were the studious type, I suppose. I'm a driver for Admiral— Oh, I'd better not say, had I? Walls have ears and all that.'

'Quite right. Excuse me, I think my family are heading off.'

She ducked through the crowd in the chancel, only to find her parents were deep in discussion with some earnest-looking academics and there was no escape yet.

'Fran Morgan! Hello there. What the bally ho are you doing with yourself these days?'

Fran swung round to see another schoolfriend, this time in the pale blue of the WAAFS. Like Ailsa, she thought, and felt another wave of sadness wash over her, then a rush of anger.

'Can't really tell you,' she said, tapping the side of her nose, 'but let's just say I'm heading into enemy territory any day now.'

'You're a spy? Goodness, how marvellous. All I do is sit on a wireless listening to German pilots talking to each other.'

She shuddered and Fran felt instantly terrible for her stupid lies.

'I have a friend doing that too,' she said. 'Well, more reading Morse, I think.'

The girl pulled a face.

'I was hopeless at Morse. Good job I got my German higher cert, though I tell you, when I hear them shouting for Mutti as their planes go down, I rather wish I hadn't.'

Fran gave her arm a pat.

'Let's hope someone shoots Hitler down, and then perhaps we'll all be allowed to go back to normal life.'

'Whatever that is!'

'Indeed.'

The girl melted into the crowd and Fran leaned back against a pillar, feeling weary. It wasn't even midday yet but already she wasn't sure how much Christmas cheer she could take.

'Come on, old girl,' Rob said, appearing at her side. 'Ben and I have had quite enough of this. Let's leave the olds to their chatting and head home for a bit of liquid cheer, shall we?'

Finally, Fran felt a smile tug at her lips.

'Sounds perfect.'

It didn't take long to get tucked safely into their own sitting room, the fire lit and mulled ciders in their hands.

'So you're back in England then?' Fran said to her brothers. 'That must be a relief.'

Ben shrugged.

'Depends on your point of view. We're not desperately staunching blood from bullet wounds any more, but now we're treating the longer-term injuries. Sometimes it feels worse. These poor blokes have had time to look at their lost limbs and realise that this is it for the rest of their lives. It's so sad.'

Fran gave him a quick squeeze, but Rob said, 'Don't feel too sorry for him, Frannie. There's a certain young nurse who's making him feel a lot better about it.'

'Rob!' Ben protested, but he was blushing cutely.

'You've met someone? That's wonderful, Ben. What's she called?'

'Rita. She's a nurse and she's from Bristol and, well, I like her a lot.'

'Wedding bells?' Rob teased.

But his younger brother looked straight at him and said, 'Maybe.'

Rob grimaced.

'Fair enough. Lucky you.'

'No one for you, Rob?' Fran probed.

'Nah. I'm too jaded for love.'

'That's not true,' Fran protested. 'Love is what stops you being jaded, right, Ben?'

'Right,' Ben agreed. 'But come on, Fran, that sounds like the voice of experience. Who've you met? Some clever young chap in whatever mysterious office you work in?'

Fran flushed.

'Not exactly. And it doesn't matter anyway, it's over now.'

Ben frowned.

'Are you sure? It doesn't sound it to me.'

'Yes, well, I'm not the one who went away, am I?'

'Ah. Right. Sorry, old girl. But it is a war, you know. People have to go away for all sorts of reasons. It might not be, you know, personal.'

'It feels personal.'

'It usually does. But hey, is he the one who sent you the mystery gift?'

'Mystery gift?'

Ben leapt up and went over to the Christmas tree in the corner. They'd dug up their usual tree from the garden yesterday – glad they had their own as, with lumberjacks in the forces, supplies were short – and had a lovely time decorating it with their childhood baubles. Overnight, Santa Claus had come, even German planes unable to stop his magical sleigh, and they'd opened their presents this morning, so what was Ben talking about?

'I forgot it was here. It arrived a couple of days ago, addressed to 'the Morgan household' so I opened it up and inside was a pressie for you. It was so small I put it into the tree to be sure it didn't get lost. Ah, here it is.'

He reached into the branches and produced a tiny gift, neatly wrapped in silver with a red bow. Fran took it, hands shaking. Could it be?

'Open it,' the boys urged.

She fumbled the bow and the whole thing came open to reveal a lovely silver locket, not dissimilar to the one Fran had taken back, but designed to look like a miniature book. Tears sprang to her eyes and she slid her nail into the clasp and eased it open. Nothing. No tiny portrait, no lock of hair. What did that mean?

'It's empty,' she said.

'Maybe it's waiting for a photo once you're together again.'

'Maybe,' Fran agreed, but she wasn't so sure.

This felt more like a parting gift, a book for Fran's future that did not have Valérie in it. Tears stung her eyes again and this time she let them fall.

'Don't cry, Fran,' Rob said. 'You've got us.'

'Thank you,' she wept.

It was good to know. And at least her family's love was soft, unassuming, unquestioning. Not like Valérie's, which had burned like a flame – glorious while it was alive but swift, it seemed, to die. She took the locket and put it back into its bag. She didn't need Valérie's consolation gift, thank you very much. She'd decide her own future, her own way, however much it hurt. Already she was looking forward to being back in Bletchley Park.

Steffie

Steffie stood beneath a red-ribboned garland, listening to carols on the gramophone and the hum of happy guests at her parents' Christmas drinks, and wished she was anywhere but here.

'I know, darling,' her sister crooned from her self-appointed position at the centre of the gathering. 'I'm sooo lucky. Wonderful to have found joy amid the pain of war. I'm the happiest girl alive.'

Steffie glanced at the canapés circulating the drawing room and wondered if she dared stuff two mini cheese scones into her ears to block out some of Roseanna's gushing, then felt uncharitable. Barney Fotherington had proposed to her sister this morning – an emerald under the tree – and of course she wanted to talk to everyone about it. At least with this many people in the house, Steffie was spared some of the exuberant joy. As soon as the guests went and she had to sit down to Christmas dinner with the happy couple and her delighted parents, it would be even worse. She already knew that it would be turkey with lashings of wedding plans.

Roseanna was keen to get on with it because 'who knows what might happen with, you know, the invasion...' Steffie was sure that young Barney would bag himself a cushy job in an HQ far from the front line, but then told herself not to be uncharitable. Roseanna was absolutely right and she should seize happiness with both hands. Steffie only wished she'd had the chance to as well.

'I know,' she heard Roseanna say, voice low. 'I feel so terrible for poor Steffie-poo. I wish I could do something to help her heal. Well yes, I understand that, but I'm so happy I want everyone to feel that way.'

It was sweet, Steffie knew, but she hated being an object of pity. Being in love was so much more fun. With a guilty look around, she ducked away from the party into the quiet of the

sitting room and sank onto a chaise longue. In all the excitement
of the engagement this morning they'd run out of time to open
their presents before the guests came and a small selection still
sat decorously beneath the tree. Lord knows how her mother
had got hold of a fir in wartime London. When she'd asked,
Julianna had murmured something vague about a 'kind man
bringing it in from the country,' and Steffie had known better
than to press further. She glanced idly at the presents. One
stood out, wrapped in brown paper dotted with hand-drawn
stars. Leonard had handed it to her before she'd left for London
two days ago, startling her.

'That's so kind. I'm sorry. I didn't get you anything.'

'Neither did I expect you to. Don't get your hopes up, it's
nothing special but, hey, happy Christmas.'

'And to you, Leo.'

She'd given him a kiss on his cheek and then made for the
door, embarrassed. When she'd looked back, he'd been standing
there, fingers to the spot she'd kissed, looking dazed, and she'd
wondered if she'd done the wrong thing. But he was the one
who'd said Brits were reserved and, besides, his family were
Italian – surely they kissed each other all the time?

She reached for the package. In the other room the sound of
hearty clapping signalled that someone was making a speech.
Steffie turned the parcel over. It was small and square. Choco-
lates, maybe? Some American luxury would be nice. She gave it
a shake but there was no rattle. Hmm.

Taking another sip of her wine, she slid her nail under the
tape and released the packaging. It came away to reveal a blank
white square. Steffie frowned at it in confusion for a moment
before she came to her senses and turned it over. She gasped.

There, drawn in charcoals, was a beautiful picture of
Bletchley Park. In the foreground, two ducks flapped on the
pond and past that were the lawns, the funny old mansion and
half of the original Hut 4.

'Nothing special?!' she murmured. 'Leonard D'Angelo, you dark horse!'

She held it at arm's length to admire it. The perspective was perfect, the detailing impressive, and she loved it. The time would come, she supposed, when the war would end, her job at Bletchley Park with it, and she was hugely touched that he'd thought to give her this beautiful memento of an amazing time in her life.

'What's that you've got there?'

She jumped but it was only her father, sidling in with a backward glance to be sure her mother hadn't noticed him sneaking away.

'It's a picture of BP.'

At least with Anthony a member of the Twenty Committee, she didn't have to be coy about where she worked.

'It's very good. Did one of your friends draw it?'

Steffie thought about this, but not for long.

'Yes,' she agreed. 'A good friend.'

'That's nice.' He sank onto the sofa beside her, stretching out his legs with a contented sigh. 'Dinner will be a bit ghastly for you, I expect.'

'It's nice to see Roseanna so happy.'

'She's had an easier ride than you, my darling.'

Steffie grimaced.

'Couldn't have been much harder. First, I was separated from Matteo by the war, then we fell out over me working, and when we'd finally sorted all that out...'

'I let SOE ship him into enemy territory. I'm so sorry, Steffie. I should have got him a nice adjutant's job like Barney, kept him safe for you.'

Steffie shook her head.

'He wanted to go. He knew he could be the biggest help as a double agent.'

'And he was. It wasn't his fault that our lot made a huge

cock-up of the damned armistice. Rotten job all round. Apart from you, of course. I heard you were marvellous, darling.'

'You did?'

'I did.' Her father put his arm around her shoulders and held her close. 'I'm proud of you, Stefania Carmichael. Occasionally, I'll admit, I've thought it a shame I didn't have a son to follow in the old footsteps but, by George, you're doing a grand job of it, girl.'

Steffie's heart swelled. God, she missed Matteo but she had her family, she had her friends, and she had her work, and right now that would have to do. She looked again at the picture of Bletchley Park, expertly caught by Leo's clever charcoals, and smiled.

'Looks like 1944's going to be a big year, right?'

'You better believe it,' Anthony agreed. 'Buckle up, girl – it's time to really go to work now!'

PART TWO

1944

TWENTY-TWO

JANUARY 1944

Steffie

Steffie walked into the St James's Street offices on New Year's Day in her new suit – a Christmas present from her mother – feeling ready for anything. It was 1944 and time, as Leo would say, to kick some German ass. She waved to her father, chatting to Masterman at the far end, and then smiled at a new figure she recognised.

'Air Marshal Tedder.' She stepped up to shake his hand, seeing him struggle to place her. She wasn't surprised. The Twenty Committee couldn't be more different from the last time they'd been together. 'I'm Stefania Carmichael. We met in Cairo. You gave me a lift back to base out at Heliopolis and I was mad enough to recommend my friend Ailsa for your listening station on Malta.'

'My goodness, yes! Splendid to meet you again. Your friend did a marvellous job.'

'And nearly got killed doing it.'

'Really? Damnation.'

'Not to mention accused of being a spy.'

'What?'

'Wrongly accused. As was I. It was the American attaché, Bonner Fellers, in the end.'

'Gute quelle? You were one of the gels caught up in that?' Tedder squinted at her. 'I tell you what, they make you females of sterner stuff than they used to in my day! It was well spotted, that.'

'Thank you, sir.'

'Arthur, please. Are you well, Stefania?'

'I'm good, thank you, sir.'

'Still at Bletchley?'

'Yes. I'm here as their representative, as a matter of fact.'

'Are you indeed?' Arthur Tedder clapped her on the back. 'Well, good for you. And the wireless operator? Ailsa, did you say her name was? How's she?'

'Very good, sir. Working out in Ceylon now with the husband she met in Malta.'

He laughed heartily.

'Wasn't all bombs and spies then, hey? Good stuff. Oops – looks like we're being called to order.'

He pulled out a seat for Steffie to sit at his side and Steffie saw her father looking over in surprise and smiled proudly that she'd made her own connections in his world. She drew her notebook out of her new satchel – a Christmas present from her father – and settled into the meeting.

'So,' Masterman said. 'There's been movement on D-Day.' A stir went round the room and he waved to Tedder. 'I've asked Air Marshal Tedder to brief us, so listen up well.'

Tedder rose.

'On twenty-fourth December, General Eisenhower was appointed Supreme Commander of the Allied Expeditionary forces.'

'Eisenhower?' someone asked. 'Why an American?'

'Those reasons are not for this committee,' Tedder said

repressively. 'But let's say that Eisenhower has the sort of calm temperament ideal for an umbrella role in this vital operation.'

'He means Monty's too bullish to play the politics.'

'I mean,' Tedder said, 'that General Montgomery, a superb frontline tactician, is to be used to best advantage in command of all ground forces on D-Day. The two men will work closely together. Indeed, they already have. Only yesterday they studied the plans for an amphibious landing by three divisions and have both called for it to be expanded to a five-prong attack: Sword, Gold and Omaha, plus Juno and Utah. This will enable us to operate on a wider front from the off, stringing out enemy defences and increasing our chances of securing vital ports.'

'Makes sense,' Anthony said.

'It does, but it also increases the amount of landing craft needed as we have to get our boys ashore fast to give them a fighting chance. It's been estimated that we'll need at least a hundred more, so the invasion is delayed.'

There was an audible intake of breath.

'For how long?'

'One month, to June fifth, the next full moon. The Americans can send materials across the Atlantic and we have all shipyards on standby for the moment they arrive. That, on top of our existing converted Thames lighter-boats, should be sufficient for a five-pronged attack on the beaches of Normandy. As long, at least, as the entire strength of the Wehrmacht is not lined up waiting. And that, gentlemen – and lady – is where you come in. We have to keep as many German troops as possible away from the Normandy beaches. Bevan?'

He gestured to Johnny Bevan, head of the London Controlling Section, who set out the strategic plans for double-cross deceptions.

'If this is going to work,' Bevan said, standing up, 'it needs to be our most coordinated and wholesale deception. We'll never be able to hide the invasion of Normandy, but we must create the illusion of possible invasion sites elsewhere to keep Jerry occupied and out of the way. We're working on plans to suggest invasions in Norway, the South of France and the Balkans.'

'And how are they going?' demanded someone at the back and Steffie turned to see a new man had joined the committee. 'David Strangeways,' he introduced himself with a jaunty smile. 'Head of Ops B for Monty.'

'David is back from some neat deception work in the Med to help with the big one,' Masterman told the rest.

'And in the nick of time,' David said, turning piercing eyes on them all. He was a man bristling with confidence and clearly happy to shake up the committee. Steffie leaned forward, interested. 'Surely if we want Jerry to believe we're going to hit the Pas-de-Calais, we need to convince him there are troops in Kent?'

'Of course,' Bevan agreed tightly. 'We have plans for fake troops movements and dummy tanks to simulate a six-division force down there.'

'Six divisions?' Strangeways threw up his hands. 'That's not going to keep many Panzers back, is it?'

'More will be hard to simulate.'

'On the frontline, perhaps, but not on our own soil, far from their reconnaissance. The forces don't need to actually be there, just to look as if they are.' He paced around the room, ripe with energy. 'I suggest that we need to make Jerry think that we have two full invasion forces ready. One aimed at Normandy – as you say, Johnny, there's no way we'll be able to hide that completely – and another in Kent ready to hit Pas-de-Calais. The latter is the more obvious attack-site, with only 20 miles of sea to cross against the 250 to Caen, so it shouldn't be too hard to convince them we're eyeing it up. Do we have any intel on where Hitler believes we'll attack?'

'Steffie?' Masterman asked, and Steffie found herself in the glare of David Strangeways's intense eyes.

'Abwehr reports suggest that Hitler is favouring Calais. It's what he would do.'

'Exactly!' Strangeways beamed at her. 'What's the first principle of deception? Be sure you're thinking like the enemy! If the Fuhrer wants to believe we're coming for Calais, it will be far easier to convince him he's right.'

Bevan harrumphed.

'What you say is true, David, but what forces do we make the Germans believe are there? The Abwehr has the fine detail of all our units, right, Steffie?'

'That's right,' she agreed awkwardly, not wanting to annoy the dynamic new arrival. 'The weekly situation report provided by FHW – *Fremde Heere West* – details them every week.'

'What about the American units?' Strangeways asked, stopping at her side.

She looked up at him.

'They're doing their best to pin those down.' She thought hard about her work in the last week. 'We read a message the other day about the First US Army Group that shows they're trying—'

'Stop!' Strangeways put up a hand and she froze. 'Say that again.'

'Erm. I said, we read a message the other day about the First US Army Group.'

'Which is?'

'A unit newly arrived in Britain under General Bradley, but it's only small.'

'Do they know that?'

'They don't know anything much about it, but they're trying to find out.'

Strangeways clapped his hands in delight.

'Perfect. Thank you…?'

'Stefania,' she supplied. 'Stefania Carmichael, Bletchley Park representative.'

'And actual genius!' he said, blowing her a kiss. He looked to the others. 'It sounds good, right – the First US Army Group. It sounds... big.'

'It does,' Masterman agreed cautiously.

'Important,' Strangeways said. 'What did we just say is the first principle of deception? Be sure you're thinking like the enemy! The Germans know there's going to be an Anglo-American attack, but they don't know the extent of our cooperation and will be unable to conceive of different nations working in full harmony. It goes against everything the Nazis stand for.'

A ripple of awkward laughter went around the room and he smiled.

'Hitler is far more likely to believe that we'd run a British invasion from one site and a US one from another. They'll also believe that the US one will be the biggie. If we can make them think Normandy is a diversion to draw troops away for the true invasion later, it will play into our hands. Do you see, gentlemen – it will keep them near Calais not only when we invade, but for days afterwards, maybe even weeks!'

His eyes were alight with the idea and Steffie felt the rest of the committee being infused with his enthusiasm. The idea was big and bold and incredibly invigorating. She scribbled frantic notes.

'It's worth exploring,' Masterman was saying. 'But how do we create the illusion of an entire army group?'

'Fake tanks, planes and landing craft,' Strangeways said promptly. 'I've got a set-building friend at Shepperton studios. I'm sure he'll be up for it.'

'That's good.'

'And we can put out wireless signals from SLUs that mimic the activity of inter-battalion comms across Kent. Fake station IDs, fake Morse orders, fake supply demands, the works.'

Masterman nodded and now Tar Robertson stood up.

'I can get the agents drip-feeding a picture of American

units heading for Kent. Brutus, Treasure and Tricycle are all building trust with their Abwehr handlers and Admiral Canaris sometimes feels as if he's on our side, he's so obligingly credulous. We can start to ramp up the ratio of fake info to chickenfeed any time now. They love Garbo and he's doing a grand job of "recruiting" more agents into his entirely fictious network – a network, note you, that they are paying for. And handsomely too.'

'Who have you added now?' Masterman asked.

'Let me see, we have his brother in Aberdeen and a wealthy Venezuelan student in Glasgow. A Gibraltarian waiter working in Chislehurst, a Greek deserter, an Indian poet, and an anti-Soviet South African. Then there's the ex-seaman living in Swansea, who has been joined by several others to form the Brothers in the Aryan World Order – a group of fiercely anti-semitic Welshmen, dedicated to bringing national socialism to the valleys.'

Masterman frowned.

'Are you sure you're not going a bit far, Tar? That sounds ridiculous.'

'To us it does, but to the average Nazi it sounds entirely plausible. As David has already said, the point is to get into their world view. They're jolly keen on the brothers and have wired over money for a recruitment drive.'

'Hmm. Well, don't overdo it. Could be they're stringing us along and these agents are actually reporting into them.'

'Most of them are made-up, John, so it would be hard for them to report to anyone.'

'True.' Masterman shook his head. 'Sorry, Tar, you're far too convincing.'

'I do my best! Don't you worry, we'll work our agents to build whatever picture suits. I can send the waiter to Ramsgate, the deserter to Canterbury and the Aryan frigging brothers all along the south coast. Whatever you need, you give us a shout.'

'Thanks, Tar. Thanks, David.' Masterman nodded to the two men, who took their seats again. 'Miss Carmichael, we're going to need your ears on this one. If we go for this, it will be vital we know what the Abwehr think is going on. We're going to need the weekly FHW reports and everything else you can get us.'

'Yes, sir.'

'Perfect. Listen up, all of you! None of us around this table will be stepping into the waves on fifth June 1944 to face the German guns, but every one of us can do their utmost to be sure there are as few of those guns as possible. Understood?'

'Understood,' they chorused back, Steffie as loud as the rest.

She felt a thrill run down her spine. The Germans had taken Matteo from her but now she was coming for them. They were all coming for them, real forces and fake ones alike. First steps, St James's Street, last ones, Berlin.

TWENTY-THREE

FEBRUARY 1944

Fran

'You want me to get on that?!'

Fran looked from the rickety motorbike to Gilberte Brossolette in astonishment. Gilberte shrugged in a way that reminded her painfully of Valérie.

'I find it the best way to get around Londres, especially at, er, short notice.'

Fran looked again at the petite woman before her, elegant even with a heavy leather jacket over her trouser suit, and wondered at the sort of life she lived. Pierre had been away in France for months now, working hard to cement the *Conseil Nationale de la Résistance* after Jean Moulin's tragic death. The Germans were desperate to secure Pedro – his codename – so Gilberte must be worried sick but, somehow, she kept calm, picking up a lot of Pierre's administrative tasks here in England, on top of keeping an eye on their two children, coming into adulthood in a turbulent world. Fran was full of admiration for her, but that didn't mean she wanted to get on her motorbike.

'Is it safe?'

Another shrug. 'Not if a bomb falls on us.'

'Well, no.'

'But otherwise, yes, it is safe. My friend Margarite is an excellent mechanic and keeps it in top shape for me.'

Fran looked again at the bike, wondering what it would look like if it was in poor shape but then supposed that was only the bodywork. If the engine was good, who was she to complain?

'In that case, yes, thank you.'

She took the leather jacket Gilberte was offering her and shrugged it on. It was surprisingly supple, with a woollen lining that was marvellously soft against her neck, and she had to admit that she felt 'cool'. The American word made her shiver. It was the one she'd thrown at Valérie when they'd argued about her becoming a *résistante*.

'Nice jacket,' she said, determinedly pushing thoughts of her one-time girlfriend away.

She'd heard nothing from her since the mystery present at Christmas and each day that passed, she was training herself to think of her less.

'It's Pierre's.'

Gilberte paused astride the bike, lost in thought.

'You haven't heard from him?'

'*Non*. They tried to get him out before Christmas but twice the plane failed to land. Cloud, or some such. I don't know. I don't think the British pilots understand the risks the *résistants* are taking. Night after night those people go out to set up a landing site, breaking curfew, taking torches that will attract German attention, standing in the open where they could easily be found. Those are all huge risks to themselves and their families, but if the pilot doesn't think he has a perfect view, he circles over the top and heads off back across the Channel to a warm dinner on a nice, safe base.'

'Pilots have the worst death rates of all the forces,' Fran reminded her gently.

Gilberte looked back at her.

'In combat, yes. Landing in a field in rural France, not so much. Ah! I am so worried for my Pierre. I heard the other day that he might attempt to come home by boat. There are some fishermen in Brittany who may be happy to take him.'

Fran put a hand on her shoulder.

'That would be good.'

'If it works. It is February, Frances. The seas are rough.'

'As are the skies. He'll do it, I know he will. He'll be back soon.'

'Thank you, Frances.' Gilberte put her own hand over Fran's. 'And now, come on – we have a meeting to get to.'

She handed Fran a helmet and gestured to the leather seat behind her. Fran slung her leg nervously over the bike and settled in behind the Frenchwoman, but as Gilberte kicked the engine into life, it shuddered through Fran's body in an instant thrill.

'Wow!' she gasped.

Whoever Margarite was, she knew how to tune an engine and Fran gave in to the sensation of speed as Gilberte steered them expertly towards Fleet Street. It was only when they pulled up outside an imposing building that she felt nerves replace the thrill of the ride.

Gilberte was bringing her to meet the chairman of *Associated Newspapers*, whose flagship newspaper, the *Daily Mail*, was despised by her parents for its 'vulgar' style of journalism. It was, however, increasing in circulation all the time and, with so many men away at war, the typical reader was increasingly female and wanted articles to suit her tastes. That was where Fran might fit in; it all hinged on the interview ahead. She climbed off the bike and removed the helmet, gasping in horror as she caught a glimpse in the side mirror of what it had done to her hair. Gilberte laughed.

'It is only flattened. Here.'

She reached up and tousled Fran's hair into a style that she didn't think much better but didn't have the nerve to correct. Gilberte had been so kind to her, encouraging her writing and arranging this meeting, and if it went well, Fran might have the basis of a life after the war. Which she would need, she thought bitterly, with Valérie gone.

'Focus,' she told herself sternly. 'This is about you now.'

She followed Gilberte upstairs into a newsroom crammed with journalists, mostly older men tapping away at typewriters beneath a fug of cigarette smoke. There was a buzz to the place that gave Fran a thrill even greater than riding the motorbike and she knew instantly that this was where she wanted to be.

Her nerves grew as Gilberte led them to a private office at the back and knocked on a door bearing the words: *Esmond Harmsworth, Chairman*. This man, along with his father and uncle before him, was a legend in the newspaper world as a pioneer of so-called 'popular journalism', and Fran cleared her throat nervously as a voice barked, 'Come!' She found herself opposite an imposing man in a dapper three-piece suit, with a carefully styled head of hair and razor-sharp eyes. 'Morning,' he barked. 'Come along in. I haven't got all day. Gilberte, good to see you. And you must be Miss Frances Morgan.'

'Yes, sir. Thank you for meeting me.'

'Always keen to find new talent. Gil tells me you can write. Sent me your piece on the Albert Hall. Not bad.'

'Thank you, sir. It was quite heavily edited but—'

'They always are. Space, you know. A journalist can't afford to be precious. Are you precious, Miss Morgan?'

'No, sir. I just want to write, sir.'

'Excellent. It's all about attitude, Miss Morgan. We're not highbrow here. We write what people want to read.'

'That seems sensible.'

Harmsworth threw back his head in a sudden laugh.

'It does, doesn't it, Miss Morgan. Tell that to the literati, will you? They're such snobs about it all. "Popular press" they call it, as if that's a bad thing, but who doesn't want to be popular?'

'The proof of a newspaper's success is surely in the size of its readership?' Fran offered.

'It is, Miss Morgan! It truly is. Oh, you'll fit right in. When can you start?'

'Start? Here?'

'Of course, here. Where else?'

Fran looked to Gilberte, who stepped in.

'Miss Morgan has an important job working for the government at the moment, so she's looking to freelance for now.'

'Only until the war ends,' Fran said. 'Then I want to go full-time. I want to make journalism my career.'

'Career? Interesting word for a woman. Don't use it in the paper. Inflammatory!'

'Right, sir. Of course not.'

'But I like to hear it. Talk to Jim out there.' He waved into the hub of the newsroom. 'He runs the women's section.'

'I can write other—'

'Start there, then we'll see, yes?'

'Yes, sir.'

'Good stuff. Welcome on board.'

He stood up and stuck out a broad hand and Fran took it eagerly, trying to match his hearty handshake. He gave a nod of approval.

'You'll do,' he said, and then he was waving them away and they were tumbling out of the office and back into the buzz beyond.

Fran felt dazed.

'You'll do,' she echoed under her breath, feeling as if it was the highest praise she'd ever received.

Her enthusiasm was slightly watered down by Jim's summary of what he needed – fashion, food and feel-good friendlies – but she understood about working her way up.

She'd started at BP organising cards into shoeboxes and now she was running the entire invasion map system. Maybe it would be the same here. Today, feel-good friendlies; tomorrow, world news. First, though, the world had to sort itself out and for that, it was back to Buckinghamshire.

'Have you got time for a drink before your train?' Gilberte asked her as they came out of the offices into the fresh air of Fleet Street. 'I said I'd meet Tommy, see if he has any more news. You're welcome to come along.'

Fran nodded. She'd left hours for the interview, but Harmsworth had been efficiently brief.

'I owe you a drink anyway, Gil, that was amazing.'

Gilberte shrugged.

'Someone got me started, so it's a pleasure to help you in turn. Us women need to stick together. If you get a chance, look up an American called Martha Gellhorn – she's trying to shake things up, as you are, so she might be useful to you once you're a big-shot in Fleet Street. Oh, and when you are, I hope you'll help some other pup.'

'Pup?'

'Pup reporter. That's what you are now!' She winked at her, then threw her a bike helmet. 'But come on, Tommy will be waiting.'

Another speedy ride and Fran found herself in the French House. Tommy wasn't there yet so they grabbed a table and Gilberte ordered something called pastis. The two glasses of clear liquid came with a small jug of water and when Gilberte poured it in, the liquid turned cloudy like – well, like dishwater frankly, though the scent it released was pleasant.

'It smells like aniseed balls,' Fran laughed.

'Taste it.'

She took a tentative sip. It was soft but zingy and tickled at her tongue.

'I like it.'

'*Bon!* We will make a Frenchwoman of you yet. Valérie will be pleased.'

Fran's joy subsided instantly.

'Valérie won't care.'

'*Pardon?*'

'She's gone, Gil. We're not together.'

Gilberte peered at her.

'Why, then, has she asked to meet us here today?'

Fran's heart performed several acrobatic moves in her chest.

'Valérie has? Here? To... today?'

Gilberte nodded.

'She has finished her training and said she wanted to see you. I assumed you knew.'

'No. I haven't heard from her since she left.'

Gilberte gave her a smile.

'This does not surprise me. Valérie is a woman who throws herself into her tasks, is she not?'

'Well yes, but...'

'And this matters to her greatly, you know, to us all. It is a great shame to our nation that we gave in to the Nazi bastards and vital that, at the critical moment, we stand alongside the Allies to fight them back off our shores. You see that?'

'I do. But why should that stop her from contacting me?'

'Perhaps she can only give herself to one thing at a time.'

Fran looked at Gilberte. 'Perhaps that isn't good enough?'

Gilberte gave her a sad smile. 'That, *ma chérie*, is up to you to decide. Ah, but look, here is Tommy!'

She waved as Yeo-Thomas came hurrying into the bar. He looked over, gave them a half wave, then paused a moment, as if gathering himself. Gilberte's hand tightened around her pastis glass and Fran sucked in a breath as the air in the French House seemed suddenly to thin. Tommy came over, tried to smile, and then gave up.

'It's not good news?' Gilberte said, her voice taut.

He shook his head.

'They've got him, Gil. The bastards have got him.'

Fran felt Gilberte's body collapse and put an arm around her shoulders.

'How?' Gilberte demanded.

'We've had a message from the group in Brittany. It seems Pierre got on a fishing boat but then the damned thing was shipwrecked. The local Resistance picked him up and all was well but some bitch local women turned him in at a checkpoint and, as he didn't have a pass for the coastal zone, they've taken him in. The good news is that he gave them his fake ID as Kenneth Dodkin, British pilot, and they seem to have bought that. He's in prison at Rennes, which is bad, obviously, but not half as bad as if they knew who he really was. Then he'd be—'

He stopped himself but Gilberte knew.

'At Avenue Foch, with the Gestapo torturers.'

'Hmm. But he's not and as long as they think he's a bumbling British pilot, he should be fine.' He grimaced. 'The problem is…'

'His hair.'

Tommy nodded. Fran thought of Pierre's shock of dark hair with the distinctive white streak running through it. He'd dyed it to go to France and had presumably been keeping that dye up to date, but in prison…

Gilberte reached out, grabbing Tommy's hands.

'We have to get him out, Tommy. We have to get him out before his hair grows and they know they have the infamous Pedro in their vicious hands.'

Her whole body was shaking and Fran held her close, unable to imagine what she was going through. If it were Valérie facing torture, she'd be a wreck. And then suddenly, as if she'd conjured her up with her imaginings, there was Valérie, standing behind Tommy and staring down at Fran with an unreadable look on her face.

'Valérie!' Fran gasped.

'This looks cosy,' she said.

Fran could hardly believe her ears.

'Hardly. Gilberte just found out Pierre has been captured.'

'Oh.' Valérie blanched. 'Oh, I'm sorry. That must be, er, painful.'

'Losing someone you love?' Fran shot back. 'It is, especially when they disappear without trace.'

Valérie's shoulders tightened.

'Sometimes it has to be that way. Perhaps it is better, in wartime, not to love at all.'

Fran's heart stilled its acrobatics as sharply as if someone had shot a bullet straight into it.

'Is that what you believe?'

Valérie looked at Gilberte, quaking in Fran's arms.

'Is it not the most sensible choice?'

'You think love is a *choice*?' Fran spluttered. Valérie simply stood there, staring at her. 'Fine then. You are right. Love *is* painful. I choose not to have it too.'

'Frances...'

But Fran had had enough of Valérie's histrionics. They were wearying and she was weary enough already. She turned her attention, instead, to Tommy, who had leaned into Gilberte, his eyes afire.

'I'll go out there, Gil. I'll go out there the moment I can get a plane. I'll get to Rennes and I'll find him and I'll break him out before his hair exposes him to the Gestapo. I'll rescue him for you, I swear it.'

'It's too dangerous, Tommy.'

'For Pierre, yes. He's my friend, my best friend, and I will not leave him there. Stay strong, Gil, and we'll be back. Together. Yes?'

Gilberte looked up at him.

'Yes. Thank you, Tommy. Don't take unnecessary risks.'

Tommy laughed.

'What's unnecessary?!' He looked at Fran. 'Can you get Gil home?'

'Of course.'

'I'll get going then. There's no time to waste.'

He turned to go but Valérie was standing in front of him.

'I'll come with you,' she said.

'No.'

'Yes. You'll need help and a woman is less likely to be noticed. I'm French, Tommy, I know the area. I'll be useful to you.'

'That's true, but—'

'No buts. I want to do this.' Valérie threw a defiant look at Fran. 'Besides, there's nothing to keep me here now.'

And with that, she was gone, striding out of the French House after Tommy, leaving Fran with a sobbing friend and a broken heart. Well fine. Valérie had told her to choose not to love, so choose it she would.

Or, at least, she'd try.

TWENTY-FOUR

MARCH 1944

Ailsa

Ailsa looked eagerly out of the train window. It was growing dark but she could make out the familiar buildings of Bletchley station and sighed in relief. Rowan had, of course, chosen to go to sleep about two minutes ago, rather than the forty that would have given Ailsa some rest before she arrived, but there was nothing new there. Ailsa swore she hadn't had more than three consecutive hours' sleep since giving birth and was starting to crave it like an addict.

She looked around the carriage to make sure she had everything. Juggling a duffel bag, a carrycot and an additional case full of nappies, bottles and assorted paraphernalia had not been easy but people had been kind, especially with her WAAF uniform. She wasn't quite sure if she'd been sacked from the force for the terrible crime of having a baby, but she still felt a part of it so until anyone told her otherwise she'd soldier on.

The train wheezed to a halt about a hundred feet short of the platform and she groaned. She felt as if she'd been travelling forever and this final delay made her want to scream in frustration. She'd left Ned in Colombo back in mid-January and here they were, well into March and she was still going. The ship had taken weeks to traverse the Med and then ground up the Atlantic coast in swells that had made both her and Rowan sick, before finally docking in Portsmouth.

Problems on the train line had forced a detour to London with an increasingly tetchy baby and she'd only coped with it all by cursing Commander Keith in every way she could imagine. If he'd only let her stay safe in Colombo, she'd have six-month-old Rowan settled into a lovely routine with a nurse and would be listening in to the enemy as she was meant to do, instead of bouncing around on a succession of miserable vehicles to satisfy the British government's stupid scruples about females serving abroad. And now, within sight of journey's end, she was stuck again.

In truth, she wasn't meant to be at Bletchley. She'd been instructed to go home and, keen to introduce Rowan to her eager grandparents, she'd been fully intending to catch the night train to Glasgow. When she'd got into London, however, she'd been so daunted by the thought of another twenty-four hours of travel that she'd bought a ticket to Bletchley on impulse. There'd barely been time to send a telegram to Gloria and grab some odd-looking cheese and bread from a funny shop nearby, before hopping on board.

Hopefully she could spend a few days recuperating with her friends before making for North Uist and she cheered inside as the wheels ground into motion and the train chugged up to the platform. She hefted bags and baby into the corridor and battled with the door, wincing at the rush of chill air as it opened. Lord, she'd forgotten how cold it was in Britain! Slinging the duffel bag unceremoniously onto the platform, she cradled the carrycot, feeling with her foot for the step and wondering, yet again, how on earth Keith thought this was going to help anyone. But the next moment she heard squeals and her name being called and, before she knew it, kind hands were helping her eagerly down onto the platform.

'Fran,' she breathed. 'Steffie. Oh, it's so wonderful to see you.'

Fran and Steffie hugged her then turned to the carrycot, cooing at an inevitably wide-awake Rowan.

'What a divine baby!' Steffie cried. 'She's such a mini you, Ails. Look at that red hair! And those aqua eyes.'

'She's gorgeous, Ailsa,' Fran agreed, touching a tentative finger to Rowan, who gripped at it. 'Ooh look – she likes me!'

'Of course she likes you,' Ailsa said. 'You're going to be her godmother.' She clapped a hand over her mouth; that was not the way she'd been going to do this. 'That's to say, would you, both of you, be Rowan's godmothers? Ned and I would be honoured.'

'Ned will be terrified, I imagine,' Steffie laughed, 'but yes! Yes, please.'

'Absolutely,' Fran echoed. 'The honour is all ours. Oh, little one, wait till we get you back to the caravan. We're going to have such fun!'

And with that, Steffie swept Rowan into her arms, Fran hefted the duffel bag and baby-case, and they marched Ailsa off the platform and out into Bletchley. It had been a year since she'd left and, despite the cold and missing Ned, it was a relief to be home.

They snuggled into the caravan and she watched contentedly as Rowan bounced on Steffie's lap while Fran attempted to feed her semolina, getting far more on the caravan walls and down all their clothing than in the baby's mouth. It didn't matter. It would clean up later and she couldn't remember when she'd laughed this much.

'It's so good to be together again,' Steffie said, ducking to avoid flying food.

Ailsa reached for her hand.

'I'm so, so sorry about Matteo, Stef. I felt so useless miles away. I longed to give you a cuddle.'

'I'll take it now,' Steffie said, pulling her in close and making Rowan scream with laughter as she was crushed between them.

'How are you doing?' Ailsa asked her when her daughter had settled down.

'Ups and downs. Who knows how it will feel once the war ends and all this madness stops but for now work is keeping me sane – well, almost.'

She ducked another globule of semolina and dropped a kiss onto Rowan's sticky head. That girl was going to need a bath, Ailsa thought, but her own eyes were drooping. The companionship was wonderful after battling around the world with Rowan, but it was strangely tiring too. Or perhaps her body, knowing she was safe at last, was finally insisting on rest. Fran and Steffie had moved themselves onto the top bunks, making one of the lower pair up for Ailsa and clearing the other for Rowan's carrycot, and she could hardly wait to crawl in, but there were still things to catch up on.

'How's Valérie, Fran?'

Fran tensed.

'She's gone to France. She feels she could be more use there.'

'Right. That's awfully brave of her.'

'She certainly thinks so.'

'You don't?'

Ailsa looked nervously at Steffie, who grimaced behind Rowan's head.

'I think she's looking for a glory role rather than getting on with the vital one she was so good at here in BP, but it's up to her.'

'You fell out?'

'You could say that. Valérie says love is too painful to indulge in during wartime.'

'Or it could be the only thing that keeps us going?' Ailsa suggested tentatively.

'I'd have thought so,' was the tight answer. 'But it would seem that, for now, we're all without other halves.'

'But with our other thirds,' Ailsa suggested.

Fran smiled, her shoulders relaxing again, and both she and Steffie reached out to hold Ailsa's hands so they were linked together, a perfect triangle. It was a strong shape, Ailsa thought, and she was so blessed to have it in her life.

Two days later she was called to Whaddon for a 'de-brief' with Gambier-Parry, who'd somehow got word that she was in the vicinity. She pulled a face at herself in the tiny mirror in the caravan bathroom as she tried to get ready. She looked terrible. The slight colour that her peely-wally skin had picked up in Colombo had gone and there were bags under her eyes.

Both Fran and Steffie had been insistent that they could 'sleep through anything' but clearly they hadn't tried to sleep through a hungry baby's wails before. Ailsa had been horribly aware that they'd got work the next morning as she'd paced with Rowan, heating a bottle and changing her nappy in the cramped space of the caravan. She could get away with, at best, another night and then she'd have to make for London and, from there, North Uist. The thought of further travel was daunting.

She was missing Ned badly. While she'd had to focus on keeping Rowan alive and well on the journey, she'd been able to push her longing for her husband to the back of her mind, but with things more settled, it was bubbling to the surface like lava – and hurting as much. What's more, she felt terrible for him missing out on his daughter's development. Every time Rowan did something new, she thought 'Ned would love this,' and it pained her that all these magical firsts were unrecoverable for him. She was trying to write it down in letters but knew that by the time they reached him, their daughter would be on to some new feat. She would doubtless be walking before he saw her again.

'Cheer up, eejit,' she muttered under her breath. 'At least he's alive and loves you.'

She hated that poor Steffie and Fran were lonely but delighted with how they'd taken to their 'niece'. She couldn't imagine better aunties for Rowan and didn't want them to be separated from her. It was all too sad.

'Enough,' she admonished herself sternly.

Making sure her uniform was smart even if her face wasn't, she let herself out of the caravan and crossed the yard to the farm.

'Ooh, is that my gorgeous Rowan come to play?' Gloria asked, swooping in on them and lifting the baby into the air. She and Alfie had been delighted to meet the new arrival and Rowan had taken to them both instantly. 'Are you flying, Ro-Ro? Are you? Are you flying?'

'Ro-Ro' certainly looked like she thought she was and giggled madly.

'Are you sure you're happy to have her?' Ailsa asked. 'It shouldn't take too long.'

'Take as long as you want, my love. We'll be quite content here, don't you worry. We'll have a little play and a little walk.' She indicated the beautiful Silver Cross perambulator that Alfie had wheeled out of the back of a barn and spent all of yesterday cleaning up. 'And then, no doubt, we'll have a little sleep, so there's no rush at all.'

'A sleep sounds better than where I'm heading,' Ailsa said ruefully but she was already running late so, leaving Rowan in Gloria's tender care, she made for Bletchley Park.

It was strange walking up the familiar path and in through the big gates. Gambier-Parry was in the park, having a meeting with Travis, so she was spared the trek up to Whaddon Hall and it felt like her very first days here as she traced her way around the duck pond and into the mansion. She remembered how intimidating it had seemed when she, Steffie and Fran had been marched in to sign the Official Secrets Act on their first evening. She'd come a long way since then, she reminded herself, and she wasn't going to be intimidated by military bureaucracy. Head high, she marched in to see her boss.

'Ah, Ailsa! Welcome home. Good to have you back.'

Affability was not what Ailsa had been expecting and she shook the proffered hand nervously.

'Good to be back, sir. That is, am I? Back, I mean?'

'Good Lord, I hope so. Things are hotting up and we need all hands on deck. Perfect timing to get my top operator onto a set, I'd say.'

'Right. Yes.' Ailsa's head swam. 'I mean, it would be.'

'Problem?'

She looked at him sideways.

'Not for me, but I thought there was at your end. You do know why I was sent home?'

'I believe, Mrs Robinson, that you have had a baby.'

'That's right, sir.'

'Well done. Are you, you know, healthy and well and all that?'

'Yes, thank you.'

'Excellent. So, you can work then?'

The question threw her. She was dying to see her parents and introduce Rowan to them but the chance to do her bit to help end this damned war was enticing.

'I'd love to, sir,' she admitted, 'but I was told that it wasn't allowed by the RAF?'

Gambier-Parry considered. 'It probably isn't in the normal run, but we do things a bit differently at BP. You're a talented operator, so I don't see a problem as long as you think you can get care for it.'

'For Rowan?'

'Who?'

'My daughter.'

'Ah. Yes. So, can you?'

Ailsa had no idea. She hadn't been prepared for any of this.

'I can try, sir. I mean, I'd like to try.'

He leaned over his desk.

'Thing is, Ailsa, I've just come out of a meeting with Travis and it looks like the naval bods have got permission to put a listening station up in the park for D-Day. The thinking goes that it will enable greater speed of comms during the invasion which could, obviously, be vital to its success. So, we're going to need top operators.'

Ailsa gaped at him.

'You want *me* to work in a BP listening station for D-Day?'

'Yes. Do you think you can?'

She swallowed, her head spinning.

'Of course I can, sir. I'd be honoured to, truly. Can you give me a few days to find Rowan some care?'

'I can,' he agreed, then put up a hand. 'But, Ailsa, make it good care, yes? We have more leeway in BP, but there'll be a few people looking on, so I don't want to be made to look stupid.'

'No, sir. Me neither, sir.'

She shook his hand with enthusiasm. God bless BP! With its academics and its relaxed style of working, it had always been aside from the normal rules of the world and she'd never been more glad of that than now. Somehow, she'd been handed a chance to prove that becoming a mother didn't put paid to your other talents and, sad as she was not to be heading to her ma and pa, she had to seize it with both hands.

Ailsa left newly determined and returned to the farmhouse to find Rowan asleep under an apple tree and Gloria washing nappies under the pump.

'Oh, Gloria, you didn't have to do that!'

'It's got to be done, and I don't mind, my love. I've washed plenty of these in my time, you know.'

'I know, but it doesn't seem fair when Rowan isn't your family.'

'I feel as if she is, if that doesn't offend you?'

'Offend me? Lord no! I love it. Thank you.'

Gloria smiled.

'You look bouncy. Meeting went well, did it?'

Ailsa perched on the side of the pump and thought about it.

'I think so. That's to say, work-wise it was amazing. They want me back, Gloria.'

'I'm not surprised. I'm sure you're very good at whatever it is that you do.'

Ailsa smiled.

'Thank you, but it's not that simple now, is it? There's Rowan to think about.'

Gloria laughed and lifted a nappy up to the sun to test for whiteness. It looked immaculate; far better than Ailsa ever managed.

'Don't you worry about that. I'll take care of her.'

'You will? But Gloria, they'll want me on shift six days a week.'

'So I'll have her for six days. It's fine.'

'Really? I'll pay you, of course. I don't have all that much, but we can work something out and—'

'You will not.' Gloria hung the nappy over the line and put her hands on her hips. 'You're doing your war work, lass, so this will be mine – and a finer, happier type of work I simply cannot imagine.'

Ailsa leaped up and hugged her.

'You're a wee marvel, Gloria.'

'Away with you. We all have to do our bit. Tell you what though, it would be easier if we moved you into the farmhouse so we had everything in one place. It's spring, so the apples can go in the barn. I'll get Alfie to shift them and then we can make the loft up as a bedroom again, like when our Mary and Penny were here. Oh, it'll be like old times.'

Ailsa couldn't believe her luck.

'Are you sure? She cries at night, you know.'

'Of course she does – though I bet she won't once I have her crawling around the farm all day. Either way, it doesn't matter, the walls are that thick we won't hear a thing.'

Ailsa could have cried. In fact, it seemed, Ailsa was crying. She was still missing Ned like a hole in her very core, and she ached to see her parents, but this was work. Important work.

'God bless you, Gloria,' she said, hugging her again.

There was a long journey ahead to win this war, but D-Day was visible on the horizon and if that went well, the Nazis could be defeated and her husband could come home to her and Rowan. That was something truly worth fighting for and, mother or not, she was sure as hell going to play her part.

TWENTY-FIVE

MARCH 1944

Steffie

Steffie stared at the five-letter blocks on the paper in front of her and the translation she had written carefully above it. She was sure she'd made no mistakes, but it was still hard to believe. She beckoned Leo over.

'Can you check this for me? I want to be absolutely certain it's right.'

'Sure thing.'

He took the paper and bent over it, sticking his pencil in his mouth as he always did when he was concentrating. Before long, he looked up at her.

'I don't think you've made a mistake, Steffie. The German is perfect, the message is, is...'

'A disaster,' Steffie said. 'Thanks, Leo. I need to take this to Denys.'

She took the sheet and traced her way down the busy block to Denys's office at the far end. As usual, his door was wide open and she edged in.

'Everything all right, Steffie?'

'Not really, sir. It looks like Admiral Canaris has been fired.'

'What?'

Denys leaped up so fast that his mug of tea went flying. Taking the paper from her, he read it over, twice, then looked up, his face pale.

'Everyone – emergency meeting. Now!'

The team gathered around, exchanging worried glances, as well they might. If Canaris, the leader of the Abwehr, had been fired, that might mean that the entire set-up was disbanded. They all knew that Himmler had been gunning for the archaic secret service for the last two years, unhappy about how separate it was from the Nazi machine, and he might have won.

'Arrest?' someone asked. 'You're sure it says arrest? He's not ill, or on leave or something?'

'*Festnahme*,' Denys read out. 'That's arrest, no two ways about it.'

Leo sighed.

'I guess if we've had our suspicions that Canaris was turning a blind eye to some of the wilder stories we fed him, then his bosses may have had them too.'

'Well now they've acted on them, and with three months to D-Day. It's a potential disaster.'

'All our agents,' Steffie gasped.

She had to get onto Tar Robertson immediately. Every one of their double agents had an Abwehr handler who could be under suspicion too, and if they were replaced, then months – no, years – of careful trust-building could be thrown away overnight. Only last week at the Twenty Committee, Tar had reported that his agents were starting to drop hints about forces gathering in Kent to fit with the work David Strangeways' team from Shepperton were doing to create a smoke-and-mirrors camp and docking area. David even had the king lined up to 'inspect' it nearer to D-Day to add weight to the deception, but without Canaris's team, their careful house of cards might tumble down, leaving every Panzer in the Wehrmacht waiting for the Allied boys on the beaches of Normandy.

'What do we do?' she asked Denys.

'First thing – we don't panic. It might only be Canaris who's been nabbed and that could just as easily be a personal vendetta as an issue with the whole system. We'll need more Ultra to determine which. I'll go to Travis, get the wireless operators on double-time to pick up every bit of info on the airwaves, and I'm afraid it will be the same in here. Anyone with any leave planned for the next week, cancel it.'

Someone at the back groaned.

'Sorry,' Denys said, 'but there's an information war on and this is a potential ambush. Someone make tea, and let's go to work!'

Everyone went back to their desks and Leo went around collecting tea mugs and setting the kettle to boil in the smart kitchen area. Glancing across, Steffie smiled to see him frowning at the tealeaves as if trying to work them out but there was no time to waste being amused at the peculiarities of Americans. She followed Denys into his office.

'Can I use your telephone to call Tar, please, sir?'

'Of course, of course.'

Denys had finally spotted his spilled tea and was mopping at it with his handkerchief. Steffie lifted the receiver and asked for a line to St James's Street.

'Tar,' she said when he answered. 'I'm afraid we have a problem.'

The next few days went by in a blur. Tar Robertson arrived in Bletchley, looking dashing in the tartan trews of his uniform as a Highlander, but with deep worry lines across his handsome face.

'I have an agent in Lisbon at the moment,' he told Steffie. 'Her life could be in danger if the Nazis suspect a breach.'

Her life, Steffie noted and wondered who this woman was, out there spying on the Germans. It made simply reading their messages feel tame in comparison but then she remembered Fran telling Ailsa how she thought Valérie had gone to France because it felt more 'glamorous' than being stuck in Bletchley Park and told herself to get on with her job. This agent's life could hinge on what she read in Ultra, and so much more besides.

'We're getting no indication so far that the individual handlers are under suspicion,' she told him, 'but we're on high alert.'

'Thank you,' he sighed. 'I'll get her out as soon as I can and keep everything else flowing as normal. Well, pretend normal.'

He grimaced at Steffie, who nodded and went back to her decrypts. The news was not good. One by one they picked up reports of the cleaning out of a number of key staff in the Abwehr – all the old guard, who had come up under Canaris and spent the war living the good life while the men on the next rung down gathered intel. It was hard to tell from the crisp reports of their removal whether it was on grounds of ineptitude or corruption but either way it was a huge concern. The purge seemed to have been instigated by Heinrich Himmler, head of the SS, and all the signs pointed to him replacing the entire Abwehr with his own SD – Sicherheitsdienst – intelligence service, under the formidable Ernst Kaltenbrunner.

'We think it's a powerplay,' Steffie reported to the Twenty Committee. 'Himmler's hated the Abwehr for years because it's been out of his control, so he's reeling it in now. He's stripped out the top level but so far no sign of any changes further down.'

'It takes a long time to get a handler working well with an agent,' Tar said. 'They won't want to cut the link into all that intel, as long as they continue to believe their agents are genuine. We need to up the chickenfeed, give them a few provable truths to keep their credentials high.'

The committee swung into action and Steffie went back to Bletchley, her head whirling with secrets. She was finding it a struggle to distinguish fact from fiction these days. Tedder had returned from inspecting the frame of the First US Army Group – FUSAG – down in Kent and she'd actually asked him when the men would be arriving. He'd squinted at her and she'd covered her stupidity with what she'd hoped was a knowing wink and buried herself in her notes.

Back at Bletchley station, she turned her steps reluctantly towards the park. She'd barely seen Ailsa or her beautiful baby in the last two weeks and felt terrible about that, but at least they were both staying. Ailsa had moved into the farmhouse and Gloria seemed to be loving looking after Rowan in the day. Every time Steffie went through the yard, she saw nappies on the line or toys on the lawn, but these last few days she'd been out and back in the dark, with the energy only to fall into bed and sleep.

She showed the guard her pass on autopilot and let herself into Block G. Leo was at his desk and smiled at her as she slid into her own alongside him. She smiled back, glad of a friendly face.

'Long day?'

She nodded. 'And not over yet.'

'Only this lot to get through.'

He indicated a huge stack of papers and she groaned.

'Do you ever wish that once, just once, they could bungle the key at midnight and give us a day without new messages to catch up on the backlog?'

'Often,' he said. 'But then I remember that we'd all panic that the messages we were missing would be the ones that really counted.'

Steffie grimaced, thinking of the report of Canaris's arrest, coming in a run of perfectly ordinary decrypts.

'True. Heads down then, hey? I'll pop the kettle on before I start.'

'You Brits and your tea! I swear you need it more than oxygen.'

'It's our secret weapon!' she told him. 'Fancy one?'

'If it's all we've got.'

'I'm afraid it is.'

Tea mugs to hand they worked into the evening in compan-ionable silence. The weekly FHW report had come in and suggested that the loss of the top Abwehr people had not changed the German understanding – or, rather, misunder-standing – of the Allied positions and Steffie worked her way to the end of it, her neck knotted but her mind relieved.

'OK?' Leo asked as she stretched out her cramped muscles.

She grinned.

'I think so, though I'm never sure what this weird word of yours is?'

'OK? You know, fine, dandy.'

'Right. What does it stand for?'

He considered.

'I think it's all correct.'

'But that would be AC.'

'Not in the south – Ole Korrect,' he drawled in an exagger-ated accent and Steffie laughed.

'Whatever you say, Yank.'

'It'll catch on, Limey.'

She shook her head, unconvinced, and her stomach rumbled.

'I'm starving. Shall we go to the canteen?'

'Not sure I can face spam fritters,' Leo said. 'How about I buy you dinner down the pub?'

'Down the pub!' Steffie echoed, delighted with this British turn of phrase. 'You're going native, Leo.'

'Maybe. I'm certainly getting to like that ale of yours and would love a pint now. You?'

Steffie felt she should say no. There'd be talk if they went out to eat together but on the other hand, she *was* starving and a pie in the Dunscombe Arms sounded so much more enticing than fritters in the canteen.

'Sounds good, Leo. Thank you.'

It *was* good. Steffie suspected that the chef at the Dunscombe was being supplied by Alfie, or one of his poacher mates, as the pie was full of succulent meat.

'What is this?' Leo asked. 'Chicken?'

'Rabbit, I'd say.'

'Rabbit? Coney?'

'If that's what you want to call it. Tastes good, right?'

'Tastes great. My mom would love it. She's a country girl, grew up on a big farm out west. She goes back out there every summer – says she needs it to recharge her batteries after city life.' He smiled. 'She used to take us with her when we were kids. I loved it. Well, until the summer when...'

His face clouded and he drank deep of his ale, draining the glass and staring into it as if the past lurked in the dregs.

'Can you tell me what happened?' Steffie asked softly.

'It was a horse. It's always a horse! Mum was a brilliant rider, really brilliant. She could clear a fence like no one else I knew and she never fell off. Never. Well, until...' He swallowed and looked at Steffie. 'I don't tell many people about this.'

She put out a hand.

'You don't have to, Leo.'

'No, I'd like to. That is, it would be good to. There are so many people getting injured now, aren't there? So many young men will be going home with burns and breaks and missing limbs and it doesn't do to brush that under the carpet. Hell, our own president is in a wheelchair so disablement shouldn't be a taboo subject, should it?'

Steffie hadn't thought of it that way before, but it was an excellent point.

'You're still a person if your legs don't work, right?'

'Right! Or if your brain doesn't, for that matter. Sometimes I think about that poor kid that General Patton slapped in Sicily for having shell shock. He couldn't help it, could he, any more than he could have helped having an arm shot off? It's wrong to think some injuries are more worthy, more "manly".'

Steffie looked at Leo, his eyes lit up with the injustice of it, and felt newly intrigued by this surprisingly sensitive American. Not that Americans couldn't be sensitive, of course, that was simply another sort of prejudice.

'Tell me about your mother,' she urged.

He nodded, gathered himself.

'It was such an ordinary day, Steffie. She went out for a ride before breakfast, as she nearly always did. She loved the dawn. Still does, actually. She insisted on an east-facing apartment in New York so that she can see the sun come into their bedroom window the moment it's up. Anyway, that day everything was hunky-dory until she was heading home and came across a snake in the middle of the trail. Goddammed thing – 'scuse my language – bit the horse.' Steffie waved this away, intent on his story. 'The poor animal reared up in fright, so sudden and so high that even my mother couldn't control him, though she tried.'

'How do you know?' Steffie whispered.

He gulped.

'Because I saw it. I'd heard the hooves from my bedroom and run out of the yard to wave to her as she came back in. I saw her battle with that poor beast, but it was half-crazed with pain and fear and it threw her to the ground. Oh, Steffie, I ran then. I hollered for help and I ran so fast my legs near fell out from under me. She was on the ground, sprawled out. The horse had bolted but I didn't pay him one moment's attention. She was awake but her eyes were glassy.

'"Leo," she said. Just that, "Leo," and then the others were upon us and pushing me aside and telling her not to move, while I stood there watching and praying she wasn't going to die.'

'How old were you?'

'Nine.'

'Oh Leo!'

He gave her a watery smile.

'She didn't die. She told me later that there was no way she was going to die, not with me and my brother Alex to care for, but she'd fallen on a rock. It had cut into her right at the base of her spine, severed the nervous system, and there was no way she was going to walk again. Dad paid for the best doctors, but they all said the same – paralysed for life.'

'Only her legs though, Leo, right? Not her whole self.'

'Oh no! That stayed intact. At least, I used to catch her weeping sometimes, if I came on her unawares, but she'd always wipe her eyes and smile and pull me onto her knee. "I'm too big," I'd tell her. "I'll hurt you." And she'd say, "No you won't, Leo. Nothing will ever hurt me again."' She'd tap at her legs but I knew, even back then, that she meant more than that. The worst had happened and the only way was up.'

'She must be a brave woman.'

'She is. Brave and warm and funny. So funny. She likes to shock. Says everyone expects an invalid to be a nice, polite person and it's her mission to prove that they're as grumpy, rude and naughty as the rest of us.'

He laughed and Steffie laughed with him.

'I'd like to meet her.'

'I'd like you to, too.'

The laughter snagged. Steffie buried herself in her gin and lime and was relieved when the landlord rang out time.

'Last orders, ladies and gents, please. Last orders at the bar.'

'One for the road?' Leo suggested, but she shook her head.

'I think I'm too tired, sorry.'

'Me too. Long day.'

'And another ahead.'

'And another and another and another until we win this damned war.'

'And you can get back to your family.'

'Hmm.' Another pause, then, 'Come on, I'll walk you home.' He leaped up, offering his arm.

'You don't have to do that.'

'Oh, I do. It's late and my mother wouldn't approve of me leaving you to tread dark roads alone.'

'Well, if your mother wouldn't approve...'

He smiled and she took his arm, noticing a couple of looks thrown their way but not really caring. Leo was a warm, kind man and her friend. And, besides, it felt so nice to have his tall frame at her side as they walked back beneath the stars, his warmth shielding her from the March chill.

'Do you miss home?' she asked him as they turned up the lane to the farm.

'Oh yes. But I'm having a good time here too.' He coughed. 'Am I allowed to say that? There's a war on, after all.'

'All the more reason to seize what happiness is available, if you ask me.' She heard her own words echoing up against the farm and, confused, was glad to turn Leo in to the caravan. 'Here we are – home!'

'Your van is so neat.'

She laughed. 'Not with me in it, it isn't. I make a terrible mess.'

'No! Neat. You know: cool—' He grimaced. 'I mean, good – nice!'

'Oh. I see. You lot don't half talk some nonsense, you know, but thank you. I love it here.'

Steffie smiled at the funny van, remembering the first day she'd seen it from the field above, when she'd stormed out of her lodgings because her landlord had tried it on with her. It had looked like a refuge then, and it still did now. A light was burning behind the gingham curtains, most likely Fran working away on the articles she was now submitting regularly to the *Daily Mail*. Behind them, another clicked on in the window under the eaves of the solid old farmhouse and Steffie glanced up, imagining Ailsa heaving herself out of bed to tend to her daughter.

She looked back to Leo.

'This is my home now and I think it might be the best one I've ever had.'

He looked down at her, his face handsome in the light of the moon, his smile soft. Her arm was still in his, and she instinctively turned into him, warmed by the happy evening in his easy company. He was so close, so safe, and he was smiling at her so enticingly. Before she even knew what she was doing, she'd pushed herself up on to her tiptoes and brushed a kiss against his lips. His response was instant. His arm went around her, lightly caressing the small of her back as he kissed her, soft but sure, and she melted against him, feeling all her cares recede – the troubles at work, her friends' problems, her grief for...

Horrified, she pulled away.

'Oh, my goodness, I'm sorry. I'm so sorry. I didn't mean to do that.'

'I really didn't mind, Steffie.'

'No. I mean, thank you. But I'm not... I'm not free. That is, I'm not ready to be free. I'm not... Oh, I don't know.'

Leo stepped away, putting his hands up before him.

'I understand, Steffie. It's not a problem. We can be friends. We *are* friends, right?'

His voice was so gentle, so understanding.

'Of course we are,' she agreed. 'If you're... OK with that?'

He smiled.

'I'm A-OK, Steffie.'

'A-OK?'

'Don't ask. I've got no idea what it means either.' Then he was laughing and she was laughing too and blessing him for defusing her embarrassment with such ease. He gave her a little bow. 'Good night, Steffie.'

'Good night, Leo. And thank you.'

'Any day.'

Then he was gone, off into the night, and Steffie could only stand, one finger to her lips, and tell herself not to call him back and bury herself in his kisses.

'What are you doing, Stefania Carmichael?' she asked herself, but she could find no answers and instead dived into the caravan to bury her confusion in her pillow, at least until morning and her place at Leo's side once more.

TWENTY-SIX

APRIL 1944

Fran

Fran trudged out of Bletchley station, barely noticing the rain hammering down. Let it soak these horrible, black clothes into oblivion if it would. She'd gladly throw them out after today if she had to. She shivered at the memory of poor Gilberte, huddled into the front pew with her children either side of her, all three consumed by grief. The church had been filled with exuberant flowers from Easter, and their bright, happy colour had jarred against the sorrow of the bleak memorial service. There had been no coffin for Pierre Brossolette, no body to bury and it was perhaps a mercy they'd not had to see it for they all knew – though no one was saying it – that it would have been mangled with the worst forms of Nazi cruelty.

'Bastards,' Fran muttered into the rain.

Pierre's escape had been looking so promising. Fran had seen Gilberte in London two weeks ago when she'd taken a handful of articles up to Harmsworth, and she'd been more positive than Fran had seen her since her husband had been arrested.

'I've had word from Tommy,' she'd told her. 'Pierre is still in Rennes and they have a plan to get him out. I don't know what, but something to do with a laundry girl.'

Fran's heart had jerked at the thought that girl might be Valérie, but then told herself that was nothing to do with her any more. What had mattered was getting Pierre free, not who did it. But that hadn't happened either. Some wireless operator had let it slip across the airwaves that the glorious Pedro had been captured and that had put the SS on high alert. It had not taken them long to track down all recent prisoners and identify Pierre in Rennes.

He'd been marched straight off to the dreaded Gestapo HQ in Avenue Foch, the infamous torture chamber where Jean Moulin had died last year. No one knew what exactly had happened to Gilberte's poor husband but they'd all heard enough tales to be racked by imaginings. He had not caved, however, and several days after being thrown in there, he had thrown himself out, via a sixth-floor window. He'd been buried the next day in a quiet ceremony that no one had dared attend in the Cimetière du Père Lachaise. His grave had apparently been simply marked but by dawn the next day it had been covered in a mountain of flowers. That, at least, had been a comfort to Gilberte, if no substitute for the man himself.

Even worse, they'd had news yesterday that Tommy had been captured too, taken at Passy railway station while trying to meet a contact. He, like Pierre at first, seemed to have convinced his captors of his fake ID and did not, at least, have a treacherous lock of hair to betray him, but things looked bleak. Fran wondered if Valérie was regretting her decision to head into the bosom of the Resistance and then told herself off, again, for thinking about her.

Perhaps it is better, in wartime, not to love at all.

How often she'd heard those words in her head, spoken in Valérie's melting French accent. They were right, of course, and

Fran was doing her best to pay attention to them, but it wasn't easy and sometimes she felt like a torturer was wringing her deepest feelings out of her bit by painful bit.

She threw off the ugly simile and reached for the caravan door. It was unlocked and, as she pulled it open, she heard the comforting sound of singing. Ailsa was crooning some lilting Scottish tune to Rowan who was sitting in a high-chair at the table, bashing out time with a spoon.

'Hello,' she said from the doorway and they both turned.

Rowan let out a welcoming gurgle and Ailsa a gasp.

'You poor thing, you're soaked. Was it terrible?'

'Terrible,' Fran confirmed.

'Come in, come in.'

'I'll drip everywhere.'

'It's only water. Golly, if you worried about that where I come from, no one would ever get inside. Here.' She pulled a towel out of the bathroom and thrust it at Fran. 'Get those horrible wet clothes off and wrap yourself up. I'll run a bath. Rowan could do with a wash anyway.' She indicated the little girl who was, as usual, coated in a happy mixture of food and mud. 'You can share the water.'

Fran began obediently stripping off her hated black layers, enjoying the sensation of being mothered by her friend.

'What are you doing over here, Ails?'

'Gloria and Alfie have friends for tea, so I thought I'd make myself – and madam here – scarce. It's so kind of them to share their home with me, but they need a break sometimes. Besides, I miss the caravan!'

'It misses you.'

Ailsa smiled and grabbed the laundry basket.

'Clothes in here. I'll rinse them out in the farmhouse later.'

Fran surrendered them gladly, wrapped herself in the towel, and went to sit opposite Rowan, who offered her a squashed raisin by way of greeting.

'Thank you, Ro-Ro.'

Gloria's nickname had stuck and they all called her it now, even Ailsa. The girl's favourite nursery rhyme was 'Row-row-row-your-boat' and Fran often woke up with its jaunty tune going round and round in her head. Still, there were worse things to wake up to.

She forced herself to smile at her god-daughter. They hadn't actually had the christening yet – Ailsa wanted to wait for Ned to be back, and for her parents to make it south, so it was likely to be a while – but she and Steffie didn't need a priest's say-so to look on Rowan as their special charge. She sat opposite her, pulling a silly face that made her giggle and, by default, pulled a smile onto Fran's face as well.

'Bath's ready!' Ailsa called. 'Take all the time you want, Fran. Rowan only has it lukewarm anyway.'

Fran gave Ailsa a grateful smile and slid into the bathroom. Curling her long limbs into the tiny bath, she let the warm water seep into her chilled skin and willed it to reach her equally chilled heart.

'I heard from one of my old colleagues up at Whaddon Hall today,' Ailsa called through the half-open door.

'Oh, yes?'

'Big lad called Reggie. He's from Yorkshire but it turns out his mother was French and he was brought up bilingual.'

'Right.'

'It's useful that, these days, isn't it?'

Fran swallowed.

'It is. How did you hear from him?'

'I'm in communication with a number of radio operators in the er, in the field.'

Fran's ears picked up.

'The field?'

Ailsa came closer to the door.

'France,' she said, low-voiced.

'I see.' Fran lifted the sponge, letting warm drops fall slowly onto her knees where they protruded from the water. 'Anywhere in particular in France?'

Ailsa coughed awkwardly. Even in their own caravan, far from prying ears, they'd all been conditioned to keep absolute secrecy about their work.

'Let's just say, he's not so very far away.'

'Right.'

It had to be the north then. Normandy maybe. Bayeux even.

'He says he's glad to have someone he knows on the other end of the line. And that he's been partnered with someone else he knows from before too. From the, er, the Drunken Arms. A woman.' She peeked her head around the door. 'A French woman.'

'Valérie?' Fran gasped.

Ailsa put up her hands.

'I don't know, Fran. It's all codenames.'

'Of course.'

'Reggie is Celine, after his mother, and his partner – his partner is Elodie.'

Fran dropped the sponge. It landed with a splat on the bathroom floor and, in the other room, Rowan giggled. Elodie! The name of Valérie's revered grand-mère, the one whose exploits in the Great War and, it seemed, in this one, had scratched at Valérie's pride until the only way to soothe it had been to parachute back into France. Surely that couldn't be a coincidence?

'Fran? Are you all right? Should I have told you?'

Fran reached for the sponge.

'I'm good, Ailsa, thank you. And yes, you should definitely have told me. It's good to know she's safe whatever...'

Her sentence ran out of steam as fast as the bathwater was doing and, with a last trickle of water over her aching head, she heaved herself out to make way for Rowan. If Valérie was with this Reggie then at least she hadn't been captured and wasn't being tortured by the Gestapo.

She pictured Gilberte at the front of the church, her elegant form crumpled by grief, and counted this small blessing. Then she remembered that even if Valérie had been killed, she would not be at the front of her funeral – not because society didn't like it, but because Valérie herself had chosen to walk away from her.

Perhaps it is better, in wartime, not to love at all.

'It is,' Fran said sternly, wrapping herself in the towel again. 'It definitely is.' But, even so, she couldn't help feeling that bit better for knowing that the wild French girl who had trapped her heart was alive and well in France.

At least until D-Day.

TWENTY-SEVEN

APRIL 1944

Ailsa

Ailsa tapped out the sign-off on her latest message and waited for the return signal to tell her it had been received. She closed her eyes, trying to picture the operator, crouched somewhere in France, running their set out of an attic, or a barn, or the heart of a forest. They were so brave, those people, carrying around their radio sets in a suitcase. If they were stopped and a German soldier found it, they would be captured as a spy. That was bad news, for spies, unlike soldiers, were not covered by the Geneva convention, so could be arrested and slipped into the enemy prison system – never to emerge again. Or, at least, not alive.

Ailsa pictured Reggie, once a big, blunt Yorkshire wireless operator in Whaddon Hall and now working as 'Celine' in occupied territory, running the gauntlet of German malice every day. She only hoped Valérie could keep him safe; and he, her. Fran always shut down any attempt at talking about 'Elodie' but Ailsa knew she'd been glad to hear that she was with Reggie and she kept dropping in hints about how they were doing, however blankly they were received.

For herself, she had to admit that she was enjoying her work at Whaddon Hall. She'd sent a telegram to her parents telling them she was staying in Bletchley, and then managed to speak to them on the North Uist post office telephone. It had cost a fortune but been worth every penny to hear their dear voices, and Rowan had even gurgled out a happy laugh for her far-away grandparents. The quicker the war was won, the sooner they could all be together and Ailsa was working harder than ever.

Gambier-Parry had promoted her to sergeant, putting her at a higher security clearance, so she got to find out more about the Morse she was sending and receiving. This was not the tangled workings of Enigma, but direct messages into agents in the field. The system ran on a relatively simple book cipher so Ailsa could render code into plain text and vice versa. It meant that for the first time, other than perhaps when Ned had picked up references to Gute Quelle in Malta last year, Ailsa actually knew the content of her messages, and that gave them so much more meaning.

```
Supplies urgently needed. Guns and ammo.

Plan scheduled midnight, Tuesday 23rd.
Stand by.

Operator captured. Shutting down
network. Resume when safe.
```

All these spoke of a war being fought in the forests and fields of France, right under the noses of the Germans, and every moment that Ailsa was at work, she felt she was alongside them. She knew all their call signs and could recognise most of their fists – their own style of operating the Morse key. It made her feel close to the action but, on the flip side, if a message came in reporting someone hurt or captured, she felt as if a friend had been lost. She dreaded the day that friend was either Reggie or Valérie, but so far they were doing well.

Valérie's group, centred around a bicycle shop in Bayeux that Fran said was run by her grandmother, was very active, and very effective. The other day they had blown up a key railway line, right at the time when a German supply train had been running along it. The train had toppled, damaging five armoured vehicles, and the line was wrecked. It would take weeks to get it going again, especially as most of the work gang in the area was made up of secret *résistants*. Why the Germans thought their captives would do a good job for them was anyone's guess and she could only suppose they believed that everyone operated on fear which, thankfully, wasn't true.

'Ailsa – my office please. Now.'

Ailsa jumped to it, feeling instantly guilty. Had word somehow got back to her boss that she'd been dropping hints to Fran about the welfare of agents? But when she entered, she was relieved to see he was smiling.

'Sit down, sit down. All good? Going well? Your baby is, you know... going well?'

Ailsa suppressed a smile.

'It's all going well, thank you, sir, yes. My landlady—'

'Good, good. That's what we like to hear. You're a pioneer, Ailsa.'

'Er, thank you, sir.'

Ailsa wasn't sure she wanted to be a pioneer but if it was what was needed to do her job, then she'd take it.

'You'll recall I mentioned something to you about a listening station in BP?'

'Yes, sir, of course.'

'Well, I'm glad to say that we've been given the go-ahead. Clearly there's a certain risk to sticking bloody great aerials in the centre of the park, but we figure the Germans will be too busy monitoring the Channel to worry about flying reconnaissance all the way up here, so it's full steam ahead.'

'That's excellent news, sir. Our own SLU.'

'Quite. No use breaking codes and then sitting on our academic arses congratulating ourselves, is there?'

'Er, no, sir.'

'Getting information to the front line, that's the key, and the less loops in that particular chain, the better, especially when it comes to D-Day.'

Ailsa swallowed. Easter had been and gone, with its promise of renewal and new beginnings – a promise that was starting to ring false after nearly five years of war but that might, this year, carry some weight. That was only, however, if D-Day worked and the beachheads were established. It could just as easily all go wrong and the men could be driven back in another Dunkirk, leaving the Allies weakened and Germany in the ascendancy. And then what? Ailsa wasn't sure the country could take much longer at war, and she certainly couldn't. It *had* to work.

'I'm sure speedy comms will be vital, sir,' she said, wondering where this was going.

'Exactly, and that's where some, ah, lively discussion, has taken place. The upshot of it is that the naval snobs are insisting on bringing in some damned ratings from Scarborough to run the sets.'

'Oh.'

Disappointment surged through Ailsa.

'But I've said I want one of my own running their ship.'

'Very wise.'

'Glad you think so. We're understood then?'

Ailsa cleared her throat.

'We are? That's to say, sir, I'm not. What is it you want me to do?'

'Oh. Did I not say? I want you in charge, lass. I want you making sure the ship sails smoothly.'

'Me?' She gaped at him.

'Yes, you,' he said impatiently. 'You keep telling me you're up to the job, so prove it.'

She stood to attention.

'Yes, sir. I will, sir.'

'Good. There are a lot of men counting on us; let's do them proud.'

'Yes, sir!'

Ailsa burst out of Gambier-Parry's office feeling as if she'd grown at least two inches. This was unbelievable. Wait until she told Ned, he'd be so... She stopped herself. She couldn't tell Ned, not yet, but later, when they'd won and he was home and they were tucked into their country cottage with Rowan and any brothers or sisters who might follow, then she'd tell him.

Ailsa hugged herself. The details of this future rural idyll were hazy but the outline shape was clear. Well, clear-ish. Her parents, she knew, would be desperate to have them up in North Uist. They'd assured her on the phone that they would try and get south for a visit, but their choice of wording had been careful. They would never move away from North Uist, but there would be no work there for Ned. Perhaps they could settle somewhere between his family in Manchester and hers up past Glasgow? She had no idea where that might be and resolved to look at a map as soon as possible, but for now a listening station at BP seemed enough to wrap her head around and she went back to her set glowing with pride.

Later, shift done, she made for the farmhouse, desperate to get her hands on Rowan. She loved her job but, oh, she missed her daughter and she all but ran into the yard. The kitchen door stood open, a couple of hens attempting a cheeky raid, and Ailsa made for it, then stopped as she heard a babble of voices from within. They were high-pitched with panic and fear shot through her.

'Rowan!' She scrambled inside. 'Is it Rowan? Is she ill?'

'It's not Rowan.'

Fran came towards her, Ailsa's daughter in her arms, and Ailsa gathered her up, drinking in the baby scent of her.

'Thank God.' But then she looked past Rowan, to the back of the kitchen, where Gloria was rocking in a most un-Gloria-like way and a doctor was bending over a figure prostrate on the flagstones. 'Alfie?' she choked out. 'Is he...?'

'Not dead, no, but he's in trouble, Ails. He got his foot caught in a damned trap. Seems there's a new gang trying their luck in the woods and Alfie was taken by surprise by one of their devices. It's not pretty, not pretty at all. There's an ambulance on the way.'

'Oh no, poor Alfie.'

Fran nodded.

'Gloria's beside herself. The poor man dragged himself to the road, trap in place around his ankle and dripping blood with every step. Got picked up there by a staff car – someone visiting Travis – and brought back here. They wanted to take him straight to the hospital but he wasn't having any of it. Said his Gloria would sort him out.'

Ailsa looked in horror at the tableau at the back of the room.

'Is it still on him then? That must be agony.'

'No. Gloria flipped the catch and pulled it apart with her own hands. Must have taken nerves of steel, but she did it. Been a wreck ever since, mind you. I got back to find her cramming sheets around the wound and screaming for help. I fetched the doctor straight away and I think he's staunched the bleeding but it's touch and go if he'll lose his foot.'

'Poor Alfie,' Ailsa said again, but now Steffie came running into the kitchen.

'What the hell is going on? There's an ambulance in the lane.'

'Thank God!' Gloria pushed past her and went scrambling out, shouting, 'Here! In here!'

Steffie looked to Fran and Ailsa in confusion.

'Alfie's hurt his foot,' Ailsa said.

'All but chopped it off more like,' Fran provided.

'Hush!'

Gloria was rushing back in, clasping at Alfie's hand and murmuring to him. It was almost comic until the doctor got up to usher the medics inside, and they saw their poor, kind, mischievous landlord lying on the kitchen floor looking drained of colour and as old as the hills. Gloria clutched at him as the men went to manoeuvre the stretcher into place and one of them had to physically prise her off for access. Steffie rushed forward and enveloped the landlady in her arms.

'We've got you, Gloria. We've got you safe.'

'It's not me that matters,' she shot back, wild-eyed. 'It's Alfie. It's my Alfie. I have to go with him.' She looked at the girls. 'They will let me go with him, won't they?'

'Of course they will,' Steffie said. 'Let them get him loaded up and you can step inside too.'

'Will it cost me?'

'I'll pay,' Steffie said immediately. 'Don't you worry about that.'

She fumbled in her purse for notes, then they all stood aside for the medics to edge the stretcher through the busy kitchen. As they paused to negotiate the door, Alfie opened his eyes.

'Don't worry, sweetheart,' he murmured to his wife. 'It's only a poaching injury. Happens to the best of us. I'll be right as...' But his words were cut off in a yelp of pain as the men had to lift the stretcher over the doorframe and Ailsa winced.

'Poor Alfie,' she said for a third time, holding Rowan close.

Gloria rushed forward, determined not to miss the ambulance, and it was only once she was in, holding Alfie's hand again, that she calmed. Looking out at them as the medics made sure her husband was secure, she drew in a wobbly breath.

'Will you keep an eye on the house for me?'

'Of course,' Ailsa agreed. 'You can count on us, Gloria.'

'And I'm sorry but I won't be able to have the little one tomorrow. Or, or...'

'Don't worry about it for one moment, Gloria,' Ailsa said, because she had to, didn't she?

Alfie was Gloria's number one priority right now and the small matter of her own childcare was nothing next to that. Well, nothing for Gloria at least. For Ailsa, however...

'All going well?' Gambier-Parry had asked her earlier and she'd confidently told him that it was. How wrong she'd been. Now D-Day was on the horizon and her boss was calling her a pioneer and trusting her with a huge role, but that looked in doubt unless she could, somehow, find someone to care for her daughter. And fast.

TWENTY-EIGHT

APRIL 1944

Steffie

Steffie peered out of the window of the caravan and across to the farmhouse. It was her day off and she'd promised Ailsa she'd look after Rowan so she could go into work, but she was awake early so had time for a quiet cup of tea first. The news from the hospital yesterday had, thank heavens, been good. Alfie's leg was badly damaged but he wouldn't lose his foot, just a lot of time with it kept up high while it healed.

Gloria, home to fetch him some things, had been babbling away about how grumpy he was about it and her relief had flooded through every complaint and eye-roll. Steffie had felt as if she'd been looking at true love. Not fancy engagement parties, or glamorously posed couples but real, deep care for the person with whom you shared your life. She was so glad Alfie would recover.

With a sigh, she stared at her diamond ring, glinting in the morning sunshine flooding through the window. She'd written to Matteo's family offering to return the heirloom, but they'd replied kindly that it was hers to do with as she wished, leaving her in a conundrum. She was starting to feel like a fraud wearing it. After all, Matteo was dead now, so she wasn't actually engaged, but in her heart she still felt it. Indeed, in her heart, especially first thing in the morning, she still felt as if Matteo wasn't dead at all but living it up in Rome, waiting for a plane back to her. Realising that wasn't so was always painful.

Twisting her hand, she watched the light glint through the prism, sending a rainbow onto the table. It was such a pretty pattern, so hopeful, but Steffie was out of hope right now. Or was she? She felt a guilty prickle across her skin at the memory of kissing Leo last week. For that brief moment when she'd reached up and pressed her lips to his, it had felt so right, so wonderful. But then she'd felt his arm around her and sensed his body, taller than Matteo's, and his scent, more crisp and citrusy than her fiancé's, and felt like a cheat. Another twist of the ring sent the rainbow onto the ceiling. She wasn't a cheat, she knew that in her head, but it didn't stop the guilt.

Turning from the window to put the kettle on, her eye caught the can of condensed milk sitting on the side. Leo had brought it for her the morning after the kiss. He'd explained it away as 'a little something they were handing out from stores', but she'd known it was a form of peace offering and accepted it gratefully. Taking the saucer off the top, she dipped a teaspoon into the deliciously sweet goo and let it tingle across her tongue. A simple pleasure, but you had to take them these days. She bet Rowan would love this, she thought wickedly. Her mother probably wouldn't approve but it wouldn't hurt to have a treat from her Auntie Steffie.

She took another small spoonful and put the saucer back on before she ate the lot. Even in wartime it didn't hurt to watch your figure; she was a single woman now, after all. She put a hand to her ring and tugged. It moved up her finger but stuck at the knuckle, refusing to be taken off.

'What use are you to me?' Steffie demanded of it, cross suddenly. 'All you do is remind me of what I've lost.'

'Talking to yourself Stef?' Fran asked, emerging from the bedroom, half-dressed. 'Ooh, is that the kettle? Lovely.' She moved to make tea and then stopped and looked at Steffie. 'Steffie? Is something wrong?'

'Is something right?' Steffie shot back, then shook her head. 'Sorry – got out the wrong side of bed this morning.'

'You're wondering whether to take your ring off?' Steffie stared at her and she shrugged. 'It doesn't take a mind reader to see you fiddling with it. You do it a lot, you know.'

'I do?' Steffie gave it another tug and it shifted up onto her knuckle, pulling the skin with it. She pushed it back down. 'Do you think I should take it off, Fran?'

Fran considered.

'The easy answer is, I think you should take it off if you want to, but I guess you know that already. The question is, do you want to?'

'Exactly! And I don't know the answer. Is that stupid?'

Fran shook her head.

'Not in the slightest.' She sighed. 'I have a locket. Valérie sent me it for Christmas, but with no card or anything, so I don't know what she meant by it – or whether to put it on. It's been in my chest under the bed ever since.'

She looked so forlorn that Steffie threw her arms around her.

'Look at us pair! One with jewellery we can't take off and the other with some they can't put on!'

Fran nodded.

'Pathetic, right? I guess, at the end of the day, it's only jewellery. It doesn't actually change how we feel, or what we do, does it?'

Steffie smiled.

'Well put, Miss Morgan – you should be a writer.'

'Here's hoping!'

Fran winked at her and set to making the teas, so Steffie went back to the window. Fran was absolutely right, and in one determined move, she tugged the diamond off her finger. It looked bare without it but she felt lighter, less fraudulent. Her love for Matteo was still strong but she was no longer bound to him by anything but memories and she felt better not hiding from that. The only thing now was, what did she do with the ring?

Across the yard, the farmhouse door opened and Ailsa slid out with Rowan in her arms.

'Best make a third tea, Fran,' Steffie said, waving to her.

'Coming right up.'

Steffie ran to open the door as Fran set three steaming mugs on the table and they all sat down together, letting out a collective aah of pleasure. Rowan looked round at them, perturbed, and they laughed, which only confused the little girl further.

'Hey, look,' Steffie said, holding up the ring to the light and letting it play its rainbow onto the table again. Rowan's eyes widened and she reached out to try and catch the colours. Steffie moved the ring and the rainbow danced. Rowan was entranced.

'You've taken it off,' Ailsa said softly.

Steffie nodded.

'It's time.'

'That's good then. Not that you have to do it,' she added hastily, 'but that you feel ready.'

'I'm not sure I do. But, then, I'm not sure I ever will so best just to get on, right?'

'One foot in front of the other and one day you'll be walking freely again.'

'Like Alfie?'

Ailsa grimaced.

'Poor man. He's going to hate having to sit still all the time.'

'Better that than lose his leg,' Fran said.

'Life, hey,' Steffie said, 'a series of choices between two rubbish options.'

Ailsa looked at Fran, who smiled.

'Someone got out the wrong side of her bed this morning.'

'It's true though,' Steffie said. 'Ailsa had to choose between her husband and her baby, you've had to choose between chasing Valérie down or doing your own thing, and I've had to choose between losing myself in grief for Matteo or getting on with life without him. Always a compromise. What's so wrong with wanting it all?'

Ailsa put out a hand and squeezed her shoulder.

'You've got us, Stef,' she said.

'You've always got us,' Fran added.

Steffie looked from one to the other, her eyes filling with tears, though they were not the usual, smarting kind but something softer, more cleansing.

'I've got you,' she agreed. 'My sisters.'

She put a hand on the table and the others covered it with theirs, a pyramid of care. With a delighted chuckle, Rowan reached out and patted her own tiny one on top and suddenly Steffie knew what to do.

'Here,' she handed the ring to Rowan. 'It's yours, baby.'

Rowan took it delightedly, then went to put it straight into her mouth.

'No!' they all said as one, pulling it back.

'Stupid of me,' Steffie said, laughing. 'You take it for her, Ails. Keep it till she's old enough.'

'No way.' Ailsa shook her head. 'You can't give her that, Steffie. It's yours.'

'It was. And now it's hers. I'm her godmother, right – one of them – so this is her christening gift. Every girl needs a diamond and I'm delighted to give our girl her first one.'

'Well then, thank you, Steffie. She's honoured.' Rowan reached keenly out for the ring and they all laughed. Ailsa held it over her head. 'Don't get too attached, sweetie, I might have to pawn it to pay for childcare. Gloria's going to be far too busy with Alfie laid up to have you for a week or two, and if I duck out now, Gambier-Parry will give my job to someone else.'

'Something will turn up,' Fran said. 'Now come on, I know we're early but how about we head to BP anyway and show Rowan the ducks before work?'

Rowan was delighted with the ducks, leaning out of her perambulator to wave excitedly at them, though she stuffed the bread Steffie handed her into her own mouth, much to the birds' indignation.

'Are you sure about the diamond?' Ailsa asked, looping her arm through Steffie's as Fran showed the little girl how to feed them.

'Utterly sure. It only makes me miserable, so far better it goes to a good home.'

'Then thank you, really. Wait till I tell Ned his daughter has a diamond already!' Her face fell. 'A letter will take forever to reach him.'

'At least you *can* reach him,' Fran said. 'Valérie is completely out of contact, even if I wanted to reach her.'

'And Matteo is dead,' Steffie added.

Fran pulled a face.

'Fine, you win the "who's most miserable stakes",' she said.

They stood in a row, staring into the murky water, and then someone came running out of Block A with a rounders bat. Suddenly people were collecting on the lawn, putting down jumpers for bases and calling friends over for a pre-shift game.

'Yanks versus Limeys,' Harry Hinsley cried, and the group obediently shuffled itself into two.

There were more Yanks and Harry looked around and spotted the three of them.

'Hey, girls, we need you!'

Fran stood up.

'You're on!' She looked to the others. 'Come on.'

'What about Rowan?' Ailsa asked.

'She'll be fine in her pram, watching. She'll love it.'

Steffie looked over and saw Leo in the Yanks team.

'I'm not sure, Fran. I'm not dressed for sport.'

Fran raised an eyebrow and Steffie had to concede that the slacks and shirt she'd put on for a day looking after Rowan were perfect for sport.

'It'll do you good, Stef – run off some of that grump.'

'She's right,' Ailsa agreed, getting up and positioning Rowan's pram under a tree, safe from flying balls. 'Come on – it'll do us all good.'

And it did. The Yanks won the toss and went into bowl first. Steffie took up her position behind the others and watched Ailsa fluff her shot but dart off for first base before the backstop could retrieve the ball to dob her out. Fran followed and whacked it far across the park, scampering all the way round like a pro, the rest of the 'Limeys' cheering her wildly in.

When it was her turn, Steffie gripped the bat and faced Eugene, the self-appointed bowler. He pulled his arm back and she focused hard, swinging her bat at the ball as if she might hit all her troubles out with it. It connected with a sweet thwack and went sideways, not as far as she had hoped but far enough to set the fielders scrambling. She darted for first base, stopping there, but the fielder's throw to second went wide and, as the ball bounced across the grass, she was off again, her feet flying, round second, round third...

'Go, Steffie!' she heard her team calling and, panting now,

she made for fourth. The fielder threw, the man on fourth leaped to catch it, and she sprinted past with a split second to spare.

'Yay!'

Steffie bent over, drawing in breath as her team patted her on the back. It felt brilliant. Fran was right – this was chasing her grump away and she took her place in the field with a new spring in her step.

Leo was first up and he gripped the bat with a grimace.

'It's mighty thin, this limey bat.'

'Because we're more skilful than you lot,' Harry told him, lining up to bowl. 'Take that!'

But Leo did, slicing the ball to the left, into one of the bushes around the pond. Steffie and Fran dived to fetch it but it was well and truly tangled in the branches and Leo was able to lope round easily before they could scrabble it out.

'Nice technique!' she cried, finally throwing it back to Harry.

'Not quite cricket, as you lot say, but, hey, this is baseball.'

'Rounders,' Steffie corrected him, laughing. 'This is rounders.'

It didn't take long for the rest of the Yanks to take their turn and soon Eugene was stepping up for the last go. The Limeys, if Steffie had counted correctly, were ahead at 4 ½ to 4, so if they could stop him scoring even a half-rounder they'd win. She crouched down, ready, as Harry prepared to bowl. Eugene swung fiercely at the flying ball, but missed it, sending himself spinning comically.

'First base!' Steffie screamed at the backstop but Ailsa, on that base, was distracted by a cry from Rowan and missed the throw.

Eugene skipped past and on for second. Fran dived in, scooping up the loose ball to send it straight to fourth. Steffie ran in as backup behind Walter Ettinghausen, but he caught it with a sure hand and dobbed the base just as Eugene passed third. The Limeys went wild, running in on Walter and jumping around celebrating as if this was the World Cup. Steffie danced with the rest, feeling joy flood through her, and it was only when someone said, 'What do they think they're doing?' that she realised the American team was celebrating too.

She went across.

'You know we won, right?'

Leo stepped out of the group.

'You didn't. We won. You only got two home runs and we got three.'

'Rounders,' Steffie corrected. 'And that's true, but you only got two half-rounders and we got five.'

He stared at her blankly.

'Half rounders?'

'Yes, you know, when you get round in more than one? No? Oh, it doesn't matter. Let's both win, shall we?'

'Let's,' he agreed. 'High five!' He held out a hand and she stared at it, confused. He shook his head. 'You limeys have got a lot to learn. Like this.' He took her wrist, holding her hand up and enthusiastically slapping his own against it. 'Get it?'

Steffie nodded, dumbly. She got it. What she didn't get was why his hand around her wrist felt so enticing. Could she? Could they? No. She wasn't ready and, besides, he was American. He had funny phrases, strange gestures and, most importantly of all, he'd be heading back over the Atlantic the moment this war was done. Even considering it was foolishness.

'Good game,' she managed weakly and then turned and fled Leonard D'Angelo for the safety of her friends.

'I declare a draw,' Harry said, laughing when Steffie explained. 'And now, it's back to work, folks. The next game is the big one, but at least we're both on the same side for that.'

Steffie's heart squeezed and she took in the idyllic scene of Bletchley Park in springtime. No one would know, looking around the daisy-strewn lawn and the ducks on the pond, that in these blocks thousands of people were hunkered over plans for the mud and blood of the battlefield ahead. It was time for her, Fran and Ailsa, to sort out their own problems and get to work. D-Day was a month away and it deserved all their focus.

TWENTY-NINE

MAY 1944

Ailsa

Ailsa stood in the farmhouse door, peeping on the scene within in astonishment. She'd pushed the pram a long way around the lanes of Bletchley, trying to stride out her frustration while her daughter slept; had she perhaps overdone it?

She'd cobbled together childcare for the last three days with help from her friends and one of the lovely older operatives up at Whaddon, but today she'd had no choice but to take time off. Gambier-Parry had not been happy and had made it clear that if she didn't sort something official, she wouldn't be running the new listening station for D-Day. She'd walked miles, trying to think of a solution, but surely not far enough to start hallucinating?

Alfie was propped up in what had become his usual corner, heavily bandaged foot up on a stool, with Gloria opposite him at the kitchen table, chopping vegetables. That, at least, was normal, but between them, hands round mugs of tea and looking perfectly at home, were Ailsa's parents.

'Ma?' she stuttered. 'Pa?'

They leaped up, chairs clattering, and ran to her.

'Ailsa! Oh, my wee girl!' Mirren threw her arms around Ailsa. 'You look well. Doesn't she look well, Hamish?'

'She looks well,' he agreed, leaning in to kiss her cheek. 'Motherhood suits you, lassie.'

'The bairn!' Mirren cried. 'Where's the bairn?'

Ailsa laughed.

'Don't worry, Ma, I haven't mislaid her yet. She's right here.'

She stepped outside to unclip Rowan's reins and present her to her grandparents. They stared at her in near-reverent hush, then Mirren took a step forward.

'Hello,' she said softly.

Rowan put out a hand and touched her face.

'Meet your granny, Rowan,' Ailsa said.

Rowan gave a happy chuckle.

'May I?' Mirren asked Ailsa, holding out her own hands.

'Of course,' Ailsa said. 'Oh, Ma, of course you may.'

She handed Rowan over and Mirren took her with tears in her eyes.

'Look, Hamish – our wee grandbabbie.'

'She's a fine bairn, to be sure,' he said, also looking emotional. 'Just like her mother.'

He gave Ailsa another kiss and then bent down to talk to Rowan, babbling at her in a way that made Ailsa's heart fill up. She thought back to four years ago, when she'd left North Uist with her parents cursing her wilfulness and was unutterably glad that they had forgiven her and that she could bring them the joy of a grandchild. They were getting old, there was no denying it. Hamish's hair and beard were purest white and Mirren looked stooped and small but as they chattered to Rowan, the years seemed to fall away before Ailsa's eyes.

'How did you get here?' she asked.

Hamish glanced over.

'Oh, you know, boat, train, another train. It wasn't so hard.'

Ailsa hid a smile. Her parents had never been further south than Glasgow before they'd come to Bletchley for her wedding at the start of last year, but now they were sounding like professional travellers.

'And are you staying?' she asked hopefully.

'If we can get a room, we'd like to, aye.'

'A room?' Gloria said indignantly.

Hamish turned to her.

'Is there a pub, perhaps, or a boarding house?'

Gloria put her hands on her hips.

'I'll not have you staying in a pub.'

Hamish looked at her uncertainly.

'You, er, you don't take drink?'

Ailsa burst out laughing.

'Oh, I think we can safely say that they take drink, Pa. Alfie makes the best gin in England.'

'Then?'

'We don't send family looking for rooms,' Gloria said firmly. 'You'll stay here, with us.'

Mirren looked at her, wide-eyed.

'Are you sure? I mean, do you have room?'

'We'll make room,' Gloria said. 'We're sleeping in the sitting room anyway, because Alfie can't get up the stairs with his fool foot, so our bedroom's free. We've taken the mattress down, but we can get the two off the top bunks in the caravan and lash them together. It'll be rough-and-ready but if you don't mind that, you're very welcome.'

'Oh!' Mirren gasped, looking as if she might hug Gloria too now. 'You're so kind. Our Ailsa's really landed on her feet here. It does me good to know she's so well cared for. And the bairn too.'

Gloria pulled a face.

'I promised I'd care for our Rowan while Ailsa was at work but I've been struggling since the accident. There's so much to do on the farm and a lot of the jobs are too dangerous to have a little 'un around, so...'

'So it's a good job we're here,' Mirren said, firm in her turn. 'My Hamish is a dab hand with a job and I'm sure between us, thee and me can cope with the bairn and your husband.'

'I'm not totally useless,' Alfie objected. 'I can check a still.'

'Ever tried making whisky?' Hamish asked him, and he grinned.

'Never, but I'm always up for a new challenge. How does it work?'

Ailsa stood there and watched, amazed, as Mirren sat down with Gloria, Rowan on her knee, and Hamish pulled his chair closer to Alfie to describe the process of making his beloved whisky. It was a noisy, cosy, happy scene and, best of all, there was no place for Ailsa in it.

'Anyone mind if I go to work?' she asked and, getting an easy wave of assent from all parties, she blew Rowan a kiss goodbye, spun on her heel and made for Bletchley Park. It looked like she was back in the nick of time.

THIRTY

MAY 1944

Fran

Fran stared at the report Steffie had handed her.

'Have you read this, Stef?'

'Of course. Not bad, hey?'

'Amazing.'

Fran scanned the two-page document. It was an itinerary for the visit of a high-ranking German officer to the Panzer-armee headquarters in northern France and provided very handy details about where they were located. The Germans might as well have sent them a map.

She went over to the wall of Room 149, checking off the HQs already marked against this list. They weren't far off, but there were at least two corrections where the unit had presumably been moved. She pulled out the first pin and repositioned it and Steffie watched.

'This is amazing, Fran.' She pointed to the postcards taped all around the edges, linked with string to the relevant sections of beach. 'Did you do all this?'

'With help.'

Fran looked at Steffie, glad her friend had clearance for the room. It was such a relief to be able to talk about work after several years of tiptoeing around.

'Do you think it's accurate?' Steffie asked, moving up to the map.

'As much as it can be.'

'It looks like they're buying our deception then. So many of their Panzers are around the Pas-de-Calais.'

'Ready for FUSAG?'

'You know about that?'

'I do. You do too?'

'I'm on the committee setting it up.'

They stared at each other.

'How did we do this?' Steffie asked.

'No idea. I was just a librarian.'

'I was just a socialite!'

'Well, we're both here now.' Fran looked at the map, tracing a hand across the line of the Atlantic Wall. 'Valérie is behind there somewhere.'

'You miss her?'

'I'm trying not to. It's pointless.'

'I thought you two were so good together.'

'We were. It was a big thing for me, finding her. And she introduced me to Gilberte and to journalism, so I'll always be grateful.'

She glanced over to the side table where a copy of last Friday's *Daily Mail* sat, turned to Fran's article on 'Mending the House the Female Way'. It was a collection of rubbish about how to hammer nails, clean gutters and lag pipes, dressed up with a bit on pinnies and rubber gloves to make it more feminine, but it was in the paper and she'd been paid for it, so that was something. At least Fran knew where her future lay now, if not who it would be with.

'Valérie's moved on, Steffie,' she said, 'and she did it pretty heartlessly too. I was a fool to throw myself in so deep, but I'm climbing out. I don't... I don't love her any more.'

'Are you sure?'

Fran nodded firmly. 'Sure.'

'That's good then. See you back at the caravan tonight?'

'Absolutely.'

Steffie let herself out and Fran closed the door and leaned back against it. She wasn't sure at all. She lay awake at night wondering what Valérie had come to say the terrible day that Tommy had brought news of Pierre's capture, but what was the point of torturing herself with it? And what choice did she have anyway?

She pulled out the second pin to move it into place but then the door opened and Thomas Boase stepped in.

'Who was that in the corridor?'

'Someone from ISOS with a report on Panzer HQs. It's full of information.'

'Fabulous. If the Nazis knew we were reading all this!'

'Maybe one day they will.'

'I hope I'm around to see their faces when they find out. But for now, Fran, I have a new job for you.'

'You do?'

Fran looked askance at the mounds of paperwork in the room but Boase waved an airy hand at it all.

'I'll get some more WRENS in for this lot. This is important.'

'Go on.'

'We need someone to prepare leaflets for the troops. One for each beach, so that the men know roughly what to expect in terms of buildings and defences when they get ashore.'

Fran stared at him.

'And you want me to do that?'

'I think you're the best woman for the job, yes.'

'What if I get it wrong? What if they get out expecting a nice house to hide behind and it's not there?'

He patted her on the back.

'It'll be checked by several people, don't worry. Besides, there could be all sorts of reasons for that, including the bombardment that'll be preceding the invasion. It's simply our best estimate to give them the lay of the land, and build their confidence before they go in. Keep it clear, short and straightforward. Chatty, even. We want them to feel that we're holding their hand as that flap goes down on the landing craft.'

'You think I can do that?'

He laughed.

'My wife reads the *Daily Mail*. Showed me your article on "Repairing the House the Female Way".'

Fran was mortified.

'It's just fluff, sir. The editor won't let me write anything meatier.'

'He will. One day. It might be fluff, Frances, but it's good fluff and it tells me you're the perfect woman to guide our troops ashore.'

'Well in that case, sir, I'll give it my best shot.'

'Good stuff. Here's some guidelines from the commanders. Let me know when you've got a draft ready.'

'Yes, sir!'

Boase gave her a nod and left.

Fran sat down at the table and read through the guidelines until she reached the signature at the bottom: Dwight Eisenhower. She swallowed, then got determinedly up and went back to her map, putting her finger up to touch the first of the five landing sites – Sword beach. Time to go to work. In two weeks, her leaflet would be in the hands of boys about to try and take this beach and she had to get it bang on. Let Valérie – Elodie – take care of herself, those soldiers were Fran's main concern right now.

THIRTY-ONE
MAY 1944

Steffie

'Stefania – how do you fancy driving an old man to Dover?'

Steffie stared at Air Marshal Tedder. The Twenty Committee meeting was coming to an end and she'd been about to leave when he'd collared her.

'Me, sir? Absolutely!'

'Excellent. My own driver has asked to be transferred into active service. Wants to be involved in D-Day, brave man.'

Steffie didn't ask why the Air Marshal couldn't drive himself. A run out to the south coast in a nice car would be a change from slaving away over decrypts in ISOS and she'd love the chance to see the mysterious FUSAG in action. The Abwehr traffic was, thankfully, continuing and Tar had assured the committee that the agents were still being asked for information so they just might get away with losing Canaris. All indicators from FHW were that troops were being kept in the Pas-de-Calais in large numbers so it was vital to keep them believing that FUSAG was real and poised to attack.

The committee had recently played a masterstroke in

appointing General Patton – still on 'leave' after his blunders in Sicily – as FUSAG commander. He was a man held in near-reverence by the enemy and when it got back to them that he was in charge, they would most certainly take the force seriously. Patton had been loving his role, striding about London clubs making unsubtle references to his vital job on D-Day and throwing his weight around on the airwaves with a run of commands for his fake divisions that must, surely, be picked up by enemy listeners? The thought that there might be a Nazi version of Bletchley Park somewhere in Germany was a chilling one but for FUSAG to work they had to hope that there were at least some leaks into their system.

'When, sir?' she asked Tedder.

He glanced at the clock – nearly 3 p.m.

'No time like the present. Light should hold for hours yet and the roads are nice and clear with petrol rationing.'

Steffie blinked.

'Right, sir.'

'I'll get you a pass.' He strode through to the offices next to the meeting room and was soon back with a slip of paper identifying Stefania Carmichael as his official driver. 'Sign here. Don't see the point of it myself – I'm hardly likely to let some renegade drive me, am I? – but the military love a pass.'

Steffie signed the slip and tucked it into her bag alongside her papers from the meeting. She'd been planning to go with her father to meet Mummy and Roseanna for afternoon tea but that would have to wait now. It was a shame, but would spare her the endless wedding plans. The big day was to be in August, when Julianna believed – based, as far as Steffie knew, on no knowledge whatsoever – that the invasion would be 'all done with'.

Steffie wished she had her mother's optimism but at least planning the big day was keeping Julianna busy – and stopping her trying to find men to match Steffie up with. She could do that herself, thank you very much. Not that she would, obviously. She liked Leo, she really did, but as a colleague, a friend. Kissing him had been a madness and she was relieved that he'd done nothing to try and repeat it. Relieved and, if she was totally honest, disappointed.

'I'm all set, sir,' she said, pushing the rogue thought to the back of her mind.

'Excellent. If we get a move on, we'll be there in time for dinner in the mess and can still be back in town for a nightcap.' Steffie looked sideways at him and he grimaced. 'Do I sound terribly callous, my dear? I'm not, I assure you. I just find it doesn't do to overthink the enormity of the task ahead or one might lose one's nerve.'

Steffie nodded. She could see that. They all had to keep their heads down and do their jobs without torturing themselves about the consequences. Fran seemed to be in Room 149 all the hours now and Ailsa was working hard with Rowan safe in the loving care of her grandparents and adoptive grandparents.

'Keys, sir?'

He pulled them out of his pocket and she took them, delighted to note the discreet Bentley logo on the keyring. She, too, had been working hard and this would be a welcome change of scene. She rushed over to her father to excuse herself from tea.

'Lucky you,' he said. 'If I have to listen to another debate about roses versus lilies, I might run away to Dover myself. Give Patton my love.'

He winked at her and she was free to head onto the street with Tedder and slide herself behind the wheel of a sleek Mark V.

'Buckle up,' she said to her passenger. 'Next stop, Dover.'

The roads were, as Tedder had said, pleasingly clear and the car near-perfect and they made good time to the coast. But as they drew near, they met a mass of military cars and trucks and Steffie's jaunt to the seaside turned darker.

Many of these preparations were fake. They passed a truck carrying balsa wood on its way to be turned into pretend planes, and another crammed with curious flat rubber bags that would, when blown up, turn into realistic tanks. But there were real troops too. A large engineering corps was stationed off the road, ready to be moved along the coast to form a second wave if – when – the beachheads were established. Further down, a medical corps was readying itself to move in for the inevitable injured and seeing the rows upon rows of stretchers stacked neatly along the edge of the camp brought it home to Steffie that this was a real war, with real battles and real lives on the line.

'Sobering, isn't it?' Tedder said. 'Within the first hour of the landings every one of those will have carried at least one wounded man, probably more. And they only take the boys worth saving.' Steffie shivered. 'Sorry, my dear. Indelicate of me.'

'Not at all. If we all have to face the realities of war, we might learn never to do it again.'

Tedder groaned.

'We thought we'd done that last time. I tell you what, though, we'll all be too bankrupt to fight for a long time. This stuff costs a fortune. Thank heavens the Americans came in with their big cheque book or none of it would be possible. You've got some Yanks at Bletchley Park, haven't you?'

Steffie's thoughts flew to Leo.

'We have. They're not bad chaps, actually. Not nearly as brash as I'd been expecting.'

Tedder laughed. 'You've got the quiet ones then. Lucky you. You're about to meet brash head on. Right here.'

He indicated a turn and Steffie took it and came to a stop at the gates to an army camp, or, rather, a series of wooden supports and camouflage nets designed to look like an army camp. Only one tent at the entrance seemed to be occupied and as they drew up and got out their passes for the guard, a tall man came striding out in an impressively bemedalled uniform.

'Let them in, fella,' he called in an American accent. 'Don't you know an air marshal when you see one?'

'It could be an enemy dressed up as one, sir,' the guard protested.

The man considered.

'Fair point. Most things around here are fake, so why not the personnel too. Am I even who you think I am, lad? Monty has a double, after all, so perhaps I'm a pretend Patton.'

The guard looked flustered and Tedder got out of the car.

'Leave him alone, George. Poor lad's only doing his job.'

General Patton shook his hand heartily and Steffie clutched at the steering wheel, wondering if she could get away with staying in the car. She'd been dying to see this camp but now she was here she felt nervous.

'Steffie, come and meet George.' No hiding then! 'George, this is my driver, Stefania Carmichael.'

'Something of an upgrade, Arthur!' Patton said, winking at him, but he shook her hand as heartily as he had the air marshal's. 'Stefania! Good to meet you. Come along in and see the giddy heights of my command.'

It was giddy indeed, at least for Steffie. Patton took them round his fake camp and then out to the docks at Dover where hundreds of flimsy wood-and-canvas landing craft were bobbing in the water, twenty abreast. He showed them the fake planes lined up on a fake runway, and then the handful of real ones whose job would be to scatter scraps of tin foil across the Channel to mimic invasion vessels on German radar. At the end sat two battered old jeeps.

'We drive those up and down at night,' Patton told Steffie, seeing her looking. 'The headlights simulate planes taking off and landing. Clever stuff.'

'It really is,' Steffie said.

Patton dropped his bonhomie.

'It has to be. There's a lot of heavy artillery out there waiting to take our boys' heads off and we need it all around Calais out of harm's way for as long as humanly possible.' He took her arm and guided her to the end of the runway. It was at the top of a slope and from there Steffie could see across the rolling fields to the English Channel. It looked blue and serene today but soon it would be alive with ships.

It was the last day of May. June the fifth was less than a week away and by the time that most idyllically English of months was out, thousands of women would have lost loved ones. Matteo would be but one in a tragic crowd and Leo would be off to a similarly denuded America. The best thing Steffie could do would be to take her grief and confusion, ball it up into a fierce, focused anger, and fire it at the Germans. Freedom for Europe was going to come at a terrible price but together, fake military and real, they would make it as small as humanly possible.

THIRTY-TWO

JUNE 1944

Ailsa

'Funny seeing the farm out again, isn't it?'

Ailsa picked up a cow and gave it a long hard look. Four years ago, when Steffie had first moved into the caravan, she'd found this toy farm under the bed and they'd set it up to represent the situation in the Mediterranean. When Steffie had been sent to Egypt and then Ailsa to Malta, the 'farm' had become a way of communicating their own positions with each other and they'd used it in their letters, resulting in them all being arrested as potential spies.

Not surprisingly, they'd gone off it a bit after that, and it had been tucked away under the bed once more, but this morning Rowan had found it when Ailsa had brought her in to say good morning to her aunties. They'd set it out and she'd loved it instantly. She had no idea what the animals were, of course, but the bright colours and, above all the loud noise they made when bashed against the table, had proved irresistible to the eight-month-old.

Now Rowan was asleep in the farmhouse and Ailsa had

seized the chance to pop over and have a cup of cocoa with her friends. She'd had to brave the rain lashing down, and Gloria, Alfie, Hamish and Mirren, cosied up around the wireless listening to *The Radio Allotment*, had thought her mad. But Ailsa, knowing what she knew from BP, had found it impossible to relax. Little did those four dear people, or most of the country, realise, but tomorrow was D-Day and the knowledge hung heavy on Ailsa's soul.

She set her cow down.

'Busy day ahead tomorrow,' she said tentatively.

'Very busy,' Fran and Steffie echoed with such feeling that Ailsa realised they knew too and was relieved to have people to share the burden of anticipation.

'Actually, today wasn't as busy as I'd been expecting,' Fran said, uneasily casual.

'No,' Steffie agreed. 'The weather was terrible.'

They all nodded sombrely. D-Day had been set for 5 June since February, and troops had been locked into their holding camps on 31 May, ready to go. Many, indeed, had been loaded into boats last night, but there had been storms in the Channel and Eisenhower had sent out a reluctant order to postpone the invasion for twenty-four hours.

Messages had gone out on the BBC French service to inform the many Resistance groups across northern France, but Ailsa had still had to answer panicked messages from the field. Two days ago, from Algiers, General de Gaulle had declared the Gouvernement provisoire de la République française and the *résistants* were desperate to pave his way back into France. It was good that the invasion was going ahead today or it might be hard to hold them back.

Ailsa was installed in the new listening station in the middle of BP. It had been set up in the old Hut 8 last week and Ailsa had been involved in all of the testing and tuning. The fresh-faced naval ratings from the wireless station up in Scar-

borough had looked astonished to find a woman in charge, especially one in a WAAF uniform, but their egos weren't Ailsa's
concern and she'd soon got them in order.

'This will be a battle situation,' she'd told them at the end of
an intensive week's training. 'Our ability to help the men
fighting the enemy will rely on accuracy and speed. D-Day will
be the worst but, assuming the beachheads are established, the
attack will continue for days – indeed, weeks – and our ability
to relay messages in both directions will be vital to the progress
of the Allied expeditionary force. I expect absolute focus,
concentration and effort.'

They'd saluted her smartly and she'd given them a sharp
nod and marched out, escaping to the one lavatory she'd finally
persuaded the carpenters to fence off as a Ladies, to breathe a
sigh of relief that they'd accepted her authority. It was going to
be hectic and they had to work as a team. She'd kissed Rowan
goodnight with extra tenderness this evening, aware that she'd
be lucky to see her for more than a few minutes in the days to
come.

Thoughtfully, she picked a horse out of the box of toys and
set it opposite the cow. Steffie reached for a blue tea towel from
the side and, folding it neatly, placed it along the table between
the two animals. Ailsa swallowed. Back when they'd set this
farm up, the horses had been the British army and the cows the
German one. They'd been separated by land masses then, as
they were now, but in less than twelve hours, that distance
would be closed and they would be face to face for the first time
since Dunkirk.

Fran reached into the box and lifted out several more
'British' horses, standing them at the shoulders of the first one, a
strong, active group. In response, Fran picked out a 'German'
cow but, instead of putting it with the first, moved it down the
tea towel, towards what Ailsa assumed was the Pas-de-Calais.
Steffie searched through the box and found a white horse, then

set it across from them – a ghost horse. The airwaves had been rammed with messages in the last few days, and Ailsa had picked up her share of comms from units she was pretty sure didn't exist. There was something called FUSAG, a supposedly vast force of American troops stationed in Kent, but Ailsa knew for a fact that several of those units were actually in Portsmouth. The fact that so many German troops were down the coast from the invasion sites suggested they didn't share her knowledge. God, Ailsa hoped so.

There were two more cows in the box and Steffie set these with the first but then trotted one away in a south-westerly direction. Ailsa watched, puzzled.

'I hear its Rommel's wife's birthday tomorrow,' Steffie said, taking a sip of her cocoa. 'He's throwing her a party in their hometown of Ulm. Isn't that nice of him?'

'He's got leave for that?' Ailsa gasped.

'Must have,' Steffie said, not quite meeting her eye. 'Well, you know, with the storms in the Channel, nothing's going to happen right now.'

'No. No, of course not. That makes sense.'

'So why not have a party several hundred miles away?'

She gave Ailsa a slow, deliberate wink. If this was true, it was amazing. Rommel was Germany's most fearsome on-field commander and his absence would be a huge boon to the invaders.

Fran picked up the other cow and moved it south.

'Ideal time, then, to send officers on a training course, wouldn't you think? Get some practice, in case of invasion. I hear there's a perfect place for it down near Rennes.'

Ailsa gaped. If her friends were to be believed, the Nazis really didn't think the Allies were coming for them yet. The element of surprise would be a huge advantage and she was glad that Eisenhower had taken the tricky decision to go for it. From what she could gather, tonight was the last one for some time when the conditions were right for a seaborn invasion. The men needed the moon full enough to provide some light to sail by, and the boats to hit Normandy at half-tide. The Germans had set defensive spikes to prevent landing at high tide but with skill – and timing – they could be negotiated by the flat-bottomed landing craft sooner, the rising water allowing the bigger boats in once the first wave had hopefully taken out the German defences.

It was all, as far as Ailsa could see, down to very fine margins and, if they couldn't attack tonight, they would have to wait for 19 June for the same conditions. That was a long time to stand troops ready and keep the plans from the enemy, so it had been a tremendous relief when Eisenhower had given the go-ahead, but now it felt terrifying. She thought of Ned, out in Colombo, listening to Japanese messages detailing German defences, and shook her head at how this damned war had clamped its hold around the whole globe. It had to stop and soon. She drained her cocoa.

'We should get some sleep,' she said. 'We're going to need it.'

There was no doubting that, but as she let herself out of the caravan to re-join her baby in the farmhouse, she doubted any of them would get much. There was an armada of over 150,000 men about to set sail for Fortress Europe, and the whole of Bletchley Park would be there with them every step of the way. How, knowing that, could anybody sleep?

PART THREE
D-DAY

6 JUNE 1944

The men sail in darkness, meeting at the centre of the Channel in a location known, with gruff British humour, as Piccadilly Circus, then fanning out to creep up on the beaches of Normandy. As the first rays of a dull sun appear over the horizon, those on deck see more ships than sea. They are an armada, a force, an invasion. The wind is up and waves squall over the men as they clamber down nets into the landing craft, standing shoulder to shoulder, sardines in a tin, as the flat-bottomed boats roll in the swell. Soon they will be cast adrift from their mother ships and piloted in, their hulls scraping over the top of the spikes meant to keep them out, before the big iron flaps at the front go down and – bang – they are running at the guns.

'Keep moving,' they've been told, over and over. 'Don't stop, don't lie down, don't look for cover. Run for the top of the sand because if you stop, you're dead.'

They are ready. The wait has been too long and the night's delay was agony. They want to charge. They want to shoot at the men who have kept the world trapped in hell for the last five years. They want to end this and, young and strong and eager,

*they believe that today, they can. They have to believe it; what
alternative is there?*

*In their pockets they carry guides – small brown books that
tell them what to expect when their boots hit the sand. They are a
comfort, a reassurance. Someone has been here before, not like
this perhaps, but they have trod these shores and left a print for
the new visitors to follow. The booklet details the depth of the
beach, the houses overlooking it – a selection of fine dwellings,
many with the Tudor cruck-frame that will, strangely, remind the
invaders of home. They are grand, picturesque. Above all they are
solid, a wall to hide behind. For the booklet also details German
batteries, concrete boxes from which the enemy can – and will –
shoot at them. If they can get behind them, they stand a chance
and in the front boats, many a soldier pats his pocket and thinks
of his guide. Hit the sand and run. Thirty paces to the big house
with a garden that once held laughing holidaymakers and you're
on your way.*

*In the middle of England, far from the coast, the author of the
pamphlet is waiting too. No waves lash at her blackened face,
there is no gun in her hand, no sergeant at her back, but she is
waiting all the same. She's given up trying to sleep, given up
even trying to drink her tea, and is heading for Bletchley with her
friends. Fran, Steffie and Ailsa are not the only ones to march up
the muddy track to the park before the sun is up. There will be
many, many enemy messages in the airwaves today and the
8,000 workers in the bucolic park must catch, decode and inter-
pret them, then send the Ultra back out to the men with the guns
to turn them into victory.*

*On the French coast, the planes begin their bombardment of
Rommel's dreaded Atlantic Wall and two hundred miles further
south, Rommel stirs in his bed, turns over and snuggles down to
sleep off the excesses of his wife's birthday party. There will be no
such luxury for his men. On Sword beach, on Gold and Juno, on
Omaha and Utah, the first iron flaps slam down into the*

churning shallows, and the first shots of the invasion are fired.
Lookouts in the enemy bunkers set up a frantic alarm and
German soldiers leap to their guns, but it is clear, already, that
they are too few.

Inland, another army waits, a secret army. The Resistance,
called out by messages from the BBC, leap into action as the
German guns sound out. Theirs is not an invasion. Theirs is a
rising up, a furious internal attack on the men who have had an
iron grip on their country for too long and who must be thrown
out. For months, they have been receiving arms from Britain, in
planes coaxed out of Churchill by Yeo-Thomas, a man who is,
even now, plotting an escape from a concentration camp with no
idea that the résistants he worked so hard to unite and supply are
in place to help the Allied cause – to blow up railways, roads and
bridges, to fling grenades and shoot Nazis and clear the way for
the soldiers coming storming towards them. They are ready all
across France but here, in Normandy, they are most concentrated
and behind Sword, a young woman in dark clothing, her face
blackened like the soldiers and her grandmother's bold heart
beating in her slim chest, checks the grenades on the belt around
her waist.

'Allez,' *she murmurs to herself.* 'Il est temps de mourir,
chiens allemands.'

In the German bunkers, alarms are sounded and guns
manned. Bullets spray the invaders with cruel intensity and all
around young men fall, bravery spraying from them with their
blood as they call out for their mothers. Their fellows have no
choice but to leave them. 'Keep moving. Don't stop, don't lie
down, don't look for cover or you're dead.' *They know, now, how*
bitterly true that is. But they are starting to make it up behind the
low dunes, behind the fancy houses, behind the German defence.
The beaches are turning into beachheads.

In Bletchley Park, all is activity. In her listening station, dead
centre, Ailsa strides the hut, tuning sets, checking messages,

ensuring their smooth passage out to the decoding units. In between, she gets on her own set to monitor messages from the operators in the field who trust her as their contact back home, their link with the world that is coming, at speed, towards them.

In ISOS, Steffie frowns over a mountain of decrypts. All night the bombe machines have been whirring to crack the key to today's codes and now that they have it, it must be applied to every message crackling across the German airwaves. Again and again, Steffie translates the words, Warnung, Alarm, Kampf Stationen. *Panic ripples across the slips of decrypts and then, more vitally, action plans – troop movements, recalling of officers.*

At 10 a.m., worn out after watching a late film with Eva, Hitler wakes and is told the news. Rubbing his hands, he goes to his map-room, sure the next few days will see the Allies thrown out of Normandy and the anticipated 'real' attack in Calais repulsed. For too long Allied troops have been lurking over the Channel and he is glad they are finally here and can be sent slinking back to the negotiating table to plead terms with the Führer of Fortress Europe.

But the Allies are not here to plead terms. They are here to win. Sword is taken, then Juno and Gold. Utah follows and even Omaha, though the sand is thick with bodies of young Americans, doomed in their bravery to lie forever beneath a simple white cross in a foreign field. In Hut 3, Fran moves around her plans with Peter Lucas. Room 149 sits empty now, its job done. This is no longer a plan but a reaction.

Decrypts and direction-finding locations flood in and they battle to keep pace with the battle. They cannot stop the Germans moving their troops, but they can make sure that Montgomery and Eisenhower know they are coming. Or not coming.

In the Pas-de-Calais, several thousand German soldiers wake, as usual, to a pale, invasion-free dawn and go sleepily to the parade ground to train for when the great First US Army

Group hits them. In London, Tar Robertson's double agents keep up the news of the forces in Kent, where Patton inspects his blow-up tanks and balsa wood planes, and wishes he was part of the pounding further west.

'Allez!' Valérie's word is no longer a murmur to herself but a call to action.

She springs from the coarse grass at the back of the German battery at Hermanville-sur-Mer, a hundred comrades with her, and runs. At the rear, huddled into a gap in a hedge, Reggie clutches his radio set and wishes he had not felt the need to be brave. At first he'd loved being able to use his passion for the wireless in the service of his country but in time it had shamed him not being in uniform. He had sensed eyes on him, heard whispers as he passed, felt the brush of a white feather. That was why he'd volunteered to come to France but now, with guns all around, he thinks he'd take a hundred feathers. He'd strap them to himself and cluck around Skipton market because at least then he'd be alive.

The woman he has been paired with awes him. He remembers her from the Drunken Arms, back when BP was less than a thousand people and they all knew each other. She was quiet then, petite and alluring with her glossy hair and well-fitting clothes. Now she is an animal. As Elodie, she has cut her hair to a boyish length and dresses in utilitarian black. She talks with passion of throwing the Germans out of La France and he watches her running at them with fire in her dark eyes, one hand pulling the pin from a grenade, the other lobbing it with startling accuracy into the pin-slit of the concrete battery. She is reaching for a second before it explodes.

Reggie sees Germans run from the battery and huddles further into the flimsy protection of the hedge. He sees the résis-tants crouch into the grass, lift their guns, shoot them down like metal figures in a fairground attraction. From the far side, Allied soldiers are arriving. They are going to win, Reggie thinks, and

realises it surprises him. He has always been a pessimist. The
Germans are going down. A few minutes more and they will all
be safe, this tiny corner of France taken for the Allies.

He shuffles forward and that's when he sees her, Elodie. She
has not crouched. She has not stopped her personal advance. She
lifts her third grenade and that's when a young German, fighting
for his life, lifts his gun, captures the ragged figure in his sights,
and shoots. She goes down with a wail of fury and Reggie,
babbling with fear, fumbles out his radio set and does the only
thing he truly knows to do – call home.

In BP, Ailsa, fresh from tweaking a recalcitrant set, picks up
her headphones and hears a familiar fist. She sinks onto her chair
and grabs a pencil. It's from 'Celine', she's sure it is, although the
Morse is erratic and the message, she rapidly realises, not in code.
She tuts but as the words emerge, she stops caring about protocol.
She stops caring about anything but the terrible words she is
transcribing onto the slip.

Elodie down at Hermanville. Repeat, Elodie down.
Wounded. Badly wounded.

Her hands fly to her mouth and then she is up, scribbling on
a bit of paper, and grabbing an ancillary.

'Get this to Hut 3,' *she orders,* 'fast.' *She writes again.* 'And
this to ISOS.'

D-Day, it seems, has come to their part of Bletchley in the
worst possible way.

THIRTY-THREE

Fran

'No sign of the Panzers moving west yet.'

Fran scanned the latest message and pressed the pins that marked the tank units in the Pas-de-Calais more firmly into place. It was five hours since the first men stormed the beaches and as far as they could tell it was going well. There were too many injuries, but there would always be too many injuries. Here in Hut 3, they could not think of individuals but of the whole – and the whole was advancing. It was strange being back, but her job in Room 149 was done so she'd re-joined her old team. To be honest, they were working slickly without her and she felt like a bit of a spare part, but she was doing her best and it was astonishing to see the invasion in action almost first-hand.

Sword was secure and the army were starting to unload the tanks and armoured vehicles that would lead the battle for France. D-Day was only the beginning. It would be a long, hard march to Paris and an even longer one to Berlin, but at least the march had begun. And it wasn't only the troops. Wireless operators had been unloaded onto the beaches with their SLU vans to send captured Enigma back to Bletchley Park. Every medic available was on a hospital ship and Fran knew, from hints from Ben, that her brothers were due to leave on HMHS *Dinard* tonight. She prayed they'd stay on-ship, safe from the bullets, if not from their effects.

Even journalists were being shipped over with their notepads and cameras to feed news back to an eager public. Gilberte had told her that the American, Martha Gellhorn, had been refused a pass for being female and had talked friends of hers into smuggling her over as a nurse. The world, it seemed, was heading to Normandy and Fran could only hope the advance continued.

'Message for you, Fran.'

'For me?'

She turned in surprise as Peter Lucas handed her a torn-off scrap, and opened it up. It was Ailsa's writing, small and neat but running off the page with haste. She read it, read it again.

Valérie hurt. Meet me at the duck pond.

Her head swum and her body flooded with horror, as if it were she who had been shot with an enemy bullet.

'Valérie,' she murmured. The word, banished from her lips for so long, sang through her heart before another followed it, far too fast. 'Wounded?'

The pain told her one thing – she loved her still. However hard she'd tried to drive that love away, it was not to be banished. The thought of Valérie suffering tore at her every fibre and, with grim humour, she saw the irony of realising this as she might be taken from her.

'Something's happened,' she said to Peter, hearing her voice shake. 'Something bad. Can I go?'

'Go,' he agreed, unquestioning.

Fran burst from Block D and ran up the short path to the duck pond. It was a grey day but the flowers were opening their petals and the ducks quacking with gay innocence between the flourishing rushes. Ailsa was there, her hair red in the few strands of sun peeking through the heavy clouds, and Fran ran to her.

'What's happened?'

'I don't know any more, Fran. I'm sorry. Here.'

She thrust a Morse slip at Fran and she scanned the words. They were painfully brief. She knew Hermanville, of course – Hermanville-sur-Mer. She had marked it on a thousand maps and collated a thousand postcards showing its once-pretty seafront. But what did wounded mean? It could be anything from a scratch on the cheek to a lost limb, to bleeding spreading through the internal organs until... *Stop it*, she told herself. Imagining the worst would do no good. She clutched at Ailsa as Steffie came bursting out of Block G and running towards them.

'What's wrong?'

'It's Valérie,' Fran heard Ailsa tell her over the rush of her blood pounding around her skull. 'She's wounded.'

That word again. God, why did the damn woman have to go to France? Why did she have to put herself in danger? Why did Fran have to care?

'I'm so sorry, Fran,' Steffie said. 'But you have to try to trust. There are hospitals out there, doctors. They'll treat her.'

'Hospitals,' Fran repeated. 'Doctors.' An idea lit up in her head. 'My brothers are doctors.'

'Exactly. They're good ones, right?'

'Good ones who are heading to Normandy on the hospital ship tonight,' Fran agreed.

'So, they'll help her,' Steffie said. 'They'll look after her.'

Fran nodded but she knew one thing – no one would look after Valérie like she would. Ailsa pulled back to look into her face.

'Fran? What are you planning?'

'There's a journalist called Martha Gellhorn, an American. She petitioned the *New York Times* to let her go to D-Day with the press corps but they said no.'

'Because she's a woman?'

'Exactly.'

'But?'

'But Gilberte says she's got herself a nurse's uniform and a sympathetic doctor who's signed her onto his staff. She's going to Normandy.'

Steffie grabbed her.

'No, Fran. You can't go.'

Fran pushed her away.

'Why can't I?'

'It's too dangerous.'

'Not as dangerous as letting Valérie die without telling her how I feel about her.' Steffie bit her lip and Fran pressed her advantage. 'What did Matteo do, Stef? Did he lie in his hospital bed waiting to die, or did he find a fishing boat to get to you – to tell you what you meant to him, to die in your arms?'

'You don't know Valérie is dying, Fran,' Ailsa said.

'I don't know that she's not.' Fran looked from one friend to the other. 'I have to get to her. Or, at least, I have to try. If I can reach Southampton, I bet my brothers will get me onto their ship.'

'Won't that get them into trouble?'

'Maybe, but they got me into trouble hundreds of times when we were kids, so they owe me. Besides, this is important.' She grabbed at her friends. 'I have to see her, girls. You knew that, Ailsa, when you sent me the message. You knew that if it was Ned, you'd feel exactly the same. And you know it, Steffie, because you've been there. Help me, please.'

Steffie looked at Ailsa and the two gave reluctant nods.

'I can get a message to Reggie,' Ailsa said. 'I can tell him to tell Valérie you're coming. I can tell him to get her to a hospital and to wait.'

'Thank you.'

'And I can get you to Southampton,' Steffie said. 'Come with me.'

She dug in her bag, producing a small slip that said 'Official Driver', then marched them up the path to the right of the mansion and round the back into the stable yard. Fran looked around; she'd never been here before, never needed to. She spotted the cottage where Dilly Knox had cracked so many codes with his early team of female staff. Dilly was dead now and the cottage staff had been moved into the concrete blocks, expanded from pen-and-paper wizards into a vast decoding machine. The pretty building stood empty but across from it, in the old stable block, a man was tending one of several smart-looking cars.

'You can drive?' Steffie asked her.

Fran nodded. Her father had bought an Austin 7 to take the family on holidays and they'd all taken turns driving it around the remote campsites her parents had favoured to 'get back to nature'. She didn't actually have a licence – testing had been suspended before she could get one booked – but she was competent enough. The beautiful cars ahead of her now looked more daunting than the cosy Austin but she could do it.

'Good.' Steffie marched up to the garage attendant who blanched at the sight of her.

'Can I help you?'

'I need a car.' Steffie flashed the pass. 'Air Marshal Tedder requires it urgently.' The man examined the pass and looked nervously to his precious cars. 'Don't worry,' Steffie told him. 'It won't be me driving.' She looked back at Fran and Ailsa. 'This chap doesn't appreciate an Italian style of driving but he doesn't need to worry, does he, Fran? You're perfectly safe, right?'

'Right,' Fran agreed with a firmness she was far from feeling.

'So,' Steffie said, waving the card imperiously. 'Let's not keep the air marshal waiting.'

'No, miss.'

The garage man reached for the keys to the nearest vehicle and handed them to Fran. With her heart in her mouth, she slid into the driver's seat and inserted the key. The engine turned over with a purr.

'Does it have fuel?' she asked, trying to sound confident.

'Full tank, miss. Where are you going, if I'm allowed to ask?'

'Southampton,' Fran told him, checking in the glove compartment for a map. 'I might be a few days.'

'I'll need you to sign then.'

'I'll do that,' Steffie told him, waving Fran on.

'Thank you,' Fran called. 'Tell Peter Lucas for me, will you?'

'Will do,' Steffie called back. 'He'll understand. The air marshal has to come first!'

She threw her a wink and guided the garageman into his office. Grateful not to be watched, Fran engaged the clutch and felt the car respond instantly. Within moments, she was easing it out of the garage and turning it through the gates of Bletchley Park and south. Was this madness? Others might certainly think so, but for Fran it felt like the sanest thing she'd done this year.

The sun was setting over a crammed Southampton dock when Fran pulled in. She looked nervously around. From the plush safety of the Rolls-Royce this had seemed like a bold quest but now, with so many military vessels and vehicles crowding for space, reality hit her hard. Could she do this? She thought of the booklets she'd so carefully compiled to guide soldiers onto the beach, never imagining that it would be she who set foot on that sand. It would look different now, of course, though adrift in a car with no connection into the information lifeblood at BP, she couldn't tell in what way. Was Hermanville taken by the Allies? Right now, there was only one way to find out.

Sliding the Rolls into a set of spaces marked out for officers, she locked it up and slid the keys into the pocket of her work trousers. She'd come with nothing, she realised – no coat, no spare clothes, not even her handbag. She had her BP pass around her neck and the keys to an implausibly fine car and that was it. She was tempted to turn around and drive back to Buckinghamshire again but then thought of Valérie lying in some rough hospital tent, fighting for her last breaths, and renewed her resolve. If Martha Gellhorn could get to Normandy to write articles, Fran could get there to find the woman she loved.

Turning her back on the car, she strode towards the docks where several big, grey ships were being embarked. She cast around for the one with the distinctive red cross of a hospital vessel, spotted HMHS *Dinard* dead centre, and marched up to the sailor standing at the bottom of the gangplank before she could lose her nerve.

'Nurse Morgan reporting for duty,' she said in her crispest grammar-school accent.

He looked sceptically at her.

'You're no nurse.'

'I am!' she told him indignantly. 'I'm a senior sister and have been at a Whitehall meeting about medical provisions so have been delayed getting here. Thank God the Rolls moves fast or I might not have made it at all.'

She dangled the keys and he shifted, impressed, and looked at his clipboard.

'I don't have a Nurse Morgan here. Just two Dr Morgans.'

Dare she? She smiled at him.

'I'm delighted to hear that the navy are finally enlightened enough to use my proper title. You'd have thought everyone would see the sense in ratifying female degrees in this day and age, wouldn't you?'

He blinked, confused.

'Both Dr Morgans are on board, miss, that is, ma'am, er, Doctor.'

'Really? There must be a mistake. I'm sure Ben – that's my brother – must be here but I am the other Dr Morgan.' Had she overplayed this? Nothing in her high school drama classes had prepared her for wangling her way on board a battleship, but she was in deep now and had to swim on. She pressed his hand. 'Don't worry, I won't tell. It must have been crazy here today.'

'You don't know the half of it. I've been run off my feet for weeks.'

'It'll be worth it when we win. So, can I go on board? My other nurses are here, I assume, and no doubt running riot.'

'There did look to be a few lively girls.'

'Too right. Giddy lot they are. They'll soon sober up when we get to the beaches.'

She gave him a grim look and he nodded but still didn't step aside.

'Your pass doesn't say Dr Morgan.'

'No. I told you, not everyone is enlightened enough to recognise my qualification. Tell you what, fetch Dr Benjamin Morgan and he'll vouch for me.' He glanced up the gangplank. 'And hurry up, sailor – there are people dying while you hang around fretting about whether I have a degree or not.'

'Yes, ma'am.'

He saluted then shouted up to his fellows on deck to fetch Dr Benjamin Morgan. Fran stood, crossing everything she had behind her back and praying Ben would stand up for her. It felt an age until the sailor returned, a curious Ben in tow. He leaned over the railings.

'Frances? What are you doing there?'

'Waiting to be let on board by this jobsworth who doesn't believe I'm a doctor.'

Ben barely blinked.

'Really? How old-fashioned. There's no one better with a severed limb,' he shouted down. 'Let her on, man, and we can all get on with doing our jobs.'

'Sir.'

The sailor saluted and stepped aside and, just like that, Frances was on board. She walked up the gangplank with as much dignity as she could muster and gave a bemused Ben a business-like handshake.

'What the hell are you up to, Frannie?'

'Affairs of the heart, Ben.'

'Your chap's out there?'

She swallowed.

'Not a chap, Ben, a girl.'

He raised an eyebrow.

'I see. Makes sense of why poor Jack Parsons could never get anywhere with you.'

Fran stared at him. She remembered Jack. He'd always been turning up on his bike with random gifts – slightly fluffy chocolate bars, an old typewriter, a dried moth. She'd thought he was a bit odd, but it turned out that had been an attempt at courtship. It seemed like something from another time now, another life.

'Does it bother you?'

'Not if it doesn't bother you, but what's she doing over there?'

'She's French. A *résistante*. I've had word she's wounded.'

He looked down at her, his eyes kind.

'That's horrible, Frannie. I'm so sorry.'

'Me too. We fell out. I didn't want her to go, she said I didn't understand. Then I think she came to try and make up with me but, well, events got in the way and I let her go. That's why I have to get to her, Ben, in case...'

She welled up and Ben ushered her through a metal door, away from the prying eye of the deck sailors. Inside, the entire space was laid out with slim bunks.

'That's a lot of beds.'

'And they'll all be full within an hour of getting there, with more on the floors. Believe me, Fran, I've seen it before. It's awful. We've had reports of hundreds wounded, more dead.'

'We've taken the beaches?'

'I believe so but if the Germans bring in reserves, it could all change. Battlefields are never static, sis.'

'I know that,' Fran said, picturing the ever-changing maps and plans on the wall of Room 149. Even before the actual attacks, they'd shifted all the time, so God only knew what it was like out there now. 'But I have to go. I have to try and find her. I love her, Ben.'

He sighed.

'Rob is going to kill me but, come on, if you're sure, let's find you a uniform. We set sail in an hour.'

'Thank you.' She took his arm, squeezing it affectionately. 'Thank you so much.'

'You might not thank me when you get there,' he said grimly. 'And I tell you now, if there are Germans on the beach, no nurse is going ashore, not even a bonkers pretend one, agreed?'

'Agreed,' Fran said and followed him meekly along to stores.

An hour later she was dressed in crisp white, her car keys and her BP pass in a bag at her waist and her heart in her mouth as the HMHS *Dinard* cast off for Normandy, and for Valérie. She only prayed she wasn't too late.

THIRTY-FOUR

Ailsa

Ailsa sidled back into the listening station to find Gambier-Parry standing in the centre of the room, arms crossed.

'Been somewhere important, Mrs Robinson?'

Ailsa cringed. Whenever her boss was cross with her, she became Mrs Robinson.

'Yes, sir,' she said, following the never-apologise-never-explain approach she'd always fallen back on as a teenager. It hadn't worked then, mind you, and from the look in Gambier-Parry's eyes, it wasn't going to work now.

'Something more urgent than the invasion of Europe, was it?'

'Something equally urgent, but on a smaller scale. I had to get a message to a friend.'

'A friend?' He stared at her. 'I've entrusted you with running this unit, and you're darting out for gossip?'

Ailsa felt her blood start to boil and told herself to stay calm.

'It was not, in any way, "gossip", sir. If you must know, a

good friend's had bad news from Normandy – a possible loss of life.'

Gambier-Parry huffed.

'Yes, well, that's terrible obviously, but there's going to be a lot of it about this week – and more if we don't all do our jobs.'

'Sir.'

Cheeks flaring, she turned to check on the eighteen men in her charge, horribly aware that she was reinforcing every reason cited by the military not to employ women. She felt as if she were letting the side down and couldn't meet anyone's eyes as she applied herself to checking sets and ensuring the smooth flow of messages around the wire trays.

'Don't worry about him,' said a young WREN, brought in to shift slips around. 'Everyone's snappy today.'

'Not surprising,' Ailsa said, giving her a rueful grin.

The girl patted her on the back, picked up the nearest tray, and was gone. Ailsa felt bad for needing the comfort of one of the lower staff members and then reminded herself that there was nothing wrong with that. Perhaps it was the people who didn't need comforting that should worry, not the other way round.

Certain that everyone was working as they should, she sat at her own desk, tuning in to Reggie's line. Nothing. She ground her teeth in frustration, burningly aware that she'd promised to tell him that Fran was on her way. When she'd been trapped in a fallen-down air-raid shelter in Malta, it had only been the sound of Ned's voice telling her he was coming to rescue her that had kept her from kicking the place down in panic. It could make a huge difference to Valérie's chances of survival to know that Fran was trying to reach her, and it would make all the difference to Fran's happiness if Valérie survived. But she could do nothing until Reggie tried to call in again so, for now, she could only leave the line open and get on with her other tasks.

'Mrs Robinson, ma'am, I've got a problem with my signal.'

Ailsa tugged her headphones off, leaving them connected so she'd pick up the sound of any message being transmitted, and went to help.

'You've got to keep your hand steady on the dial, Jim,' she told him. 'There are so many messages flying around that nearly every frequency is operating so you've got to be certain to keep yours stable. Here,' she leaned in, 'hold it as you'd hold your girl on the dance floor – firm but gentle.'

Jim blinked at her.

'I don't have a girl, ma'am.'

'Then hold it as you hope to hold a girl when this mess is over.'

He smiled.

'There is one I dream about. Poppy she's called and she's so sweet.'

'There you go then. Poppy's there, Jim, tune into her.'

She left him with a slightly dreamy look in his eye but a steady hand and soon he was scribbling down his messages with new intent. Gambier-Parry gave her an approving nod, though if he'd heard the content of her advice, he might not have been so pleased. It was probably far too feminine to pass muster.

Ailsa glanced to the door, willing him to leave. What was it with her and bosses? She'd rubbed Commander Keith up the wrong way out in Colombo and now Gambier-Parry over here. Was it that she was as stubborn and wilful as her mother had always told her, or were they unreasonable? Either way, he wouldn't approve of her leaving a line open for Reggie, and she looked guiltily to the headset. It crackled and she made a dive across the room for it, almost knocking over the returning WREN in her haste.

'Steady now, Mrs Robinson,' Gambier-Parry called.

'Agent in the field, sir.'

'Down here? Thought we were doing all that up at Whaddon?'

She cursed herself.

'We are, sir, but I brought my agents with me. They're used to my fist, and it was felt that it wouldn't do to disrupt the relationship this close to D-Day.'

She prayed he wouldn't ask who had felt that as it had been entirely her own decision, but it was standard protocol to keep direct links alive where possible so he merely nodded.

Please go, she willed him. What was the point in him putting her in charge of the unit if he was going to waste his own time here too? She saw him glance at his watch but then her set crackled again and she yanked on the headset and tapped out the Q code for 'receiving you'. She glanced around for her codebook but already the message was coming in direct.

```
Elodie in hospital at Hermanville. Wound
serious. In surgery. Under professional
care.
```

Ailsa bit her lip. She thought about how to word the next bit but the quickest, simplest thing was the truth. In swift Morse she tapped out:

```
Tell Elodie Frances is on her way. Tell
her she loves her.
```

There was a long pause, then:

```
Will do.
```

Ailsa breathed a sigh of relief, then sensed a heavy presence at her shoulder and turned.

'Tell her she loves her?' Gambier-Parry said. She looked at him, shocked. 'You think I can't read Morse, Mrs Robinson? I run a radio comms operation, of course I can read Morse –

certainly enough to know when it is being abused. What the hell do you think you're doing?'

His voice had risen and all eyes turned their way. Slowly, Ailsa took off her headset and stood up.

'I'm sorry, sir. We have an agent down and I was sending words of comfort.'

'Operationally important words of comfort, were they?'

'No, sir. They were not. But they were personally important to two scared people.'

'I see. And while you were doing that, what were your team up to?'

She looked around. Her team looked back.

'I believe, sir, that they were doing their jobs, as I have shown them and as they are more than capable of doing without constant supervision. I am here to run the operation, not to nanny the operators.'

Gambier-Parry sucked in a breath.

'I'm beginning to think, Mrs Robinson, that you would be far better off as a nanny. Or, at least, as a mother – as nature intended you to be.'

Ailsa drew herself up tall.

'And as I am, proudly and lovingly so. I just happen to think that having a baby has not impacted on my ability to do my job.'

Gambier-Parry shook his head.

'I've done my best to agree with you, Mrs Robinson, but it is clearly not the case. You are messaging friends.'

'I am messaging my agent. If she happens to be a friend, I acknowledge that and believe it makes my relationship with her even more effective.'

'Not if it stops you doing your job.'

'But it's not stopped me!' Ailsa was shouting now but so what? Her patience, stretched to breaking point for far too long with the rigid, male ways of working, had snapped. She was going to lose her job, that much was clear, so she might as well have her say first. 'I happen to believe that caring for my colleagues makes my work better, not worse. I happen to think that being sure that they are well, emotionally and physically, makes for a happier workplace and—' She put up a hand to stop him interrupting her, 'I happen to believe that a happy workplace is a more effective one.'

'Which is why,' Gambier-Parry spluttered, 'it will be better for everyone when this war is over and women can get out of the workplace once more.'

'And leave you all miserable? Perhaps you're right. I'll get my things. Thank you for the opportunity and I'm sorry that I didn't live up to your expectations. Actually, no, forget that – I'm sorry that you didn't live up to mine.'

She turned to her desk to grab her bag, her anger already falling into sadness. She'd loved this work, taken pride in being involved at such a crucial level and hated having failed. But as she turned for the door, Jim stood up, scarlet in the face but with a determined set to his shoulders.

'If you don't mind me saying, sir,' he said to Gambier-Parry, 'I think Mrs Robinson is the best boss I've ever had.'

Gambier-Parry looked astounded.

'You're, what, twenty?'

'Nineteen, sir.'

'How many bosses have you had?'

'Oh loads, sir. I've been in five listening stations already and had at least two bosses in each and not one of them has helped me to understand my job as well as Mrs Robinson, or made me enjoy it as much neither.'

'I see.' Gambier-Parry looked around the room. 'Does anyone else feel like this?'

There were a few coughs and foot shuffles but then, one by one, more of Ailsa's men stood up.

'She knows how to explain things so I get them, sir,' one said.

'And she doesn't shout if I ask a second time, sir.'

'She let me have ten minutes' break when I was upset about my mum taking ill, sir, and I felt that much better for it, I could concentrate again. If that's how girls do it, sir, I think that's all right with me, sir.'

The lad looked desperately uncomfortable but he stood his ground and Ailsa felt her whole being swell. She looked to Gambier-Parry.

'Well, Mrs Robinson,' he said. 'It seems you have the confidence of your team.'

'It's very kind of them to say.'

'They don't want to lose you. Perhaps it is I who is out of place. This is Bletchley Park after all – there are strange ways of doing things around here but, by golly, they seem to work.' He shook his head, but then smiled. 'Put your bag back on the hook, Ailsa, you've got a team to run.'

He gave her a nod, then strode across the room and left. Ailsa looked around at the young men who had so bravely stood up for her. They looked uncertainly back.

'You heard the man,' she said. 'Back to work. We've got a war to win!'

'Yes, ma'am,' they said as one.

Ailsa smiled and turned off her own radio. She had sent her message, done her bit, and maybe struck a tiny blow for female bosses of the future. Now, she could only put her head down to her task, and leave Fran to find Valérie as best she could.

THIRTY-FIVE

Fran

The sun rose over a scene that surely only a crazed Dante could dream up. HMHS *Dinard* was moored off the coast of Sword and, standing on deck with her brothers, Fran had a first-hand view of what a sea invasion looked like. They were anchored just inside a sweep of ancient ships, tugged across the Channel to form a 'gooseberry' harbour wall, their rusting bulk breaking up chop and providing nominal shelter for the mass of craft operating within their curve. All around them, vessels were lining up to take their turns landing on the beach now that the tide was reaching the high line above the spikes, and a more curious set of vehicles Fran could not have imagined.

She watched as a long, thin tank with chain flails on the front was rolled through the shallows and, with a roar, began ploughing up an open stretch of the beach, chains whirring like crazed arms, setting off flashes and bangs as mines exploded. Another had huge spikes in front and was driven into the dunes where it proceeded to tear into the hedges at the top, breaking up any barriers behind which the enemy could lurk.

The beach was crowded, tanks of various sizes jostling for space with American jeeps and canvas-topped trucks and men were running around guiding them onto the road to make space before the tide dropped too far to get the rest off the waiting ships. Fran even saw soldiers pushing bicycles ashore and for a moment felt as if she were in a skewed Sunday afternoon jaunt.

Along the pockmarked promenade at the top of the sand, a selection of villas stood, tall, proud and bemused-looking, one with a hole in its roof, one with rubble for a garden, all sporting the flag of the regiment that had taken them as a base. Fran recognised them from the postcards she had pored over in Room 149 and was glad to see at least some of them intact.

'There,' Ben said, pointing. 'It looks like the hospital is inland – can you see the flag?'

Fran followed her brother's finger and spotted a red cross on a white flag flying in what looked like it might be the centre of the tiny town. It wasn't far away – maybe a street back from the front, though of course she had to get ashore first.

'This is a bad idea,' Rob said reprovingly.

'We're sending the other nurses in,' Ben told him, pointing out the uniformed women waiting in a huddle nearby.

'Not the *other* nurses, Ben. Fran is not a nurse.'

'I can do nursing.'

'And she is our sister. What would Ma say if—'

'That won't happen,' Fran told him. 'The Allies have this whole area secured.'

'And if she's not here, this friend of yours?'

Fran wanted to tell him Valérie was more than a friend but sensed there was only so much her conventional older brother could take. She remembered him meeting her in London one time when he was fresh from treating men in Africa. He'd been shaken, scarred by the limits of his profession in the face of man-made carnage, and he was about to face it again. She felt mean for adding to his worries, but she had to do this.

'I can take care of myself, Rob, I promise. And you can't stop me, you know.'

He groaned.

'I know! But please, take care, sis. I don't want to lose you.'

Fran reached up to kiss his cheek.

'I won't go out of the Allied zone, I promise.'

'We'll be here, waiting for you.'

'Thank you.'

He looked as if he might say more but landing craft were pulling up alongside, loaded with wounded, and someone was calling for all nurses to muster. Leaving her brothers, she ran to join them. A few looked askance at her but they were from several hospitals and no one questioned her as they were led to the boats. They had better things to worry about.

Man after man was being lifted out of the smaller boat by a pulley that hooked onto either side of the stained stretchers on which they were lying. Their uniforms were wet and bloodied and most of them had their eyes closed against the sight of their own maimed bodies. Fran glanced back to Rob and Ben, but they were already gone, into the hospital to prepare to treat all the poor youngsters carved open by enemy fire.

These men should be playing rugby and taking girls to hops, not lying in the filth of someone else's blood as their own seeped out to join it. Was Valérie like this too? Pain shuddered through Fran at the thought and she took a step up to the railings as the last of the men was brought on board. She had to find her. Dying or living, she had to tell her that she loved her.

'All aboard,' someone urged the nurses, gesturing to the now empty craft.

'Down that?' one asked, staring at the cargo netting thrown over the railings.

'Think of it like school gym,' Fran advised and, before she could lose her nerve, flung one leg over the top and felt for a foothold. It wasn't easy. The swell was high and the net slammed back and forth against the metal sides of the ship so that she had to cling on for dear life as she felt her way down. Eager hands reached up to help her and, with relief, she landed.

The relief did not last long. The flat-bottomed boat had little defence against the roiling water and she had to clutch at the sides to stay upright. This time yesterday, she thought, men were crammed into these to run at the German guns. She'd already seen some of the results of that terrible sacrifice and, with the stretchers being thrown back onto the craft with them, she knew there was worse to come. Another girl's hand crept into hers as they cast off and she held it gratefully but they hadn't far to go.

'Brace yourself, ladies!' called the pilot, as they drew close to the beach, but before they could do anything, the giant flaps at the front went down and water flooded in, covering their feet and swelling up around their ankles. The girls squealed but eager young soldiers were wading in to help carry them ashore and Fran found herself swept into burly arms like something in a Hollywood movie. She didn't like the feeling of helplessness but at least it kept her dry and it was a relief to see an uninjured man, so she thanked him as prettily as she could manage when he set her on the shore and looked eagerly for the hospital.

'This way, ladies,' a soldier with a nasal accent instructed them. 'Sergeant Lee Derrington at your service, Fifth Battalion of the King's Liverpool Regiment.' He saluted smartly then indicated a track laid with rough boards. 'Up this 'ere. Don't look left.'

They all instantly looked left and stumbled at the lines of corpses laid out along the top of the sand, eyes closed, hands crossed over empty lungs and still hearts.

'I said don't look left,' the sergeant barked. 'You're here to make sure there are no more of them poor gits, so don't go upsetting yourselves.'

The girls huddled closer as they followed the track between

two houses and onto a street. Fran found herself in a pretty French square. To one side a café was doing a roaring trade to happy servicemen, looking as if they had popped over for a holiday, save for the mass of supply trucks and service vehicles trundling past.

Fran saw a waitress kiss one soldier as he was swung into his truck, thought how quickly people seized at a moment of love, and was comforted. But now the hospital was before them – a makeshift set-up in the lower floor of the Mairie. A bedraggled French flag, presumably rescued from hiding in some basement, flew proudly from the flagpost and Fran thought how happy Valérie would have been to see that.

Valérie.

Was she alive? Was she here? Tugging self-consciously at her borrowed uniform, Fran headed in through the open doors with the other, real, nurses and looked around. Men packed the space, some on beds, some on stretchers, some laid out on tables or the floor. They were, at least, out of their uniforms, washed and with the worst of their injuries hidden beneath rough blankets, and Fran scanned those closest to her. Men. They were all men.

A doctor was passing and she grabbed at his arm.

'Do you have any women here?'

'Apart from you lot?'

'Women patients. I'm looking for one in particular, a French girl, a *résistante*.'

'Last time I looked, we hadn't got barbaric enough to sign females up to the battlefront yet. This way. Well, save you poor lot, hey? This way.'

Fran followed him through the line of beds, searching frantically.

'Is this Hermanville?' she asked an orderly as she passed him checking a patient.

'*Oui*,' the man in the bed said. Fran froze.

'You're French?'

'I am.'

'Are you with the Resistance?'

'I was. I'm stuck here now while they fight without me, but I will be out again soon, will I not, Doctor?'

The orderly shook his head.

'You've lost a leg, Raoul. You're not going anywhere in a hurry.'

Fran winced with pity as the man's face fell and he looked under the blanket as if to check. The orderly patted him sadly and moved away and Fran slid in at his side.

'Do you know a girl called Valérie? Valérie Rousseau?'

'Elodie's granddaughter? *Oui*, I know her. She is very brave girl, very – how you say? – bold?'

'That's her,' Fran agreed, feeling tears welling up at the thought of her bold, bolshy, devil of a girlfriend. 'Do you know where she is?'

His face fell again and his eyes filled with tears. Fran felt her own well in response. Had she got this far only to be deprived? Of course she had. She was a fool to think it could be any other way. She'd marched up a beach marked with as many corpses as there would once have been sandcastles and wind-breaks. Was one of them Valérie? Was she going to have to walk the line of death until she found her, drained of the vigour Fran had loved so much.

'They took her away.'

She looked up. The man's eyes were drooping and she clutched at his hand.

'Please, was she alive?'

'She was alive. Barely. Bastard German shot her. They took her away.'

'Who did? Who took her?'

'Her comrades, of course.'

'Where to?'

He shrugged.

'Home, I assume.'

'Bayeux?'

But he was already asleep, his face relaxing as he was carried from his pain for a time. Fran was glad for him but felt as if her own was only increasing.

She's alive, she reminded herself. Or at least she had been when she'd left here. Now the question was, how far was it to Bayeux and how on earth was she going to get there? She turned for the door but a truck was pulling up outside and someone shouted, 'New arrivals. All hands on deck!'

With a stomp of boots on the wooden floor, soldiers began arriving with stretchers.

'Attack out at Cresserons,' one called. 'Ambush from a hedge. Bastards took out loads of our lads.'

Fran shivered. She could hardly grab a bicycle and go jaunting across Normandy as if this were any old summer. It was war out there and she'd promised her brothers she'd keep safe. She looked down at the poor souls arriving. On the nearest stretcher lay a man, groaning in agony, his hands clutched to one eye while blood oozed between his fingers. The other focused on Fran.

'Help me, Nurse. Please, help me.'

What could she do but obey? She was desperate to see Valérie but at least, if she was alive, she had family around her. These poor men had no one. Guiding the stretcher to a bed, she looked for bandages and thought with dark irony of how proud her parents would be if they could see her now. Then she was prising the man's fingers from his face and looking into a missing eyeball, and she thought of nothing more but the horror before her.

THIRTY-SIX

JUNE 1944

Steffie

Steffie rubbed her eyes and forced herself to concentrate. It was three days since D-Day and she felt as if she'd been working non-stop. The whole country knew about the invasion now and the papers and wireless were full of it. Everywhere you went, groups were huddled around sets, hungry for news. It had even been playing in the pub when Steffie had trudged wearily home late on D-Day, older men silent over their pints as they glued themselves to the reports from the brave journalists following the soldiers into Normandy. She had paused in the open doorway to listen.

'Today, our boys struck the first blow for freedom,' some young man called Richard Dimbleby had told his rapt audience. 'Five beachheads have been secured and even now, as the sun goes down on the day history will forever know as D-Day, they are starting to unload the tanks and trucks that will one day roll into Berlin and cease Hitler's reign of terror in Europe.'

It had been grandiose but nonetheless true, or so they all hoped. The men in the pub had nodded approval and muttered about sausages for Christmas, as if it would be a straight march from here. Steffie knew differently. There were many battle-hardened German troops in Europe and, although the Allies had caught them by surprise on the beaches, they were defending the Norman hinterland with ferocity.

The Allies had got within sight of the vital port of Caen but been driven back and were dug in around its edges. Trying to get up the Cotentin peninsula to Cherbourg was also proving difficult and the only port they would be able to rely on for now was the one they were constructing at Arromanches out of vast 'mulberry' units, dragged across the sea and clipped together to form an artificial harbour. The only town that had been captured was the pretty one of Bayeux but for Steffie and Ailsa, that was the one that mattered.

'Valérie's family were from Bayeux, weren't they?' Ailsa had asked Steffie when their brief breaks had coincided earlier today.

'They were. Let's hope she's there.'

'And that Fran gets to her.'

'In safety.'

They'd both shivered and for a moment Steffie had cursed herself for securing her friend that damned car. Questions were already being asked about why Air Marshal Tedder, who was with Eisenhower at Southwick House above Portsmouth, had requested it and it was her name on the chit. She was considering getting a train down to Southampton to get it back. A girl in Switzerland had showed her a neat trick with the wires beneath a car's steering wheel to start it – it was amazing the things you learned at finishing school – so she was confident she could manage that, though less confident she'd get a day off to get that far before the authorities came knocking. At the end of the day, though, it was only a car; it was Fran that mattered.

Last night, despite being so tired she'd seriously considered matchsticks to keep her eyes open, Steffie had gone to the cinema for the late newsreel. Ailsa had told her she'd seen Fran in the Albert Hall out in Colombo and Steffie had combed the grainy pictures from Normandy in the foolish hope of hitting the same luck. All she'd seen, though, had been 'plucky' men waving from the back of trucks and giving thumbs-ups from stretchers.

There had been a brief pan across a vehicle-strewn beach to show a line of bodies, German prisoners digging their graves, but the camera had not dwelled on the dark sight. The BBC was sworn to the truth – a fiercely held edict, set against the known lies and propaganda put out by German-controlled stations – but it also preferred to give hope to the millions of people back home who had loved ones fighting.

'Cup of tea, Steffie?'

She looked up to see Leo reaching for her mug. She felt as if she'd been living on tea since the boats landed but she nodded gratefully.

'Yes please, Leo.'

He smiled at her.

'Even I've started drinking this stuff. Curiously comforting, isn't it?'

She laughed.

'I suppose so, though it has its limits.'

He looked at her more closely.

'Do you have anybody out there?'

Steffie jumped. It was a fair question but not one she'd been asked before. She shook her head.

'My father is in the forces but he's too old for active service.' She thought of Anthony Carmichael, vigorous in the corridors of Whitehall. He was active, for sure, as everyone at Bletchley Park was active, but not on the front line. 'And I have no brothers, just a sister.' A thought hit her. 'Do you?'

He gave a little nod.

'My brother, Alex – Alexandro. He was at Omaha, I think.'

'No!' Steffie stared at him. There had been terrible losses at Omaha. 'Have you heard anything?'

He shook his head.

'No news is good news, right?' he managed tightly, but his eyes were clouded with worry and instinctively Steffie leaped up and threw her arms around him.

He stiffened at first and then, when she didn't let go, his arms went around her and he held on so tight that her heart ached for him. She didn't want him to hurt. She didn't want anyone to hurt, but especially not him, and now it was her holding on too. Eventually Leo pulled gently back.

'Best get that tea,' he said softly.

Steffie smiled up at him. 'You're getting more British with every day that passes.'

'I hope so. I like it here.'

Her heart fluttered dangerously. 'You do? You mean...?'

'I might stay. Perhaps. If I had a job, you know. If I had a, a reason.'

The air between them seemed to shimmer with something that might, if she let it, become possibility. Dare she put herself through that again? Love made you vulnerable to hurt, didn't it? Look at poor Fran, somewhere in Normandy risking great danger to seek out Valérie – for love. She gave Leo an awkward smile and sat down at her desk. With a chink of mugs, he went off towards the kitchen and she let her eyes follow him. That one kiss they'd shared had been so sweet and she could feel her body craving another, but was it sensible?

With a sigh, she took a new decrypt from the top of the pile and set to translating it. What she read was enough to banish all thoughts of kisses from her mind. She scanned it once, then again, then leapt up.

'Denys!'

The whole of ISOS looked up and Denys came rushing over.

'What is it, Steffie?'

'They're moving the panzers. They're moving the panzers from Calais to Normandy.' She looked at her boss. 'I have to call Masterman.'

He nodded.

'Do it. Now.'

He ushered her to the phone on his desk and, with trembling hands, she lifted the receiver and asked to be put through to the St James's Street offices.

'Masterman,' came a crisp voice.

'John. It's Stefania Carmichael. They're moving the panzers.'

John Masterman cursed.

'Already? How many? Where to?' She gave him the details she had so far. 'Right, leave it with me. Tar!' she heard him shout across the office. 'Time for your agents to go to work.' He came back to her. 'Thank you, Stefania. This is most helpful. We'll see what we can do.'

Then he was gone and she could only sit back and look around the many men and women battling to read enemy messages and pray better news came in soon. One thing was for sure, there would be no leave to go and hot-wire cars in Southampton. If the Panzerarmee was on its way west, it would be all hands on deck here and all hell in Normandy.

'Stay safe, Fran,' Steffie willed her friend as she made it back to her own desk.

'Did you say something?'

Leo was back with her tea. She took it and looked across at him.

'Can you keep a secret?' He spread his hands wide. Of course he could keep a secret, he worked in BP. Steffie grimaced. 'Sorry. This is a personal one but it's burning me up not being able to talk to anyone about it. Well, my friend Ailsa knows too but she's working all the hours, like us, and looking after her baby girl in between.'

'Rowan,' he said. 'I met her. Cute little thing.'

Steffie smiled. 'She is.'

'But that's not what's worrying you, I'm guessing.'

'No. It's our other friend, Fran. She's, er, she's gone to Normandy.'

His eyes widened. 'How? Actually, forget that. Why?'

'We had word that someone she loves is hurt.'

'Ah. And she wanted to be with them?'

He said it so simply, so acceptingly. Steffie nodded.

'Do you think that's mad, Leo?'

'I think it's what we're all fighting for – the chance to love and the freedom to go wherever that love takes us.'

Steffie stared at him.

'It is,' she agreed, looking into his kind eyes. 'It so is.'

Love would always be a risk. It could always hurt you, even without bombs and guns and tanks to cut across its path, but at the end of the day, it was what made life worthwhile. Steffie swallowed. It was time to stop hiding, time to stop dwelling in the past where love was sad but safe.

'Leo,' she said. 'I'd really like to kiss you again.'

A smile spread across his handsome face, lighting up his eyes, and he leaned closer.

'I'd like that too, very much – though perhaps not here.' They both glanced at the desks all around them, filled with hard-working decrypters. 'What time do you finish tonight?'

Steffie groaned.

'If the panzers are on the move, we'll be lucky to finish at all,' she said.

Leo reached out and put a hand over hers.

'I can wait, Steffie. I'm not saying it won't be hard, but I can wait. I promise you now, I'm not going anywhere so we have all the time we need.'

Steffie felt warmth steal through her. She picked up her pencil and looked down at her next decrypt, but couldn't resist another peek at the warm, kind, totally gorgeous man at the next desk. He peeked back. God, but she wanted to kiss him! Tonight, with the whole of the country playing a high stakes game to try and end the war, she was painfully aware of how short life was and desperate to seize happiness where she could. Work had to come first right now, she knew that, but, Lord help her, it was going to be a very long shift.

The news came in at ten o'clock. It was someone else who got the message this time but they jumped up to announce it to the whole room.

'The panzers are turning back!' They all crowded round the man, who waved his slip as if it contained a huge win on the horses. 'The Germans have declared a state of emergency in the Pas-de-Calais and are turning them back.'

Steffie's heart leaped and she longed to call Tar to find out what his agents had said but knew he'd be busy. There would be time to find out at the next Twenty Committee meeting and, besides, she could make an educated guess. His trusted agents would have sent panicked messages about FUSAG and the Germans, fearing a second attack from wood-and-canvas landing craft filled with make-believe American troops under a general they respected as much as one of their own, had decided to keep their fearsome Panzerarmee waiting in Calais. The invasion force in Normandy had more time to establish themselves, and Fran more time to get safely to Valérie.

Steffie wept at the news, silent tears of relief. Leo took her hand, led her quietly from Block G and, by the light of the moon and the quacking of the ducks on Bletchley Park pond, kissed her at last.

THIRTY-SEVEN

Fran

'Hey, you!'

Fran jumped as someone tapped her on the shoulder. She was taking a much-needed break from the seemingly endless nursing duties in Hermanville to drink a quick but utterly delicious coffee in the café across the way. It was a lovely day, the bad weather having finally subsided in the Channel, and she'd been drawn instinctively towards the seafront but the moment she'd crested the dunes, she'd seen the hive of military activity and turned hastily back. She wanted the postcard beach, not the army camp version. Now though, as a man came up to her table, she almost wished she'd stayed on the sand.

'Can I help you?'

'I think it might be more that I can help you. I hear you want to get to Bayeux?'

'You do?' Fran's heart raced. 'That is, I do. Yes. Very much.'

She'd told a couple of the nurses about her 'friend' in the town but had no idea how it had got to this man, not that she cared if he could help her.

'As it happens, I've got a truck heading in that direction this afternoon. There's a seat free.'

Fran couldn't believe her ears. She flung her arms around him.

'Thank you. Oh God, thank you so much.'

He flushed right to the tips of his already sunburned ears.

'There now, we all know what it's like. I just hope I get a lovely girl like you prepared to chase across France for me one day.'

Fran gave him a smacking kiss on his pink cheek.

'You will,' she promised him. 'You definitely will.'

'Yes, well, be outside the hospital at two sharp and you'll be on your way.'

He brushed her off, but he was smiling fit to burst and so was Fran. Then she remembered that, even if she got to Bayeux, she might only be in time for Valérie's funeral and fear flooded through her once again.

'Only one way to find out, Fran,' she told herself sternly and, draining her coffee, went back to her nursing duties until her lift arrived.

The truck, when it came, was filled with fresh-faced soldiers, sitting on strange wire mats, who heaved Fran into the back with much jocularity. She found herself bouncing out of Hermanville and towards Valérie's hometown with ten lads desperate for female company. They started with the usual 'what's a pretty thing like you doing out here?' lines but, those out of the way, they settled into talking to her about their sisters, their mums, and their wives, grateful for any reminder of the life they were fighting to preserve.

The sun was shining and, away from the beaches, the countryside was lush with meadow flowers and fruit trees. It might have been possible to believe you were on a simple country jaunt, save for the pockmarks carved into the hillsides by bombs and the stricken faces of the inhabitants of every village as they saw you coming.

They passed through one tiny place that had taken a direct hit to its centre. Homes lay in rubble and spades stuck out of it, ready for renewed digging, while those who had survived huddled, all in black, around a priest singing Mass over a line of fresh graves by a spireless church. It was not just soldiers who were being killed in this growing Battle of Normandy, but the civilians unlucky enough to find themselves in its path and Fran cursed Hitler to hell and back for what he had done.

'I swear he's the most evil man on this planet,' she said as a girl with one arm in a sling and younger sibling on her hip, raised a pleading hand to their truck.

'He is that,' the soldier next to her agreed, pulling his precious chocolate ration from his pocket and tossing it to the girl, who cried a pitiful *merci* after them. 'But we'll get him. We'll get him and we'll put him on trial before the whole world and then we'll cut his sodding head off. And that'll be too good for him 'n all.'

The others chorused agreement but now they were turning off the road into the middle of what seemed at first to be a meadow but, as the truck swung around, turned out to be an airfield in construction. The soldiers jumped up and began heaving the mats they'd been sitting on out of the truck. Fran jumped out too, keen not to be in the way, and stood at the edge of the site taking it all in.

Several army tents stood either side of a long line of the mats, hammered into the ground to, she assumed, make a temporary runway across the soft grass. Pegs marked where it would extend to and two engineers were installing lights at the far end and setting up flags to guide pilots in. The mats were being flattened into place by a big roller and Fran marvelled at the machines the Allies had brought onto their newly taken beaches.

The runway was nearly complete and men ran to deliver these final mats. In the next field along, a farmer and his daughter were busily harvesting yellow hay in the sunshine, forking bundles onto the back of a rickety cart drawn by two beautiful Percherons. One of the horses looked up with a startled whinny and, following his big eyes, Fran saw a plane circling in the blue sky, smoke coming from its underside.

'Stray!' someone shouted. 'Looks in distress. Clear the runway!'

Amidst much shouting, men and machine were hastily cleared and, heart in mouth, Fran saw the distinctive sleek shape of a Spitfire come swooping down. In a squeal of brakes and a cloud of fumes, it landed on the matting, skidding to an only slightly sideways halt right alongside the horse and cart. A cheer went up around the field and, as men rushed to put out any possible fire, Fran felt the giddy thrill of having been present at an important moment. Many more planes would land and take off here, she was sure, but she had seen the first.

'Got 'ere in the nick of time,' the lance corporal in charge of the unit said, coming to stand next to her.

'It's amazing.'

'It's necessary. And now, we've got to get on. We're off to base a few kilometres to the west of Bayeux but we can drop you above the town if you're happy to walk in?'

Fran clutched at the side of the sturdy truck.

'Is it safe?'

'Should be. We've got that whole area so secure that I hear they're thinking of sending that frog general over. De something funny.'

'De Gaulle,' Fran said. 'General De Gaulle.'

'That's the one. Keen to get his feet on home soil. Wants to make sure us Brits don't nick it in the Germans' place, I reckon.'

He winked at her, though Fran knew more than most that there was a grain of truth in his joking. De Gaulle had been

fighting for a free France from the moment he'd fled the occupied zone in 1940 and he wouldn't stop now. Valérie would
be so excited if he was coming to Bayeux. At least, she would
if she was alive to know it. Fran looked back at the farmer's
daughter, waving enthusiastically at the Spitfire pilot as he
swung himself from his cockpit with a swagger, then turned
her face south – to Bayeux and, one way or another, to
Valérie.

The truck dropped her at the top of a hill.

'There it is, love. Follow the bloody great spires and you
can't go wrong.'

The lance corporal pointed to an elegant dome showing
above the green horizon, two smaller points flanking it. Fran
nodded but couldn't quite persuade her legs to jump down from
the safety of the truck.

'Can't we take her in, boss?' the man next to her said.

'Sorry, son, I'd love to, but we've got to get on. We can't be
taking jaunts to deliver damsels in distress.'

'King Arthur would,' the lad shot back.

'Yeah, well, King Arthur didn't have Colonel Marshall
barking at him if he was late, did he? Tell you what, here!' He
chucked Fran a tin helmet. 'That'll keep you safe.'

'Chivalry isn't dead,' the soldier muttered, leaping down
and offering Fran a hand. She took it and, with no choice,
swung herself out of the truck full of men who now felt like her
best friends. 'Stay low, hey,' her escort said, then with a grimace
leaped back into the truck, which pulled instantly away.

Fran gave a tiny wave and then turned and looked down the
road to Bayeux and, more nervously, to the hedge-lined fields
either side. There could be a German sniper in any one of
those. Would he shoot at a girl in a nurse's uniform? Probably,
but she was here now and doubtless safer in the town than up

on the hillside, so putting the tin hat firmly on her head, she gathered her dwindling courage and set out.

It was quiet and she was disturbed by nothing more than a rabbit jumping from the wayside. It looked at her a moment, then turned its white tail and hopped away. Fran crouched, getting her breath back, then marched on. Her heart was pounding in her chest and the only way she could stay calm was to picture the maps on the walls of Room 149 and talk herself down the routes she had traced in string so many times. It felt a lot longer on foot but, at last, she hit the first houses of the town. An old man was ushering his wife into their home with a basket of fruit over her arm and Fran could have wept at the normality of the tableau, but now she had made it here alive, she had to find out if Valérie was alive too.

Alive and wanting you.

The thought buzzed into Fran's heart like a fly – small but persistent – and yet again she questioned the fool motive that had sent her so far from all she knew. All but Valérie. She would just have to tell her how she felt, and take whatever came next.

'*Excusez-moi.*' She stopped the couple. '*Connaissez-vous un magasin de bicyclettes?*'

The old man looked at her, his grey eyes sharp.

'*Vous cherchez le magasin d'Elodie Rousseau?*' Fran blinked in surprise and the man tapped the side of his nose knowingly. '*Tout le monde cherche le magasin d'Elodie Rousseau. Elle a les meilleures bicyclettes.*' He threw her a sudden, wicked wink. '*Vous le trouverez sur Rue Saint-Martin, derrière la cathédrale.*'

'*Merci. Oh, merci, monsieur.*'

He reached out and patted her arm.

'*Non. Merci à vous, ma fille. Bonne chance.*'

He pointed her down the road and, feeling slightly more hopeful, Fran went as instructed. Bayeux was very pretty and she traced her way down cobbled streets, between buildings of soft yellow stone, seemingly untouched by bombs or guns, and felt curiously reminded of her own hometown of Cambridge. Stepping out into an open space, she found the cathedral looming up before her, majestic in its beauty, but there was no time to stand gawping at the past when her own future was in the balance.

Tracing her way around the cathedral, from the imposing square front to the softer, rounded rear, she found a sign on the buildings nestled behind: Rue Saint-Martin. Heart beating so hard now that she swore it might give the church bells a run for their money, she moved slowly up it and there, discreet but clear, was an ancient metal bicycle bearing a sign that read simply: *Bicyclettes* with beneath it in far smaller letters: *Famille Rousseau*.

Fran glanced right and left but no one was around so, snatching her tin hat off her head and laying it next to the old bicycle, she ducked through an archway and found herself in a small courtyard. Several bikes stood on stands and two men were sitting in one corner, drinking tiny coffees and smoking. A woman emerged in the doorway behind them, making Fran jump. She was tiny, with cropped white hair, a lined face, and razor-sharp eyes that fixed intently on Fran.

'*Bon après-midi, madame. Nous pouvons vous aider?*'

Could they help her? Fran had no idea. She tried to speak but her throat was so dry that nothing came out and she had to cough pathetically to clear it.

'*Je... Je cherche Valérie Rousseau.*'

'*Valérie?*' The woman pushed past the two men and came darting across to Fran, at surprising speed for her considerable age. '*Vous cherchez ma Valérie?*'

Fran noted the use of the possessive – my Valérie. Was this, then, the infamous Grand-mère Elodie? She looked sad. Did she? Did she look sad, or did she look scared? Or French? Fran's mind raced as fast as her heart.

'Elodie?' she asked tentatively.

'*Peut être,*' the woman said – perhaps.

She crossed her arms over her birdlike chest and the two men came over to stand protectively at her shoulders. Fran swallowed.

'*Est-Valérie ici?*' she squeaked.

'*Peut être,*' the woman said again, her eyes boring into Fran.

She was sure now this was the infamous Elodie, provider of the best bicycles and the most penetrating information in northern France. She coughed again.

'*Est-elle...?*' She scrabbled around in her mind for the word for alive. '*En vie?*' she tried.

'*Vivante? Peut être.*' Fran's heart tolled. '*Qui veut savoir?*'

She shook herself. Who wants to know, she had asked, and of course, they were afraid. She could be anyone – a German spy maybe, sent to chase down the escaping *résistante*. That had to be it, right? Surely that was it?

'*Je m'appelle Frances Morgan,*' she started. '*Je suis—*'

But she had no chance to say what else she was, or to explain anything further, for all three of them were falling upon her, kissing her cheeks and repeating her name with the same soft inflection that Valérie always gave to it.

'*Frances! Ah, Frances, tu est ici! Je suis Elodie, oui. Je suis la grand-mère de notre cher Valérie.*' She clutched Fran's arms in a vice-like grip, reaching up to punch a kiss onto each cheek. Did this, then, mean...? '*Entrez.* Come in. This way. Please. Valérie, her heart break for you, *ma chérie. Elle est gravement blessée –* injured. Bad injured – *Mais maintenant...* Come. Quick. You must come.'

Elodie Rousseau took Fran's hand and led her through the doorway, turning her up a narrow wooden staircase to an open door at the top.

'Please...'

She stood back, ushering Fran inside and, awash with

emotion, she stepped into the room. It was a simple bedchamber, set beneath beamed eaves, with a mullioned window looking right out onto the cathedral, not that Fran had any time to notice such detail for there, in the bed, was Valérie. She lay beneath a white coverlet, her dark hair short and scraggy against the pillow, her full lips still and her eyes closed.

'Go,' her grandmother urged. 'Wake her. Is good.' Fran looked back at her and she smiled. 'Is good, really. I leave you.'

Then she was gone, clattering ostentatiously down the stairs. Fran crept up to the bed but the sound of her grandmother's noisy departure had woken Valérie and her eyes fluttered open.

'Frances?' She shook her head as if she thought she might still be dreaming. 'Frances, *c'est toi?*'

'*C'est moi*,' Fran said.

'You are here? In Bayeux? Why?'

Fran laughed, the last few days of worry and fear fading away in an instant.

'To see you, of course, Valérie. To see you and to tell you that I love you.'

'You do?' Valérie went the cutest pink against her pillows. 'You love me? Even though I am a stubborn, stupid Frenchwoman with no idea how to – how you say – arrange her priorities?'

'Even though you are a proud, brave, crazy Frenchwoman who wanted to fight for her country, yes.'

Valérie pulled a hand out from beneath the restrictions of the coverlet and grabbed at Fran's.

'I was wrong, Frances. I knew it the minute I got out here. I was thinking all the time of La France. I was thinking of how I should serve her and of what she might think of me for not standing by her in her hour of need.'

'But you were—'

'I know, I know. I told you – I am a stupid, stubborn Frenchwoman.'

'You are *my* stupid, stubborn Frenchwoman – and I love you for it. Well, I love you despite it.'

Fran smiled down at her but Valérie still looked distressed.

'You are too good, Frances, too kind. But listen, this is *importante*. I was thinking always of France when I should have been thinking always of Frances.'

Fran laughed.

Very good, Valérie. Very neat.'

And now, at last, Valérie smiled.

'I have been working on it,' she admitted, her eyes finally sparkling with a hint of the glorious mischief Fran knew so well. 'I have been working on it in case I was ever, somehow, granted a chance to see you again. I even wrote it down so that if I... if I could not give it to you myself, you would at least read it from my hand.'

Fran swallowed.

'Are you badly injured, Valérie?'

'They say so. Do you want to see?'

'No!' Fran put up her hands. She'd seen enough injuries in the past three days to last her a lifetime. If she'd thought the medical profession wasn't for her before, she was sure of it now. 'Just tell me you'll recover.'

'I will now.' She patted the side of the bed and Fran sat tentatively down, careful not to brush against her. 'It is my chest. Pig German shot me. I lost a lot of blood.' A shadow crossed her face at the memory but she pushed it away. 'But not as much as he did. I shot him from the ground. He died in front of my eyes.'

Fran shivered.

'I'm so sorry, Valérie.'

'About the German?'

'About you! I was so scared you were dead.'

'How did you even know?'

Fran smiled.

'It's a long story. Reggie told Ailsa that "Elodie" was down, and Ailsa told me and Steffie got me a car and then my brothers got me on a ship and, and here I am.'

'It was not, I think, that simple.'

'It feels it now that I am here. May I kiss you, "Elodie"?'

But at that Valérie shook her head vehemently.

'I am Elodie no more. There is only one Elodie, my *grand-mère*, and that is as it should be. I was trying too hard to be her instead of making the most of being myself. You knew that, Frances. You knew Valérie – and, perhaps, liked her?

'*Loved* her.' Valérie flushed again and Fran leaned in closer. 'Can I, then, kiss you, *Valérie*?'

Now the sparkle filled Valérie's eyes.

'I thought you'd never ask, *chérie*.'

Then Fran was bending over and Valérie's hand was snaking up around her neck, caressing it with wonder, as their lips met and her battered heart swelled with healing happiness.

'You can stay?' Valérie asked, when finally they parted.

Fran thought about it. Her brothers would be worried, her friends too, not to mention all the authorities she had defied along the way and the car she had more or less stolen. All for love; all worth it.

'Not for long. Perhaps until De Gaulle comes to Bayeux?'

'De Gaulle?' Valérie half sat up then winced. 'The general is coming here?'

'Oi! You look more excited than when you saw me.'

'Well, he is very handsome...'

'He is not! And you wouldn't care even if he was.'

'He is De Gaulle, Frances...' Valérie teased and then she shook her head. 'I would not care, not if he was the most handsome man in the world, or the most beautiful woman. I care for no one but you, Frances, not now, and not ever.'

Then she was reaching up to kiss her again and Fran felt her future open up before her, rich with peace and laughter and love.

Four days later, they stood together amidst an overexcited crowd in front of the Mairie. Or, at least, Fran stood; Valérie leaned heavily on her, too proud to accept the creaking bath chair that her grandmother had proudly produced.

'Never!' she'd proclaimed.

'Never?' Fran had asked. 'What, then, will I push you in when you are a grandly grumpy eighty-year-old?'

Valérie had softened.

'When I am eighty, Frances, I will let you push me in a bath chair, but for now, your arm please.'

It had taken her a long time to get down the stairs without pulling too much at the slowly healing wound, but they had started early and, besides, they had positions on the balcony so did not have to worry about saving a place. Elodie Rousseau was a legend in these parts, running the most efficient Resistance ring in France with piercing efficiency and deceptive, white-haired innocence. She smoked Gauloises, drank pastis and could assemble the hidden parts of a gun in seconds. After four days in her household, Fran could see why Valérie had wanted to emulate her.

'Perhaps, if we have a daughter, we could call her Elodie,' she'd said to Valérie last night.

'How on earth would we have a daughter?' Valérie had laughed, but Fran had been serious.

'We could adopt. There will, sadly, be many orphans needing loving homes when the war is done.'

'And you would subject them to me?'

'They would be the luckiest children alive.'

Valérie had cried then.

'How did I ever leave you, Frances?'

'It doesn't matter – as long as you never do it again.'

'Never.'

Now Fran felt Valérie's hand sneak into hers as they heard cheers at the bottom of the town. Bayeux, heart of Normandy, was the first place to be declared officially unoccupied and every last occupant was out to await the arrival of General De Gaulle, self-proclaimed liberator of France. The press had descended in force and yesterday Fran had spotted a woman writing eagerly in a notebook and been sure it was Martha Gellhorn. She'd made it then, as Fran had made it.

'You should be making notes too,' Valérie had said when Fran had told her later, and Fran was.

While Valérie slept, she wrote all she could in one of the strange, squared notepads they favoured in France. She was a journalist now, after all, and this was not an opportunity she could afford to miss. She'd sent a telegram to Esmond Harmsworth informing him that she was 'on the spot' in Bayeux and offering to send news and, with no one else available, he had agreed. She was poised to telephone in her report from the local post office as soon as De Gaulle had made his speech and was determined to seize the opportunity this had offered her.

She'd sent telegrams, too, to Gloria at the farmhouse for Ailsa and Steffie, and to HMHS *Dinard* for her brothers. Even the Nazis didn't bomb hospital ships, so she was fairly confident Rob and Ben would be fine but also very aware they didn't have any such assurances about her.

We are both safe, well and happy.

She had seen little need to say more. There would be time for the details another day but for now she would make the most of seeing the arrival of the leader of the provisional French government into the first town in France to proclaim it. And here he was, coming up the street with the crowds waiting reverently either side for him to pass and then falling in behind, like a giant human train.

People pressed flowers upon him and he took them with a smile and passed them to helpers drowning under their colourful mass. Those at the back chased around the side streets to come out and see him again, children darting between their legs, giddy on the thrill of a tall man with big ears and a stiff wave, who strode up the street like the movie star he did not in any way resemble.

De Gaulle reached the Mairie and they left the balcony to join him in the room, dark behind its heavy drapes, and he shook their hands with such genuine vigour that Fran warmed to him. He was an angular, awkward, truculent man but he had stood up for France when all the other leaders had laid down and he deserved this day. She remembered meeting him in the Connaught Hotel in London a year ago, when he'd been an exile operating from beneath a portrait of Napoleon, and thought that there was a lot to be said for truculence. Being nice, sadly, did not win wars.

Fran lingered at the back of the grand party, as they headed back onto the balcony behind the general, to more uproarious cheers from below. She looked down at the giddy joy of a people granted freedom and felt a fraud to be looking in on their private celebration. But with Valérie clutching tight at her arm, and her family pressing around her, she was a tiny part of it. Besides, via the *Daily Mail*, she would be able to share it with the world so that they, too, could feel the joy of the first step to victory.

And so, as General De Gaulle stepped up to the microphone to address the people with the usual cries for *patriotisme, fierté, bravoure* and, of course, La France, Fran held Valérie close and savoured every last, glorious, loving moment of liberation.

EPILOGUE

AUGUST 1944

They gathered on the grass in the sunshine, the women in their prettiest dresses, and the men their crispest shirts, so that even the graves behind them seemed cheerier than usual on this hot August day.

'It's warmer than it was for our wedding,' Ailsa murmured to Ned, waving to the pretty Bletchley church that had been covered in snow for their nuptials.

She leaned against him to be sure that he was really here, safe at her side. Although the war was going well in Europe, the Japanese were still hurling themselves against the Americans in the Far East and they'd feared Ned would be stuck in Ceylon for ages. Then, in a strange quirk of wartime fate, he'd caught malaria and been shipped home.

'God bless the mosquitos,' he'd cheerfully told Ailsa when Steffie had driven her and Rowan down to Portsmouth to meet him off the boat.

His pale skin, wasted frame and shadowed eyes had told a darker story but the doctors were satisfied the disease had receded and Gloria had been feeding him up with her usual exuberance so he was well on the way to recovery. Now he bent to drop a swift kiss on her lips.

'Can you believe we only got married a year and a half ago and here we are – a proper family.'

They both looked fondly to Rowan. Although only ten months old, she was making a determined effort to walk and was clutching tightly to one each of Fran and Steffie's hands as she tested her legs along the path, merrily oblivious to the back pain she was inflicting on her doting godmothers.

'I'm not sure that's doing her christening gown much good,' Ailsa said ruefully, glancing to her mother, who had brought the precious heirloom down from North Uist.

'It's a good job I had to take the fabric off the hem to make it bigger around the chest,' Mirren agreed, 'or she'd have trampled it into the dirt by noo.'

'Sorry, Ma.'

'Och now, don't apologise. It's a dress to be worn, so it is, and it can easily be adjusted back for the next one.'

'Next one?' Ailsa laughed, but she felt Ned's hand slide around her waist and found herself wondering if, perhaps, a brother or sister for Rowan wouldn't be rather lovely.

Peace seemed to be close at hand after all. The Germans were retreating and two weeks ago the Allies had marched triumphantly into Paris. One of Valérie's uncles had appeared at the caravan with a whole crate of champagne and they'd had an impromptu party, stringing handmade tricolours around the farmyard, making Valérie laugh, then cry and then – much later – sing 'La Marseillaise' at the top of her voice.

Valérie had returned to Bletchley at about the same time as Ned, still nursing a nasty wound but limping around at Fran's side with a near-permanent smile on her pixie face. Ailsa clutched tighter at Ned's arm as she watched Fran share a fond smile with her girlfriend. Both she and Fran, she suspected, had come nearer to losing their partners than they wanted to know and she could only thank God that they were all here, safe, today.

She looked to Steffie. The shadow of Matteo's death lingered around her friend. She was still thinner than she'd been when they'd first met, quieter and more serious too, but Leonard was slowly coaxing smiles out of her once more and it warmed Ailsa's heart to see it. His brother, Alex, was staying with him, on crutches from an injury on Omaha beach but grateful to be alive, and Ailsa had been delighted to include him in today's celebrations. The more family the better, if you asked her. The other day Steffie had confided that Leo had been offered a government post in London after the war and Ailsa had seen a happy future in her friend's shy smile and been glad of it.

Not that they were there yet. Hitler was still blustering nonsense about fight-backs and strong stands and they all feared that there would be much needless destruction before he could be brought to his senses. Steffie, who, as far as Ailsa could gather, read many of the high-level German messages as part of her work in ISOS, said he had no senses to be brought to and the Allies would have to march all the way into Berlin before the world was rid of him, and Ailsa prayed they could do that fast. You could smell peace in the summer air, as sweet as the jasmine on the bushes at the edge of the church-yard, and everyone was ready for it. Next week would be exactly five years since the Nazis had invaded Poland – five years of sacrifice and destruction, of loss and pain. It had to stop.

Ailsa shook away her dark thoughts and focused on the many friends and family around them. *This* was what they were all fighting for. *This* was life – nothing to do with borders, or power, or who ruled where, just the happy rhythms of ordinary, everyday love.

In the doorway of the church, the vicar cleared his throat.

'Are we ready to welcome a new life into our community, ladies and gents?'

'We're ready,' Ned agreed.

All eyes turned to Rowan as Steffie and Fran, flanked by Leonard and Valérie, turned her to walk towards the church. Ailsa let go of Ned and crouched down to encourage her daughter on and, as she did so, Rowan shook herself free of her godmothers and, her face creased with concentration, set out alone.

'Oh Rowan,' Ailsa gasped. 'You're walking!'

She held out her arms and, giggling wildly, her daughter took the last few tottering steps and fell into them to raucous cheers.

'That girl knows how to make an entrance,' Ned laughed, kissing his daughter.

'She's storm-blessed,' Ailsa said and they both shook their heads remembering the tropical hurricane that had brought Rowan into the world.

'I'll take the vicar's blessing, thank you,' Ned said, lifting Rowan into his arms to carry her to the church as the other guests began to head inside.

Ailsa dropped back, taking Fran and Steffie's arms as Leonard, with a smart bow, offered Valérie his own. The three friends looked around at the people of Bletchley Park, filing into the church as if they were any old workmates and not the men and women who were quietly and systematically breaking down the German defences from the heat of rural Buckinghamshire, and smiled.

'Who'd have thought,' Fran said, 'when we stepped out of a train onto Bletchley station that dark night back in 1940, that the war would bring us to this. You've got a family, Ailsa, I'm starting up as a journalist and Steffie is all but running the secret service.'

'I am not!' Steffie protested.

'Give it a year or two. Travis will surely retire soon and I can think of no one better to be the next C.'

Steffie nudged at her.

'Idiot! The war's changed all our lives, for sure, but the best thing it's given me is you two – the sisters I never knew I had.'

'And the ones you'll never have to be without again,' Ailsa confirmed.

Then, arm in arm, Steffie, Ailsa and Fran ducked into the cool of the church, into the smiles of friends and family, and into peace at last.

A LETTER FROM ANNA

Dear reader,

I want to say a huge thank you for choosing to read *Code Name Elodie*. I loved writing about Fran, Steffie and Ailsa in *The Bletchley Girls*, so it was a real treat to be able to carry their story into the second half of the war and all the way up to D-Day. If you want to keep up to date with all my latest releases, just sign up at the following link. Your email address will never be shared and you can unsubscribe at any time.

www.bookouture.com/anna-stuart

I have, obviously, always been aware of D-Day as a critical point in the Second World War, but when I came to research it in more detail for this novel, I was fascinated by the vast and complex logistics that went into landing so many men in Normandy to start the advance on Berlin. Reading about the many and varied people preparing for the invasion in different ways intrigued me, perhaps especially the web of lies woven around the unhideable truths to give the Allies every possible advantage. Bletchley Park and the people who worked there were critical to the success of both the real and fake plans and I loved giving Fran, Steffie and Ailsa key roles in the build-up to D-Day.

If you enjoyed this novel, I'd be very grateful if you could write a review. I'd love to hear what you think, and it makes such a difference helping new readers to discover one of my books for the first time. I also love hearing from my readers – you can get in touch on my Facebook page, through Twitter, Instagram or my website.

Thanks for reading,

Anna

www.annastuartbooks.com

 facebook.com/annastuartauthor
 twitter.com/annastuartbooks
 instagram.com/annastuartauthor

HISTORICAL NOTES

You'll find more information on Bletchley Park and its outposts at the back of *The Bletchley Girls* but here are a few additional notes on elements key to *Code Name Elodie*:

The bombing of Bletchley Park which opens this novel is, I confess, anachronistic. Bombs did drop on Bletchley Park, one in the stable yard, one in the road, one near the Elmer's School at the entrance, and one so close to Hut 4 that it knocked the whole thing off its foundations. However, in reality, that happened on 21st November 1941. Having had no room to include this dramatic and terrifying threat in *The Bletchley Girls*, I took what I hope is a forgivable liberty of transposing the event forward two years for an impactful opening to this novel.

General De Gaulle is a fascinating man. These days he is hailed as a hero of France, with streets and squares named after him all over the country, so that it is easy to forget that for much of the war he was a little-known exile whose only real weapon was the BBC. Not a natural charmer, De Gaulle was an awkward oddity with limited social graces but driven by a passion for his country that saw him refuse to give up fighting when almost all his compatriots had done so. Churchill supported him but found him tricky, especially when Roosevelt took against him, and the man must have had the obstinacy of a bull to keep fighting for recognition as the post-war leader of France.

From a back-street office in London, De Gaulle played a sly and clever game, working with the resistance, holding control of the provisional French government set up in Algiers in 1943 (no mean feat without American backing) and quietly establishing a civil service that went into France behind the invasion to claim Mairies and control regional government, ensuring instant liberation rather than Allied occupation as the Germans retreated.

From the moment he escaped his homeland, in considerable danger, in June 1940, De Gaulle established 'Free France' to stand up against the collaborationist government of Petain (his onetime mentor). He battled to get this alternative 'government' recognised and insisted on being included in conferences and negotiations so that his country, despite offering little concrete contribution to the liberation of Europe, emerged as one of the four conquering powers post-war. They even got a portion of Berlin – not something afforded to, for example, beleaguered Poland who never collaborated but ran an official government in exile out of London throughout the war. De Gaulle was a man with little grace, but much passion and the French people understood what he had done for them, so it was a joy to me to be able to conclude this novel with his triumphant entry into Bayeux, the first liberated city in 'La France'.

The resistance characters mentioned in this novel were all inspired by real people and all lived lives as dramatic as depicted. Pierre and Gilberte Brossolette were a very brave couple who, as shown, escaped their Paris bookshop – a hotbed of resistance activity – after their teenage son was briefly arrested. Pierre was instrumental in pulling together various resistance groups in the occupied north, whilst Jean Moulin did the same in the unoccupied south.

Moulin, with his rakish hat and scar-hiding neckerchief, is the more well-known face of the resistance these days, but Brossolette did just as much work, for longer, and at great risk to himself. He was, as shown, captured after being shipwrecked trying to get back to England. His lock of white hair is genuine, as was the need to get him out of prison before it began to grow back – a gift of a detail for a novelist! Sadly, he was found out and had to kill himself to escape torture, though I'm pleased to report that Yeo-Thomas, after various daring escapes from prisons and concentration camps, miraculously survived the war.

Gilberte Brossolette was an admirable woman in her own right, carrying on much resistance coordination from British shores, and working for the BBC to support French interests. In 1946, she was one of twenty-one women elected to the *Conseil de la République* that formed the interim government of France and she served as a senator until 1959.

Grand-mère Elodie is a fictional character, though inspired by a woman called Marie Drouet, a grocer from Bétheny, near Reims who, despite having a shop to run, four children to care for and a fifth on the way, spent World War I transporting the wounded from the battlefields of the Somme to hospital using her plough and donkey. She also informed French artillerymen about German positions via slips of paper displayed in her shop windows and she seemed to me a strong person on whom to loosely base the formidable Elodie.

The whole Rousseau family are made up, though based on many brave, real-life families, but the resistance in Bayeux was, indeed, run out of a bicycle shop near the cathedral so this seemed too good a detail to pass up.

Operation Mincemeat was a real deception that has recently been immortalised in the very enjoyable Colin Firth film of the same name. It was dreamed up by Ewan Montagu and all the documents and personal touches described in the novel were truly added to the dressed-up corpse of a dead tramp named Glyndwr Michael. In reality, the picture of Major Martin's fictitious fiancé, Pam, was drawn from a selection brought in by girls in government offices, and the letters (of which the quotes in this novel are direct) were written by a friend of one of those girls, but it seemed to me that Steffie could easily fill that role for this story and I enjoyed giving her a small part in this unusual – and very successful – element of the invasion of Sicily and Italy.

The Italian peace negotiations, a huge coup for the Allies, were, I'm afraid, as much of a mess as depicted in the novel – including the petty dispute over which Italian general had the highest rank to negotiate in Lisbon. The armistice seems to have been signed in something of a rush and publicised without due attention to the German response in Italy and the resultant taking of Rome by the Nazis and hideous loss of life across the country could have been avoided with greater care and planning. Thousands of Italian soldiers and civilians were massacred and Rome, a city that could so easily have been secured, was not taken for another whole year. It was not the Allies' finest moment and led to many personal tragedies, as exemplified in poor Matteo's death.

The rounders match between the Americans and the British at Bletchley Park did take place, although on July 4th 1943, rather than spring 1944 as shown in the novel. It also did result in both sides believing they had won due to the different scoring systems of rounders and baseball. It seemed, to me, a lovely example of Anglo-American cooperation – and confusion – and I was delighted to be able to use it as a small part in Steffie and Leo's love story.

D-day is, obviously, an important part of World War II but it was only when I really started looking into it for this novel that I understood the length and depth of planning that went into that most vital invasion on so many levels. The military planning and equipping were obviously crucial but the logistical arrangements to get 150,000 men (many of them still in America just a couple of months before) across the channel were vast. And done in such secrecy that Rommel really was off at his wife's birthday party on the critical night.

What's more, although we tend to think of D-day as a one-off scramble up the beaches, it was really just Day One in the two-month Battle of Normandy that led to the liberation of Paris and the Nazi retreat into Germany. Taking the beaches was vital not as a standalone exercise, but to create a way of unloading more men and equipment to drive Hitler out of 'Fortress Europe'. Along with these came the medical staff and journalists who offered me the chance to get Fran onto French soil to find Valerie.

Even more fascinating to me was discovering the Twenty Committee, the double-cross programme, and the 'strategic deception' that led Hitler to believe there was a vast American battle group in Kent. This kept many of his lethal Panzers in the Pas-de-Calais, not just for a few days but a whole month, giving the Allied Expeditionary Force in Normandy a far greater chance of success. Men still had to fight, of course, and men still lost their lives but there is little doubt that without Patton's fake planes and boats, or the elaborate network of invented and double agents feeding lies to the Abwehr, many more would have done so. I hope that, in part, this novel has shown how many different elements went into the D-day landings and to how many people – brave soldiers, clever officers, smart planners and thousands of ordinary workers just like Steffie, Fran and Ailsa - we owe their success. I thank them all.

ACKNOWLEDGEMENTS

This novel is dedicated to Norman, who is not a friend, editor, family member or secret (indeed, not so secret) lover, but a motorhome! We bought him in 2021, but 2022 was our first year to truly put him through his paces as an on-road home and mobile office – and he performed both tasks admirably.

We took Norman to Normandy (surely his spiritual home?!) in autumn 2022 to research D-Day for Fran and Valérie, then had the not-so-arduous task of taking him all the way down to Lisbon (via Granada, Cordoba, Seville and Faro) to check out that amazing city for Steffie's visit. Along the way, I wrote the majority of this novel sitting at the table in the back while my husband drove, shopped, cooked and did all the tiny tasks that Normans seem to require!

I drove some of the way too, partly because I enjoy it, partly to give Stuart a rest, and mainly because it's rare to see women driving motorhomes and I wanted to do my bit for on-the-road feminism. Most of the time, however, I wrote. It was a joy immersing myself in Bletchley Park in the 1940s only to look up to find that olive trees had given way to orange ones and we were close to a new place to spend the night. My reward for getting up early and writing a chapter was a chance to swim in the Atlantic or visit a Spanish mosque, and it was a wonderful way of crafting a book that I intend to repeat in the years ahead. So thank you, Norman. And thank you Stuart, co-pilot, domestic god and number one support.

A mention should also go here to our fellow traveller,

Cookie – our admirably well-behaved collie cross who took Europe in her stride and sat as devotedly at my feet in the motorhome as she does in my office. She will never know what I do, nor what a help her supportive presence is when I'm stuck or frustrated or running out of ideas, but I'd like to record my appreciation all the same.

Thank you, too, to my children for growing up into responsible (well, semi-responsible) adults so that we could hit the road for five whole weeks without you! A special shout-out to Alec for keeping the house standing and just about tidy while we were gone. Seriously, though, all my love to the four of you for being you and making our lives so rich.

On a professional note I want to thank, as always, Natasha and the fabulous Bookouture team for bringing this novel to life in such an enthusiastic, dedicated and informed way. I most definitely couldn't do it without you and am so glad to be working with you all. And the same goes for the wonderful Kate Shaw for her ongoing support and hard work on my behalf. Dream team!

I'd like to thank Eilidh Beaton for doing such a wonderful job reading both this novel and *The Bletchley Girls* as audiobooks – and my mum for being such a kind and enthusiastic listener.

And, finally, you readers. I grew up loving books and my life has been hugely enriched by the many and varied stories I have been lucky enough to read in my fifty years. It is an honour and privilege to see my own books on people's shelves – real and virtual – so thank you for reading and do, please, keep getting in touch. It means the world.

Made in the USA
Coppell, TX
02 April 2024